I'LL MEET YOU AT THREE FORKS

By

David G. Bishop

Acknowledgments

I want to thank the following people for their help, guidance and understanding:

Barbara Bishop for her knowledge, her patience, her encouragement, and for being my sounding board,

Helen Keezer Burton for her friendship, writing expertise, and literary guidance,

and finally,

Brent Crump who inspired me with his wit and love for life and because he always wanted to "hear more"

Table of Contents

BOOK 1 – ADVENTURES IN THE SHININ' MOUNTAINS

CHAPTER 1: AMBUSHED

The night was ending and the sun had begun its tireless climb up the eastern sky. It would be a while before it crested the peaks of the distant rugged mountains but already, there was enough light so that images among the trees were no longer a blur. A man could see his sights good enough to shoot if he had to. Clinton Jeffries stood a good way back from the creek that wound its way through the serene valley. A shallow mist rose from its slow rippling waters into the cold October morning. He gently stroked the muzzle of the bay mare calming her with soothing whispers "easy girl, it's awlright, shh." This was no time for the horse to whinny.

The traps he'd set the morning before needed to be checked but he had to be careful. Yesterday, he'd seen Indian sign while scouting out new trapping grounds in the valley to the west. The tracks he'd found and the then-cold cook fires told him there were seventeen or eighteen of them, no more than twenty for sure. "Blackfeet," he'd thought, "probably up here after elk...too high for buffalo and the deer started movin' down weeks ago." Pondering this a moment, a new thought reached his mind. "Maybe they're huntin' something else...maybe they're huntin' me."

As he stood in the shadows, his keen blue eyes slowly scanned the trees and openings for movement. Carefully, he listened to the sounds of the morning as they rose above the sluggish gurgling of the stream. He searched for something in the air, anything that might tell him danger was about. Far away, a hawk shrieked calling to its mate, squirrels chattered, and the normal twittering of the birds in the willows lining the creek was like gentle music; everything seemed normal. He dropped the reins of the horse, allowing her to wander and feed. He knew she wouldn't go far but would stay back in the trees where there was still some grass that the frosts had not completely killed. He slowly moved to the stream and proceeded to check the traps.

More than two hours had passed when he at last reached the end of the trap line. Normally, it wouldn't have taken so long but he had been extra careful to move slowly and cover his tracks. "No sense advertising you're about" he thought.

The morning's catch yielded him two fine, fat beaver. After skinning them out, he reset the traps and hid each carcass where only the ants and flies would discover it.

His legs ached as he climbed up the bank from the cold water. It had been seven years since he'd left the farming community in Tennessee and come to the mountains. It seemed like the streams got colder each year or maybe it was because he was just getting older.

Strapping the pelts to his back, he took up his rifle and headed back downstream. Walking on the same side of the creek where he'd left the horse, he decided to move farther back into the woods; it was safer there. He figured to come up from behind the animal, keeping it between him and the brushy little stream. If there were Indians waiting for him, they'd be expecting him to come from where he'd been trapping. Hopefully, coming from this direction he'd be able to spot them first and slip away without being noticed.

He made good time heading back and was careful not to make noise. He'd learned long ago if you expect to keep your hair in this country, you'd best act like an Indian. The course he'd taken through the trees had led him to a natural path that angled sharply away from the creek, so that by now, he was at least two hundred and fifty yards back into the woods. At this point he left the path and again took up a line that ran in the downstream direction and was parallel with the creek. He knew when he finally came even with the place where he'd left the mare he'd have to go some distance back toward the stream to get her. "Better this way than back-trackin' straight down the creek," he thought. "It may take longer but it's safer."

An hour had passed since he'd waded from the cold water. The sun was up full and the air was warming. The walk had driven the pain from his legs, but his buckskins were still wet and cold. He now drew near the place where he must be extra careful. He calculated that the horse could be no further than three hundred yards ahead and perhaps a hundred yards to the right.

He decided he'd leave the pelts here and come back for them when he got the horse. If he had to make a run for it, he couldn't carry them and there was no sense letting those red-sticks have them. If everything was safe, he'd be on his way to camp within the hour. A thought suddenly raced across his mind and he silently mouthed the words "probably'd be a damn good idea to pull outta this here part of the country...it's gettin' too crowded for my well bein'."

Quietly, he pushed the pelts under the side of an old fallen pine, checked his rifle to see that it was primed, and set out to find the horse. Moving very slowly, he inspected everything ahead of him. Nothing seemed out of the ordinary. He'd gone about a hundred yards from where he stashed the pelts and still he could not see the horse. He knew, though, she wasn't far off. Carefully he crept ahead through the gray, leafless quaking aspen, watching, listening, and straining to make out even the faintest warning. But nothing came. Hell, maybe he was being too careful. The other men in the fur company had always said he was too damn much that way. They'd always made fun of him and accused him of being antsy. The funny thing of it was, though, he was still alive and many of them had gone under.

As his thoughts returned to the present, he saw the horse. She stood about thirty yards ahead of him through the trees. She hadn't wandered far and appeared to be calm, standing there cropping grass. Clint crept closer, all the while surveying the situation. Everything seemed all right, but...sometimes he just got this gut feeling that things weren't right. He had that feeling now but everything looked safe. "Maybe I oughta just belly on back outta here and high-tail it for camp" he thought, "I could come back tomorrow for the horse; she'd be all right here tonight and she shouldn't stray too far...there's plenty of grass and water."

Clint laid there for what seemed like an hour, trying to decide, trying to be smart. It was times like these that made you want to give up trapping and get the hell out of the mountains. Well, the time had come to decide; daylight was wasting. He looked around once more and almost unwillingly, began to creep forward. He moved ahead swiftly in a crouch toward the horse, his eyes constantly searching about him. Still, nothing! As he approached the mare, she raised her head quickly, her body stiffened, and she acted as though she might bolt; but then, his scent came to her and recognizing him, she seemed to relax. Now, he came to a full upright position. Walking quickly up to the horse and grabbing the reins, he thought, "All right, so I am antsy like they say, but it's better to be safe than..." He barely heard the whir of the arrow before it slammed into his thigh. Two more whistled past his back as he reeled in pain. The air was suddenly filled with what sounded like a million screaming voices from hell. He had hold of the saddle but the horse was terrified. White showed around her eyes and she bawled loudly and started backing away. Clint hung on to the reins and, staggering, managed to swing himself into the saddle. He spurred the horse violently and she charged downstream directly toward the creek.

As if from nowhere, an Indian appeared just ahead of him and off to the right. "Those red bastards were waitin' for me after all" he thought, "but this hoss ain't down yet and I'll sure as hell take some of 'em with me fore I go."

With bow drawn, the Indian steadied his aim on the advancing rider. Clint lowered himself to the horse's back and at the same time cocked the hammer on the big Flintlock gun. Almost simultaneously, the Indian let loose his arrow as Clint touched off the .50 caliber. In the rush of the moment, the arrow went off the mark, narrowly missing the rider. Clint's bullet, though, was right on target and at thirty feet, it caught the warrior square in the chest. A spray of bright crimson filled the air as the ball burst from his back.

As Clint raced by the crumpling body, another Indian leaped from the brush at the side of the stream and rushed toward him, tomahawk in hand. Clint brought the now empty rifle up and swinging it like some monstrous club, hit the Indian square in the face just below the nose. He saw the fine structure of the man's features collapse giving way to the twelve-pound gun and felt the life-taking thump vibrate up through the stock. The man's assault with the hatchet had been cut short but not before he had severely lacerated the mare's shoulder.

More arrows came and Clint swung the horse from side to side dodging them as he galloped away. Behind him he could hear the screaming war hoops intensify as the braves realized their brothers had fallen. Clint knew they'd soon be mounted and after him. All this had happened so damn fast and, except for the initial sting of the shaft, he had been too scared to think about the pain. But now, it washed over him in a wave; his head whirled and he almost passed out. Blood streamed from the wound and he clenched his teeth and spurred the horse harder.

"Damn, the fat's in the fire now "he thought "how in Hell's name am I gonna get outta this mess? This horse is cut bad...she's bleedin' more than me...won't go too much further, I reckon."

Clint chanced a quick look behind him and was surprised to see that the other braves weren't yet mounted and after him. "Musta had their horses ditched far back in the trees," he thought. Another wave of pain shot up his leg. The shaft of the arrow had broken in the turmoil but what was left of it was solidly imbedded two inches above his right knee. "Probably in the bone..." he thought, "...sure as hell hurts."

His mind raced as he steered the mare up onto a long narrow mound that had once been the bank of the stream but which now stood by itself some twenty yards from the water. The course of the river had changed years ago, leaving the bank standing high and dry. A thick row of willows, however, still grew along its base where the river had once been. Off to the left of the mound, stubby sagebrush grew and there were many rocks. "I've gotta git hidden fore they catch up to me" he thought. "It's my only chance; I can't out run 'em and I sure as hell can't out fight 'em....there's too many...and this damn leg don't help matters either."

He'd trapped in this valley for the last two weeks and knew the lay of the land well. Right now, he had to think and think straight. It was becoming harder to concentrate. His leg wouldn't leave him be and for the first time since the arrow hit him, he was beginning to grasp the realization of what was happening.

"C'mon, think you fool...where can I hide? How can I ditch these bastards?" The questions came over and over but the answers didn't. "I'd better find a place soon," he thought, "they'll be on me 'fore long, and then...?"

It suddenly came to him, "They'll be expectin' me to high tail it out of here. They won't be expectin' me to hide. Not here! Not this close! It's my only chance." With that, he galloped close to the edge of the mound and threw himself from the saddle toward the willows. The impact of his body crashing into the brush knocked the wind out of him and he struggled to gain his breath. The mare, half out of her head with fear and pain, galloped wildly down the length of the mound and out of sight.

As his head began to clear, he knew he must conceal himself quickly. The Indians would soon be along. He hunkered into the low, dead brush that was growing in and around the base of the willows and tried to blend in as best as possible. An ugly thought began to roll around in his mind, "What if they don't fall for this? What then?" Death would not come easy at the hands of these boys. They knew how to make you hurt real bad before you finally pushed off. He'd once come across what was left of a trapper the Blackfeet had caught and tortured. They had cut off his genitals and then, strip by strip, had skinned him alive; what was left of him was only fit for the buzzards and the insects. Seemed as though Indians had a way of taking you right to death's door and then bringing you back for another round of pain. He couldn't believe anyone was capable of doing what they'd done to the man.

His thoughts suddenly snapped back to the present. "I know they'll catch the horse before too long and then they'll come back lookin'. If they just ride by without spottin' me, I can be gone before they get back...make it to the creek and lose 'em...maybe."

He hadn't long to wait. The riders screamed their war whoops as they raced toward him. "That horse oughta be easy to track" he thought, "I hope to hell they're so intent on catchin' up that they don't look down here." With his face pressed into the brush, he didn't so much as breathe, when the Indians rode by, their ponies passing within ten feet of him.

Seconds later they were past him and he could hear them galloping away. "Hot damn," he said, "I fooled 'em. I gotta git goin' now." Quickly, he took out his knife and cut off a piece of soft buckskin from the strap of his hunting pouch. He hurriedly wrapped it twice around his leg and about the stub of the arrow protruding from the hole in his leg, tying it off with a square knot. Then, he reached for his rifle. It was gone. "Where the hell....must have lost it when I jumped. God-damn...ain't got time to hunt for it now." He cast one last look for the old gun that had saved his bacon more than once but it was not to be found.

Gaining his feet, he made for the stream. His leg was throbbing but it held him. "No sense bein' careful to hide my tracks here," he thought, "They'll easily find where I unloaded into those willows and know I made for the creek. They'll find my rifle too, sure as hell...damn."

He stood in the water at the edge of the stream, trying to decide which way to go and how to outsmart them. He had fooled them once; he knew they would not easily be fooled again. This had to be good. Thoughts raced through his head, "Downstream is probably my best bet; the current would carry me faster that way but there isn't much cover below here. Upstream though, there's plenty of beaver dams - lots of downed trees, willows, and snags...thicker'n molasses in some of those places...that's where I'm going." With that, he fought his way upstream through the current to the edge of the far bank. He was careful to stay in the water, thereby leaving no sign for the skillful eyes that would soon be here looking for him.

"The hard part," he thought, "is gonna be gettin' away from this creek and into the backwaters of the beaver ponds without leavin' a trail. They know they got me and they'll be careful to look under every log and rock."

Suddenly, it came to him. He had trapped this very spot four days ago and remembered a place where he had stepped on what appeared to be solid ground only to have it give way under his weight. He had gone into a hole clear up to his crotch. He remembered thinking how these old beaver runs could be damn dangerous and how lucky he was that he didn't nut himself, sinking in like that.

The branches of a river birch hung into the water directly ahead of him. "If I'm careful," he thought "I can climb up those branches and not leave my tracks in the mud. That hole's somewhere just ahead and off to the left. I gotta be careful here." Clint moved slowly, cautiously, applying every bit of skill he had. He had to make absolutely certain that nothing was disturbed; no leaf could be turned, no twig broken. If he made a mistake, it would cost him his life. The bad part was, he had to hurry. He didn't have much time.

At last he saw the place where he'd fallen through the bank. A small channel that had been cut out by a beaver when the water was higher, was now visible and was apparently, what had been the undercut in the bank that he had stepped through. So far, Clint had managed to keep himself out of the mud and not leave any tracks. This he accomplished by painfully slithering from willow pile to willow pile. After each move, he would check his trail to see that nothing betrayed him.

Now, he was at the edge of the small channel and had to lower himself into it without leaving footprints in the muddy bottom. Mossy, stagnant water about a foot deep filled the channel. Carefully he knelt and lengthened out over the willows easing himself chest first into the water, much as a beaver would. It smelled foul as he pulled himself along, using the small willows and sticks that lined the channel as handholds.

Floating nearer the place where the bank had given way, he saw there was much more of an undercut than could be seen from above. In fact, there was a hole that went back in under the bank for what appeared to be six or eight feet. This would have to do.

The slimy water continued right on into the hole and he guided himself in. "Hell; I'd rather go in feet first," he thought, "but there ain't no room to turn around in this here ditch. Hope to hell there's enough room in there; I don't like tight places."

Pulling himself further into the hole, Clint discovered that it was actually an old beaver house. The entrance had been tight going in but now he found himself in what seemed like a small room. It smelled of animal, thick with a musk-like odor. He crawled up out of the water to a drier place. The available light coming in from the tunnel was scant and he could hardly see a thing. He had bumped his head coming in so he knew the ceiling wasn't very high. He wasn't complaining, though; this was better than trying to make a fight of it out in the open where he would die for sure.

He felt safer now and reached to see if his knife was where it should be. Quietly he slipped the trusty blade from its sheath, holding it at the ready. One thing was for certain, if they tried to take him from this hole, they'd have one hell of a time on their hands and he'd get at least one of them.

He suddenly felt a wave of exhaustion roll over his entire being, covering him like a heavy blanket. "Jesus, I'm so tired. I need to rest for a bit. Probably should say a prayer...Lord, if you can hear me, I sure could use a hand right now. I've gone and gotten myself into a sure enough fix. I'd appreciate it if you could....." his eyes closed and without finishing, he drifted off to sleep.

For some time, he dozed in a fitful, twitching, half-sleep. Partly, it was from fatigue. Mostly, it was from shock. Clint awoke then with a bone-chilling shiver, realizing he'd dozed off but he couldn't imagine for how long. The light coming in from the small entrance was much dimmer now. He could only guess that it must be late afternoon; this time of the year the days were short.

"Don't know whether I can last the night in this hole," he thought, "I'm soakin' ass wet and it's so damn cold in here the Injuns won't have to kill me, I'll freeze to death first. Daresn't leave till it's full dark, though."

As he mulled over a plan of escape, he reached down to feel the wound the arrow had made in his leg. Since he hadn't moved much, the bleeding had subsided. Unfortunately, the pain hadn't. For as his hand clumsily groped at the wound, a fiery stinging rushed upward letting him know that it had not gone away. He almost screamed as he quickly drew his hand away.

Always before, he had been able to endure pain fairly well. He remembered the bruises and cuts he'd gotten from fights with Indians; also, when he'd turned in his pelts to the company, near the outpost, there were always drunken trappers, half out of their minds with liquor and spoiling for trouble. He'd been stabbed three times during those go-rounds. And then there was the old she-grizzly that had charged him, clawing his arm and chest clean to the bone. After killing the bear, his compadres had taken an awl, a bone needle and some fine deer sinew, and sewn him up like an old leather sack. All those times he had been able to just grit his teeth and bear it. But this pain was different; it wasn't like it had been before. The others had burned and were festery for a few days and he had ached for a while afterward. But this was deeper, a real no shit, God-awful burning that sunk clear to his marrow; no, by God, clear to his very soul. He wondered if he'd ever be able to walk normal again if he managed to get out of this mess.

During his indulgence to the agony, he was suddenly shocked back to reality. The light from the hole through which he had entered and that which he had been blankly staring at during those waves of pain, suddenly dimmed to the point that nothing was now visible.

"The sun goes down fast, but not that fast," he thought, "Damn! Something must be in front of the hole. No, something is coming in through the hole...they've found me."

His guts were tying up in knots. He again brought the big knife up and braced himself for what was about to come. He would only have one chance and he'd have to make it good.

"Maybe I can kill this red bastard and his friends won't ever know what happened to him," he thought. But the reality was, he knew they'd hunt him down for sure if one of them came up missing.

Now he could hear the breathing and he felt the vibrations of movement coming closer.

"He's almost within arm's length now...I'm gonna take him...just a little closer. Now!"

Clint lunged with all the strength he had left. In the dark, cramped space and in his weakened condition, the blow fell short and his knife stuck into the mud. He'd missed.

Struggling to recover, his hand brushed against the thick hair of his adversary. Suddenly, there was a surprised growl and a snapping of teeth. The fox had been taken completely by surprise and bolted from the small room back out through the opening.

"Holy shit," Clint whispered, "a goddam fox. He musta been usin' this place fer a den. I thought it was an Injun for sure. Why didn't he smell me...must be all this mud and goo I got coverin' me? Holy shit!"

The incident with the fox had again drained the strength from him. Once more, he closed his eyes and drifted off into some kind of half-sleep. His semi-conscious memory was taking him back to the time he had boarded the keel boat on the banks of the Mississippi River. His sister had been there to hug him and tell him goodbye. All that day she had been sniveling and carrying on like an orphaned calf. Every time he had packed another piece of gear in his knapsack, she had started in bawlin' again. Women! He just couldn't figure them out. He did love his sister though; she had been the only family he'd had since his folks died and it now came to him what she was feeling. He had been so excited at the thought of going to the mountains to hunt and trap that he hadn't considered the fact this might be the last time he would ever see her. When he climbed the gangplank of the keel boat, he hadn't been able to turn around to wave goodbye for he knew if he did, she would surely have seen the tears that filled his eyes.

Once again, he was pulled back to consciousness, awaking with a chill; he was freezing cold. The dim light that had previously illuminated the opening to the beaver house had given up to the night. Outside, it was totally black.

"Can't see my hand in front of my face," he whispered to himself. "Sure is dark. Time to get movin'."

He hoped the Indians had gotten tired of looking for him and had left. He knew he couldn't stay here any longer or he'd freeze to death. He inched toward where he remembered the opening of the beaver house to be. Feeling along the walls, he began sliding out. Immediately, his leg reminded him that it was still there but he kept going. Coming out into the night, he paused, listening for any unnatural sound. Behind him somewhere, the river whispered in its timeless, familiar voice. Nothing else moved. Clint's eyes strained to see but the sky was overcast and the night was dark as pitch.

"Appears I'm gonna have to feel my way back to camp," he whispered "this otta be real interestin.'"

Since he had crawled from the beaver house, he'd remained kneeling; he hadn't tried to stand. Now came the test.

"Hope this damn leg will get me back and then the boys can fix me up."

The boys, Jim Tucker and One-thumb Jack Harris, were two of his best friends. Clint normally didn't trap with others, even friends, but these two had been with him when he first came to the mountains and had taught him the ways of a mountain man. He had willingly let them convince him to come with them to this place. They had said there were "loads of beaver for the takin." They had been right. The trouble was though, there were also a passel of Injuns - and Blackfeet, to boot!

Clint rose slowly from the wet ground testing the leg. The pain was there and as he put more weight on it, it stabbed at him unmercifully. He took a step and almost fell. Not because the leg let him down, but because he was stiff and shivering and the mud was very slippery. Regaining himself, he tried it again. This time he made it. It hurt like hell but he made it; the leg held. His eyes were now beginning to make out obstacles that lay in his path.

He had a good sense of direction, as did most mountain men, and he thought he had a pretty good idea which way it was to camp. He knew it wasn't that far, maybe a mile straight on, as the crow flies.

"Hate like hell to leave a trail straight back to camp," he whispered to himself, "but I'm freezin' to death and I got no choice with this bum leg. If I can get there afore daylight, me and the boys can saddle up and high-tail it outta here before those red devils pick up my sign. If I don't make it before daylight it won't matter anyway, they'll have me."

Clint struggled through the marshy bottom and finally reached the sharp hillside that marked the edge of the stream bed. So far, the leg was supporting him. It hurt and had started bleeding again; he could feel it running warm down to his foot. He stopped for a minute and retied the buckskin bandage he had placed over the wound. Moving slowly up the shallow incline of the hill, he became suddenly aware of something else in the night. It had started to snow.

"Well, that about caps it," he whispered in a disgusted tone. "If this ain't been one helluva day. I get arrow shot, lose my horse and rifle, share a hole with an irate fox, have to stumble my way through the dark with a bunch of heathen devils on my trail, and if that ain't enough, it's gotta snow. Shit!"

The storm had begun with only an occasional flake falling here and there. But now, it was really coming down. One good thing about it though, it was brighter and lightened the ground ahead of him; he could at least see better. Also, with it falling this heavy, it would rapidly cover his trail. Maybe he could get out of this mess after all.

It seemed like hours since he'd crawled from the muddy burrow and he supposed he was nearing camp. "Only a hundred or so yards to go," he thought "and I should be there." Moving among the trees was difficult and he couldn't help but make noise. "Best give the signal," he whispered "I'd hate like hell to scare those boys and have 'em shoot me after comin' this far."

With that, he put a cupped hand to his mouth and gave the hoot-hoot of an owl; then, listening for a moment, he continued his limp toward camp. Ahead of him, he could hear anxious shuffling and the click of a rifle's hammer being set to fire.

"That you, ole hoss?" came a whispered voice; it was One-thumb Jack Harris.

"Yeah, it's me and I'm shot up," Clint answered.

"Here, let me help you." Harris came running and threw his shoulder under Clint's arm, helping him into camp. "Hell, when you didn't come in by dark we thought maybe you'd holed up somewheres to ride out this storm. Didn't know you'd had a run in with Injuns."

The camp was well concealed in the hollow of a small hill. A thick stand of heavy pines surrounded it and there was much dead-fall about. Among the pines, the men had constructed a lean-to shelter. Its size was adequate to house them and their possibles and one would almost have to walk right up on it to recognize it for what it was. From a distance, it resembled just another pile of dead fall. Behind it, some forty yards or so, lay a well-hidden pasture. There, a tiny spring trickled from the ground and last summer's grass fed the men's horses.

As Clint ducked in through the dimly lit door, he began to speak, "Them sons-a-bitches jumped me this mornin' over on that small creek where we were scoutin' yesterday. My horse got all cut up and I had to ditch her. When I baled off her, I lost my rifle and damn near broke my neck. I tell ya, it ain't been a good day." He paused only a moment to catch his breath. "We need to pack it in and get shed of this place about as quick as we kin. I don't know how many of 'em there are but they're gonna have our hair if'n we don't."

Attentively, the two men helped him onto a warm buffalo robe that lay next to the glowing coals of a small cook-fire.

"Now calm down ole hoss," Harris said. "We'll get outta here soon as we kin but that's one bad blizzard out there; it might not quit for days. Besides, you look like you couldn't go another step." Motioning to the other man, he continued "Jim, throw a hunk of that jerked meat to this ole' boy; he looks half starved."

Clint caught the meat that Jim Tucker threw to him and took a big bite. When he could again talk, he said "Thanks, Tuck. That tastes real good. I was hungry."

With knapsack in hand, Jim Tucker moved to Clint's side. Taking a closer look at him he asked, "How bad you hit, bud?"

Clint, finishing off the last of the meat, choked out "Pretty bad, I think. Took an arrow just above the knee; I think the head is stuck in the bone. You're gonna have to dig it out, Tuck."

Jim Tucker took out his knife and cut away the crude bandage that had been hastily applied. He then slit Clint's buckskin leggings up from the bottom so he could get a better look. Blood seeped from the wound and he brought forth a clean piece of cloth from the knapsack. He reached for a small jug that sat in the corner. Tipping it, he doused the cloth with water. "This ain't gonna tickle, hoss; lemme wipe it clean and take a closer look." With that, he raised one of the tallow

17

candles and held it close to inspect the wound. "Sure as a cat's got an ass, that arrowhead's stuck square in the bone. It's gonna be a sombitch to get out but if you're figurin' on walkin' again, we're gonna have to do it." With that, he carefully laid the knife blade in the coals of the fire.

Seeming half-dazed, Clint raised himself onto his elbows and leaned his head back. He took a deep breath, looked at the men and said "You'd better get to cuttin', Tuck. Time's a wastin' and them Blackfeet will be here first thing tomorrow." Putting his hand on Clint's chest and pushing him back down, Jim Tucker handed him another large chunk of jerked meat from the knapsack. "Alright Bud," Tucker said "you'd best clamp your teeth around this and get prepared. Shit, I wish we had some whiskey. It'd make this a whole lot easier. Harris, hold this candle close so's I can see what the hell I'm doin'."

This wasn't the first arrow Jim Tucker had removed. When you lived in this country, you had to do some doctorin' now and then; that's just the way it was. It was expected that a man would help another man when needed. They had to take care of each other because nobody else would.

Jim Tucker drew the knife from the fire. Its blade glowed orange in the dim light. "Jesus, I hate doin' this," he said "it always makes my guts feel weak and my balls tighten up and ache real bad." Leaning close with the candle, one-thumb Harris softly scolded, "Maybe it does make your balls ache Tuck, but that's all in your mind. He's gettin' the real thing here, all that pain and..." Clint had heard enough, "For Christ's sake, will you two stop all this damn talk and just get on with it. If you keep this up and I'll have to take the damn thing out myself."

With a deft hand, Tucker drew the knife from two directions toward the protruding shaft. Clint felt only the first deep slice of the searing blade. The pain that had come before was but a shadow of what was pulsating through him now; the leg was screaming at him. His teeth sunk deeper into the jerked meat and his body convulsed. From deep in his throat came the low rumble of words being jammed together. "Oh-my-Gawd.....help me, hel..." His tortured eyes rolled back in his head and a sudden blissful blackness engulfed him.

"Jesus Tuck, he's gone and died on us," Harris cried.

"No, he ain't neither, you damn fool," Tucker scolded, "he just passed out. It'll be easier now." Then, under his breath, Tucker added, "For both of us."

CHAPTER 2:
NEAR DEATH – THE JOURNEY TO BLACK ELK'S CAMP

Jim Tucker crouched in the low doorway of the lean-to shelter and gazed out at the falling snow as it drifted silently to the ground, filling up the woods around him. His shoulder was propped against the doorway and he sucked slowly on an old briar pipe. He held it tightly in his teeth letting the smoke roll up from the corner of his mouth and over his fine features. "Wish to hell we had some decent tobacco," he said. "This KinniKinnick I got from those Crow last summer tastes like a mixture of cedar bark and horse shit. It's gonna be a long time til we git us some honest-to-God tobacco and whiskey."

Three days had passed since he'd dug the arrow from Clint's leg. Fever had set in from infection and Clint passed in and out of consciousness. One minute he was sweating profusely and ringing wet with perspiration. The next minute would find him freezing and the men would have to bundle him in robes to stave off the cold. "Think he's gonna make it, Tuck?" Harris whispered. "I don't know," Tucker replied, still gazing out at the snow. "I've seen men die from arrow wounds before but ole Clint there is a pretty tough nut; he can take it. What worries me is the gangrene. We may end up havin' to cut off that leg just to save him." When he heard those words, Harris became suddenly very sober. "You know hoss, if that were me and I knew I was gonna lose a leg, I'd just as soon go under. Wouldn't be no sense livin'- a man can't get along in this country with only one peg."

Again, without turning, Tucker took a big drag on his pipe and said, "Maybe we oughta try to get him to Black Elk's camp and see if they can do anything for him. They got ways of fixin' a man up, using herbs and roots and such. Yessiree, I think they might be able to help. What do you say, Harris?"

Hesitating, Harris answered with a grunt and shrugged his shoulders, "I don't know," he said. "I don't much care for Injuns and I don't know that they can help him any better than we can." Pondering the question some more, he added, "But, I guess it wouldn't hurt to try. We don't know where Black Elk's camp is though."

This time, Tucker turned as he spoke. "I think I know where he is," he said, pausing. "I'd lay you a dollar to a dog turd they're camped at the same place they've been winterin' for the past ten years; they're up on the Beaverhead. There's plenty of game and good winter grass for the horses; I know, cause I spent a few winters with 'em myself."

Harris stared at him for a moment as though he couldn't believe what he'd just heard. "Jesus man, do you know how far that is from here?" he blurted out. "Why it'd take us more than a week just to ride there, let alone dodgin' Injuns and tryin' to drag ole Clint here along. And besides, I..." Tucker suddenly pushed himself up and forward until he and Harris were looking straight into each other's eyes. His voice was quiet but deliberate. "Look Goddammit, if'n that were you layin' there lookin' death in the eye you'd want your compadres to do all they could for you, right?" Harris didn't know what to say. He stammered, "I...I only meant..."

"I know what you meant," Tucker said, "but you know if the situation were reversed he'd do all he could for you." With that, the conversation ended.

Jim Tucker had most of their gear packed when Harris lifted the buffalo skin door of the lean-to aside. "Our horses are saddled. Clint's gonna have to ride one of the mules," he said, not wanting to look Tucker in the eye. He still felt bad about the words they'd had. He and Tucker had been friends for a long time and this small incident seemed somehow to have driven a wedge between them.

"Clint! Clint! Wake up, we gotta go." Jim Tucker was gently shaking him when Clint at last opened his eyes. He had been dreaming of his sister and a warm fire in a far-away cozy cabin. Now, he was suddenly being dragged back from paradise to a damp, cold, hellish place that was filled with fever and pain. As he struggled to get his elbows under him, he received a sudden sharp jolt. It raced upward from his tortured leg and exploded in his brain. "Jesus Christ, this hurts," he muttered under his breath.

As he helped Clint into his heavy coat, Jim Tucker spoke to him quietly, "C'mon ole hoss, we're gonna try and get ya to Black Elk's camp. They can doctor ya better'n we kin." Clint helped as best he could but his arms were like lead and he felt very weak. "Think you can ride with that leg?" Tucker continued. "I can ride," Clint answered "I just don't know how far. Maybe you could tie me onto the saddle, that way, I can't fall off." Smiling, Tucker again spoke in a quiet voice, "Ain't nobody gonna let you fall off, hoss; we'll keep ya up there."

Four hours had passed since the three men left the shelter of the hidden camp. The snow, although it had stopped some time ago, was nearly to the horses' knees. Clint had not wanted to show the other two men how badly he felt and so had started out sitting upright in the pack saddle. Now, however, he was hunkered forward and his tormented face rested heavily against the mule's neck.

"Let's pull 'em up in that stand of pine, Jack," Tucker said pointing ahead at a dark clump that stood on the left side of the long narrow valley. "Old Clint here looks as if he could rest a bit and I need to pee."

Within the thicket of lodge pole pine, they dismounted. Harris and Tucker helped Clint down onto a buffalo robe they had spread out on the snow. In here, the trees grew close together and the snow had not been able to penetrate so easily.

The three of them, sprawled out now and resting, lay for a long moment staring at one another. "Yer the two ugliest sons-a-bitches I ever saw in my life," Clint said breaking the silence. "But yer also the best damn friends a man could ever have. Others would have gone off and left the likes of me to go it alone," he concluded.

"Ain't nobody leavin' nobody," Harris mumbled without lifting his eyes.

"You know" Clint said, gripping the thigh of his wounded leg, "This thing oughta quit hurtin' so damn bad now that the arrow's out, but it burns like blazes."

"I couldn't get it all out," Tucker said quietly in a solemn voice. "The head's buried deep into the bone. I didn't have no tools or pinchers to grab it with. Why I even broke my bullet mold tryin' to grab at it. I just couldn't get it out, Clint, I'm sorry. Maybe we can give it another go when we reach Black Elk's camp." Clint sensed the anguish in his voice and could see the concern in his eyes. "Hey, it's alright Tuck. We'll do like you said and get after it when we get to the village."

"Here, sink yer teeth into this," Harris said as he handed pieces of dried elk meat to Clint and Tucker. "How far you reckon we've come, Tuck?" It was a meaningless question and Harris knew the answer before he asked but it seemed somehow to fill the silent void that surrounded them. Clint's condition was something none of them wanted to think about but it was on all their minds. Each of them knew that arrows and bullets, if they stayed in a man's body, most always led to blood poison and that nearly always meant a slow, painful death.

"Reckon we've come five, maybe six miles," Tucker answered without shifting his eyes from the distant horizon. Continuing, he added, "We get another ten miles behind us and we'll be off this mountain and outta the high country;

most likely we'll be outta the deep snow too. Then, we can rig a travois and ole Clint can ride on into that village in style."

Turning toward Clint, Tucker grinned through his brown teeth and chuckled "Hell man, you'll look so comfy ridin' on that sling it'll make them Shoshone women wanna get neckid and jump up there to join ya." Clint grinned shaking his head in agreement but didn't say anything. He couldn't, for in his mind he wondered if he'd ever reach the camp alive.

#

Tucker had been right about the snow not being as deep in the lower country. And so, as he had said, they made a travois to carry their friend. Now, they made good time. Harris and Tucker both realized they had to reach the Indian camp and get Clint some doctoring or he'd surely die. Therefore, they rose early each morning, ate what they had as they rode, and pressed on late into the night before making camp.

On the morning of the seventh day, the men, because they were so fatigued, had slept later than usual. They rose to find the sky had turned a sullen gray. The sunlight that should have been brightening the mountainsides was not to be seen. Instead, heavy storm clouds hung low on the distant peaks and the occasional penetrating rumble of thunder echoed away through the lonely canyons.

A light soaking rain was falling, with here and there an occasional snowflake mixed in. "Did ya ever see such a goddamn dreary day in yer whole life?" Harris said, directing his question to Tucker. "Couldn't keep yer powder dry if you had to. Days like this make ya wanna just crawl inside yerself to stay warm and get away from the cold and wet. By the by, how's ole Clint holdin' on?" Tucker's eyes told the story even before he answered.

"Don't look too good," he whispered. "He's had that fever since we left and it's gettin' worse. He's dingy too; hell, half the time he don't even know who we are. If'n we don't get to that camp soon and get some decent care for this boy, we're gonna lose him."

Because of the steady downpour, the rich dark earth had turned to an even darker mud. Footing for the horses became a problem, especially on the slopes and shallow hillsides. The men had to slow down their relentless pace. The travois, however, seemed to drag easier through the slick mud and Clint rocked back and forth on it with every step the mule took. Little noises sometimes escaped his throat as he drifted in and out of consciousness.

Afternoon arrived and still the men rode on. The rain had stopped some time ago and a light breeze had taken its place. Though it felt colder, the breeze did help to dry things out. Suddenly, Harris held up his hand and signaled to stop. He sat in silence surveying the surrounding hills. Without turning, he softly whispered, "Now don't get real excited hoss but we got two bucks a taggin' us. They're off to the left, back there in the trees. Can't tell who they are - Blackfeet maybe."

Tucker calmly pulled a piece of dried pemmican from a small pouch inside his buffalo skin coat. "I seen 'em," he answered. "There's two or three more over here on the right. They been follerin' us for some time. They're Shoshone, I reckon." Biting into the dried meat he chewed for a minute, swallowed, and then added, "If'n they were Blackfeet, we'd be killed by now."

For some time, the Indians rode abreast of them but stayed well back in the trees. Seemingly, they were content to watch from a distance. They acted almost as if the white men weren't there. Occasionally Tucker thought he could see one of them looking at him directly but he couldn't be sure.

Then, as suddenly as the Indians had appeared, they were gone. Almost like the wind they were gone. Harris once more held his hand up and signaled to stop. Again, he sat for a long moment scanning the country about them. "Jesus!" he whispered, "Injuns make me nervous when I know they're about and I can see 'em. But I really git itchy when I know they're about and I can't see 'em."

He quickly checked his rifle and the flintlock pistol he carried at his waist to make sure they were primed.

"Don't git yer topknot in a tangle, Jack," Tucker said quietly. Tucker always called Harris by his Christian name when he was being serious. "Just take it easy," he went on. "Some of 'ems gone ahead to the camp to pass the word we're comin' and prepare for us. The rest of 'em will make their presence known right shortly now. You just keep yer wits about ya and don't do nothin' foolish."

Stretching forward in the saddle, Tucker arched his back and took a long deep breath. Letting it out slowly he whispered, "Ya know, I looked real close at them bucks when they'd come out in the open and I'll tell you, Jack, it worries me some."

"What worries you?" Harris asked anxiously turning in the saddle to face his friend.

"Well," Tucker continued, "I lived with these folks for nigh on to three years and it worries me because I didn't recognize a damn one of 'em. I know I been away a while but you'd think I'd know some of them boys. I hope to hell this is Black Elk's camp, else we're gonna have to make a whole bunch of new friends and real quick – and sometimes, that ain't so easy to do."

Just then, a long shrill war hoop pierced the air. It came from somewhere off to their right and was quickly joined by several others all about them. Indians poured from the surrounding gully's and low hills where one would think even a jack rabbit couldn't hide.

The screams were like that of a chorus of banshees, interrupted now and then with the grunting and whinnying of frightened horses, as their hooves clamored for sure footing among the rocks and low brush. Almost immediately, the three white men were surrounded.

A tall, lanky brave decked out in war paint and swinging a coup stick reached out and grabbed the reins of Jack Harris' horse. The frightened animal reared up and tried to pull away. This unexpected reaction caught Harris completely off guard. Losing his seat, he flew from the horse and crashed to the ground with a resounding 'thud.'

As quick as he'd gone down, One Thumb Jack Harris was back on his feet and ready to fight. Fumbling to cock his rifle, he yelled, "Goddam you, ya red sombitch, I'll have yer ass fer that." The Indian, however, had dropped the reins of the squealing horse and moved his own mount forward knocking Harris again to the ground. This time, as Harris staggered to right himself, the brave leaned forward and struck him squarely on the side of the head with the coup stick. The blow was not hard but it once more sent him reeling headlong onto the soggy earth.

A loud cheer went up from the other Indians who had momentarily ceased their yelling to watch the action. Harris was now rolling over and scrambling to wipe the mud from his face. "It's every man for hisself," he screamed as he looked about anticipating the next blow.

Once more regaining his feet, Harris' grit-festered eyes caught a glimpse of Jim Tucker and he couldn't believe what he saw. Tucker appeared to be having the time of his life, laughing as though he were crazy. Another Indian that Harris hadn't seen ride up had his hand on Tucker's shoulder in a gesture of friendship and was laughing along with him.

It took only a minute for Jack Harris to clear his head and grasp what was happening. The terrible fear that had filled him only moments before was now waning and a feeling of intense anger grew in its place. He had been scared, hurt, and humiliated. The pain and fear he could handle, the embarrassment he couldn't.

"Tucker, you no good son-of-a-bitch, you set me up. And for that, I'm gonna gut you out." With a deft hand, Jack drew the large hunting knife from his belt and prepared to charge.

"Put the knife away, Jack." The sound of Clint's voice stopped Harris dead in his tracks. It took him and Tucker both by surprise. Clint had been unconscious so much the last few days that they had almost forgotten about him. "What the hell's wrong with you, pullin' a knife on your compadre?" Clint scolded. "Tucker's been your friend forever and now you're tryin to kill him."

Without lifting his eyes to meet the other man's, Harris quickly replied, "He set me up, Clint....made a fool of me in front of these red bastards. The word will get out through the whole damn village and I won't get no respect from any of 'em."

Hearing the allegation, Jim Tucker cut in, "Jack, I didn't set you up; I was scared too until I saw Black Elk here ride up" he motioned toward the stately Indian and continued to speak, "By that time though, you were flat on the ground and rollin' around like a gut-shot wolf. To be right honest about it Jack, you looked kinda funny and I...." Tucker couldn't hold it back any longer and he and the Indian again began to laugh.

That's all it took, One Thumb Jack Harris charged. Like a mad bull. He came on, head down with hackles bristling. Accepting the charge, Jim Tucker calmly waited until just the right moment and then pulled hard on the reins of his horse causing the animal to rear up. Jack Harris lifted his face just in time to see the flailing hoofs, then everything went black.

The blow caught him just under his left ear and knocked him cold. Again, the Indians cheered loudly. Jim Tucker climbed down from his horse and walked to where Jack lay. Rolling his unconscious friend over, he scolded, "Ya hot-headed sombitch. One of these days, it's gonna git ya kilt."

Jack was still breathing, and outside of an ugly knot on the side of his head, didn't seem to be hurt that badly. Motioning to two braves that had gotten down from their horses to look at the fallen man, Tucker began to lift Jack up. The men came to his aid and together, started to carry Jack and lay him over the saddle on his horse. "Hold on there" Clint said lifting himself onto one elbow. "Why don't you put him on here where I'm at and I'll ride his horse? I'm gettin' tired of this damn thing anyway." With that, Clint lifted the buffalo robe and stiffly climbed down. "By the way," he added, grimacing, "how much farther is it to the camp?"

"'Black Elk says it's not far," Tucker answered with concern in his voice. "But are you up to ridin'? You been unconscious for three days."

Clint answered the man sharply. "I'm up to it. You just help me get aboard this ole cayuse and I'll take it from there."

Once Clint was in the saddle, Tucker and the two braves finished putting Jack Harris on the travois. As he climbed onto his horse, Tucker grinned at the Indian that had been at his side before Harris's headlong charge and said in Shoshone, "This one will have a very bad headache when he wakens." The stately man shook his head in agreement and they both laughed.

"Is he gonna be awlright, Tuck?" Clint broke in.

"Yeah, I think so," came the reply. "He's pretty damn hard-headed." The laugh then disappeared from Tucker's face. "Clint, I'm sorry this happened. I guess I shoulda known he'd go crazy. He's flat-assed scared a Indians."

Clint nodded in silent agreement; and then, with a slight tone of disgust added, "Yer right! Somebody coulda got killed." Pausing a moment, he went on, "I somehow always thought he was your friend." Tucker caught the meaning in Clint's words but said nothing.

The Indians now accompanied them as they rode toward the camp. Looking up, the men noticed that the sky ahead looked strange. It seemed even darker and more ominous than the menacing storm clouds that had accompanied them throughout the day.

Shortly, they reached the edge of the shallow bluff on which they had been riding and stopped to gaze at the sight below. It was breathtaking. The Beaverhead River wound its way through the beautiful, wide valley. In a long sweeping bend, it angled off to the northeast toward some distant, low hills that appeared to just bump up from the valley floor. Here and there, small groves of cottonwood trees and river birch intermingled with the heavy growth of willows that lined the stony banks.

The scene was only made more pristine by the nearly two hundred lodges that lay directly below the men, nestled between the bluff and the river's edge. Among them, small groups of children ran about, dogs barked, and the occasional whinny of a war pony echoed from the large remuda at the edge of the camp. The smoke from the numerous cook fires was what had caused the sky to appear so dark. It rose in drab-gray pillars and spread out under the low clouds to form the eerie, inky blanket that hung above them.

Riding down the hill into the camp, the men were soon engulfed by a large group of people who shuffled from the lodges. Clint's leg was on fire and his head was spinning. It was all he could do to stay in the saddle.

On the ride to the camp, Tucker had explained Clint's injury to Black Elk. When the people met them, the stately chief made some hand signals and, at the same time, issued what sounded like orders. The words had barely escaped his mouth when three hefty squaws stepped from the crowd and steered Clint's horse to a large wikiup near the center of the encampment. Gently, they helped him from the horse into the lodge. Tucker watched as his suffering friend disappeared behind the rawhide flap of the lodge. "Well," he thought, "We made it. Now, if they can only help him."

It was several hours before Jack Harris regained consciousness. When he finally did awaken, his head felt as though it would explode and his whole body ached. Even his skin was sore to the touch. A knot the size of his fist blossomed on the side of his face and an angry red welt formed a slight crescent just below his right eye.

With his fingers pressed hard against his temples, Jack Harris tried to recall the incident. As his memory jogged into place, he again felt the familiar hatred building in him and his thoughts ran wild. "Those sons-a-bitches...foolin' me like that...sidin' up with them red bastards and then makin' me out to look like some sort of a damn fool. First chance I git, I'll put their ass in a sling and see how they like it, especially that Tucker. Him and his goddam Injun wife and the rest of his blanket-ass in-laws. I'll fix 'em...I'll fix all of 'em."

"Well, I see ya finally decided to come back among the living." The voice was that of Jim Tucker as he slid the buffalo skin flap aside and entered the lodge where Jack lay brooding. "How's the head?" he asked in a friendly tone.

31

"As if you really give a shit," came the reply.

"Appears as though you ain't any happier than the last time I talked to you," Jim said in his usual soft voice. Kneeling to stir the coals of the small fire, he went on, "I told you I was sorry."

"Sorry ain't good enough," Jack broke in "you goddam near kilt me with that knock to the head...and I ain't forgettin' it either. One of these days I'm..." He then became suddenly quiet and turned away from the sympathetic eyes of his old friend. Jim knew he could not reason with this man and he rose up and turned to leave.

"Where's my horse?" Jack said in a curt voice. And before Jim could answer he followed the first question with another. "And what about my possibles? Where they at? I hope to hell one a yer red relations didn't go south with 'em."

"Yer gun and yer possibles are over there on that robe. Yer horse is hobbled and is feedin' less than fifty yards that way." Jim pointed back across his left shoulder and then paused for a moment looking his one-time friend in the eye. "Now," he continued, "if you have any other questions, look me up when you can talk civil to me. I ain't gonna tell ya again that I'm sorry." With that, Jim Tucker lifted the flap of the lodge and was gone.

Jack mumbled, rolling a plan of action around in his aching head, "First thing in the morning, I'm gonna get my shit together and be gone high and wide from this place. Yes sir, come this time tomorrow, I'll be a long way down the trail and that's a fact."

CHAPTER 3:
JACK'S REVENGE AND THE BEAR

Through the afternoon, Jack Harris drifted in and out of sleep. During his waking moments, he tried to devise ways to get even with the two men he had one time considered his partners. The nagging pain in his head, however, would not let him sort out the details and his mind ran in circles.

By the time the evening shadows were upon the land, he'd managed to rest enough so that he no longer felt the dizzy confusion. "Reckon I oughta pull outta here tonight," he thought. "I ain't tired and all my stuff is right here ready to go. Hell, I could be loaded and gone in ten minutes...only problem is it'll be damn dark; I wouldn't know where I was goin'." He paused a moment then, cursing himself and smiling, "hell, I don't even know where I am."

Jack was suddenly aware of someone coming in through the lodge's entrance. Turning toward the figure, he spoke out, "Tucker, I got nothin' more to say to you. I..." His words stopped right there. It wasn't Jim Tucker who had entered the lodge. It was, rather, a young girl. In her hands, she carried a piece of greasy buckskin wrapped around, what appeared to be a large chunk of roasted meat. Within the scant light of the lodge, Jack could make out the fear in her eyes as she knelt and offered him the steaming mass.

"You understand American?" Jack said before taking the food. There was no answer. Reaching out to take it, he could not help but notice how beautiful the girl was and his eyes quickly took the full measure of her. Beneath the loose-fitting buckskins, he could make out the gentle rise of her breast and the womanly spread of her hips below the fine, slim waist. The fading light deepened her skin to a soft copper color and tiny fires danced in her black eyes.

She suddenly sensed the lustful stare that engulfed her. Somehow, it made her feel naked and dirty and she quickly lowered her face to avoid his eyes.

It had been a long time since Jack Harris had been with a woman and the all-consuming urge was now upon him. "Yer a right purty thing, you are," he whispered as he slowly lifted his crippled hand to touch her cheek.

"Wen," she said pushing the meat toward him. At the same time, she skittered backwards out through the flap of the lodge and was gone. Jack made a sudden, half-hearted grab for the girl as she disappeared into the dusk but his now-pounding head reminded him he shouldn't move so fast. Still, he crawled to the entrance and watched her walk quickly away, finally disappearing into a nearby lodge.

"Damn," he cursed himself in a low voice, "I'd sure like to have me some of that. I swear I could teach her a thing or two. Don't much like Injuns but I got me one helluva hankerin' for a woman and she looks fit."

Jack threw back the heavy buffalo skin that covered the lodge's entrance, leaned down on one elbow, and gazed into the cold night air. Stars were beginning to appear in the coming darkness and as he lay there, he slowly ate the roast meat and thought of the girl. "Wonder if her pa would like to do a little tradin'? I'd let him have a packet of vermillion or some beads for a few hours with his daughter." Jack rolled the proposition around in his mind and then, in a whisper, answered his own question, "Sure he would. Maybe! Hell, it won't hurt for me to ask; all he can say is no, and if he does that, I'll just take what I want anyway."

Finishing the meat, Jack wiped his greasy hands through his hair and then laid his head on his forearm; minutes later, he was sound asleep.

Several hours passed and the small fire that warmed the lodge had about exhausted itself. As the damp, cold crawled over his body, Jack Harris woke with a start. "Gawd," he whispered in a shivering voice, "it's colder than sin in here." He quickly rolled away from the lodge's opening and groped about for the small stack of brush that had been left to feed the fire. With the palms of his hands he formed a small cone and began to blow gently through it onto the smoldering coals. Small orange sparks responded to his coaxing and crackled wildly against the rush of his breath.

Once he had the fire going, Jack crawled back to where he had fallen asleep and began pulling the hide over the entrance to shut out the cold. In doing so, his eyes once again fell upon the lodge in which the girl had entered. Suddenly, all the thoughts and feelings of a few hours ago rushed back into his mind. "Reckon it's time for me to go a courtin,'" he whispered as he quietly rose to his feet and stepped from the lodge.

The morning broke clear and cold with a thick blanket of frost covering everything. Jim Tucker stepped from his lodge and stretched his arms above his head. His breath came out in long billowing clouds of steam. "Chilly this morning," he whispered to himself and slowly made his way toward Jack's lodge. He hadn't been able to sleep much during the night because of the situation between him and Jack. They had been friends for many years and had been in some tight spots together. And now, they were at each other's throats.

As he walked toward the lodge, his mind tried to sort it all out. "I guess most of this is my fault and I think I owe our friendship one more try."

Lifting the flap of the teepee, he stepped in. It was dark and his eyes could not make out his friend lying among the many robes. "Where the hell are ya, Jack?" he asked, straining to see. There was no answer. The warming fire had long since gone out and the place was as cold inside as out. "Hell, he's up and gone," Jim whispered. "I guess I should have tried to reason with him more last night, but sometimes he just makes me crazy. He can be downright obnoxious." With that, Jim turned and stepped back into the morning light.

He had returned to his lodge and was preparing to go hunting when he heard the screams and wailing. It was the death chant; he knew it all too well. "Now what the hell's goin' on?" he thought as he stepped outside.

Several people were gathered near one of the lodges and there was much commotion. The intensity of the group grew and those that wailed were being joined by others. Black Elk was suddenly among the people motioning for them to move away. Jim hurried to his old friend's side. "What has happened?" he asked.

Black Elk's eyes were filled with tears as he answered, "It is tragedy, my friend. Someone has murdered Otter and his family." He dropped his face and wiped away the tears. "He was my dearest friend; we were boys together. His wife was..." He could not go on, and seemingly embarrassed to show his feelings, turned away from Jim.

"May I look?" Jim asked. Black Elk nodded and Jim stepped through the lodge's entrance. The smell of blood hung in the air. As near as he could tell, there were four bodies. One was that of a man, Otter, he supposed. Two of the others were women, one older, probably the mother of the man or the other woman. All, had been stabbed numerous times and the man's throat had been cut. For the most part, the lodge was not cluttered and Jim surmised that no struggle had taken place. It appeared someone had crept in and killed them while they slept.

The fourth body was that of a young girl, perhaps fourteen, no more than seventeen for sure. There were no knife marks on her naked body. She was beautiful and looked as though she were only asleep but her head lay at a strange angle. Her neck had been broken and from all else he could derive in the dim light, he concluded that she had been raped.

As Jim turned to leave, his eyes fell upon a length of buckskin clutched tightly in the girl's hand. Slowly, he pried the stiff fingers apart revealing the thing. His heart seemed to stop for a moment as he gazed at the familiar talisman strung on the buckskin thong. So many times he'd commented about it and so many times Jack Harris had told him "This here's my lucky piece; I don't go no place without it."

Exhausted and weak from the previous day's ride, Clint lay in a death-like sleep. He did not hear the man enter the lodge.

"Clint!! Clint, wake up." The voice he recognized as Jim Tucker's but it seemed to be coming from a very distant place, somewhere far back in his mind. He stirred momentarily and repositioned himself under the warm robes. "Wake up, dammit, we're in a heap a trouble." This time the voice was closer and someone was shaking him.

Clint's eyes opened, trying to focus in the dim light. It was Jim Tucker alright. "What's the matter?" Clint stuttered in a raspy morning voice.

"Listen and listen good," Jim whispered. "It looks as if ole' Jack went crazy last night. He up and murdered some of these people and the whole damn camp is buzzin' like a hornet's nest. I know your head ain't real clear about all that's been goin' on lately, but you gotta know these folks are fixin' to skin us out. They figure we're as guilty as him."

Things were falling into place now and Clint remembered the goings-on of the day before.

37

"Black Elk's tryin' to calm em down," Jim went on, "but if he can't, all hell will break loose and me and you are gonna' be wolf bait."

Thinking for a moment, Clint asked, "Where's Jack now?"

"He high-tailed it outta here sometime last night" Jim answered. Then going on, he said "That's another thing...he stuck a knife in one of the boys that was guardin' the horses. The young man ain't dead but he's in purty bad shape. Jack also took about a half dozen head of their stock when he left."

"Smart," Clint said. "He'll use those horses to cover his sign lettin' one go every now and then just to confuse things and slow down the trackers. Jack's a mighty crafty old bird when it comes to stayin' alive."

"If'n they decide not to kill us, I'm goin' along on the search party...I think it's fittin'," Jim said. "Jack was my friend but he shouldn't a done this...I knew the folks he killed and they were decent people."

Jim paused for a moment and his voice took on a low, urgent tone, "You listen here Clint, I know you ain't too mobile, what with that game leg and all, but if'n you hear a lot a commotion goin on, you'd best try and slip out the back of this lodge...crawl if you have to. There's a thick grove of aspen about a hundred steps back; before I go, I'll tie a horse in there. With Black Elk and me away there won't be nobody here to speak for you...it could be bad."

"I'll be alright," Clint said "and I'll heed your words. I know enough of their lingo to understand what they're sayin' but the fact of the matter is, I couldn't outrun em' anyway Jim...hell they'd have me 'fore I got ten feet and you know it."

Jim looked at his friend without speaking, knowing that he was right.

"Well, you look out fer yer topknot just the same," he said and slipped out through the lodge's entrance.

#

Jack Harris moved at a steady pace, keeping the horses in the stream so as not to leave any tracks. There were four of them besides the one he rode and all were tied nose to tail so that they followed in a single line.

He had been traveling all night and was tired but his keen eyes didn't miss a thing. He was a man on the run and he had to be careful and smart. He kept scanning the banks of the brushy river looking...looking, watching for something...anything that would aid him in his escape. It would have to be good and he wouldn't get a second chance.

This wasn't the only time Jack Harris had had to run for his life. Others had tried to catch or kill him but he had always managed to come out on top. He had always gotten away. He knew he had a good head start but he also knew that as soon as the bodies were discovered, the whole tribe would be after him. They would know that he would try to hide his tracks in the river and they would follow it coming fast, trying to overtake him.

"There!" he said to himself, staring toward the right at a small tributary stream running into the Beaverhead. "That could be just what I need." With that, Jack slid from the back of his horse and guided the string of animals toward where the small stream merged with the larger. Here, he tied the reins of his horse and the lead rope to the string of ponies to a stout clump of willows. Reaching into his possibles sack, he brought forth a length of rawhide and stuffed in into the pocket of his coat. Moving quickly, he went to the last horse in the string and cut the knot that secured it to the other animals.

The small stream was about ten feet wide where it joined the other. Brush lined its edges and here and there large jutting rocks choked the water volume down to small, rushing, noisy, white torrents. Jack guided the horse up the stream, over the snags, and through the tangles of willows.

When he had reached what he thought to be a far enough distance from the main river, Jack began to search the shoreline. His eyes fell upon a patch of wild roses that were clumped in and among the willows on a steep bank. Tying the horse off to an overhanging tree limb, he hurried to the thorny briars. With his knife, Jack cut several of the largest stocks, stacking them in a bundle and trimming them to a near two-foot length.

When the bundle had reached the size of his forearm, he took the length of rawhide from his coat, wet it in the stream, and lashed it tightly around one end of the rose stalks. Then, moving back to the horse, he gently slid the sharp bundle of thorny roses under her soft belly, near her flanks; the free end of the rawhide he looped over her back.

"Gotta do this quick," he said to himself, "else she'll kick me from here to Sunday."

Holding the loose end of the rawhide in one hand, Jack gently raised the rose stalks up to meet the tender flesh with the other. Then, he firmly pulled at the rawhide strap; this caused the bundle to bend around the horse's belly much like a thorny girdle.

As he secured the rawhide strap to the other end of the rose stalks, the horse began to react. At first it was like a nervous twitch. But the more she moved, the more the thorns dug into her flanks. Jack barely had time to untie the guide rope from the limb when the mare went crazy. In her panic, she tried to turn about in the willow lined stream and run back the way they'd come. Jack though, slapped her on the side of the face with his hat and headed her upstream. Now, the faster she ran, the more the thorns cut into her soft paunch.

Jack stood watching her as she crashed wildly away up the boulder strewn stream. "That ole bugger'll run til she drops with them briars a diggin' into her," he whispered to himself. "Hate to do that to a good horse but she oughta leave plenty of tracks to foller soon as she breaks away from this stream; that'll give them red bastards somethin' to do while'st I hightail it in a different direction." With that, he returned to the other horses and continued downstream.

#

Jim Tucker rode at Black Elk's side as they made their way down the Beaverhead. The Indian leader had managed to calm his people through his explanation that these men were honorable. He had noted that Jim was his blood brother, married to one of the daughters of the tribe and Clint was badly injured and ridden with fever; neither man could have had any part in what happened. Just the same, Jim had tied a horse for Clint in the trees out back of the camp where he said he would.

Leaving camp, they had seen where Jack had traveled along the river's edge and finally entered the water with the horses but they couldn't be sure whether he'd gone up or down the stream. Several of the camp's warriors headed upstream in case he went that way.

"We should've left earlier," Jim thought to himself. "At least we'd a had some chance at catchin' ole Jack. These fellers take too long to get goin'. Hell, by the time they get their war paint on and do all them religious things they do, the trails got cold and ole' Jack's done slipped away."

"Tucker, you say something?" It was Black Elk, speaking then. Trying to find the right words, Jim spoke slowly, "No my friend, my mind was wandering and my lips were trying to follow." Pausing for a moment, he went on, "I was thinking what I would do if I were Jack. How would I get away and where would I go to spend the winter?" Black Elk watched his friend sort through his thoughts; patiently, he waited for the answers to the questions.

"My guess is Jack will use the river for his getaway...yessir, that's what he'll do; you can hide a whole lot of sign in a river. Here and there he'll release a pony to throw us off the trail and slow down the trackin'. Then, he'll look for a good size stream runnin' into the main branch and follow it to its head. Yup, and when he comes out he'll cover his tracks as best as possible and beat it over the mountain to the next valley. Then..." it was here, that Jim paused for a long moment thinking. "Then, I believe he'll head south and ride like hell; he'll winter in the high desert country. Not too much snow there and game is plentiful." Looking at Black Elk he smiled a half smile and said, "That's what I'd do."

#

Jack Harris knelt in the shallow edges of the Beaverhead looking around and contemplating his next move. "Time to give 'em another set of tracks to follow" he said to himself. He stood and removed the large knife from the sheath that hung at his side. Carefully, he cut another of the Indian ponies loose from the string. He then led the horse through the waist deep water to the opposite side of the river. Once there, he released the pony and slapped it as it stepped ashore. "Yaw! Get on outta here horse," he yelled as the animal bolted away. He knew it would make its way back to the camp but in the by and by it would cause some of the braves to spend time tracking it.

It was late in the morning now and the dark scattered clouds threatened a storm. Only here and there did they allow the sun to peek through. A light breeze from the south had come up and as it touched Jack Harris' face, he pulled his horse to a stop and scanned the sky. "Damn," he muttered to himself, "it looks like a storm's comin'. That'd help this ole beaver out some. Rain or snow would likely hide my tracks and I could give 'em the slip for sure."

Pausing a moment longer, his keen eyes studied the lay of the land before him. Less than a mile ahead, the river swung more toward the east bringing it close against the rugged mountains. "I gotta find me a way outta this river a fore it storms," he whispered. "I need a place...a way...a trail where they can't follow me." Looking at the rugged side hills ahead, he whispered, "Maybe that's the place...maybe." He rode on.

#

"I think we should ride like hell down this river and try to catch up with him." Jim was speaking to Black Elk as they rode with the tracking party. "Jack's slicker'n a greased pig, Black Elk, and if we don't catch up to him quick it's gonna storm and we'll lose him for sure. He'll slip away without leavin' a track." The wise Indian studied the face of his friend and listened carefully to what he said. "Yes, I think you're right. We'll let the others try to find the man's track and you and I will ride ahead." Black Elk spoke to his braves and then he and Jim rode across the river. They worked their way out of the heavy willows and took off at a gallop downstream.

#

Jack was now at the place he'd seen from a distance. The mountains were indeed close to the river here. Two hundred yards ahead he noticed a heavy growth of willows coming out from a steep canyon that had before, been hidden to his eyes. "A stream!" he said "a stream that will take me to safety."

Jack rode to the confluence of this stream and saw that it was almost as large as the Beaverhead itself. "This'll do," he whispered. "Now what I have to do is let this last horse go. Best to let him go downstream a ways..." Jack sat for a long moment and laid out the plan. "Release the horse...high tail it back here and ride to the head of this river...then, find me a place where I can slip out and be gone."

A half mile downstream was another canyon that came directly down to the river. It also had a stream in it but it was only a trickle. "Good place," he whispered to himself as he prepared to let the last of the Indian ponies go.

Jack swung down from his horse, tied him off to a large willow near the shore and cut the line that held the last pony. Carefully, he made his way up the small stream making sure not to leave much sign. He wanted them to find only the things a man would overlook when he was running for his life, a broken twig here, a small stone overturned there.

As he made his way ahead, the pony suddenly started acting up. It pulled back on the lead rope and began whinnying. Jack held on and yanked hard on the rope. "C'mon, God dammit," he cursed "I ain't got time for this." The horse, seeming to calm down, came along. But within ten steps, it again violently reared, jerking the rope from Jack's hand and setting him flat on his backside in the mud.

"You son-of-a-bitch," Jack screamed as he watched the horse disappear down the narrow stream bed. "Them damn Injun ponies are wilder'n March hares," he cursed. "Well, at least she'll leave a set a tracks to follow."

Picking himself up from the mud, Jack heard a small grunt behind him. Turning, he suddenly saw what had caused the horse to bolt. Less than eight feet from him stood a huge grizzly bear. Its head was lowered and its close-set beady black eyes stared unwaveringly, burning holes through him. The bear seemed puzzled by what stood before it.

Jack didn't move. His heart was racing and his gut was tied in a knot. He could feel his pulse pounding at his temples. He'd had run-ins with bears before and he knew they were nothing to trifle with. He also knew they were unpredictable, some would run and others...well, he didn't want to think of that right now.

His rifle was loaded, as always, but he'd have to nail the bear smack between the eyes if he hoped to stop it. A bullet any place else would only make it madder. "Don't panic," he told himself, "let it make the first move."

The bear did not move other than to raise its head and sniff the air, trying to make out the strange scent. Then, clearing its nose, the bear suddenly snorted, blowing out a large gob of mucus. So close was the animal, that the gooey mass landed smack on the front of Jack's coat.

Before he could stop himself, Jack's temper flared and he stood cursing the thing and bringing his rifle up. "You filthy bastard. Nobody or nothin' blows his nose on Jack Harris and gets away with it."

At the sound of the man's voice, the bear jumped backwards, almost as if to run. In that same moment, Jack fired. The fiery hot rifle ball hit the animal directly in the teeth, knocking a good portion of them out before ripping through the side of its jaw. In agonizing pain, the bear reeled backwards, pawing at its shattered maw.

With the shot, Jack was off and running; running for all he was worth. Through the smoke, he could not tell if he'd made a fatal shot. He didn't dare turn to see where the bear was; he only hoped he could reach the horse and be gone from here. Hell, the Indians that were tracking him probably heard the shot. Now he'd really have to do some tricky dodging. His only hope lay in the possibility that it would storm. He knew if it did, he could lose them. Other than that, he could only ride like hell over the mountain and pray that he had enough head start.

Thirty yards ahead of him stood the horse, tied just as he had left it. In ten long strides, he was at the edge of the river. Three more and he'd be home free. Just then, the animal reared backward, stumbling on the stony bottom of the river to keep its footing. Wild-eyed and snorting, it broke free from the willow and stampeded toward the distant shore.

Jack knew, without turning, what awaited him. With a deft hand, he yanked his large hunting knife from its sheath and wheeled to meet his fate. The bear had run him down and was now coming forward on its hind legs.

Looking up to its ten-foot height, Jack could see the grizzly's ears laid flat back against its head. Its thick neck was arched in a forward bow and its muscular forelegs with their three-inch long claws were raised and poised to do battle. The wound to the bear's face caused its jaw to droop at an awkward angle, producing a somewhat sinister, blood-drenched, smile.

"Yer one ugly sombitch," Jack screamed, charging headlong into the bear's grasp. Wildly, he slashed with the knife. But all too quickly, the huge limbs closed round him. He felt his backbone and his ribs snap like twigs as the bear unleashed its fury. The pain was unbearable and he screamed with what air was left in his lungs.

Slamming him to the ground, the bear bit into Jack's left shoulder, taking his whole upper chest in its wounded mouth. Viciously, it shook him, biting and chewing, and shaking some more. Again and again, Jack stabbed at the musty underbelly of the beast but his strength was gone and both of his arms were broken. He could not breathe and he felt like a rag doll, as the thousand-pound bruin had its way with him.

Jack's broken ribs had punctured a lung and blood gurgled up in his throat causing him to choke violently. This enraged the beast all the more and it bit him again and again about the face and the neck.

And then, he heard something, something familiar, something from a faraway dreamland. It was a sound, a friendly sound; it was the sound of a rifle shot. He suddenly felt the powerful body go limp and a tremendous weight began smashing him into the ground.

Jim's shot had hit the bear just behind the ear and killed him instantly, dropping him squarely on top of Jack. Jim and Black Elk struggled to roll the animal off the man but he was so heavy they couldn't move him. They ended up using a fallen log to pry Jack loose.

What they found when they uncovered him was something neither of them had ever seen before. So badly was he mauled and bitten, that he was almost unrecognizable. It appeared that every bone in his body had been broken. His face had long gashes with the bone showing through in several places. Large chunks of his hair and scalp had been ripped away and one of his ears was torn off. The bear had also clawed him viciously about his back and shoulders and his ribs and entrails were visible.

Surprisingly, Jack was not dead. Both men were astonished when the mutilated body began to moan and twitch.

"Jack! Jack, it's me...Jim. Jack, can you hear me?"

"I hear ya pard," came the gurgling reply. "God, I'm so broken up. Look at me… just look at me."

Jim sat there in sad amazement wondering how a human being could live through such a mauling.

Struggling to get the words out, Jack whispered, "Jim, I'm sorry for what I did to those people. One thing led to another and - well, you know how I am. Tell Black Elk I'm...I'm sor ..." Never finishing the word, Jack's body went limp and a small wisp of breath escaped his lips. Both men knew it was over.

After a while, Black Elk turned to his friend. "The Great Spirit saw to it that he paid for what he did. The bear was sent to take vengeance on this murderer."

Jim placed his hand on the shoulder of his long-time friend and replied, "I guess yer right. He got what was comin' to him. But I can't help feelin' bad. He was my friend and I will miss him."

Together, they buried Jack where he lay. Afterward, they piled stones on the grave to keep the animals from digging him up. Jim lashed two sticks together in the form of a cross and pushed it into the soft river bank.

As the two men mounted their horses, Jim cast one final look over his shoulder at the mound of rocks with its rugged marker. "So long, Jack," he whispered, "I hope God smiles on ya."

The journey back to the Indian camp was spent in silence, neither man spoke.

CHAPTER 4:
HEALIN' TIMES

The December morning was brisk. A heavy frost lay over the land, adding a chilly sparkle to all things it touched. Jim Tucker and two braves rode silently from camp toward the river. As they passed the lodge where Clint was recovering, Tucker leaned from his horse toward it and said in a half-whisper, "You awake Clint?"

For a moment, all was silent. Then, an equally quiet reply issued forth, "I am now. Where the hell you goin'?"

"Seen some geese flyin' along the river at daybreak, headin' downstream," Jim replied. "Peered to be they was lookin' fer some place to set down. Me and my two brothers-in-law, here, thought we'd see if we might get lucky. Geese would taste good for a change; I'm gettin' damn sick of eatin' deer." He paused for a moment and then added, "Yer welcome to come along if'n yer up to it."

Again, the answer was slow coming, "Leg's too stiff, Tuck. Besides, this cold makes it ache like you can't believe. You go ahead; I'll go with ya next time." With that, Jim Tucker nudged his horse forward and the three men rode quietly from the camp.

Clint, still only half awake, turned on his side and pulled the heavy warm buffalo robe further up over his head. The early drowsiness of morning caused his mind to wander and carried his thoughts back in time to when he was a boy. He suddenly thought of his mother and although he could not clearly see her face, he did remember her features. She had been a thin woman, small in size with high cheek bones, pale blue eyes, and a pointed nose. Her hair was light brown and long days in the summer sun would turn it even lighter; he recalled how it stuck to the side of her brow when she would sweat and how stringy it looked at the end of the day when she would be so tired, she'd come into the cabin and collapse on the bed without eating supper or even getting undressed.

And then, there were her hands. He remembered how rough and strong they had become from plowing and doing chores. And yet, when needed, they could thread a needle and stitch a fine new dress or make up a batch of whompin' good cookies. Mostly, he remembered their gentle touch, how they were always there to hold him or care for him when he skinned a knee or became ill.

A quiet tear suddenly escaped Clint's eye tracing a path down across his cheek. Where had time gone? It seemed only moments since those loving hands were upon him. And yet, it had been years ago and in a place so far away.

"Shit," he sighed wiping his cheek,"I gotta get myself up and movin' instead a lyin' here feelin' all melancholy and sad."

With that, he sat up, stretched, and looked around. In the dim light of the lodge his eyes could barely make out the prostrate forms of Black Elk and his wives and children huddled under their warm robes.

The small fire in the center of the lodge had reduced itself to a heap of glowing coals. The warmth of it, however, and the aroma of last night's roast venison still hung in the air as Clint rose and moved silently toward the door.

Stepping from the warmth of the lodge into the morning air, Clint was immediately immersed in the winter's chill. So shocking was his first breath that it spewed back in a gut-wrenching cough of steam and spit as his lungs rebelled against the bitter cold. He quickly placed his hands over his puckering mouth.

"It's colder'n a whore's heart," he mumbled, "always makes me wanna pee."

Most Indians relieved themselves where ever and whenever they felt the need. But Clint had never gotten used to that and always walked away from camp to where there was some privacy.

This morning, he was moving a little slow as he made his way to a nearby grove of trees. The cold made his leg ache. It had been over two months since he'd arrived at the camp. In that time, the squaws had worked on his leg using poultices made from roots and dried moss. At night, they would bind the wound, tying pieces of cooked, fatty meat over it. This seemed to draw the poison out.

When Clint became stronger, Black Elk's three wives often took him to a nearby hot spring. There, they would help him undress and he would spend hours soaking in the soothing warm water. Afterward, they would dry him and gently massage his leg to keep the muscles working. It had always astounded him how dedicated these women were to helping him get well. Then, one day at the hot spring, he noticed them giggling and making gestures about the size of his genitals. He knew then, they were enjoying this as much as he was.

Although he often longed for a woman, Clint had no desire to get involved with these women, for to do so would most certainly result in a slow, painful death. After all, they were the chief's wives and it would not be wise to embarrass the man in front of his tribe. Clint did think, however, that since these women had been so good to care for him, he owed them something. So, upon finishing his bath that day, he boldly stood before them in all his manliness, flexing and strutting back and forth until they could stand no more and they all burst out laughing. After that, however, whenever they went to the spring, they took one of the village men along.

Despite the doctoring and good care, the leg continued to bother him. Clint asked Jim to make another attempt at removing the arrowhead but he refused, saying that the leg was healing on its own and that they shouldn't mess with it right now. Also, he suggested that if it continued to bother him after it healed, Clint should probably travel back to the settlements and have a real doctor perform the operation.

Although the process was slow, the wound did heal and Clint seemed to get around well enough. Not wanting to re-injure it, he deliberately walked stiff legged and favored the limb while it healed. He didn't know how the leg would be if he really had to put it to the test. Hopefully, it would grow stronger before that time came.

Finishing his morning pee, Clint hobbled back to the lodge and drug out the heavy buffalo robe that he used for sleeping. He spread it out fur-side up next to the lodge where he had a commanding view of the river. Carefully, he lowered himself onto the large robe and proceeded to wrap it about him. The winter sun was now above the crest of the mountains and its warm rays poured down on him making him feel most comfortable.

The usually gurgling river lay hushed beneath a solid blanket of ice and only the occasional voice of a small bird in the willows at the river's edge could be heard. Looking out upon the expanse before him, Clint realized how much he loved winter mornings; their absolute cold and surrounding silence were so crisp, so unyielding. Yet in their own way, they created within him, a sense of peaceful solitude, some small, inner voice that whispered "You belong here; this is your home." It suddenly occurred to him that if God ever decided to start the whole world over again it would surely begin on a morning such as this.

As Clint sat pondering the thought, the report of a far-off rifle shot reached his ear. "Must be Tucker," he thought to himself. "Probably caught up to them geese. Hope he had enough sense to use pepper shot on 'em."

Clint had done that many times as a boy. Instead of loading his rifle with a single bullet, he'd add extra powder, cover it with a hard patch of paper, and dump in a handful of lead shot. It'd kick like hell and your shoulder would bruise up the next day. But if you took your time and were sneaky, you could line up several geese and take 'em all down with one shot.

Within the hour, Clint could make out the three horsemen returning to camp. When they got near enough, he knew that Tucker had done exactly as he thought, for hanging across one of the Indian ponies was a nice string of geese.

"Not bad for one shot, huh?" Tucker yelled out.

Clint smiled acknowledging his friend's success and answered, "We're gonna eat good tonight."

CHAPTER 5:
ORDEAL IN THE WATER AND FOND GOODBYES

Winter was a long time going. Clint's confinement to camp during his recovery had about driven him crazy. Once, he had ventured forth with Tucker to search out some elk that had been spotted by one of the camp's hunting parties. His leg had been feeling alright and so he had decided to go along to break the monotony. It was, however, only a matter of minutes in the saddle before his leg let him know he'd made a mistake. The pain forced him to turn back.

Clint rode straight to the lodge and once inside, pulled his britches down to inspect the leg. He found it had turned an ugly dark purple all around the scar. Apparently, it hadn't healed as well as he thought. After that, he stayed close to the lodge and took it easy.

Spring finally arrived and the ice disappeared from the river. But now, it ran wild and muddy. Each day the melting snow from the surrounding mountains forced it ever higher up its banks. Mornings and evenings were still on the cool side but the days were pleasant. Many of the trees and bushes were beginning to bud out, anticipating the coming summer.

Black Elk's camp was preparing to leave the Beaverhead and return to their summer hunting grounds. Each year, at this time, the whole tribe worked together readying themselves for the mass migration. Everyone had a job to do, even the children. Clint was amazed at how quickly they prepared for the trip. It took them less than a day to pack it all up.

Jim Tucker walked up as Clint was putting the last of his belongings into a deerskin parfliech. "Need a hand?" Jim said, smiling.

"Nah," came the reply, "I can handle it." Clint finished tying the flap down on the big leather bag. "What now?" he asked.

"Now, we all sit down to one last, big meal and then it's off to the hills. This here dinner though has a whole lotta religious ceremony tied in with it. You know, sorta like thankin' the Great Spirit fer gettin' em through another winter. They get mighty reverent, they do."

The two white men sat on a buffalo robe that had been spread out for them and watched the women stir the large cooking pots. Chunks of venison, elk, and buffalo had been put in the kettles early that morning. Various roots, herbs, nuts and whatever else they could find had been added to enhance the brew as it cooked through the day. The aroma it gave off made Clint's mouth water; he was ready to eat.

The feast began with the beating of drums and a call to the Great Spirit to bless the people and allow them a safe journey. At the same time, several braves with painted faces performed a ceremonial dance around the cooking pots. The women of the tribe scurried about between the writhing dancers, serving their men. Two women, whom Clint had never seen before, brought large servings of meat to him and Jim. They whispered what sounded like a blessing as they handed it to the two men. Jim answered with a brief thank you in Shoshone and the women went away smiling.

The meal was delicious. Everyone ate until they could eat no more. The drums were now silent and the dancers had retired to claim their share of the tender meat. Groups of people sat around laughing and talking, enjoying each other's company. "It hasn't been a bad winter," they were saying, "and truly, the Great Spirit has been good to us."

Clint leaned back on one elbow and wiped the grease from his beard. "Gawd Jim, that was one fine meal. Can't say as I've ever et one any better. These folks treat us real good. You know, it makes you feel like we're part of a big family."

Jim knew what Clint meant and just shook his head in agreement.

"Peers to me as these folks have taken to you too, Clint," Jim said, without looking at his friend. "You been grateful to 'em fer helpin' ya and you've been understanding of their ways. Yes sir, I do believe they've accepted you as one of their own." Clint thought for a moment and then replied, smiling, "Don't appear to me as they had much choice in the matter. You just kinda dumped me in their laps and they couldn't do anythin' else. I am mighty grateful though. I do believe I'd a gone under or worse yet, lost my leg if'n it hadn't a been fer these folks." Jim smiled and shook his head in agreement.

For a long moment, Clint sat thinking about what Jim had just told him. It gave him a good feeling, like he belonged somewhere. He hadn't felt that way in a long time, probably since he'd left the settlements

"Excuse me pard," Clint said standing up, "but nature's callin' and I gotta make a quick trip to the trees."

Hurriedly, he made his way out of what was left of the camp toward a thick grove of trees near the river bank. It was quite a ways downstream from the campsite and he had long-ago selected it as his private place. He chose it because it afforded him the solitude he desired and also, it was far enough away, that everyone else in camp would not use it. After an Indian camp had been in one place for a while, it got mighty aromatic. There were only so many bushes to go behind and when they got used up, whew.

Clint had just finished his business and was walking from the trees when he heard the commotion. What had before been a friendly, relaxed, get-together had now, suddenly turned into something else. He could hear women screaming and frantic shouts filled the air. Everyone was up and running toward the river.

In an instant, he knew what was wrong; he had seen the children playing near the water when he walked to the trees. Swiftly he cut to his right and fought his way through the thick tangle of willows. The raging river ahead of him churned violently as it fought against the trees and brush that now stood in its path.

Clint reached the edge of, what had before, been the river bank. Here, the trees ended and it was open water ahead of him. He waded into the water up to his chest and stood clinging to a firmly rooted river birch. Carefully, he scanned the swollen river as he heard the cries of the people getting nearer.

The surface of the undulating, muddy mass was an uneven contour of ever-changing hills and valleys, created as it rushed over the rocks and snags that lay below in its belly. In the afternoon's fading light, Clint strained to catch a glimpse of the child he suspected had fallen in. Nothing could he see as he stood in the freezing deluge. The movement of the river was almost mesmorizing as it swirled and churned its way around and past him. "Jesus help me," he said out loud, "if there's a child here help me find him."

Almost before the words had left his lips, he saw the girl's gasping face and delicate arm with its tiny hand rise from the abyss and then go under as quickly. Clint launched himself forward with every ounce of strength he possessed. The river closed around him. Now, he too was engulfed in its power.

"C'mon little one, where are you?" he thought as he fought the current to get in line with where he thought the girl would pass. Suddenly, almost violently, he was struck in the chest by something he could not see. Clint's natural reaction caused him to grab at whatever it was that had almost knocked the wind out of him. His strong hands instantly recognized the small, struggling body as the current pressed her against him. Quickly, he lifted the child above the torrent trying to allow her a needed breath. As he did, the child's weight forced him down and he gasped to gain a lung full of air, before the brown water washed over his face.

Clint strained to hold onto the child as the heaving brown mass forced him ever downstream. Each time he managed to come in contact with the bottom, Clint would push off trying to get closer to the shore. It was impossible to hold the child and make any attempt to swim. She was in a panic scratching and clawing at him; he couldn't believe how strong she was.

Ahead, the river made a wide turn to the left. This meant that the might of the current would force him and the girl even closer to the willow lined shore. The problem was that once it made the lazy arch to the left, the river quickly reversed its path, making a sharp turn back to the right. It was at this point also that it began a narrow trek through a small gap in the low surrounding hills. Eons ago, many large boulders had sloughed off the steep hillsides and rolled into the river. Clint had seen this place on one of his jaunts from camp and had, at the time, thought how rugged the small canyon looked. He knew if they didn't get out before they reached the boulders, they wouldn't get out at all.

Quickly, Clint forced the child away from him, holding only a handful of her thick long hair. Then, with all the strength he possessed, he stroked and kicked to reach the willows. The child, feeling herself being pushed away, fought even harder. Clint felt the stinging pain of her fingernails as they dug into the flesh of his arm.

The willows were now going by in a blur. As he surfaced to take a quick breath, Clint's eyes searched the shore for something to grab hold of but there was nothing within his grasp. Twice, he felt his hand dash against pieces of submerged brush but too quickly, they were there and gone.

Through it all, Clint had only been concerned with saving the child's life. Now, the bitter realization that he too may die, suddenly filled his mind. A jolt of panic shot through him and he imagined himself being pulled beneath the surface, losing that last breath, seeing that last light of day disappear as he unwillingly gave in to the murky grave. "No Goddammit, no," he screamed and stroked even harder.

Try as he might though, Clint could not seem to reach the willows. The coldness of the water and the exertion he had expended holding the child came in on him with a crushing force. He was suddenly exhausted, worn out. His resistance to the river and his willingness to survive were gone; he had tried. God, how he had tried. But now, perhaps, it wouldn't be so bad to just let go, just give in. He couldn't think straight now, nothing made sense.

Then, somewhere above the roar of the river came a familiar sound. "Clint! Clint! Grab hold here, quick." The words came to Clint's ears but he couldn't imagine who was saying them. Now, rising from the torrent before him, was a horse - a giant, beautiful horse. And sitting astride the horse was Jim Tucker. This had to be a dream and yet, there he was, big as life.

Jim seemed to be screaming something at him. It was hard to understand. "C'mon you crazy sombitch grab hold a my hand fore ya drown."

Clint could not respond, he was too weak. Jim reached down and snared Clint around the neck and shoulder and then spurred the horse toward shore. The horse in a wild panic scrambled to gain his footing on the slick bottom and stumbled his way back to the willowy shoreline. When they were within the protection of the brush, Jim eased his grip on his friend and let him down.

"Where's the girl?" Clint said, suddenly becoming aware of what was happening.

"Right there in your hand," Jim replied. "Now, let go of her hair and I'll try to help her."

Dismounting, Jim carried the child to dry land. Clint staggered along behind, coughing and still not sure of what was happening. Many of the villagers were now arriving and there was much noise and confusion. Jim wrapped the child in a blanket that someone offered and at the same time shouted something in Shoshone. Several people immediately began to gather grass and dry pieces of sagebrush. From somewhere, a flint and steel were produced and one of the braves hurriedly started a fire.

Clint was soaked and freezing cold as the reality of the situation slowly crept back into his mind. A buffalo robe was wrapped about him and he was escorted to the newly made fire. The girl, crying and shaking violently, was now being calmed by her mother. Gently, she caressed the child, rocking her back and forth and singing quietly in her ear.

The warmth of the fire and the comfort of the heavy robe soon had the child smiling. The villagers were now gathering around Clint smiling and whispering unfamiliar words. Many of them reached out gently touching him about his head and shoulders. From across the fire, the girl's mother looked at him and nodded. Although she said nothing, her eyes told him thank you.

"You all right?" Jim asked, kneeling at Clint's side.

Clint looked at him for a long moment before answering. "Thought I was a goner there for a minute," he replied.

"Couldn't believe my eyes when I looked up and saw you there on that horse. You saved my bacon, Jim."

"You saved the girl," Jim quickly put in. "That was a hell of a thing you did."

Then, neither man said anything more. Quietly, they watched the fire, concentrating on the crackling heat and reliving the near brush with death. Tomorrow, this would be but a memory and they would all be on their way to the summer camp. But right now, the weight of it hung on each member of the tribe and especially on the two white men who had become their true friends.

#

Clint was busy readying his horse when he heard the cheerful greeting from his friend.

"Mornin' Clint," Jim said as he led his horse into the circle of light given off by the small fire.

"It'll be dawn soon and we'll be on our way. I kin hardly wait to get shed of this damn place. Seems as though we been here forever."

"There, that oughta do it," Clint said tying off the rolled buffalo robe at the back of the saddle. Quickly he took a mental inventory of his belongings, knife, hatchet, possibles sack, shooting pouch, and rifle. Everything seemed in order.

When Jack Harris had been killed by the bear, Jim brought his rifle back to camp and presented it to Clint.

"Here," he'd said, "this'll get you through 'til you git a new one. It ain't much to look at but it shoots plumb center. Besides, I do believe he'd want you to have it."

Now, in the dim light of morning, Clint once more inspected the rifle. The deep scratches from the bear's claws showed through the heavy tallow grease that he'd rubbed into the aged maple stock. Clint had cleaned and re-cleaned the gun a dozen times and had, on occasion, gone away from the camp to fire it. Jim was right, it did shoot center.

"Jim, there's somethin' I been fixin' to tell ya," Clint said, fussing with the saddle cinch. "I won't be goin' with ya to summer camp."

The momentary silence caused by the remark was suddenly broken by Jim's gentle laugh.

"I knew all along you wouldn't be goin'," he laughed. "You ain't the community kind and I figured it was only a matter of time for you lit out."

"You know I'm plumb grateful to these folks and all they done for me," Clint offered, "But, I got this itch to git goin'..." Clint turned then to face his old friend, "you know how it is?"

Jim smiled and shook his head. "Yeah," he said "I know just how it is."

Clint then swung himself up into the saddle. "Jim, I ain't good at sayin' goodbye, so if you would, tell em for me."

"I'll do that my friend," Jim answered. "You take care, now. Keep your eye on the skyline and yer nose to the wind. We'll cross trails again sometime."

Without looking back, Clint spurred the horse up onto the same embankment along which they'd first ridden into the camp so many months before. Upon reaching its crest, he turned the pony to the northeast. Ahead of him, the shadowy mountains stood silhouetted against the morning's dim sky. Through his tears, their outline was a blur.

CHAPTER 6:
GOLD FOR THE TAKIN'

Several months had passed since Clint's departure from the Indian village. His leg was no better. Each time he exerted himself, it would stab at him with shooting pains. Then, within minutes, it would begin to swell and turn dark purple. The arrowhead, lodged in the bone, was obviously cutting into the surrounding tissue, causing internal bleeding.

He knew he could not survive in this condition. This was harsh country and a man had to have all his faculties about him. Clint remembered that soaking his leg in the natural hot springs near the Indian camp had given him some relief from the nagging pain. And so, upon leaving Jim and the rest, he headed to an area that he'd run across some years back while trapping. It was a high place where great streams of boiling water roared out of the ground. There were bubbling mud pots and azure blue pools. Stinky, they were, and all of 'em hot enough to scald a man.

Some, though, were located at the edge of a great lake. And where they overflowed into that lake, a man could soak his aching' bones and not be exposed to gettin' burned. Also, there was game a plenty and trout for the taking.

He would try this for a while. If the leg continued to bother him, he'd have to return to the settlements and seek some professional doctoring.

Clint made his camp some distance from the place where he took his daily baths. It was well concealed in a piney draw that lay a good half mile back from the edge of the lake. He'd not seen any Indian sign since he'd arrived but he knew they visited the area frequently.

Each day he would walk from the camp to the bath, varying his route so as not to leave a distinct trail. This would exercise the leg and at the same time, keep him from having to hide his horse. There wasn't much cover near the hot spring and a horse stood out like a sore thumb.

After his bath, he'd generally lounge around, fishing or drying some fresh killed meat. Sometimes, he would just pass the day away, watching the clouds roll by or snoozin' in the warm sun. Life was good here but to his dismay, the leg seemed no better.

One afternoon, he decided to follow the perimeter of the lake for a ways. Meat was getting short and maybe he could come onto some buffalo - take a nice fat cow. That'd be good for a change. He hadn't had hump ribs for some time and the thought of it made his mouth water.

Clint left camp, riding in a southeasterly direction. The country was a series of low rolling hills wooded in lodge pole pine and groves of silky green quaking aspen, their brilliant white trunks shining in the afternoon sun.

Between many of the low ridges were grass filled parks. Elk and deer abounded in these areas. Several times, he had excellent shots at these animals but passed them up in anticipation of bagging a buffalo.

As he mounted the top of a rolling hill, he pulled the mare up behind a stand of thick quakes and dismounted. Carefully, he stalked forward to a point where he could see the lush grassy meadow below him. It stretched away to the east, ending at the lake's edge. To the west and his far right, it petered out into small groves of quake, with here and there a pine intermingled.

Among these patches of trees, moved several large dark forms. He studied them for a moment and then a faint smile crossed his lips. "Buffalo," he whispered.

Quickly, he lifted the frizzen of the rifle, checking its powder charge. Once satisfied that it was ready to fire, he moved ahead to find a place from which to shoot. He wanted only to fire one bullet, no more. More than one shot could lead unwanted visitors directly to you.

Inching forward, he took his time. Great patience was required here. One must make sure the wind is in his favor and avoid making any sudden movements. All that done, Clint arrived at a fallen tree laying near the edge of the large meadow. The sneak had taken him nearly an hour. Lengthening afternoon shadows reminded him that most of the day was gone. If he wanted to bag one of these critters he'd best get it done soon.

The nearest animals, a large cow and a newborn calf, were perhaps 60 yards in front of him and slightly off to his left. Both were facing directly at him, lying on the ground enjoying what was left of the fleeting sunlight. The young cow he had selected, stood at a quartering angle away from him and was nearly twice the distance of the cow and calf. It would be a long shot but he couldn't get any closer without being seen.

Slowly, he pulled the hammer back to the full cock position and took a dead rest over the fallen tree. He nestled into the gun, making it comfortable upon his shoulder. Taking a deep breath, he placed the sight a little high and just back of the front shoulder.

"That should do it," he thought. "Take her square through the lights."

Slowly he released the air from his lungs. At the same time, his finger tightened on the trigger. The blissful silence of the afternoon was then interrupted by the booming crack of the big rifle. A billowing cloud of white smoke filled the air in front of him, not allowing him a full view of his quarry. He did not, however, have to see what had transpired, for the hollow-sounding "thwack" that followed the rifle's report told him that the animal was hit.

Clint struggled to get away from the smoke to see if the cow was down. As he did, he could hear the thundering hooves of the frightened herd disappearing into the distant trees at the far side of the valley. When he finally got a clear view of the area, no carcass was in sight.

"She's run off," he said in a disgusted tone. "Damn, I may have to shoot her again."

He reloaded the rifle and struck out to find the blood trail he knew would be there. As he did, he paced off the distance. He had reached a count of 146 paces when at last he came upon the blood spore.

"Not a bad shot if I do say so myself," he commented.

The trail was not hard to follow. There was a great deal of blood and it was bright red in color, indicating the animal was hit in the lungs. She wouldn't go far. Instead of following the rest of the herd, the cow had run back to the right, going into the trees near the head of the valley

Clint carefully watched ahead as he followed the meandering blood trail. He had gone, perhaps, a hundred yards into the trees when he at last saw the crumpled body, lying near an unusual outcrop of boulders. Skillfully, he approached the downed animal, slowly circling her, checking for any sign of life. Many's the careless hunter that had been gored or trampled, running up to check their kill.

The cow had died running; Clint could see the skid marks where she'd plowed up the ground with her nose. Now, he set about the arduous task of fleshing her out. Before doing so, however, he walked back and located his horse.

"Best get what meat I need from this old girl and be on my way," he said to himself. "Nights a comin' and the wolves and bears will want their share. I sure as hell ain't givin' em' any of mine."

As he cut the chunks of meat away, he laid them out on one of the pink colored boulders that lay adjacent to where the cow had dropped. This would keep the meat out of the dirt until he packed it up to take back to camp.

Skinning and cleaning a buffalo takes its toll on a knife's edge. And so, as he worked, Clint would often sharpen his knife, using the old whetstone he'd brought to the mountains. This was the only original thing he owned now. The rest of his gear he'd lost in the run-in with the Blackfeet.

As he began to hone the dulled blade of his skinning knife, Clint sat down on the large boulder, next to where the meat was laid out. Something hard poked him in the fanny and he raised up to brush it away. It was a piece of rock, dull yellow in color, and about the size of a rifle ball.

"Well, I'll be damned," he whispered, rolling it around in his hand. "This here looks like gold."

Quickly, he searched about for more of the yellow rock. It was then that he noticed the boulder upon which he was sitting had a solid streak running through its top as wide as a man's arm. It was fairly soft and with the point of his knife, Clint pried several chunks of it away.

"I reckon I'm a rich man," he smiled. "Now I can buy me a new gun."

Through the rest of the afternoon, Clint tended to the buffalo meat. He filled the two parfliechs that he'd brought from camp, taking only the choicest cuts of back straps, tongue, and hump-ribs. If he dried this much meat, he'd have enough to see him on his way. For during the last few days, he'd made up his mind to return to the settlements and locate a doctor who could patch up his ailin' leg. He knew it was only a matter of time before he'd be caught in a situation where he'd have to run or fight for his life. If that happened, he'd go under for sure because he couldn't count on the leg to support him. In the days that it took the meat to dry, Clint readied himself for the journey. He didn't stray far from camp knowing that if he did, the critters that were about would help themselves to his curing food supply. Only once did he venture out, returning to the place he'd found the gold. Here, he worked to fill two large leather bags with the heavy metal. Not having seen much gold in his life, Clint was surprised at its weight, it was heavier than the lead he used to mold bullets.

"Damn," he said, straining to tie the heavily laden bags to the horse's back. "A man could ruin his baby-makers liftin' that stuff."

Afterward, he gathered many smaller rocks and stacked them atop the large, gold laden boulder, thus hoping to conceal his discovery. However, in placing them, he couldn't help but notice that they too contained noticeable traces of gold. There was really no way to disguise it so he mounted his horse and rode toward the lake. At the shoreline, he dismounted and stacked up a large pile of rocks

"I think I could find this place again," he murmured, lifting the last stone into place, "but this here pile of boulders will be a good marker just in case I ever need any more of that gold."

Once he'd made up his mind to leave the mountains, there remained only one other decision to make, that being, which way to go. If he went north, following the shoreline of the lake, he would come to the large river that flowed out from it. This river was called the Yellowstone and it ran even further north and east before eventually joining the Missouri.

He had been this way several times and knew the route well. He also knew that for many miles it was terribly rugged country, steep and heavily wooded. There were high mountains, deep gorges, and large waterfalls. Often too, there were Indians along this path. The hunting and fishing was good here and so they frequented the area.

His other choice was to go south taking a circuitous route around the southern end of the big lake and continuing in a southeasterly direction. This way would take him across the Absaroka Mountains and down along the great divide to the Wind River. Coming out onto the plains, he'd continue to follow the Wind River to the place where it joined the northward bound, Beaver River. At this point he'd cross over and head straight east. It would be a much shorter route and with his leg being so bad, it would be the best way to go.

The Absaroka's were a beautiful stretch of country and he'd trapped and hunted them often. They too, had high peaks and rugged canyons, but the way through them was very passable. Only one thing bothered him about going this way. He'd been to the edge of the mountains several times and had heard his companions talk of the rolling hills and hollows that stretched east for hundreds of miles to the great Missouri River. But he'd never, himself, ventured out onto them.

Oh, he'd come up the Missouri all right, back when he was a green kid. He and the other 150 hunters and trappers in Manual Lisa's outfit had followed the river up to the mouth of the Yellowstone. Some of them, him included, had gone beyond that point, to the Musselshell and on to the Judith, finally reaching the great falls. It seemed like a hundred years ago.

Sometimes at night, sitting by the cook fires, the trappers would talk of the plains country, telling him of the gentle rolling hills with their brushy draws chuck full of deer and bear and grouse. They spoke too, of herds of strange animals that roamed the flat-topped mountains and sage covered valleys; they called them goats. A curious critter was how they described them, havin' dark black horns with a prong at each tip. Fast they were, and pretty, too, being a light brown on the back and white on the belly. Some say they can damn near outrun a rifle ball.

They also talked of the mighty herds of buffalo and the fierce tribes of Indians that hunted them. They said if you could manage to keep your hair and travel far enough east, you'd come upon the Platte River. Following it, you would eventually reach the Missouri.

He remembered the Platte and the place where it dumped into the Missouri. On their way to the mountains, Lisa had ordered that they bring the boats ashore and make camp there for the night.

Jack Harris and he had been assigned to gather wood for the fires. While they worked, Jack talked about the Platte saying it was the shortest way to the mountains. He said the river was too shallow to accommodate the large boats but a man on horseback could follow the Platte west and be to the Shining Mountains in a smidgeon of the time it takes to arrive there by boat.

It had sounded so easy and he hadn't forgotten Jack's directions, God rest his soul. But a man has a way of seeing things and places in his mind that may not be so. He gets fanciful ideas and starts makin' plans, then when he gets there, it ain't nothin' like he thought. That kinda thinkin' can get you killed in this country.

It was for this reason that Clint harbored a small seed of doubt in the back of his mind. Several times he'd asked himself if he'd made a wise choice by comin' this way. Hell, he knew nothing of the country he was headin' into. But each time, he'd put the thoughts away by concentrating on the beauty of the surrounding wilderness. It was something. Still, the doubt ate at him and made him uncomfortable.

CHAPTER 7:
STORM

The Wind River was beautiful. It sparkled under the morning sun and its bubbling voice mixed with the sounds of the insects and birds. Nature's music filled Clint's ears as he tended to his horses. It had been a long hard ride from the big lake and now it was time for a bath.

First, he led each horse into the stream, giving them each a good wash. Afterward, he washed himself and rinsed out his buckskins. The cold water felt good on his leg, seeming to numb it. The riding had been difficult. No matter which way he shifted in the saddle, he could not get comfortable. Each step the horse had taken had caused him pain. Now, it just felt good to stop and rest.

While his buckskins dried, Clint hunted about through the brush for some berries. On the afternoon before, while riding to his campsite, he'd noticed wild raspberries growing here and there. If they were ripe they'd be mighty tasty. He hadn't eaten anything sweet for God knows how long.

It was because he was used to walking quiet, that Clint was able to come onto the big bear without being seen or heard. It seems that someone besides himself was fixin' to dine on sweet berries. As he stepped around a large thicket of willow, Clint came face to face with the bruin. The animal had apparently been dining on the sweet fruit for some time for his face and chest were spattered with seeds and bright red dripping juice.

Immediately, the bear rose up on its hind legs. There they stood, face to face, a naked man and a messy black bear, staring directly into each other's eyes. Had it not been so frightening, it might have been funny but Clint was not laughing. He'd committed the unthinkable sin - he'd walked out of camp without his rifle.

"What the hell do I do now," he thought, grasping for answers. "No knife! No gun! Hell, maybe I oughta just pee on him."

With that, a crazy thought popped into his head and without further consideration, he quickly raised his hands above his head and screamed at the top of his voice. It completely caught the bear off guard and it whirled about and streaked off into the brush. Clint too, spun about and scurried to get his rifle.

"My God," he said, scolding himself, "I ought to be whipped for pullin' a stupid ass trick like that. Could a got myself killed."

"I'll go along with that," came an answering voice. "There for a minute, I thought that bear was gonna have you for dinner. Yer kinda skinny though and whiter'n my uncle's pet goose."

Again, Clint's heart leaped into his throat. Two times in one day was too much. Quickly he turned to face the chuckling voice.

"Sweet Jesus! You nearly scared me to death. Who the hell are you?"

"Name's Larch," came the answer "Theodore Larch, but you can call me Ned, everyone else does." Behind his cheerfulness, the man had the eyes of a hunter. Carefully, he looked Clint over, measuring him up. Apparently satisfied that he posed no threat, he again chuckled and asked, "And who might you be, neighbor?"

"My name's Jeffries, Clint Jeffries and if you'll pardon me a moment, I'll get my clothes on."

"That's probably a good idea," the man laughed, "I think you're scarin' my horse."

As he dressed, Clint looked toward his rifle leaning against the nearby river willow. The man's cautious eye caught his glance. For a moment, he was still but as he climbed from his horse his deep voice issued forth, "You made one mistake today, neighbor. Don't make another one. I don't want to have to kill you but if you go for that rifle, I'll shoot you where you stand." He paused and then added, "If it was your life I wanted, I could have shot you before. You'd have never known what hit you."

"I guess you're right," Clint answered, considering the man's words. "You'll have to excuse my manners, I ain't used to bein' around people."

The buckskins were cold and clammy as he slid them up over his rump.

"God I hate climbin' into wet clothes," he whispered. "Somehow, it don't seem natural."

Ned Larch had walked past him to the edge of the camp and was now looking back from the direction he'd come. "All right, come on in Lou," he yelled.

Clint stood there watching him and wondering what was going on. In a few moments, he heard horses approaching.

"That there's my wife and her sister," Larch commented, pointing to the oncoming riders. "Didn't want 'em gettin' in the way just in case I had some trouble with you. You understand?"

Clint understood but he didn't answer the question. As the women drew nearer, he could see they were Indian. From the look of their clothing and their accoutrements he guessed them to be Blackfeet. As he studied them, so too did they study him. Their intense stare led him to suppose they hadn't seen many white men.

Ned Larch walked toward them as they entered the camp. Softly he spoke to them and they both dismounted.

"You speak any Blackfoot, neighbor?" Larch asked.

Then, before Clint could answer, he added, "these girls are Piegans. They live further north than the Blackfeet but they're blood kinfolk to 'em and they speak nearly the same language."

Clint knew a little of the Blackfoot language. Jim had taught him a few phrases and key words when they first started trapping together. During long winter days and at night around the fire, Jim would converse with him in the tongue and make him practice.

"Could save yer hide someday," he'd say. "Might need it if'n you get yourself into a tight pinch."

"No I don't, Ned," Clint answered, not wanting to share that information. "Can't say as I ever learned it."

Satisfied with the answer, Larch again said something to the women and they started unloading the pack animal they had in tow.

"I told 'em to cook us up some food, neighbor. I hope that's all right with you?"

Clint nodded and went about finishing getting dressed.

It didn't take the women long to put together the meal. They spread out a soft buckskin mat and upon it laid out some dried elk meat and some flat bread-like biscuits. From the stream, they took up some water in a pottery bowl and mixed into it what looked like dried, mashed up meat. To this, they added some wild onion and other herbs. Together, it made a kind of watery brown looking soup but it didn't taste half bad. The biscuits were hard enough to break a tooth but when sloshed about in the soup, they softened up and tasted good too.

It still wasn't clear to Clint exactly what Ned Larch wanted. Most people in these parts were careful who they took up with. It wasn't that people, white people that is, weren't friendly and glad to see each other. It's just that one had to be careful. This was a savage land and the men who survived it weren't always honorable. And so, Clint waited, knowing that whatever it was Ned wanted would sooner or later come out.

Before they ate, Ned introduced his wife and her sister. "Neighbor, this here is my wife, Lou." He wrapped his huge arm around her shoulder and pulled her to him. "I call her that cause her Injun name don't make no sense. Besides, I can't say it with just one mouthful of air."

Grinning, he turned his attention to the other woman. "That gal there is my wife's older sister, Storm. Her Injun name is WaNeha-eo. That means Sky with Storm Clouds About. They couldn't a named her better. She's seen some hard times."

The woman lowered her eyes realizing that Larch was talking about her. Ned patted her on the knee and continued to speak. "Yes sir, she's seen some trouble, she has. She married a buck a few years back and he treated her all right. You know, as well as any buck treats his squaw. Then, he found out she couldn't bear him any children. Well, he ups and marries another woman, brings her into the teepee and turns Storm, here, into a slave. She done all the dirty work around the camp while the other woman just laid about breedin' an takin' it easy. When she began to complain, he beat her. The beatin's got to be an everyday thing so she lit out and come to find her sister." Larch paused for a moment and picked up the remaining piece of elk meat that lay on the buckskin mat before him. Popping it into his mouth, he went on. "When her husband found out she'd left, he come to our camp lookin' for her; had blood in his eye, too. He rode right up, jumped off'n his horse, and drug her from our teepee by the hair. Then, he proceeded to beat her with his quirt. I didn't dare step in bein' as how he had five other fellers with him. They don't like me anyway 'cause I married one of theirs and they'd have taken my hair and not thought twice of it.

Afterward, he tied a leather thong around her neck and made her walk behind his horse all the way back to camp, nigh onto ten miles it was. Wasn't bad enough that he done that but then he led her smack through the middle of the village. Everybody in camp was laughin' at her. She was disgraced in front of her own family.

That night, as a final insult, he decided he was gonna have himself a little bit, so he climbed in under her buffalo robe and set about pokin' her. Only thing he didn't figure on was that she'd hidden a knife in her moccasin when she was fixin' dinner. She did a little pokin' of her own. When she got through, he was stone dead. The other woman in the tent didn't pay any attention to the commotion, as it was a common occurrence. When the other woman had gone to sleep, Storm gathered up what belongin's she had and scooted outta there. Also, before she left, she cut off his balls and stuffed 'em in his mouth.

She rode to our camp again. But this time, when I found out what happened, I thought it best to high tail it out of there. I'm sure when they came lookin' for her, they'd have killed all three of us. Since then, I've done about everything I know to try and lose 'em and I think I've been successful. I don't believe they'll find us now.

I tell you though, it made the hair on the back of my neck raise up a little when I heard you comin' yesterday. You rode within a stone's throw of our camp and I thought at first you were those Injuns."

While listening to the story, Clint casually watched the woman Larch called "Storm." She was taller than most Indian women he'd seen and she was trim; he supposed it was because of the hard work she'd suffered. Though she looked like her sister, she was not as round faced. Both were very pretty but her face was longer and her mouth seemed somewhat drawn down at the corners. She carried a loneliness on her cheek and a sadness in her eyes that seemed to reflect the agonizing heartache and pain that Ned Larch had so vividly described.

"She'll not get close to another man," he thought. And then, in a whisper to himself, he murmured, "what a shame."

The meal was good. Clint thanked the women and moved a few feet backward, taking advantage of some nearby shade.

"Where you headed for now, Ned?" he asked, brushing some loose sand from his britches.

"Don't rightly know. I ain't too familiar with this part of the country. Gotta find someplace though, where game's plentiful and winters are mild. Maybe some special place along the big river. I'll know it when I see it."

For a moment, he paused and looked about, as though that special place might be right there within seeing distance. "I'm not much on trappin' or tryin' to get rich. I just like to hunt and fish and be left alone. Once a year though, when I run outta tobacco and my ball and powder are gettin' scarce, I travel north to the Missouri and trade what furs I've collected; usually, I meet up with some of the company men or sometimes even the French. They're always willin' to take prime fur in exchange for a few of their supplies."

Ned Larch reached down and began taking off his moccasins. Kicking the last one free, he got to his feet and walked to the river's edge. There, he waded in the rippling water, scuffing his toes along the sandy bottom.

"Whew, that feels good." Ned bent over and scooped up some water, washing it over his face and the back of his neck.

"And what about you, neighbor?" Ned asked. "Where you headin'?"

"Back to St. Lou I reckon," Clint answered.

With the mention of the word Lou, Larch's wife looked at Clint and smiled.

"Took an arrow in my leg last year, just above the knee. The point's still in there; buried in the bone. It causes me some grief, so I'm gonna find me a doctor that will take it out."

Without turning, Larch began to speak again. "Wouldn't mind taggin' along with you as far as the Missouri, if it's all right. Reckon I could meet up with some parties travelin' to the mountains; maybe do some tradin' with 'em. We could use some supplies."

"It's all right with me" Clint answered, "It's a free country and besides, I could use the company. I think it fair to warn you though, I'm headin' due east to the Platte. I never been that way before and it might be rough goin'." He paused for a moment waiting for some reply. When none came, he went on.

"Anyway, I figured from there I can build a raft or a bull boat and float to St. Lou. It'd be a whole lot easier on my leg ridin' a raft instead of a horse."

Ned Larch nodded his head in agreement. "Sounds good to me, neighbor. Let's get goin'."

By midafternoon of the next day, they had arrived at the confluence of the Wind and Beaver Rivers. Here, they stopped to rest and eat. While Lou gathered wood and built a small fire, Storm caught some trout from the deep riffle where the rivers came together. Clint and Ned tended to the horses, tethering them in a nearby grove of cottonwood trees where there was good grass.

"Ned, my leg's kinda stiff from all that ridin'. I think I'll walk on down the river a ways and give it a workout. Maybe it'll loosen up some."

The other agreed, nodding and Clint quietly slipped away through the thick brush. Moving ahead at a slow pace, his keen eyes searched the wooded stream banks, taking in all the sights and sounds of nature's presence. The smell of the cottonwoods filled his nose with a sweet perfume that reminded him of times gone by. Times, when as a boy, he had stalked the white-tailed deer and laid ambush for the wily turkeys that abounded on his father's farm.

"Those were shinin' times," he whispered.

An hour had passed when at last Clint arrived back with the others. Storm was the first to see him coming. And though she quickly dropped her eyes, pretending not to care, Clint could see that she seemed relieved.

"How's the leg, neighbor?" Larch asked.

"It's sore," Clint answered, bending over to take one of the skewered trout from the fire. "I'll be all right but I think we outta finish up here and high tail it. There's lots of Injun sign about and we'd play hell to make a fight of it against any kinda huntin' party."

Larch listened intently and when he at last spoke, it was to the women. He told them what Clint had said and instructed them to finish up quickly.

As the women struck camp, the men filled what skins and flasks they had with water. There was no telling what lie ahead nor how far the next stream might be. This water would have to see them through.

When they'd finished, they forded the wide stream and rode out of the stony river bottom, up onto the low sage covered hills. Ahead of them lay the vast expanse of the great prairie, stretching out as far as the eye could see. Behind them, the purple hazed mountains loomed large and beautiful. It would be four days before they finally lost sight of them. It would seem like a lifetime before they saw them again.

CHAPTER 8:
INJUN TROUBLE

The first two nights after leaving the Wind River were spent in dry camps. Though they had crossed many creek bottoms, no water had been found. It was late into the third morning when the horses began picking up the pace. They could smell water nearby so the riders held a slack rein and let them have their heads. A half mile further on they arrived at a small stream, which ran off in a northeasterly direction.

Here, they decided to stop for a while. Meat was running low and the horses were tired from the lack of water. The women began setting up camp while Clint and Ned tended to the horses.

"Soon as we finish here, I think we should nose around a bit, Ned; see who's about; also, scare us up some fresh meat."

"Yeah, I was thinkin' the same thing," Larch replied. "I figure if one of us goes upstream and the other down, we can get a good look around and we outta run onto somethin' that's palatable."

Ned Larch was the first to leave the camp. Walking away, he spoke to the women in Blackfoot, telling them that he would return soon and to have the cook fire burning. Smiling, he passed by Clint and headed up stream.

"I'll go this way, neighbor. Good luck!"

Clint nodded and finished tethering the horses in the grassy meadow where they'd chosen to camp. As he gathered his possibles and prepared to leave, a soft voice fell upon his ear. "I go with you?"

It was Storm, speaking in her native tongue. He'd not before heard her voice directed at him and for a moment he was caught off guard.

"I go with you?" she repeated, nodding her head. When he did not answer, she knew he could not understand so she quickly "signed" the words in the sign language used by all tribes.

For a moment, he was silent, pondering the question that had come so unexpectedly. He wasn't used to having someone along to scout and hunt with, especially when it was a woman. Storm looked directly at him, wondering if he understood what she had asked. A look of disappointment was beginning to fill her eyes when at last, he spoke.

"Yes," he answered, signing the reply and nodding also, "You can go."

With that, she reached into the leather bag lying at her side and brought forth a pair of buckskin leggings and a large, sheathed, skinning knife. Quickly, she dropped to the ground and slid into the leather britches. Again, she reached into the bag, this time producing a heavy belt. This, she used to secure the leggings around her waist. Finally, she slid the knife under the belt and moved it to her side; she was ready. Smiling to himself, Clint motioned for her to follow him. Together, they headed down stream.

#

An hour had passed since he'd walked from the camp and now, Ned Larch lay at the upper edge of a grassy rise, watching the buffalo graze before him. It was hard to believe what he saw. The stretching prairie contained thousands of the huge beasts, their bulky bodies blending together to form a brown, shifting carpet that reached to the far horizon. Here and there, small clouds of dust rose skyward, stirred up by frolicking calves or large bulls, dusting themselves against the biting flies.

Downstream, Clint walked at an easy pace following the meandering creek along its shallow riffles and deep water curves. Here and there he caught the flash of a trout as it swirled to take an insect or minnow. Being always alert, he would often stop to listen and survey what lay ahead.

Storm walked a few paces behind. Following his hand signals, she would stop when he stopped and only walk on when he motioned her to come. She was happy to be along, although it felt unusual to her. Indian men didn't allow their women to hunt with them. It was only when the men returned to camp with a slain animal or when the entire tribe traveled to attack a buffalo herd that the women were allowed to participate. And then, it was only to gut, skin, and butcher whatever was killed.

Also, it was pleasant for her to be in the company of this man. Through the short time they'd been together, he had made a special effort to be her friend, pointing out unusual rock formations or animal tracks or even the lightning in a far off storm; anything that caught his eye. She found herself somehow drawn to him and as such, had asked to come along on the hunt. He was easy going and made no demands on her.

The creek bottom they traveled was thick with cottonwood, willows, and river birch but the land that stretched beyond was open, rolling prairie. One could see for miles across this seemingly ocean of grass. It was because of this that Clint suddenly motioned to the woman to stop and get down. His keen eyes had detected something on the northern horizon. From their concealed position, he pointed out the slowly progressing line of horsemen moving towards them. When she recognized what he was showing her, Storm uttered something in Blackfoot and at the same time, used sign language telling Clint they must get back and warn the others. Sharing her urgency, he nodded, grabbed her hand, and headed back the way they'd come. Once concealed by the thick cover, they made straight for camp at a dead-run.

Lou was taken by surprise as they rushed into camp. Storm quickly told her of the approaching riders and upon hearing the news, Lou gasped. Holding her hand to her mouth she looked off in the direction Ned had gone. Clint tried to explain that there wasn't time to warn him; he'd just have to go it on his own.

While the women finished breaking camp, Clint untied the horses. The approaching riders were too close to make a run for it and there was no way he and the women could make a fight of it. The only thing they could do was hide, move downstream into the thickets and hope they weren't discovered. Then, when night came, they could slip away into the darkness, undetected.

Clint handed the horses' reins to Storm, motioning for her to go on ahead without him. As she did so, he took up a piece of dead sage and brushed away what tracks and sign he could. Finishing, he quickly caught up with them and was now leading them into a thick stand of willows. There would be ample cover here unless the riders came directly up the stream's bank; in that case, they'd be seen.

Clint motioned for the women to hold their hands over the horses' noses. This would keep them quiet. As they followed his directions, he slipped away to see where the riders were. Quietly, he made his way to the edge of the thicket. What he saw, made his blood run cold. Only two hundred yards away were five Indians. All, were decked out in war paint and armed to the teeth. Single file, they rode along the stream's edge.

The situation was not good. They'd probably have to fight their way out. Quickly, Clint fell back to where the women were hiding. The look on his face told Storm what was happening. In sign language, he told the women to mount and get ready to ride. When they heard him shoot, they were to get away upstream and find Ned. A troubled look crossed Storm's face as Clint related the plan. For a moment, she cast a questioning look and began asking him if there wasn't another way. He recognized her concern and grabbed her hands, stopping her question. As she looked into his eyes, she understood what he had to do.

Clint moved away toward the advancing riders and in doing so, looked for a vantage point from which to shoot. Taking them by surprise like this, he could fire, retreat and load, and fire again. If he was lucky, he would narrow their ranks enough to drive them off. If he wasn't, his hair would be hanging from some brave's lodge pole and Lou and Storm would become slaves.

He could not recognize what tribe the men were from as he aligned his sights on the lead rider. The man was large, over six feet he guessed. His face was painted half white and half black with the dividing line running at an odd angle from the hairline above his right eye, down across his nose and under the bottom left side of his jaw. In one hand, he carried a heavy buffalo skin shield; with the other, he held the horse's reins and a feathered lance. Over his shoulder and across his back was a bow and a quiver of arrows.

As Clint was about to squeeze the trigger, a rifle shot rang out from somewhere, far off upstream.

"That's gotta be Ned," Clint whispered, holding his fire.

The leader of the Indians quickly reined his pony in, holding his shield up at the same time. Turning about, he said something to the others and the group separated. Three of the men rode through the stream and out onto the prairie. The leader and one other brave rode from the stream bed out onto the open ground on the other side of the stream. Together, they galloped toward the sound of the distant rifle shot.

Within the cover of the willows, Clint and the others stood frozen as the Indians rode past. When they had disappeared, Clint swung up onto his horse. Speaking what Blackfoot he could and signing the rest, he told Storm to go further downstream and find a safe place to hide. He told her he had to help Ned and that he would return soon. With that, he rode through the stream, following after the Indians.

In his mind, Clint could picture what was going to happen. Ned had apparently run onto some game and shot it. Right now, he'd be cleaning it, up to his armpits in blood and not thinkin' about Injuns. They'd find him and run him down. He might get a couple of them first but they were on horses and he was afoot. He didn't stand a chance.

Keeping his horse close-in, near the edge of the brush, Clint galloped ahead. His eyes scanned back and forth, searching for the ponies and riders he knew lay ahead. Suddenly, another shot rang out. This one sounded very close. Clint slowed his horse, straining to hear any commotion that might be going on ahead of him. Off to his right, he then saw the ponies and the man who was guarding them. The man saw him at about the same time and dropped the reins of the standing horses. Shouldering his bow, he quickly fit an arrow to the string.

Clint, in the meantime, had drawn a bead on the man, placing his sights center of the man's chest. As he fired, the man turned slightly to draw the bow. The ball caught him just to the left of center, killing him instantly. In a flash, the untethered ponies were stampeding away, their hoofs clattering against the rocky stream bed.

Now, Clint was reloading. He knew the others had heard his shot and would be looking for him also. Taking no time to measure the powder charge, he tipped the horn up and poured it straight in. If it was too much, so what? It would just kick a little harder. He didn't even take time to patch the ball. He pushed it into the muzzle with his thumb and rammed it home with the hickory rod.

Maneuvering the horse through a small stand of cottonwood, Clint's trained eyes suddenly caught sight of movement in the trees to his left. Quietly, he dismounted, holding the horse's reins tight in his hand. He carefully brought the heavy rifle up and rested it against the rough bark of a nearby tree.

The Indian had not seen him and continued to sneak forward, looking for whomever it was that had fired the shot. As Clint took aim at the skulking figure, he heard behind him the crackling of brush and a low grunt. He never got the shot off, for a war club came crashing down across the side of his head, narrowly missing his ear. The man's charge sent Clint reeling forward into a kind of somersault. Rolling to one side, his eyes came to focus on the painted face of the brave as he scrambled to regain his footing. It was a black and white face, an angry face with hate-filled eyes. It was the face of the big Indian he'd seen earlier on.

Blood was running down across Clint's brow; he could feel its warmth on his cheek. Also, his skull felt like he'd been kicked by a mule. The Indian, now on his feet, again raised his war club and rushed forward to finish the white man. As he did, Clint raised the cocked rifle and pulled the trigger. A resounding boom belched forth from the muzzle just as the brave lunged. The shot hit him in the brisket just below his throat and exited viciously out his back, sending a spray of blood to cover the surrounding trees.

"Jesus Christ," Clint yelled, grabbing for the bloody wound at the side of his scalp. His head was spinning and he felt like he would throw up. The shrill scream behind him suddenly sent a new wave of fear pounding through his already muddled brain. Again, he rolled to one side, coming up with his knife at the ready. In the excitement and pain, he'd forgotten about the other Indian. It was too late, however, for the man was upon him. His forward motion knocked Clint backward over the sprawled-out body of the man he'd just killed.

Clint lay wedged between two trees as the Indian stood over him. Raising his lance, he smiled sullenly at the helpless white man stretched out before him.

"What a helluva way to die," Clint thought, as he prepared for the burning pain. "I'm goin' under for sure...God help my soul."

"Kaboom," came the report. Before Clint's eyes, the brave standing above him, suddenly became headless. His body wheeled backward, writhing and twisting in an ever-increasing pool of red.

"Shit, hoss! I thought you was a goner."

From somewhere beyond his sight, Clint could hear Ned's voice

"That sombitch was gonna skewer you, boy. Cut yer hair and yer nuts off and take em' home to hang on his lodge pole." He paused for a moment, then went on. "Well, I fixed his ass; he ain't gonna lift nobody's hair no more."

Clint looked up to see a large hand being thrust down towards him.

"C'mon neighbor get up off'n yer back and let's see if we can find those ladies. We'd best skedaddle, just in case these fellers got friends here abouts."

While Ned rounded up his horse, Clint knelt at the stream's edge and washed cold water over the gash near his ear. His head ached badly and he still felt sick to his stomach.

"Nasty gash ya got there, neighbor," Ned commented. "Yer bleedin' like a stuck hog. Gonna leave one helluva scar."

He paused for a moment and then with a hearty laugh, he added, "hell, it's a good thing he hit ya in the head. If he'd a hit ya anywheres else, he'd a probly kilt ya."

Somehow, Clint managed a small grin as Ned helped him climb aboard his horse.

"Here," he said, handing Clint his rifle. "I'll lead this critter and you hold the side a yer head on, so's it don't fall off. We'll get one a them women to stitch you up soon as we find 'em."

"Before we go Ned, there were five of them Injuns. I shot two and I figure you shot two, what about the other one?"

"Strangled the son-of-a-bitch," he answered. "He was tryin' to put the sneak on me. Comin' up from behind. When I shot his friend, he jumped me. I was too quick, though. Got my hands around his throat and it was all over. That's when I heard you shoot. I was mighty thankful to hear that shot. I reckon you saved my bacon. I couldn't have gotten them all."

On the way back, Ned led the horse to the place where he'd shot a young buffalo cow. Taking what meat they could carry, Ned remarked, "no sense leavin' this fine animal to the buzzards and the flies. Especially when it near cost us our hair." Grinning, he looked up at Clint and whacked him on the thigh. "We're gonna eat good tonight, neighbor. Yes sir!"

CHAPTER 9:
BUFFALO, CYCLONES, AND SUCH

Five days had passed since their run-in with the Indians and now, Clint leaned forward in the saddle gazing down from the high bluff at the wide riverbed stretching out before him.

"That's gotta be the Platte," he whispered to himself, "wide and shallow, just like Jack said."

Right now though, it wasn't very wide; maybe a hundred feet at the most and no deeper than a man's knee. The distance, however, from where he stood to the opposite high bank told him there had been times when a torrent of water filled this riverbed.

Clint gently scratched at the stitches lining the side of his head above his right ear. It was a nasty wound and would have surely split his skull had it landed more directly. Lou had been the one to sew him up. Using a bone needle and some deer sinew, she had done a good job. Least ways, that's what Ned said. He supposed the itching meant that it was beginning to heal.

Turning his horse about, Clint rode back down from the bluff and waved to the others to come on.

"River's just over this knob, Ned" Clint shouted, signing the words to Storm and Lou at the same time. Between what Blackfoot he knew and the amount of sign language he'd had to use in the past weeks, Clint was becoming very proficient in making the women understand him.

When the group finally reached the river, they dismounted near a stand of cottonwood. All of them were hot, dirty, and tired of riding. The long hours on horseback over the last two days had about done them in. They would make camp here for the evening.

After unloading the horses, Clint and Ned led them out into the shallow water, allowing them to drink. The women already had their moccasins off and were splashing and playing about in the slow running water. Its cool wetness felt good against Clint's bad leg as he tried to kneel and submerge it. Since the Indian fight, the leg had really stiffened up on him; it seemed worse now than it had ever been. Storm, watching him, noticed the strained look on his face as he tried to bend the injured limb.

"How far you reckon it is to the Missouri, neighbor?" Ned asked.

Clint thought for a moment before answering. "Can't really say, Ned, but I'd believe it's a good long ways." He paused for another moment looking downstream and then went on. "Ole' Jack Harris once told me it'd take the better part of a month to reach the Stoney Mountains if'n ya followed the Platte from its mouth and headed due west. Seeing' as how we been ridin' together for ten days or so, I'd think we got a ways to go, yet."

When the horses had drunk their fill, they were taken back and tethered to the cottonwoods. Ned located a campsite some two hundred yards downstream. It sat above the high north bank of the riverbed and was nestled between two barren bluffs. The north and west edge of the campsite was lined with a thick stand of juniper and pinion pine, thus providing a natural windbreak.

There wasn't much left of the meat they'd taken from the buffalo Ned had killed. Most of it they'd eaten along the way and fearing they might be followed, had not stopped to hunt.

After the fight, when they'd located the women, Lou and Ned had attended to Clint's head. Storm had hurriedly cooked what she could of the buffalo, roasting some on a spit and hanging the rest on stones she propped up near the fire.

Suspecting that more of the fierce Indians might be about, the group had ridden out before dawn, giving up the safety of the thick brush at the creek's edge. Pressing hard, it had taken them five days to arrive here at the Platte. Although they felt some relief in reaching the river, they knew they were not out of danger. This was a rugged country filled with hostile Indians, rattlesnakes, wild animals, drought, and starvation. So far, they'd been lucky; there had been plenty of game for the taking. But Clint knew it wasn't always this way. Water conditions or herd migration or, any one of a number of things could change the situation, bringing on starving times.

While Lou bustled about the campsite laying out the robes, Storm prepared their dinner. Clint discovered there were large fish in the shallow waters of the Platte. They looked like the suckers he'd caught when he was a boy except they were much larger. The two men cut some thick willows and after a few minutes of carving, fashioned some sharp spears.

In less than an hour they were back at camp with five of the large fish. The women cleaned them and packed them in mud brought up from the river's bank. Laying them on stones near the fire, they baked the fish. When the mud had completely dried and become solid, they broke it open with a rock and ate the steaming white meat within. This, combined with some wild onion and a type of bread Storm created using cattails, made for a delicious meal. After eating, they laid down to rest. And although it was only mid-afternoon, they each slept through to the next morning.

As they followed the Platte eastward, Storm rode at Clint's side; seemingly, happy to be there. Often, he addressed her in her native tongue. Pointing to an object he could identify in Blackfoot, Clint would say the word and then watch for her reaction. She would listen attentively and correct him if he was wrong or if he pronounced it badly. She seemed to enjoy this attention and her eyes shined happily. Sometimes, he would catch her smiling at his miserable linguistic attempts. But, he was learning the language.

The country around them held much game, just as Jack had told him. There were grouse and quail on the rolling hills, deer in the hollows, and ducks and geese along the river. Also, they encountered many of the strange goat-like creatures running in large herds.

One afternoon, meat was getting scarce and Clint shot one of the fleet footed animals. Handing the reins of his pack horse to Storm, he climbed down to clean the animal. As he began, he noticed the strong smell of the creature. The further he went with the butchering, the worse the smell became.

"I don't know about eating' this critter," Clint commented, "he smells pretty bad."

Ned laughed his usual laugh and commented, "Aw, what the hell neighbor, meat's meat I always say."

That evening, they roasted the animal's back straps and hindquarters. It took only a few bites of the queer critter to tell them that here was an animal not fit to eat. It had a strange, bitter taste and left a layer of grease on the roof of your mouth. When each of them had tasted it, they all looked at each other with their mouths full, no one dared to swallow. They all began to laugh, each turning away to spit out the nasty stuff.

"I been hungry before," Ned remarked, "but there'd have to be starvin' times fore this child wrapped a lip around another of those critters." They were hungry but still laughing when they climbed under their buffalo robes to sleep that night.

For several days, the weather had been very hot with only a slight morning breeze to stir the air. Today though, a strong wind gusted up from the south, hurrying the wispy clouds along their way and dulling the brilliant blue of the summer sky.

A large tributary of the Platte had joined it, running in from the south. The river now, was quite wide. It was here that the small band of travelers stopped to gaze in amazement at the sight before them.

On the far bank, grazed a herd of buffalo the size of which was unimaginable. They surely must have numbered in the tens of thousands for one could not see a break in the brown mass from horizon to horizon. The dust and the odor created by the large beasts carried across the river on the strong breeze, its acrid stench burned the travelers' eyes and made it difficult for them to breath. Also, there were clouds of biting flies hovering above the herd of buffalo. Their buzz created a background hum that only added to the surrounding discomfort.

"Jesus," Ned remarked, "that's the reason I lit out from my pa's farm. I never could stand the smell of cow shit; made me puke every time I had to milk them damn things."

"Yeah, well you better get used to it," Clint laughed, "cause there's a sea a buffalo out there and they seem to be headin' the same way we are. We ain't gonna be rid of 'em for some time."

Ned said something in Blackfoot which sent Lou and Storm rummaging through the leather parfliech that was strapped to the packhorse. They came out with some remnants of an old homespun cloth shirt, probably one that'd belonged to Ned. Again, Ned spoke and Storm rode down off the high bank and into the water.

There, she leaned down and soaked the ragged piece of cloth. When she rode back to the group she handed the shirt to Ned. He quickly tore off pieces for each of them to tie over their faces.

"There," he said, "that outta make breathin' a little easier."

Many of the buffalo wallowed in the cool mud at the river's edge. Others had crossed the river and were directly in the group's path. Since buffalo, particularly bulls, can be very aggressive, Clint decided to lead the group away from the water. They would go north for a ways and then turn back to the east, riding a parallel path to the river.

At a half mile's distance, Clint signaled the others to again head eastward. None of the buffalo had strayed this far from the river and it made the going easier. The smell of the herd, however, had not diminished. The gusting breeze that carried the odor had now grown to a strong, steady wind.

"That wind's signalin' a storm," Clint said pulling his horse to a stop. Pointing to the thin whirling clouds above them, he went on, "When you see those mares-tail clouds, you'd best find some place to hole up."

Storm, who was riding at his side also reined in her pony and tried to wipe the dust from her eyes.

"Here, let me help you do that," Clint said taking the cloth from her hand. Gently, he held her chin as though she were a child and wiped her cheeks and forehead. Cleaning the corners of her eyes, he noticed she was staring at him with a certain longing.

"Yer a dirty little critter," he laughed. She couldn't understand his words but the look on his face and the twinkle in his eye caused her to imagine what he meant and it made her join in the laughter.

"Ned, I believe we outta look for some kinda shelter and get these women and animals where they'll be safe. There's a bad one comin' an if'n it's got lightnin' with it, it could set that herd of buffs stampedin' our way. We wouldn't have a chance."

Storm recognized the concern on Clint's face and silenced her laughing. Quickly, she signed out the question "Is it the coming storm?"

Clint understood and answered her "Yes," he nodded and moved his palm toward his face, "bad storm coming."

Gazing about, Ned pointed to an outcropping of rock at the base of a small, far-off butte.

"Those rocks might afford us some protection," he said, "looks to be about the only shelter we're gonna find."

Clint agreed and they hurriedly rode toward the butte.

As the afternoon inched toward sunset, large storm clouds could be seen in the northwest sky. Their huge billowy heads rose to great heights and brilliant rays from the departing sun highlighted their outline. Below them was a deep blackness that blurred out all details of the western horizon.

Clint and the others had reached the rock outcropping and were preparing for the coming deluge. The rocks had at one time been part of the bluff and had, through the centuries, sloughed off; they were much larger than they had first appeared.

The corner of one of the huge stones, had fallen on a smaller stone. This created a sort of cave about three feet high and twenty feet long. This would have to do. At least it would protect them if the buffalo stampeded this way. After checking for snakes and varmints, Clint motioned the women to get everything under the rock.

While unloading Clint's packhorse, the two women struggled with the heavy leather bag.

"Here, let me give ya a hand with that," Ned said, reaching out to help. "Holy Hanna! What ya got in here neighbor; feels like it's full a lead."

"Nope! It's gold," Clint answered. "Didn't know ya was in the company of a rich man, did ya?"

"You're spoofin' me, right?" Ned replied, a serious tone creeping into his voice.

"Not at all, Ned. Found a vein of it up in the high country. Figure I can buy me a new rifle and some traps after I get my leg fixed."

"You can buy a helluva lot more than that if'n it's all gold," he answered. Then, pausing a moment, he asked, "care if I take a look at it?"

"Go ahead," Clint answered, "have yer self a look."

Ned was suddenly quieter and more serious than Clint had ever seen him. It gave him an uneasy feeling. Hell, maybe he should have just left it where he found it. He really had no use for it anyway. He could work and earn enough for doctorin' and buyin' a new rifle and traps.

"Yes sir, that's gold all right," Ned commented. "You'll need to watch yer back when ya reach the settlements. There's them about that'd slit yer throat for half that much." With that, Ned tied the top of the bag closed and set it aside.

Clint was tying the tether of the last horse when Storm ran up to him. "Clint! Clint!" she said in broken English and placed her hand to her ear.

He'd never heard her call his name before. In fact, he didn't know that she knew how. It pleased him and he smiled at her. But the urgency in her face caused him to take notice.

"What?" he questioned, looking into her eyes.

Again, she held her cupped hand to her ear and pointed toward the advancing storm. Then, he could hear it, a deep whining roar. But what the hell was it?

Calling to the others, he took Storm's hand and walked out from behind the large boulders. What he saw caused the breath in him to stop short in his throat. Storm gasped and grabbed his arm, stepping behind him as if to hide.

On the near horizon, a huge black cloud hung in angry suspension above the grassland prairie. Below it, swung a giant funnel shaped figure. It was black and looked like a giant finger moving in a jagged path. Sometimes it would lift from the earth and skip along. But where it touched down, clouds of dust and brush and whatever else lay in its path were flung high into the air. It was advancing toward the grazing buffalo.

"Sweet mother of Jesus," Ned yelled as he rounded the boulder, "What's all the commo...." His words were suddenly cut short by his surprise. "Holy shit, it's a cyclone cloud," he said.

"Yeah!" Clint added, "I read about 'em once and heard my Pa's friends talk about 'em but this is the first one I've ever seen."

Just then, another sound reached their ears, a sound that drown out the howling funnel cloud and sent a new bolt of fear through the tiny group. It was the sound of rolling thunder only louder and without end.

"The buffalo are running," Ned yelled. "I hope to God they don't come this way. We better get to shelter."

Before they reached the safety of the cave, the rain began. Within minutes, it was a torrent, coming down so hard that Clint could not see out to the place he'd tethered the horses. Curiously, there were dense clouds of dust being kicked up by the stampeding animals that now ran all about the place they lay. This and the storm's descending blackness, added an extra element of fear to the deafening melee that surrounded the huddled group.

Just beyond their stone fortress, a hundred thousand hoofs pounded the ground to a pulp. At times, the lightning would streak across the face of the clouds, exposing the great beasts in their blind anguish. The vision seemed a wooly blur with here and there a hooked horn, or bawling maw; and everywhere were the bright reflections of white-eyed panic.

In their rush to seek cover, Clint had lifted Storm up and ran with her in his arms. Throwing her before him, they had piled in under the great boulder. He then pulled her to him and wrapped a heavy buffalo robe around them for protection. Within the mounting fury, he could feel her at his chest, trembling and softly whimpering when the lightning flashed. Tenderly, he caressed her, trying to suppress his own fear while reassuring her that everything would be all right.

Almost as quickly as it started, the storm ebbed. The buffalo had disappeared somewhere into the murky blackness and with them the earth-shaking roar. The angry storm front with its huge thunderheads, whirling funnel cloud, and fierce lightning had also passed on. Now, instead of a blinding torrent, the rain had settled into a soothing rhythm, its gentle voice seeming almost apologetic. Only an occasional distant flash interrupted the returning peacefulness.

Watching the fleeting rampage disappear to the far horizon, Clint held Storm securely in his arms. It had, of course, been for her protection but now, his touch upon her body kindled a glowing flame that had been lit the first time he saw her.

Because of the ordeals she'd had to endure in her marriage, the beatings and humiliation Ned had spoken of, Clint had believed she would never look at another man. And yet, through the past weeks, she had ridden with him, hunted with him, and been attentive to his wounds. Now, she was lying here peacefully content in his arms.

She seemed to be asleep but he doubted it after what they'd just been through. He could not clearly see her face in the darkness but her breath was warm and even and fell softly upon his chest where the neckline of his buckskins lay open. Gently, he bent to kiss her. Her response was a mirrored image of his increasing passion. Lovingly, they wound together under the heavy robe, almost seeming to become one. In the heat of the moment, however, they had both forgotten they were not alone.

"Well, that was one helluva storm, eh neighbor?" bellowed Ned's booming voice.

So abruptly did the question destroy the moment that Clint forgot where he was and sat straight up. "Bonk," echoed the sound of his head against the rock ceiling.

"Damn! That hurt," he remarked, trying to gain his bearings. "Liked to knock my head plumb off my neck. Hell, I think I'm bleedin'."

Next to him, he could hear Storm laughing at his embarrassment.

"Yeah, well you hit it pretty hard, neighbor," Ned chimed in. "Heard your skull pop clear over here. An I'll bet that damn rock didn't move an inch, either." Pausing a moment, he laughingly added, "Next time yer of a mind to do some breedin', you'd best move out in the open, that way you won't hurt yourself."

Clint could stand no more of this and slid out from under the giant rock. He quickly moved to where the horses were tethered and away from any more of Ned's teasing. Behind him, he could hear Ned speaking to Lou in Blackfoot. Her responsive laughter reached him and he could feel the heat of embarrassment warm his cheeks. Two or three times Ned called out to him to come in out of the rain but the obvious humiliation would not let him.

When at last the laughter had been replaced by snores and deep breathing, Clint slipped back under the huge boulder to get some sleep. The steady rain had soaked his buckskins and he felt chilled clear through. Also, his leg ached terribly. Quietly, he removed the soaked shirt and moccasins. The pants would have to stay on, that's all there was to it. He'd never hear the end of it if Ned were to find out he was lying there buck naked.

Thinking that Storm was asleep like the others, he gently lifted the heavy buffalo robe and slid under its edge. No sooner had he laid his head down to rest than a soft warm hand touched his shoulder. She had not gone to sleep after all, but had instead waited for him to return. Feeling the dampness of his cold skin, she whispered something he could not fully understand and then, ever so gently, began to massage and warm him.

Her touch was like fire upon his skin and her strong hands worked deeply into his shaking flesh. He trembled at each caress, anxiously awaiting the next and the next.

When at last she reached the belt line of his britches, she placed her thumbs under the top edge, pushing them down.

"You want me to take my pants off too?" Clint whispered.

Again, she pushed.

"All right," he whispered, "but I'll probably live to regret this."

When he at last had the buckskin britches off, he slid back under the warm robe. This time, instead of greeting him with her hands, Storm met him with her whole body. Rolling on top of him, it only took a moment for Clint to realize that she too, was naked.

Now, her breasts pressed upon his chest and her moist lips nipped at the edge of his neck...his chin...his ear; all the time, sighing and whispering in low tones. With her nails, she drew small circles over his shoulders and down his sides; each time reaching a little lower; each time coming threateningly closer.

He too, became quickly caught up in the lovemaking and his hands followed their natural instinct. Almost frantically, his mouth searched for hers in the darkness. With his fingers locked into her thick hair, he brought her face to his, kissing her deeply and passionately; whispering love words; words she could not understand but knew full well, the meaning of.

"I think I am in love with you," he said. "I think I loved you from the very first time I saw you."

When at last they were one, the intensity was radiating but subdued. They wished they were alone and could scream out in lustful cries but they knew they could not. Instead, their writhing movements were deep and firm. Heat seemed to pour out from between them as though, in some strange manner, they were being fused together - locked at the heart if you will.

The silent explosion that ensued was like nothing either of them had ever experienced. Clint felt lightheaded, as though he would pass out. Storm could not seem to catch her breath and with each try, released an exhausted whimper.

When the intense passion had faded, what remained were two content and sleepy people. Curled tightly in each other's arms, they soon drifted off to sleep. Through the rest of the night, in his semi-conscious slumber, Clint would suddenly waken, checking to see if she was still there, and comfortable. Tenderly, he would kiss the back of her neck and press his face into her long hair. Inhaling, he would breathe her scent into his lungs, into his mind, his heart. Something new had come over Clinton Jeffries, something he hadn't felt for many years.

The narrowness of the space in which they lay kept them in darkness long after the sun had risen. The extra rest was good for them after the harrowing experience of the night before. Ned was the first to awaken. He yawned and whispered something to Lou, kissing her on the cheek. She said nothing but smiled at his affection.

"Damn, this hoss has gotta pee real bad," he whispered, sliding out from beneath the huge boulder. Before rising, he slipped the heavy buckskin shirt over his head. Now, standing fully erect, he pulled it down over his face and brought his hand up to brush back his long hair. When his eyes finally focused on what lay before him, he could not move. He could not even speak. Time seemed suspended and he forgot all about what had brought him out in the first place.

"Clint," he whispered. "Clint, wake up - come out here."

Clint lay half asleep, still holding Storm and languishing in his thoughts of the night before. Ned's voice was solemn and carried a sense of urgency. More than that, it was the first time he'd ever called Clint by his name. Usually, he simply referred to him as neighbor.

"Clint," he said again. "You gotta get out here an' see this."

"All right Ned, I'm comin,' I'm comin.' Jus' lemme get my britches on."

When he at last was out of the shelter of the big rock, he gazed toward the scene that had Ned so transfixed.

"Jesus H. Christ," he whispered, more to himself than to Ned. "I ain't never seen the likes a that."

Neither man could comprehend the destruction that lay before them. Yesterday, the area surrounding their rocky refuge had been rolling grassland with here and there a small grove of trees or brush. Now, that landscape was a bleak, trampled, muddy mess devoid of all living things. Nowhere could a blade of grass be seen, no brush, no trees, nothing. Nothing, that is, except the mangled bodies of the many buffalo caught up in the whirling inferno that had so suddenly swept down from the sky. As far as the eye could see, huge lifeless lumps dotted the tortured earth.

"Look at that, Ned...over there." Clint pointed to an awkward stack of brown wooly carcasses. "My gawd, they're stacked up like cord wood."

"We lost two horses last night," Ned remarked. "Musta broke loose in all the excitement. If they got caught up in that mess they're probably nothin' more'n wolf bait this mornin'."

Taking one last look at the carnage, Ned sighed "I'll finish gettin' dressed and see if I can round up those horses. If we don't find 'em, it's gonna be a lot tougher goin' from here on out."

CHAPTER 10:
RAFTING THE PLATTE

Four days had passed since the terrible storm left its mark across the prairie. Ned had not been able to locate the missing horses and it had greatly slowed their daily progress. In order that everyone could ride, they'd built two travois to carry their supplies. Also, the women doubled up and were riding one horse. Every other day, the men traded the horses they were riding with the two that pulled the travois. That way, none of the horses were overworked or badly chafed from the lodge poles that were tied across their backs.

Except for the bloated carcasses being devoured by the wolves and birds, no buffalo were in sight. Because of this, Clint and Ned thought it better that they return to the river bank to continue their journey.

The level of the river had risen a good deal since the storm. Its muddy current now roiled and rolled, carrying brush, trees, and dead animals in its wake. Clint's leg was giving him fits. Riding was better than walking for him but the time he spent in the saddle between rest stops grew shorter and shorter. Also, his knee had stiffened to the point that when forced to bend it, he grimaced in pain and tears welled up in his eyes.

During one of their brief rests, Clint came up with an idea.

"What do ya say we build a raft, Ned, and put me and all our goods on it? That way, I can give this leg a rest and you'll each have a horse of your own."

Ned thought a moment before answering.

"The river seems to be makin' good time," he mused "not as fast as a horse can walk, mind ya, but it's steady." Pausing and then nodding, he went on. "Sounds like it might be the best thing to do, what with yer leg so bad and all. Yeah, I agree. Let's get at it."

While Clint rested, Ned and the women scouted the nearby draws and stands of trees for wood to build the raft. Most of what they found were crooked, gnarled, or half rotten logs. Normally, Clint would not have considered using them but this was a desperate situation and they really had no choice.

Within a few hours, Ned, Lou, and Storm had managed to drag several logs to the river's edge. Here, Clint helped drag the logs into the water and lash them together with leather strips cut from one of the buffalo robes. When it was finished, the raft looked more like a log jam than a raft. The important thing, though, was that it held most of their gear and Clinton Jeffries, to boot.

Since their night together under the rock, Clint and Storm had acted like young lovers, touching and holding hands and doing whatever else inspired them. Each night had been one of heated passion and wild love-making.

"Probably," Ned told Lou, "that's why Clint's leg is so bad.

He claims it's from spendin' too much time in the saddle." He smiled and subtly added "Now I wonder which saddle he's referrin' to?"

Although Lou couldn't understand all of Ned's words, she grasped his meaning and both of them broke into laughter.

Because of her feelings, it was hard for Storm to ride on ahead and leave Clint to float the river by himself. She had suggested riding with him on the raft but it was already heavily laden and any extra weight would put it too low in the water, thereby getting their gear wet.

Before shoving off, Clint carried two extra logs out to the raft. One was long and thin and would be used for poling.

The other was short and thicker and could be whittled into a paddle. He definitely needed a paddle and the whittling would help pass the long hours of boredom. As he waved goodbye, Clint watched the three riders move out ahead of him. Within a half hour, they were out of sight.

Time on the river passed slowly and the sun beat hot against his face. In two hours' time, he had fashioned a paddle from the short log and now he dabbled it in the water, turning the raft to and fro, testing his control over the clumsy craft, but mostly he was killing time. In the peaceful solitude of the river's drift, his mind ran to the Indian girl he had so madly fallen in love with. Closing his eyes, he could see her now before him, each fine detail leaping out to tug at his heart, his mind. His vision revealed the squareness of her shoulders, the way she held her head, her fine slim calves and ankles. Never mind that her legs were a little bowed. He didn't care, he loved her anyway. Then there were the little things, like the softness of her skin and the small blue vein that showed through just above the elbow on her left arm. Breathing in slightly, he remembered the scent of her and the fine wispy hair at the back of her neck that he'd caress and nuzzle his face into. In this mood, he drifted between consciousness and sleep, reality and daydreams. At times, he'd raise up and survey his surroundings. Being satisfied, he'd again drift off with Storm on his mind.

Watching the sun disappear below the brilliantly orange horizon, Clint began to scan the shoreline for the camp he knew his friends would have made. But, it was long after dark when he at last caught sight of the small fire that marked the site. Yelling out, he summoned the group to come and meet him and help unload some of the gear for the evening.

"Got some buffler meat cooked up fer ya, neighbor," Ned hollered. "We ate some time ago but we saved ya some."

"Sound's tasty, Ned," Clint answered "My stomach's so empty it thinks my throat's been cut."

Storm was the first to reach Clint as he staggered ashore, pulling the raft. His leg was stiff and almost let him down when he waded out at the river's edge

While Clint ate, they all sat around the fire, talking. Mostly they spoke in Blackfoot but Clint still had a time understanding and so the discussion was interrupted with bits of English thrown in here and there. Clint was pleased with himself at how much of the Blackfoot language he'd managed to learn in the short time they'd all been together. Storm, likewise, had learned a good deal of English listening to the two white men converse.

"Lookit' all them stars up there," Ned whispered, holding his hand up to shield his eyes from the fire's glow. "The Almghty did himself proud when he built those. Did ya ever see anything so beautiful?"

"Yeah, I believe I have Ned," Clint answered, watching the firelight dance across Storm's cheek. At his reply, Storm saw the light in Clint's eyes and responded with a soft smile.

That night, the love they shared carried a far deeper meaning. Holding each other, they both realized how much their relationship had grown. This was a woman Clint could spend the rest of his life with. This was the man Storm had dreamed of, the strong warrior who would rescue her from her tormented existence. Each felt they were a part of the other and it was wonderful.

Three days of riding the raft had made Clint restless, he longed to have a horse under him again and be free to move about as he wished. The rest had done his leg some good though. The pain had lessened and some of darkness under the skin had gone away. His knee, however, was still stiff and at the end of the day, when he'd come ashore, he walked without bending it.

Now, he lay awake watching the sky lighten in the east. Storm lay at his side in peaceful sleep. He listened to her breathing and then turning toward her, he reached up and gently brushed back a lock of hair that had fallen upon her cheek. The sun would be up soon and he'd have to climb onto that damn raft again.

Whispering to himself, he mumbled, "Maybe I outta get up and go for a ride, see what's about. We're near outta meat anyway...maybe I could scare up a deer...do me some good to get shed of this camp for a while...get my butt back in a saddle."

Within a half hour, Clint was leading the horse from camp. "No sense wakin' the others," he thought, moving silently away up a nearby draw. Before mounting, he checked his gear and made sure his rifle was primed.

Near the top of the bluffs overlooking the river, a well-worn game trail meandered in and out of the brushy draws. Coming upon the trail, Clint surveyed its surface looking for the familiar heart shaped tracks of the deer he knew abounded here. While riding the raft for the past three days, he'd seen several of them standing on the hillsides or drinking at the river's edge.

The trail however, held no sign of deer and so he moved on. A half-mile or so back of these bluffs were some small hills, covered with thick brush. "Surely," he thought, "there will be some game there." And so, he headed the horse toward them.

Working in and out of the small canyons and draws of the hills, Clint managed to scare up only two rabbits and a covey of quail. He'd crossed some deer tracks but they were not fresh. Neither did he see any fresh droppings.

Heading east, he decided to ride to a prominent, jutting point that stuck out from the surrounding lower, hills. It lay some three or four hundred yards ahead of him and off to his left. If he hadn't seen anything by then, he'd ride back to camp. Approaching the place, he looked carefully for any sign of movement within the brush, his trained eyes all the while checking the ground for tracks or droppings. Slowly, he climbed down from the horse and proceeded on foot. Rounding the point, he observed a well-used trail leading toward the river.

Clint tied the horse to a nearby stand of brush and went on foot to investigate the trail. Cautiously, he knelt to see what game had come this way. What he saw instead were pony tracks. Indians had come this way, riding in the direction of the river. For a long moment, he studied the imprints, trying to determine how many of them there were and how long ago they'd passed here.

There were perhaps four or five different sets of pony tracks. He couldn't tell exactly how old the tracks were but he guessed the party had passed here within the last two days.

Riding back to camp, Clint was careful not to skylight himself on any of the low hills. He kept to the draws and rode as quietly as possible. From the bluff above their camp, he could see Storm and Lou rolling up the robes and packing the horses, preparing for the coming day's ride. Ned was busy with something at the river's edge.

"Mornin," he said to Storm, swinging down from the horse's back. She smiled and hurried to greet him with a hug. Holding her about the shoulder, he walked to the river's edge where Ned was dressing a fine fat whitetail deer.

"Where the hell'd ya git that?" Clint asked. "I didn't hear ya shoot."

"Got him with my knife," Ned replied, without looking up. "Saw ya ride out; figured ya was goin' huntin'. I was just layin' there tryin' to build up enough courage to get up and pee, when I sees this buck swimmin' across the water. Comin' right for us, he was. Well, I jes' let him git close enough so's he couldn't git away, then I jumped in, swum over to him and cut his throat. Simple as that!" Smiling up at Clint, he added "Did you get anything, neighbor?"

"Nope, I never saw a critter to shoot at." Clint paused for a moment and then went on. "Did see some Injun tracks, though. Peers to be four, maybe five of 'em. Prob'ly a huntin' party. Looked like they were headin' for the river. You'd best keep yer nose open today and tell them women to do the same. I wouldn't ride too far ahead either, in case one of us has trouble." Ned shook his head in agreement and handed the back straps and one ham of the deer to Lou and Storm who stood waiting to cook their breakfast.

While the women cooked, the men saw to it that the horses were packed and the raft loaded. Then, the four of them sat near the cook fire and ate their fill of the roasted meat. What was left would be packed into a parfliech and loaded aboard the raft for later.

"Before we leave Ned, there's somethin' I want ya to do for me." Reaching out to take Storm's hand, Clint went on, "I don't speak good enough Blackfoot to make Storm understand how I feel about her, so I'd like ya to tell her for me."

Ned looked at Clint's face and then into his eyes. "Ya got it real bad for her, don't ya?"

"Yeah, I do," Clint answered. "I know she cares for me too but I need to tell her some things." Pausing a moment, he went on, "I need to tell her that she has become my life. She is the moon, the stars and all things to me. She is the only woman I've ever really loved and I would lay down my life for her. Tell her I want her for my wife and I want her to come with me to St. Louis to get my leg doctored."

Turning to look at Storm, Ned relayed the message. Immediately, a smile crossed her face and she turned to look at Clint. Ned went on with the dialogue, speaking with as much sincerity as came with those words that were spoken to him. When he at last came to the part about them going to St. Louis together, Storm's eyes saddened and she lowered her face. It was clearly evident to both men that something was wrong.

"What is it, Ned?" Clint queried, "Ask her."

But before the other could ask, Storm began to speak, "Tell this man that I too have found something wonderful with him. He is the most tender, caring, and gentle man I have ever known and I love him truly. I would be proud to be his wife but..." for a moment she hesitated. "But I cannot go with him to the white man's town. I would not fit into that world. I would be frightened and miserable and it would cause him pain. It would also cause problems between us and I do not wish to risk losing him over that." Ned spoke the words just as he had for Clint.

"What are we to do, then?" Clint asked.

Seeing his concern, Storm continued, "Tell him I will wait for him at the place we make our camp, near the meeting of the three rivers. I will wait for him to come and be my husband. We will then be together, forever."

Ned relayed the rest of the message. "She says she'll wait for you and meet you at three forks." When he'd finished, Clint looked into Storm's eyes, nodding his head. Then, he leaned forward and tenderly kissed her.

"I'll meet you at three forks," he whispered. "You and I will be together, always."

The words he spoke, she could not understand. But the meaning in Clint's eyes was very, very clear. Storm held her hand at her mouth and a small tear traced down her cheek. Lou had sat quietly through all the back and forth talk and when it finally ended, she burst into tears, hugging her sister tightly.

"You have found a good man," she whispered through her sobs. "He truly loves you...I am so happy for you."

#

The sun beat down on Clint, as he lay stretched across the crude raft listening to the flowing water gurgle about him. Smiling, he recalled the events of the morning. Storm had agreed to become his wife and he was very pleased. He wished she would go with him to St. Louis but he understood how she felt. It would be difficult for her or anyone to enter a strange world where nobody speaks your language and everyone looks and acts differently. He supposed she was right and it instilled within him a new respect for her. Along with being beautiful, thoughtful, and all the other things he loved about her, she was also, smart. She held a wisdom about people and the way they felt and acted. Again, he smiled.

Before he'd shoved the raft out into the current, Storm had rushed to the shore to kiss him and present him with a gift. "I will see you tonight," she said, signing the words at the same time. Holding his hand, she tied a woven horsehair bracelet about his wrist. "This was given to me by my father. He said the one who wore it would always find happiness. I want you to have it." She smiled then and added "I will build a fire tonight and I will wait for you."

Her words had somehow warmed him when she said them. It was as though he suddenly belonged somewhere, belonged to someone, had meaning once more in his life.

Tonight, he would tell her more things, run his fingers through her dark hair, kiss her at the back of her neck, and whisper words of love she would understand.

The day drug on, and although the river seemed to have picked up speed, the hours spent doing nothing caused Clint some uneasiness. Ned and the women rode close, being cautious about the Indians Clint had spoken of. But the raft drifted slowly and it was tiring to hold the horses back. Clint could see they were dragging along, stopping frequently so he could catch up.

Ned," he yelled out. "Why don't you ride on ahead? We ain't seen no Injuns and I'm just slowin' ya down. You can make better time without waitin' for me. Find us a good campsite and cook up some food. I'll be along later."

Ned waved his hand and hollered back. "Alright, neighbor! We'll see ya when ya come in." It was not long before they disappeared from his view.

It was a beautiful day. The sky was brilliantly blue and the gentle breeze blowing in from the west rippled the river's surface. Clint, with nothing else to do, stretched out on the raft and peacefully dozed the morning away. Only an occasional biting fly would stir him. It was early afternoon when he at last sat up and looked around.

"I need to git ashore," he said to himself, picking up the hand-fashioned oar. "Nature's callin' and I'll be damned if I'm gonna use the river again. Can't stand the thought of it floatin' right there along with me for the rest of the day." Digging the oar into the brown water, he stroked for shore.

The river, at this point, was more than a hundred yards wide. Trees grew along its northern bank, with here and there some tamarack, a few cattails and a thick stand of bulrush. The water near the shore was very shallow. Clint got behind the raft and wading, guiding it into an opening between the brown, course grass. Once there, he jammed the longer of the two poles through an opening in the raft into the soft mud below. Taking up his rifle, he stiffly waded ashore. It was fifty yards to the steep rise of the bank ahead of him. Trees grew along the top of the bank. Here, he knew he could find some welcome shade and a place to relieve himself in comfort.

When he'd finished his business, he walked a ways along the steep bank and then hunkered down next to a large juniper tree. He'd stuffed the bag of roasted deer meat inside his shirt before leaving the raft. This, he brought out and proceeded to eat.

The country here was much flatter and fell away to the distant horizon in waves of knee-high grass. Far away, he could make out animals grazing in the sea of green. Buffalo, he guessed - perhaps wild horses. They were too far away to identify.

Looking about, he casually glanced back up the river to where he'd beached the raft. Quickly, he spun about, responding to what his eyes were seeing. Far up the river, beyond the place he'd put into shore, four mounted figures were crossing over; crossing from the far shore to the side he was on.

"Got to think fast," he whispered. "Can't make a fight of it here, they'd have me in a minute. Ned's too far....might not even hear the shots....gotta get back to the raft. That way, they gotta come to me out in the open."

Keeping what brush he could between he and the Indians, Clint slithered down the steep bank and low-crawled toward the beached raft. The fifty yards separating him from the water's edge was covered with sparse low growing grass and stands of bulrush. If they weren't looking directly this way, he might make it to the raft, unseen. But then, he'd have to push off and paddle like hell to get to a point where it would be difficult for them to reach him. If he got enough water between he and them, he could pick em' off one at a time if they came at him.

The first thirty yards he managed without incident. Then, the ground became swampy and he had to raise up some to keep from getting his powder wet. All the while, he kept a steady watch on the advancing riders. Through the last ten yards, he threw caution to the wind and in a crouching, stiff-legged run made it to the heavy raft. Throwing his rifle and possibles bag aboard, he pulled the long pole from the mud and pushed for all he was worth to get the raft out into the current. Once it began to move, he lowered himself into the water, hoping not to be seen. The water here was less than two feet deep and so he continued pushing with his legs, forcing the raft further away from shore. Only then, did he dare look back to see where they were.

He was not surprised to see that two of the riders had turned back toward the distant bank and that the others were whipping their mounts forward in bounding jumps to gain the shore.

"Damn," he whispered "they've seen me. They're purty smart too, gittin' on both banks and havin' me in the middle." Pausing a moment to think, he went on. "They gotta come to me, though if'n they want me. An' when they do, I'll make 'em pay."

By the time he jumped aboard the raft, the water was well above his waist. The current had hold of it now and was pushing it along at its usual slow pace. Clint grabbed the oar he'd fashioned and paddled hard to gain the center of the wide river. Behind him, he could hear the war whoops of the two closest braves as they rode toward him at a full gallop.

Believing he was far enough from the shore, Clint stowed the oar, took up his rifle, and turned about to face the oncoming Indians. The two that had crossed back to the other side had at last reached the shore and were also at a full gallop, trying to catch up to him. Lying there waiting, he piled what he could of the gear up to act as a shield against the arrows he knew would soon come. It only protected him on one side though and that would be a problem when they started shooting from both sides. The only thing in his favor was the width of the river. From either bank, it was a long shot with a bow. They'd have to ride out into the river to reach him. He knew he had the advantage here, his rifle could reach either shore with ease. What worried him, was an all-out charge. If they did that, he would be in serious trouble.

The two Indians closest to him had finally come even with the hulking raft and had reined their ponies to a steady walk, presumably waiting for the others on the distant shore to catch up. Clint readied himself for the fight. Quickly, he grabbed his hunting pouch and the attached powder horn. These, he laid where he could easily reach them to reload. From the pouch, he took two of the round lead balls and placed them in his mouth. They'd be easy to get to there and wouldn't roll away in the heat of the battle.

When at last all four braves were even with the raft, the leader began yelling and motioning his hand for Clint to come ashore. Surprisingly, the man spoke English.

"White man," he ordered, "You come. You come here, now. We trade."

Clint had no intention of doing as the man ordered. Even if these Indians were friendly, a white man alone, with a rifle and a sack of goods was a mighty tempting target and, usually, fairly easy pickin's. If they didn't kill you, they'd most likely steal your gun, your horse, your clothes, and anything else they had a mind to.

A thought suddenly crossed his mind, "If that Injun speaks the language that good, he damn well understands the meaning of the word, no."

Raising himself up a bit, Clint mustered all the gruffness he could in his voice and hollered back "No! No trade! You go away, now."

For a moment, there was total silence. The remark and its tone caught the Indians off guard. Clint could see them talking among themselves, trying to decide what to do next. A subtle smile found its way to his lips.

"Got yerselve's a pesky white boy to deal with, huh?" he whispered. "Ya want my rifle and ya want my hair but ya don't wanna die to git 'em." For a moment, he paused, still smiling "Well, if ya expect to kill this ole' hoss and take his possibles, you're gonna have to sacrifice somethin'"

Once again, the brave called out to him "You not be afraid. We not hurt you. Only want trade."

"I got nothin' to trade," Clint hollered back. Then, sharply waving his arm he added "Now, git."

Again, there was talk among the braves. It was up to them now. The line had been drawn and he'd just have to wait and see what happened. If they charged, he'd kill the leader first, then the next closest, and so on. That was the plan. He figured he could get three of the four before they were close enough for a good bow shot. The fourth one, he'd have to deal with when the time came.

Clint wondered if Ned would hear the shots and come to help him. He hadn't seen his friends for three or four hours, and he doubted they were within earshot. No, he'd just have to go this one alone.

The leader of the Indians rode his pony further out into the river, stopped, and began yelling to the two braves on the opposite shore. Clint could not understand what they said for they spoke in a tongue unfamiliar to him. The others shouted something in return and the leader turned back toward the shore. Now, they rode single file on each bank, content to follow the drifting white man, seemingly biding their time, waiting for the right moment. At least that's what Clint thought. He watched them carefully but they made no advances toward him nor did their leader call out to him again.

The afternoon wore on and the sun began its descent down the western sky. Daylight was fading fast. A covering of high, dense clouds had also moved in from the northwest further darkening what remained of the light. Soon the darkness would come and with it, the Indians. With the cloud covering there would be no moon or starlight. It would be pitch black. Clint fully expected it would be then that they would swim out to the raft and attack him. If they did, he'd be hard pressed to fend them off. Four against one was not good odds and his only hope would be to swim for it and try and lose them in the darkness.

Just as the sun was about to set, a strange thing happened. The leader of the Indians turned his horse toward the river and stopped, watching Clint float by.

"Here it comes," Clint whispered, preparing himself for the fight.

Now, all the Indians stopped and turned toward the river. But instead of charging, the leader and his companion waited until the raft was well past them and then the two of them rode across to join their companions on the far shore. Clint watched in amazement when the four of them turned back upriver and rode away to the west. In their departure, not one of the Indians turned to look back at him. It was as if he didn't exist or perhaps they'd just grown tired of the game. Whatever the reason, Clint was happy to see them go.

Because of the heavy cloud cover, the night was as dark as pitch. Clint couldn't see his hand in front of his face. The raft, being a slave to the river's current, would often turn about as it floated and since the blackness revealed no reference of direction or location, he soon became disoriented. Now and then, he'd hear a coyote or prairie wolf cry out and it would give him some idea where the shoreline was but the darkness was like a blanket over his head. Peering into it, he strained to see the fire he knew Storm would have blazing.

Time passed slowly for him now. He'd been awake since dawn and he found himself growing sleepy. The ordeal with the Indians had been stressful and it only lent itself to his fatigue.

"Damn darkness" he whispered, laying his head on his arm "Can't see nothin' and can't keep my eyes open long enough to even see that." In a matter of minutes, he was asleep.

#

"We need more wood for the fire," Storm said to Ned, raising up from the buffalo robe. "Jeffries will be coming soon."

"I'll help ya there, darlin,'" Ned answered in English, rising and slapping the dust from his buckskins. "It's a mighty dark night. Ole' Clint oughta be able to see this fire for miles."

Storm and Lou had prepared some wild onions and berries they'd found growing in a shallow draw leading up from the river. This along with some fish that Ned had speared, was what they ate for dinner. A large portion of this she set aside for Clint.

Long into the night when the others had fallen asleep, Storm kept a vigilance over the blazing fire, feeding it when it died down and gathering wood and sage when the supply ran low. All that day she had remembered his words and the look in his eyes when he spoke them. She loved this man and would be his wife, as he had asked, forever and ever.

Now, she waited for his deep, familiar voice to split the darkness, beckoning for her and Ned to come and help him get ashore. She longed to rush into his arms and feel his strength engulf her. She needed him to kiss her and tell her he loved her and cuddle her in his arms until morning. She had never known such joy. But now, an aching worry gnawed at her. He should have been here by now. He couldn't have missed the fire. Maybe something had happened to him or maybe he had gone to sleep and not seen the fire.

Quickly, she shook Ned's shoulder.

"Wake up," she said "Jeffries has not come in yet and I am worried for him. He may have fallen asleep. You must use your rifle to awaken him."

Reluctantly, the big man rolled over and picked up his rifle.

"All right," he answered "All right! It's against my better judgment to tell everyone in the whole damn countryside where we are but I guess I better if'n ole' Clint's gonna git home tonight."

With that, he cocked the hammer, pointed the muzzle toward the sky, and pulled the trigger. The resounding boom brought Lou out from under the buffalo robe, screaming. She immediately began to swing her fists in the air, trying to fight off whomever it was that had attacked them. One blow caught Ned squarely on the cheekbone just below his eye.

"God dammit' woman," he squealed, dropping the rifle and grabbing for his swelling face. "Ya bout broke my jaw. Hell, I prob'ly won't be able to chew for a month. I'll starve, git skinny, and blow away to dust. Then you'll be sorry."

Lou was enough awake by then to realize what she'd done. She was crying and spouting apologies in Blackfoot and she had her arms around his neck, trying to kiss Ned's face better. "Ouch!" he cried "Ouch! Yer makin' it worse. Let go a me woman," he yelled again, pushing her away.

As worried as she was, Storm could not help but laugh at the scene before her. They were quite a pair. Her sister, so serious about everything and Ned, so carefree and crude. One thing, though, she knew for sure. They loved each other more than anything. Ned had practically had to fight the whole tribe when Lou had brought him to their camp. Had it not been for Lou speaking up to her father who was an influential man among his people, he might have let them kill Ned. But, seeing the look on his daughter's face and watching her flying fists strike out at those who would hurt her man, convinced him to step in and spare Ned's life. From that day on, Ned was considered a friend, brother, and son to the tribe. However, there were many braves in the camp who hated white men and would just as soon have put a knife to him.

"You shoot once more," Storm said. "Maybe this time, he'll hear it."

When he'd reloaded, Ned Larch held the rifle in the air and squeezed the trigger. The thundering boom echoed from the far shore out onto the prairie and then quietly died on the night breeze. For an hour, the three of them sat beside the fire listening for Clint to call out but no call came. Sleepiness soon took over and the three of them retired to their robes for the night.

"Don't worry, Storm," Ned whispered, reaching out to touch her shoulder. "Clint understands the ways of the wild and can take care of himself, proper. He'll prob'ly meet up with us somewhere downriver in the mornin.' Until then, you'd best git some sleep."

Storm said nothing but only shook her head in agreement. Then, raising up on one elbow, she placed the last of the wood and brush onto the fire. In its crackling light, Ned could see the silent tear trace down over her cheek.

"I hope to hell the boy ain't gone and got hisself killed," Ned whispered, nuzzling his face into Lou's long hair. "That girl has had enough bad luck in her life."

CHAPTER 11:
THE BIG RIVER, KEELBOATS, AND LOST LOVE

It was not the light of morning that awakened Clinton Jeffries but rather the slapping of waves against the sides of the raft and their wet spray upon his face.

"What the hell," he whispered, sleepily gazing around. Suddenly, he was wide awake and up on one elbow. The surface of the water was covered with waves. Rolling and crowning, their white tops were being driven before the blustering wind. It stung his face as he tried to understand the situation. Carefully, he scanned each bank to see if the Indians had returned. But now, the banks seemed much farther away and looked somehow different. His mind then ran to Storm and he searched the distant shore for any sign of her or the camp. She would be worried sick at his not getting in.

"I must have fallen asleep," he whispered, "but something's not right here. The sun's not in the right place. It should be ahead of me, not off to the left."

Quickly, he grabbed the long thin log that he'd used to pole the raft. Jamming it down through a hole between the logs, he tried to touch the river bottom. At nearly its full length, the log was wrenched from his hand by the current. He had not touched the bottom. He knew then that he was no longer on the Platte but, instead, had reached the mighty Missouri.

The raft was being blown along at a rapid pace, keeping up with the advancing waves. Taking up the hand-carved paddle he'd made, Clint stroked at the river trying to drive the raft toward the far west bank. If he could reach that shoreline, he would walk back to the confluence of the rivers and meet up with Storm. But try as he might, he could make no headway against the river's power.

Next, he tried stroking for the east bank; it was nearer. Toward this end, he made some progress but he was drifting downstream at a rapid rate. It was nearly an hour before he had the raft close enough to the shore to beach it. When at last he had it secured, he climbed the steep bank and gazed about. Nothing! There was nothing for as far as he could see. Clint was a man used to loneliness but somehow, at this moment, it seemed to weigh heavily upon him. He'd give anything to see Storm's face.

When unloading the raft, he rummaged through his gear for something to eat. All he could find was two pieces of jerky from the last buffalo they'd killed. One piece, he stuffed in his shooting bag. The other he stuffed in his mouth. It was tough but he was hungry and it tasted good. He'd made up his mind to hike back up the river and try to reach Storm. He had to say goodbye to her one more time, to tell her how much he loved her. If only he'd not fallen asleep.

He couldn't carry all of his belongings and make any time, so before he left, he hid them in a shallow gulley and covered them with pieces of dry brush. The raft, he could not disguise but it looked so much like a pile of driftwood, he wasn't worried that anyone would recognize it for what it really was. He pulled it as close to shore as possible and forced the long pole through an opening in the logs and deep into the muddy bottom. That should hold it until he returned. On the bank above the raft, he selected a good size tree, standing in an opening by itself. Upon its bark, he slashed a not too obvious cross to mark the location of his goods.

By late afternoon, he'd traveled some distance up the river. The way was not easy, for the bank was brushy and heavily rutted with washes. He found the walking to be easier if he stayed back from the shoreline a ways. His leg had supported him so far but it was aching badly and he knew it would not be long before it stiffened up on him. Along the way, he shot a small deer that had come to the river to drink. Since it was nearly dark, he made camp and enjoyed a meal of roast venison. With the first light of morning, he was again on the move, traveling north to find his companions.

#

Ned Larch had not slept well, worrying about what had happened to Clint. Now, as he saddled his horse in the pre-dawn light, he recalled Clint talking about the Indian sign he'd seen on the nearby hillsides.

"Damn, maybe I should'a paid more attention to what Clint said and hung back a ways," he mused. "He couldn't have missed that fire we built for him, it lit up the whole damn countryside." Pausing a moment, he went on "I guess I'd best ride back and see if I can find him."

About five miles from the place they'd camped, Ned found the tracks of two ponies. He suspected they were Indian ponies but whomever it was, had been riding downstream and had crossed the river to the southern bank. Backtracking upstream, he discovered that they had been following the river for some distance. Returning to where they'd crossed, he too turned his horse into the water and proceeded toward the south bank. Climbing out on the far shore, he rode back and forth searching for the tracks he knew would be there. Once he'd located them, he found that they joined two other sets of tracks. All, had then ridden away to the south.

Again, he backtracked upstream and found that these two sets of tracks had also followed the river for some distance.

"There were four of 'em," he whispered, speaking to himself. "Had ole' Clint trapped out there smack between em' on that floatin' log pile, follerin' him along, waitin'... "

Climbing down from his horse, Ned's keen eyes unraveled more of the story that lay on the ground before him.

Again, in a soft voice he issued, "Peer's as though there weren't no struggle here on the bank as there ain't any human footprints or blood about. Also, none of them horses left deep tracks in the mud and soft dirt which means only one man rode away on each horse. Hmmm..."

For a long moment, he pondered the situation, rolling it over and over in his mind. At last he spoke again, "Unless they killed him in the river and he sunk, I'd believe he got away. Question is, where the hell did he go and what happened to my goods?" Aboard the raft had been some of the things Ned planned to trade for powder, knives, and trinkets. Now, besides his friend, he'd lost his trade goods.

When Ned arrived back at camp the women were packed and waiting to leave. He said nothing about the tracks he'd found; no sense worrying Storm any more than she already was. She could tell, though, from the look on his face that he'd not found any sign of Clint.

"We'll head on down river," he said, speaking Blackfoot, "maybe he'll turn up."

No one said much as they plodded along the high bank above the Platte. Each of them kept their feelings to themselves. Since that day on the Wind River, Ned had gotten to know Clint pretty well and held a high respect for him. But in this country, life was fragile and friends came and went. Mostly, they died, gettin' scalped or mauled by a bear or drowned or starved. It was only logical then that one not get too close to his compadres. If it came to a fight, they'd stand up for each other to the death but there was an unspoken understanding that if you or a friend went under, it was just part of the game. It was the risk a man took for the privilege of living in God's great mountains.

The sun was not quite overhead when Ned and the two women at last reached the confluence of the two rivers. There were signs about that many camps had been set here in the past. Ned figured it had mostly been boat crews and mountain men on their way to the Shining Mountains who had camped here. Indians didn't make such a fuss about building big fire pits and choppin' down trees for wood. White men had a way of ruinin' whatever it was they touched.

Through the day, they hunted along the banks and over the countryside for any sign of Clint or the raft. But by nightfall, they'd pretty much given up hope of seeing their friend again. Storm said very little, keeping her feelings close in. Often though, Lou would notice her staring off into the darkness, seemingly listening for his cheerful voice to break the lonely silence.

Getting her attention, Ned offered a suggestion that he thought might help Storm feel better. "Maybe we outta cross the Platte in the mornin' and look downstream on the big river. Chances are if ole' Clint got washed on downriver, he'll be tryin' to make it back here to see you. We could ease his journey some if we went to meet him." His idea brought a light of hope to her eyes and a smile to her cheeks as she nodded her agreement. She was much happier and more talkative through the rest of the evening.

Bright and early the next morning, Ned and the two women rode upstream on the Platte to a place they could cross. Ned rode into the water first checking the depth. Near its bank and for some distance out, the river was shallow. But near the center, the horses had to swim. The women waited until he was safe on the far bank and motioned them to come ahead. Their crossing was uneventful and soon, they were on their way down the Missouri to find their friend.

That morning is when Ned and the women, heading downstream, passed Clint, who was heading upstream. They were, however, on opposite shorelines and because of the width of the Missouri and the thick brush lining its banks, neither knew that the other was there.

By the time he reached the confluence of the two rivers, Clint could hardly walk. His knee had tightened up and would not bend. With each step, he winced in pain. Looking across the wide expanse of water, he knew there was no way he could cross. Awkwardly, he made his way down to a place at the river's edge where he could be easily seen from the far shore. At this point, he fired his rifle in the air and began hollering for Storm and Ned. Reloading, he fired again. There was no response, no return of fire, no movement.

"Where the hell could they be?" he wondered, reloading once more. "They were gonna camp here and trade with trappin' parties headin' for the mountains. They wouldn't have left, they had no reason to. They knew I'd come back to find 'em." It was then that a cold fear crept over him. What if that bunch of Indians he encountered circled back downstream to ambush him and came on to Ned and the women, instead. The thought stabbed at him, creating a sharp burning sensation in his stomach and throat. "I thought those red bastards gave up a little too easy," he whispered, carrying his thoughts to the next plateau. "They never even let loose an arrow." Pausing a moment, he thought it through one more time, his mind measuring each thing he knew, weighing them against the things he didn't know. Sadly, he lowered his head, "That had to have been what happened" he whispered, "they were expectin' me. They weren't expectin' to die." His voice trailed off and he slumped down on the muddy bank.

When he had at last regained his composure, Clint arose from his boggy seat at the river's edge and made his way up the steep bank. The stiffness and pain in his leg was terrible but nothing compared to the aching emptiness in his heart. She was the only one he'd ever truly loved, the only one who seemed to understand his innermost thoughts and feelings, the only one...

In a sort of stupor, he headed back downriver not thinking of his leg or the pain but instead, dwelling on the loss of his beloved Storm. At nightfall, when he could no longer see, he collapsed at the foot of a large tree. Near it, another tree lay dead, its branches dry and brittle. With the sunset, the wind had turned cold and huddling close to the dead trunk, Clint broke away some small twigs and heaped them in a mound. With his flint and steel, he soon had a warm fire blazing. For a while, he stayed awake, feeding the fire and dwelling on his misery. But his body finally gave in to the fatigue of the last two days and he fell soundly asleep.

#

The following sunrise met the world with clear skies and a heavy frost. Clint awoke to ice crystals covering his buckskins and rifle. Shivering, he quickly gathered the makings for another fire. When the warmth of the flames had at last driven away the stiffness and uncontrollable shaking, he reached into his pouch and brought forth the last of the roast deer meat. As he ate, he rubbed his leg.

"Damn, that's sore," he uttered, trying to bend his knee and get the circulation going. It was aching like crazy and he realized there was no way he could walk as he had the past few days. He decided then, to build another raft and float down the river as he had on the Platte.

When he'd finished eating, he searched along the river's bank for wood from which to build the raft. He soon discovered two large logs laying high and dry above the water line. Apparently, they had floated there during the spring runoff and had been caught in the brush that grew thick at the river's edge. He broke off as many of their branches as he could and, with some effort, rolled them into the water. Standing crotch-deep in the brown flow, he held the logs against the current and lashed them together with the strap from his shooting pouch.

"That should do," he murmured, lifting his bad leg from the water to straddle them.

Once afloat, he laid his rifle ahead of him on the logs and paddled with his hands. His legs, dangling in the icy water, once more grew numb and the shivering returned.

The movement of the river was swift and carried him along at a good rate. "No way I could'a covered this much ground," he thought, "not with this game leg and all. The water's cold but this is the only thing I could do."

The two-log raft was much easier to steer than his other craft had been and he was able to keep it near the shore. He didn't want to get too far out in the current and pass by the place he'd stashed his gear.

For hours, he floated, sitting straddle of the logs. When he finally arrived at the spot he'd beached the other raft, it was late afternoon. Lifting his rifle up and removing the lashed leather strap, he slid from the logs leaving them to float away with the current. He stumbled to the shore, cold and tired. He would make camp here and spend the night. He needed a warm fire, a belly full of meat, and a night's sleep to clear his head. Too much had happened too quickly.

Uncovering the things he'd hidden, his eyes suddenly fell upon the horsehair bracelet at his wrist. Tears welled up in his eyes and he choked back a small cry. Memories were suddenly crashing inside his head and he put his hands over his eyes.

Two days before, he had been happy, in love with a woman he cherished above all things. Today, she was gone, probably killed and scalped. The emptiness that fell upon him at that moment was all consuming. So devastated was he that he wondered if he, too, might die. And so, without benefit of a fire or food for his stomach, he solemnly climbed under the heavy buffalo robe and closed his eyes against the sunset's remaining light. Tomorrow was another day and it would be here soon enough. Tonight though, he had to have a place to hide; a place where his mind could not find him.

Clint's journey now seemed to quicken. The Missouri flowed fast and the shoreline passed by at a rapid pace. He covered many miles each day. Too, he was alone and had nobody to meet or visit with when he beached the raft for the night. To eat, he shot rabbits and speared fish. These things he concentrated on heavily, not so much because he was hungry but more because it gave him something to think about, something besides Storm. Often though, he would find himself remembering her eyes or the way she walked or the fineness of her neck when he'd lift her hair away to kiss her from behind.

It was on the afternoon of his third day alone on the river when the keel boats came into view. Men with long poles walked a steady pace forward and back on the narrow side decks of the craft, pushing the poles into the muddy bottom to propel them upstream.

"Hello, the raft," came a deep voice across the water. "What be yer name and yer destination?"

"Name's Jeffries, Clint Jeffries and I'm bound for St. Lou."

"By God in heaven, is that you Clint?" It was the voice of Afton Scroggins; he'd know it anywhere. "I thought you mighta' gone under when you didn't show up last year at the Great Falls. Where's Tucker and Harris?"

Cupping his hands around his mouth, Clint answered back "This is a helluva way to carry on a conversation. Peers as though we outta get ashore if'n we're gonna palaver."

"We need to take a rest anyway," Scroggins called out, giving a hand signal to the man at the tiller.

As the big boat swung toward the shore, Clint paddled the raft to meet it. It had been more than four years since Afton Scroggins had seen Clint. Now, when they stepped ashore, he could hardly belief the difference in the lad. The boy had become a man.

"Damned if you ain't a sight for sore eyes," he said, offering Clint his hand and a wide smile.

"It's been a while, Green," Clint answered, taking the man's huge hand in his own. Afton was the man's God given name but somehow, down through the years, he'd acquired the nickname of Green.

He was a large man, six foot four at least and strong as a bull. He was broad shouldered and had a slow easy way about him. His face was ruggedly handsome with its square set jaw and burning blue eyes. His skin was a weathered brown color as were most of the trappers and his thick sandy hair was cropped just above his shoulders.

His hands had always been what amazed Clint. They were huge and powerful. Each of his fingers would make three of Clint's. Many's the man that had tried to grip this feller down only to wind up with a broken hand or at the least, severe bruises.

"Jesus boy, you've growed like a weed. You look me straight in the eye, now."

"Yeah, but I ain't near as mean as you," Clint answered, slapping him on the shoulder and laughing. "You asked about Tucker and Harris?"

"Yeah, where are them boys? Hell, they were thicker'n thieves the last time I saw 'em. Sorta looked out for yer young ass too, as I remember."

"That they did, my friend," Clint answered with a soft smile. "Last time I saw Jim, he was with Black Elk's bunch, headin' fer their summer country. He married Black Elk's sister, you know. A good woman she is, too." Pausing a moment, he went on. "Ole Jack got himself killed by a grizzly bear."

"I'm sorry to hear that," Green offered "That's a helluva way to go. Damn, I'd a thought ole Jack could kick any griz's ass, as ornery as he was."

"Noticed ya limpin' when ya came ashore," Green said, looking at Clint's game leg.

"Yeah, I had a run-in with the Blackfeet some time back; took an arrow just above the knee and the head is still lodged in the bone. That's why I'm bound for St. Lou. Gonna find me a doctor and get myself fixed up."

"Well, you best get yerself set fer a surprise, cause you ain't gonna recognize the place. It's growin' like a weed. People movin' in from all over hell. Sorta reminds me of a big som'bitchin' ant pile, everybody scurrying about, steppin' all over one another and takin' up everythin' in sight. Amongst all that mass of humanity, I'd reckon ya outta be able to scrounge yerself up a doctor." Pausing a moment, Green looked back toward the boat. "Olley, bring us some of that cured meat and a jug a whiskey."

"Jesus, Green, you got whiskey? I ain't had a taste of mash squeezin's for more'n three years. Ole Jack used to keep a flask, you know, fer special times. He'd gimme a taste now and then but he kept it mostly to himself."

As the two men talked of past times and old acquaintances, other men, curious of why they'd pulled ashore, made their way from the boats to listen to the conversation. Clint thought he recognized a few of them but it had been more than seven years since he'd come up river and he couldn't be sure.

Some of the men in the outfit were true mountain men. Clint could tell by the way they listened and the questions they asked. Others in the group acted sullen and said nothing, their shifty eyes taking in every detail of the stranger before them. Seemingly, they were men looking to make a quick fortune or trying to hide themselves from a shady past.

Mentally measuring each man in the circle about him, Clint thought to himself "The mountains have a way of testin' a man's character, of seein' what he's really made of. Some of these fellas ain't gonna make it."

"Say Green, I noticed ya got some small dugouts strapped to the top of the keel boats. Ya wouldn't want to sell one would ya?"

"They're not mine to sell," Green answered, "they belong to the company. Gonna use 'em up-river when we reach the headwaters. It's easier than tryin' to build canoes or buffalo boats. They'll last longer too."

"Just thought I'd ask," Clint said, "that raft's uncomfortable and I can't make any time with it. Thought maybe you might be willin' to let one go."

Putting his hand to his chin, Green thought for a moment. "Hmm," he mused. "You know, we got another party leavin' St. Louis in about three weeks. There'll be four more boats filled with supplies and trade goods. We're gonna wait for em to join us at the great falls." Pausing a moment, he went on, "I reckon I could let you take one of those boats if'n you turned it over to our bunch when ya got to St. Lou. They could pack it back up river with 'em."

"Hell, I'd be grateful to ya, Green and I'm willin' to pay for its use; I don't expect to get it fer nothin'. I come by some gold when I was back in the mountains. You just name yer price and I'll pay what ya ask."

Smiling, Green answered "You keep yer gold Clint, it'd just cause trouble among the men...gold always does. Besides, where we're goin,' we don't need no gold."

When they'd finished talking, some of the men took down one of the dugouts from atop the large keel boat and helped Clint load his goods. They couldn't help but notice the heavy bag he struggled with when putting it in the boat. Stepping to the shore to see his old friend off, Green dropped a cloth sack into the dugout.

"Here's a little somethin' to stave off the hunger on yer way downriver. I wish ya luck in gettin' yer leg healed."

Thanking him, Clint pushed off into the swift current. "Watch yer topknots, now." He yelled back over his shoulder. "Them Blackfeet are thicker'n hornets and twice as mean."

The dugout swung easily into the current and moved swiftly downstream with little effort. It was good that Green had let him borrow the boat, for it would save him a lot of time and spare him the discomfort of riding that raft.

Through the rest of that day, Clint paddled, taking advantage of the river where the current was the strongest. With the setting of the sun, he selected a likely looking campsite and pulled ashore for the night. He was tired and the mounting breeze coming across the water sent a sudden chill up his back.

"A warm fire will feel good tonight," he whispered, sliding the dugout up the muddy bank. He paused for a moment then, gazing out across the eddied surface of the great river as it reflected the last brilliant hues of twilight. "Storm...I miss you," he mumbled, letting the words trail off on the breeze.

The fire had reduced itself to a small heap of glowing coals, with now and then an occasional spark leaping up to join the gusting night wind. Clint lay asleep between the warm buffalo robes snuggled up against a stand of heavy willows.

It was the sound an oar makes as it is lifted from the water to commence another stroke that brought the mountain man from his place of gentle sleep to an alert, wide awake condition. Slowly he sat up, feeling for the big rifle at his side. Finding the hammer, he grasped it firmly under his thumb and brought it back to the cocked position, all the while squeezing the trigger. With the hammer full back, he held it tight and gently released his finger from the trigger. This way, there was no click to be heard from the hammer being set - no click to give away his position - no click to warn those who were about to strike.

The night was very dark, with only a sliver of moon to cast a light. Tucked back against the willows, Clint was sure he was concealed in total darkness. The now embered fire lay between him and the dugout; it being some twenty-five to thirty feet away.

His keen ears detected a boat being pulled ashore next to the dugout.

"Let's just take his possibles from the boat and skedaddle," a voice whispered in the darkness. "The gold's bound to be here somewhere."

"Shut yer mouth, ya damn fool," another voice whispered "you'll wake him up."

With his teeth, Clint pulled the stopper from his powder horn and poured some of its contents into his right hand. As he sat there waiting, he quietly positioned himself, listening. He was ready but he would have to act quickly.

Sitting motionless, Clint could feel his pulse beating at his temples. Nothing stirred but the breeze. Then, he heard it, the soft footfall of a leather moccasin upon the grass.

"It must happen, now," he thought, "Now!" With a gentle toss, he lofted the handful of black powder upon the embers of the dying fire. The darkness was then interrupted by a loud boom and a blinding flash of fire and heavy smoke. Within that flash and etched upon his mind's eye, Clint saw the two men, one facing him, not fifteen feet away. The other crouched down near the dugouts. As the flash died away, the men were all blinded. Remembering where the closer man stood, Clint pointed his rifle and pulled the trigger. Again, a blinding flash filled the night, accompanied by the rifle's ear shattering report. Clint heard the heavy thud of a body crash to the earth near the fire. Quickly, he rolled away from where he was and prepared for whatever was about to come. Another shot then lit up the darkness, the impact of which crashed through the willows at the place he had been sitting. Once more, the night became deathly quiet. Clint's hand went deftly to the knife at his side, quietly withdrawing it from its scabbard.

For several moments, the silence hung like a black veil. Then he heard the movement. It was the hurried sound of footsteps and a rifle being tossed into a boat. Someone was sliding that boat into the river.

In an instant, Clint was low crawling toward the grunting sounds of the man struggling to free the dugout from the mud. His leg rebelled against the movement but he forced himself onward in pain. What light there was from the moon reflected from the river's surface and cast a dim silhouette of the intruder as he prepared to step into the boat and make his getaway. In that moment, Clint was upon him, his left hand coming up from behind to grab the man's bearded face and tip it upward. At the same time, his right hand drew the razor-sharp knife forcefully across the soft flesh of the man's exposed throat. It was suddenly over. The man's reflexes vaulted him forward and Clint could hear him thrashing about in the boat, as it drifted away with the current.

Still shaking, Clint returned to the smoldering campfire and scrounged about for twigs and grass to rebuild it. When the flames at last cast enough light to see the body lying before him on the ground, Clint rolled him over. The man was dead, shot squarely through the chest. It was no surprise to Clint when he discovered it was one of Green's men. In fact, it was the man who had helped him load his gear into the dugout. He suddenly remembered what Ned had told him about watching his back and how men would slit your throat to get at your gold. He now realized how foolish he'd been in mentioning it. Too many ears had been listening. He wouldn't do that again.

"Son-of-a-bitch," Clint said out loud "Ain't no amount of gold in the world worth dyin' for or worth killin' for. But then, I guess some folks just don't see it that way."

Through the rest of the night, he couldn't sleep. Instead, he sat feeding the fire and remembering the beautiful Indian women he'd fallen so deeply in love with.

\#

Dawn found him huddled once more beneath the warm buffalo robes, snoring peacefully. A heavy frost covered the ground and sparkled brightly with the sun's first rays. Somewhere across the wide river, a flock of geese greeted the morning with their harsh voices. The sound reached Clint, causing him to stir. With one eye, he peeked out from under the robe and then laid back down to snooze a while longer. When he at last arose, the sun was full up. Seeing the body of the man he'd killed brought a sickening reminder of the events of the past evening. He shuddered at the thought of what might have happened.

He suddenly felt an urgent need to be gone from this place. The men who'd attacked him undoubtedly had friends who might come looking for them when they were discovered missing. If that was going to happen, he didn't want to be here when they showed up.

As Clint loaded his possibles into the long dugout, he noticed it was not the boat that Green had given him. It was, instead, the one the two men had come in, being longer and somewhat wider.

"I guess that feller dropped into the wrong boat when I cut him," Clint whispered. "Oh well, this one's better anyway."

Taking a deep breath, he bent over and dragged the dead man away from the river, deeper into the brush. Dousing the campfire ashes with river water, he scattered them about through the grass and willows. A few of the willows he cut, using them to dust out every indication that anyone had ever been there.

When he'd finished, he took one final glance around to see that he hadn't overlooked anything. Then, pushing off, he steered the boat downstream. As he paddled, he kept a sharp eye out for the other dugout.

It was not until noon of the next day that he came upon the other boat. It had floated with the current, finally lodging itself against a large pile of driftwood that had stacked up on the outside curve of a long bend in the river. Several magpies and some turkey buzzards were busy making a meal of the dugout's silent occupant. Clint had decided to hide this body also but seeing the birds, he thought better of it and paddled on.

As he passed the gruesome scene, a feeling of guilt began to creep over him.

"By God, it was them or me," he whispered, dispelling the impending feelings. "If'n they'd a had their way, it'd be me sprawled out on some sandbar with my throat cut from ear to ear and they'd be divvyin' up shares of my gold." Then, pausing a moment, he looked down at the large parfliech that held the yellow metal. "I outta just throw that shit in the river and be done with it," he murmured. But he thought better of it and kept paddling. "By God, it was them or me," he whispered again, "them or me."

Four days later, Clinton Jeffries ran the bow of the shallow dugout onto the shore near the city of St. Louis. Green had been right, he hardly recognized the place. It had grown to three times the size it'd been when last he'd seen it.

"I reckon I'll be able to find me a doctor in this here town," he commented, "but first, I need to look up the feller that's runnin' the Company and return this boat."

With that, he shouldered his rifle and walked toward the men loading the large keel boats that were tied to the dock.

BOOK 2 – BACK TO ST. LOU AND THE SETTLEMENTS

CHAPTER 1:
DOCTORS, BULLIES, AND THE OLD MAN

Beyond the dancing glow of his cook-fire, Clinton Jeffries watched the lights of St. Louis sparkle against the growing darkness. After he'd eaten, he ditched his possibles bag, doused the fire, and headed for town. Walking the busy streets of the city, he peered into the shop windows and rummaged about in the mercantile stores. The walkways bustled with people and there were many new things he'd never seen before. The bakeries and the smokehouses emitted smells of fresh bread and cured hams and sausages. All made his mouth water. Everything was a spectacle to behold.

He too, was somewhat of a spectacle to the town's people, what with his shoulder-length hair, greasy buckskins, and woodland paraphernalia. From a distance, one would easily take him for an Indian and Indians were not welcome in St. Louis society.

As this city lay at the frontier's edge, men dressed such as he were not an oddity. Most, however, were on their way to the mountains, not returning from them, and their buckskins were usually much cleaner and in better condition. Also, Clint's size drew unwanted attention from the town folk. At six foot four, he was much larger than the average man and stood out in a crowd regardless of what he wore. But it was his clothes and his odor that had drawn the most attention.

As he walked, he would notice people staring and pointing or wrinkling their nose and laughing at him. Some, believing they were out of earshot, made stinging comments under their breath. Others, not so shy about hiding their opinions, openly confronted him with insults and obscene gestures. It was an uncomfortable, embarrassing situation and so he elected to leave the city.

"I'll spend the night camped along the river," he thought, "and at daybreak, I'll return to sell the gold. Once I have me some spendin' money, I'll git me a bath an' some new duds." Pausing a moment, he smiled and then whispered,"Waugh! I guess I smelled purty ripe to those folks; they sure'nuff turned their noses up and skedaddled when I walked into their stores. Guess that's how a skunk feels when he goes visitin'"

Content now to be alone in his camp, Clint stirred the fire and watched the swarms of angry sparks leap into the air, popping their displeasure at being disturbed and finally disappearing into the accompanying veil of rising smoke. Quietly, he spoke to the surrounding darkness, "Storm! Storm, can you hear me? I miss you so much. The short time we spent together filled an empty place in my heart. Your memory will live there forever. I will always love you. Sleep well."

The sun had not yet broken the eastern horizon when Clint shouldered the bag of gold and headed for town. Its weight was uncomfortable to carry and he had to change shoulders several times along the way.

The day before, on his journey through the streets, he had noticed a sign in the window of a building that read "We Buy Gold." It was to this store that he made his way, arriving there well before the owner.

Clint was sitting on the edge of the porch away from the door when a man finally walked up.

"We don't give no handouts here, mister," the shopkeeper said, stepping past him to unlock the door, "So, you'd best gather your things and be on yer way."

"I want to sell some gold," Clint retorted, following the man in through the narrow door. "Came upon it back in the mountains some time ago."

Taken aback by the comment, the man cast a sinister frown at him and stepped behind the counter.

"Sure ya didn't steal it?" He said sarcastically, issuing Clint a nasty smirk.

Clint's eyes narrowed at the remark and the skin across his forehead tightened.

"Look mister, I came here to sell this gold, not to take a ration a shit offn' you. Now, if you wanna buy it, fine. If not, I'm sure there's others in town who will."

The man felt Clint's cold blue eyes burning holes through him.

"I...I was only jok..." he stammered, not quite getting the words out.

"I know what you were doin,'" Clint interrupted, "and I don't like it. I apologize for my appearance but I've been in the mountains for nigh onto eight years an' I ain't had the time or money to clean up. But I ain't stupid and I don't deserve that kind of treatment."

"I'm...I'm sorry," the man said, again stammering for words. "If you want to just leave the gold here, I'll tally it up and make out a bank draft in your name."

Leaning forward so as to impress on the man his true feelings, Clint smiled coldly and answered, "If it's all the same to you, I'm gonna stand right here and watch you tally it up. I don't much trust other people handlin' what belongs to me."

With that, the man's hands began to shake nervously and he went about the business of sorting and weighing the precious metal. Inwardly, Clint smiled to himself. "That son-of-a-bitch, treatin' people like they was dirt. I got no use for a man like that. Maybe I otta just lean on him a little and teach him a lesson."

Clint watched every move the man made. Realizing he was under extreme scrutiny, the man often turned to look at his customer. Clint always returned the look with a cold, unwavering stare, focused directly at the man's eyes. He noticed then, the beads of sweat forming on the man's brow and knew he was making him nervous.

Clint was not of a mean nature but he did have a streak of mischief in his soul and this was too good an opportunity to pass up. Wanting to strike one last note of fear in the man, Clint related a story that Jack had once told him.

"You know, I remember one time up on the Beaverhead," he began. "A Frenchman named LeBlanc tried cheatin' me in a trade for my pelts. He done it 'cause I was young, you understand, and didn't know no better. Yep, he thought he'd cut a fat hog in the ass and swindle me. Well, when I found out what he'd done, I went and looked him up." Clint paused for a moment making sure he had the man's full attention. Then, pulling the knife at his side from its scabbard, he went on. "Took this here knife an' slit him from his ball bag to his bottom lip, I did. His guts spilled out there right in front of him, all green an' gooey an' oozin'. Funny thing was, he didn't even move, didn't fall down or nothin'. No sir, he just stood there in amazement lookin' at his entrails sprawled out across the ground. Some of his compadres came over and took him down. They tried puttin' everythin' back inside but it warn't no use, they just wouldn't fit. B'sides, everythin' was all covered with dirt and ants and pine needles and the like." Again, Clint paused in his story. "Took that Frenchy nigh on to four days to die. T'were a bad four days, I reckon."

By this time, the man had completely stopped what he was doing and stood open-mouthed and frozen with disbelief.

Clint then lowered his gaze and shook his head slightly as he finished his story. "Yes sir," he said, in a sympathetic tone "I always regretted that"

"What?" the man stammered "Wha...what did you regret?"

"I regretted standin' so damn close to that feller when I cut him open. Ya' see it splashed goo all over the front of me; liked to ruin that new pair a deer skin britches I had on an I couldn't get the smell out fer a month."

The man's eyes showed white all around and he swallowed hard. Saying nothing, he turned slowly and resumed his work with the gold. But after only a few moments, he turned back again, his face an ashen white color. Shiny trails of perspiration ran the length of his cheeks, gathering in drops at his chin.

"Will you excuse me please?" he said in a sickly voice. "I don't feel well. I'll be right back."

The man rushed from the store, holding his hand over his mouth. Moments later, Clint could hear him retching at the side of the building. "Serves you right, you son-of-a-bitch," he whispered, smiling.

By mid-morning, Clint had completed his dealings with the gold buyer. When he read what was written on the draft, he couldn't believe his eyes. It was far more money than he'd ever dreamed of having.

After depositing the draft at the bank, he walked into one of the mercantile stores and bought himself some new clothes, a pair of boots, a hat, and some home-baked cookies. The next stop found him at a barbershop and bathhouse. He had decided that, after enjoying a nice hot bath and getting his hair cut, he would look up a doctor and have his leg looked at.

For two hours, he languished in the heavy metal tub, paying the proprietor an extra quarter for the additional hot water. As he soaked, he ate the cookies.

"Damn, this is the life," he thought. "Beats the hell out of those cold streams. Makes my leg feel better too."

When he'd finished his bath, and gotten his hair cut, Clint strolled the main street of St. Louis. He took his time, enjoying the warm afternoon sunshine and the many shops and stores. It was along here, the barber had said, that he would find Silas Gormes, the town's only doctor.

According to the barber, who seemed well versed in the gossip and goings-on of St. Louis, there had been two doctors servicing the populace of the growing city, Doctor Gormes and another fellow named Bigsby. But, during last month's town festival, two men, drunk out of their minds, began fighting and raising a fuss. In an effort to make the peace, the good doctor stepped between them and asked them to please go outside. For all his kindliness, Doctor Bigsby received a dagger straight through the heart. Those around him said he was dead before he hit the floor.

The drunken man who stabbed him was immediately dragged into the street and hanged. His adversary in the fight was kicked and beaten within an inch of his life by the infuriated townspeople. Now, Doctor Gormes, and Doctor Gormes alone, administered to the pregnant, the ill, the injured, and the dying people of St. Louis. Needless to say, he couldn't keep up with it all.

Entering the narrow, dingy office, Clint was greeted by a sickeningly sweet smell. It seemed, a mixture of chemicals, mildew, and human body odor - that of sweat, urine, and infection. The darkly painted walls resembled a tunnel and were lined on each side with an assortment of old chairs, boxes, and nail kegs. Each held a patient.

Seated at a small table in the midst of this place of sickness sat a rather rotund woman. Her hair was pulled into a tight bun at the back of her head with a linen cap perched neatly above it. Busily, she scrawled in the ledger before her, often using the feather of her quill to wipe away the trails of perspiration that beaded on her forehead and ran in rivulets down her round cheeks.

A noisy bell attached to the door announced Clint's arrival. Without looking up, the woman acknowledged his presence. "And what might we do for you, today?" she asked in a high, nasal tone.

"I need to see the doctor," Clint answered, hesitating. "It's about my leg. You see, I took an arrow..."

"Take yer place at the back of the line and sit down," the fat woman interrupted, pointing to an empty box in the corner to his left. "The doctor will see you as soon as he can."

Looking about him, not sure if he wanted to be there, Clint offered an idea "Uh, maybe I could come back tomor...?"

Again, the woman cut short his words. "Won't be no different tomorrow," she droned. "Fact is, you'll be lucky to see the doctor today, as late as it is. You'll probably have to come back tomorrow, anyway. But, if you do, you git to keep yer place in line. Ya see, that's what I keep recorded in this here schedule." The woman seemed suddenly aggravated and looking up at last, added, "I can write, you know? I'm not just makin' fancy scratchin's on this paper." Again, she lowered her gaze to the ledger.

Clint nodded his head, in agreement - afraid to move or say anything else. He knew though, he could not stay in this office another minute. Slowly, amid the coughing and sneezing, and without turning around, he stepped back, took hold of the doorknob, and let himself out. The voice of the tattling tinny bell again rang out, causing the woman to once more raise her pudgy face. The only thing she saw this time, however, was the door closing before her.

Walking away from the office, Clint wondered if he'd made a mistake in coming here to get his leg mended. After all, he'd gotten along all right so far, even if it was sometimes difficult. However, he had only to step down from the wooden walkway to the street, to be reminded of just how bad his leg really was. Now, sharp pains raced upward from the old wound, attacking his sanity and almost taking his breath away.

"I'll come back tomorrow," he thought, wincing against the agony, "even if I have to go to the back of the line."

As he neared a large hotel, Clint noticed a commotion on the far side of the street. Many men were circled about something lying on the ground. Their laughter and loud voices drew the attention of all those within earshot. One man, in particular, seemed to be leading the group, pressing them on with increasing fervor.

"...Look here, now," he shouted, "feast your eyes on this fine example of humanity - if you can call it human. Oh yes, gentlemen, there are those who would have you believe that this is the prince of the prairie, the honorable and intelligent Red Man." Pausing, he reached into the circling crowd and lifted up what appeared to Clint, to be an old man. "As far as I'm concerned," the man droned on, "this derelict is the blight of civilization, a Godless heathen to be dealt with on the most severe level. He, and all like him, should be wiped from the face of the earth."

With that, the crowd became even wilder.

"Maybe we oughta string him up?" came a loud voice from the throng.

"Nah, let's just tar and feather him," issued another.

"Maybe you otta just leave him be?" Clint said, stepping into the circle of men.

At his words, every voice hushed. The angry eyes of the mob seemed now to focus on the tall stranger who had put his nose in where it didn't belong.

"I don't know who you are, sir," the leader of the men said, tightening his grip on the old Indian 'but it's clear you haven't had much involvement with these devils. They're not much, you know, a cowardly bunch with no stomach for a good fight."

"Well, that shows what you know," Clint retorted, looking straight into the man's narrowed eyes.

"I've spent the last seven years tradin',' livin' with,' and sometimes fightin' the likes of this feller and I can tell ya right now, they ain't none of 'em cowards. This one here, he's old and beat down but ten years ago, he'd a skinned the likes 'a you and had yer hair danglin' from his lodge pole."

The man's cold stare intensified and his lips drew together tightly. "Sir, I take this as a direct insult to my abilities as a man. Therefore, I demand satisfaction." With that, he released his grip on the Old Man. Pulling a leather glove from his vest pocket, the man attempted to slap Clint across the face with it.

Clint was too quick for him, however, and with his left hand, caught the man's wrist in mid-swing. At the same instant, his right hand doubled into a fist and delivered a thundering blow to the man's face, knocking him soundly to the ground. The rest of the men, seeing their leader lying helpless before them, backed off.

"Mister, I don't give a good Goddam what you demand," Clint said, reaching for the old Indian who had fallen and seemed somehow, oblivious to the goings on. "I just want you to leave him alone."

Looking now at the Old Man, Clint spoke softly in the Blackfoot Tongue. "Grandfather, do you understand the words I speak?"

At the sound of Clint's words, the Old Man's eyes sparkled and a sign of recognition replaced the disillusionment that had been there a moment before. With his hands, the old warrior signed out the words for Clint to understand.

"Though your words sound familiar, my son, I do not recognize the tongue. I hope you can understand this way of speaking." Clint nodded and the Old Man went on. "I thank you for your help. I was hungry and I asked these people for food. They must have thought I said bad things because they beat me and kicked me. They might have killed me had it not been for you."

Clint put his hand out to the Old Man and helped him up. He then led him away through the stirring crowd. "Come," he said, "I will find you something to eat." The old Indian didn't understand the young man's words but the gentle sound of his voice instilled a trust in his mind and he followed. When they'd rounded the corner, and were far enough away from the rowdy mob, Clint located a store in which to buy provisions. In sign language, he told the Old Man to sit down and wait for him. When he'd purchased the things he needed, Clint gathered up the Old Man and took him to his camp near the river.

"You oughta be safe out here," Clint muttered, setting the provisions near the small lean-to he'd built. "This is far enough from town that those fellers shouldn't find ya."

Seeing Clint set the sack of food on the ground, the Old Man went to rummaging through it. Upon finding a loaf of the fresh baked bread, he quickly tore off a piece and began to eat. "Here," Clint said, also reaching into the sack, "let's cut you off a piece of this." Bringing forth a large smoked ham, he easily sliced away two thick slabs. One of these, he gave to the Old Man, and the other he kept for himself. He then tore off a piece of the bread and settled back with his company to eat. Between bites, they conversed in sign language.

When he was not pushing food into his mouth, the Old Man's fingers signed out words. He explained to Clint that he was of the Flathead tribe who lived far up the mighty river, beyond the place where the water roars and spills over the rocks. Clint realized the Old Man was describing the great falls on the big river. He had been there many times, himself.

He paused once, motioning for another piece of ham. Clint obliged him and the Old Man continued.

"My village is near the edge of a huge lake, clear and clean as a maiden's eye and full of large fish."

Watching him closely, Clint realized the Old Man was seeing this place in his mind as he spoke of it. He seemed almost entranced in recalling the dusty memories. "There are many elk, bear, and buffalo. The beaver and otter are thick in the streams and large flocks of ducks and geese come there to raise their families."

"Is it far from the falling waters?" Clint interrupted.

"Yes," he signed, nodding his head. "From where the water drops, one must ride toward the setting sun, across the mountain's backbone. It is a trip of many sleeps and one which I will never make again." Sadly then, he hung his head, seeming to return to the present.

Clint recognized the sadness and reaching out, gently slapped him on the shoulder. "You might get back there someday." He said, "Hell, a feller never knows which way his stick's gonna float. One day you can be in love and be the happiest man in the world and the next, yer by yer self, lookin' at the world through empty eyes and shakin' the cold hand of loneliness." Somewhat lost in a trance himself, Clint suddenly realized, the old Indian was watching him but had no idea what he was saying.

Quickly, he apologized, signing, "I am sorry, my friend. It seems we both have an aching in our hearts. You for the loss of your homeland and I for the loss of..." He couldn't go on. Her memory flashed before him and the tears welled up behind his eyes. "Aww, shit, why did she have to die?" he whispered.

"Was she beautiful?" the Old Man signed, breaking his concentration.

"Yes, she was." Clint answered. "But, how did you know?"

Smiling, the Old Man signed "Men only get that look when they've lost a woman or a good horse." Then a sudden gleam lit up his eyes and he asked, "Was it a good horse?"

Clint didn't answer but only smiled and nodded his head, showing that he understood.

"Here," he motioned to the Old Man "take this." And he tossed him the last of the cookies he'd bought in town.

When they'd at last finished eating, they both laid back to relax. Their heads rested upon the cool grass and their eyes watched the mares-tail clouds drift past. Within minutes, both were asleep, each with his own dreams.

Sleeping through the afternoon, they were unaware of the gathering clouds stacking up in the west. An icy raindrop driven by the now biting wind woke Clint from his rest.

"Wha...what the hell?" he whispered, rolling onto his back. The Old Man was already up and heading for the lean-to.

"Eske," he murmured, signing the word for storm. "Eske."

"Right," Clint nodded, trying to erase the cobwebs of sleep from his mind. Half crawling, half walking, he too headed for the shelter. "Damn good thing I built this, Old Man," he said. "I knew there'd be some weather comin' afore long."

The shelter was fair sized. It easily held both of them, plus a stack of firewood Clint had put up, anticipating the cool weather that fall brings. The wood was stacked at the rear of the shelter, staving off the westward, prevailing wind. "That wind feels as though it could have a touch of snow with it," Clint thought to himself. "I ain't much ready for that right now and this Old Man don't even have a blanket."

Touching the Indian's shoulder, Clint signed to him, "Tonight will be cold, we can share a blanket and keep the fire going. Tomorrow, when it is light, I will go to town and buy us warm clothing and blankets." The Old Man nodded and began gathering twigs to start a fire. Sometime, deep in the night, it snowed.

Clint left the Old Man at camp the next morning, telling him to stay there. "If you come with me, those men in town might make trouble for you again. That would be bad. There is plenty of food here and you can stay warm by the fire. I will return as soon as I can."

Telling the man this, Clint wondered if he understood what he'd said. Sometimes, his sign language was weak and he could see in the Old Man's questioning face that he didn't understand. However, the man seemed to trust what he said and, whether he understood or not, made no attempt to follow.

The night had been uncomfortable to say the least, causing Clint's leg to stiffen and throb with pain. Now, the mile or so walk from his camp to St. Louis caused it to ache even worse. By the time he reached the outskirts of the city, he was limping.

Finding the mercantile store closed, Clint decided he might try to see the doctor again. It was early but the man might be at his office. As luck would have it, the doctor was unlocking the door when Clint hobbled up.

"Doctor Gormes?" Clint asked, "Are you Doctor Gormes?"

The slender man turned to face him, "Yes, I am, young man. And how may I be of service to you?"

Pointing to his game leg, Clint answered, "I took an arrow sometime back - just above the knee. My partner couldn't cut it out; said he thought the head was stuck deep in the bone."

The man stood for a moment as if contemplating what he'd just been told. Clint could now see the dark circles under his eyes. He looked tired. Doctor Gormes was not an old man in age. Yet, he seemed old for his years. He had a haggard look about him, the look of a man who'd seen too much pain, too much suffering, indeed, too much death.

"Come in, come in sir," he said, pushing the door open. "Watch your step, it's rather dark in here."

The place had the same smell Clint had noticed the day before and it almost sickened him.

"Please, remove your pants," the doctor said, leading him into his office. While Clint disrobed, the Doctor lit several lamps and began stoking a fire in a small pot-bellied stove that stood in the corner.

"It'll be warm in here, soon," he commented. "Now, climb up on the table there, sir." Resolutely, he pointed to a long table covered with a dingy, white cloth. As Clint rolled onto his back on the table, the doctor brought a light up closer. Gently, he examined the purple scar that covered the jagged projectile.

"Is this uncomfortable?" he asked, pressing at different places around the wound. Each time Clint answered yes, the doctor wrote something in a small book. When he'd finished, he told Clint to get dressed. Then he explained that the bone in Clint's leg had begun to calcify or grow around the arrowhead. It would have to come out and soon.

"I'm not sure," he said, "how much damage has been done to the bone. In some cases, injuries of this sort cause the bone to die. The leg then cannot support one's weight and has to be amputated. Most of the time, however, they heal." For a moment, he paused, "But because of the type of wound it is and because it has been so long since it happened, I believe you'll probably continue to have problems with it aching and swelling; especially when it gets cold or when you place it under strain. Eventually, it could become arthritic and cause you a great amount of pain and stiffness; probably more than it does now. But...well, I just don't know." Once more, he paused, "I operate two days a week, Mondays and Thursdays. My receptionist can make you an appointment. Oh yes," he added "You should make arrangements for lodging as you'll be laid up for quite some time. The hotel across the street is decent. My fee, mister uhh"

"Jeffries," Clint answered "My name's Clint Jeffries."

"Uh, Mister Jeffries, my fee is twenty dollars - up front. If you don't have the money, I take horses, guns, jewelry, or whatever."

"I will pay in gold, doctor."

On his way out, Clint made an appointment with the portly nurse for the following Thursday. Across the street, he registered at the hotel, securing a room for two. He would have to have help while he was mending. The old Indian would have to be the one to help; he had no choice. The only thing he didn't know was how the hotel management would take to letting an Indian live in one of their rooms. That could be somewhat sticky.

Before he left town, Clint rented a small, one-horse wagon. He didn't feel like he could walk all the way back to camp. At the mercantile, he bought blankets, clothes, boots, and a hat. He also bought a pair of scissors. What snow had fallen during the night was now mostly melted. Only in the shaded, out of the way corners was there any sign that it had even been there. The wind, however, had not gone away and it reddened Clint's nose and cheeks as he drove the wagon toward his camp.

The Old Man did not leave the fire to greet him when Clint arrived. He had the blanket wrapped tightly about him and was gnawing on a piece of the ham they'd bought the day before. Clint tossed the man another blanket before climbing down. "Here, wrap up in this," he said, "will keep you warm."

The man thanked him with his eyes and quickly placed the blanket over the top of the other one. Clint eased himself off the wagon and took up a seat at the fire with the Old Man. He too cut himself a chunk of ham, laying it on some of the fresh bread he'd just bought in town. As they ate, Clint tried to explain to the Indian what had happened to his leg. He told him that a great medicine man in the white man's village was going to cut the arrowhead from his leg. He also told him that it would be a long time before he could walk again. Then, he asked the old one if he would help him through this thing.

"If you help me," he signed, "I promise when I'm well to take you to your home, far away in the mountains."

The Old Man's eyes danced in his wrinkled face, a recognition Clint had not seen there before. Now, a smile lit his lips and a single tear traced a jagged path down his rough features. He grabbed Clint's hand and nodded his approval. "Yes," he whispered in English, "Yes."

Clint went on to explain that he would be bedridden for many days while his leg healed and that it would require they stay in the white man's teepee. He quickly scratched a picture of the hotel in the dirt near the fire. The Indian watched Clint's hands make the words and draw the picture. Nodding, he seemed to understand what had been said. Clint's face now took on a more serious meaning and the Old Man picked up on it. "I must be serious with you and tell you that the man who owns the big teepee where we will stay does not like Indians. He doesn't want them staying there. I spoke to him, however, and explained the situation and he has agreed to let you stay with me and help me until I'm well."

The man's eyes narrowed slightly and his jaw tightened as Clint signed the words. Clint could see the pain in his expression but he went on.

"To live in the white man's teepee, you will have to dress and act like a white man."

Then, motioning toward a large package he'd brought from the wagon, Clint said, "Here, these are for you."

Quickly, the Old Man seized the bundle, tearing away its paper cover. There before him lay a new shirt, woolen pants, long underwear and socks, a pair of high moccasins, a heavy, plaid coat with a wolf- skin collar, and a flat-brimmed fur-felt hat. The Old Man wasted no time shedding the blankets. Mumbling in his native tongue, he hastily removed his clothing, dropping it in a heap and replacing each piece with something new.

As he dressed, Clint continued to explain the rules of the hotel. "You must remain in the room with me at all times. You cannot walk about in the halls. You cannot speak to or mingle with the white men who live there." The man watched him carefully, seeming to understand what he meant.

At first, the old Indian looked suspicious at what Clint said. But, upon seeing the new clothes, boots, and hat, he seemed to relax some. When, at last, the Old Man had finished dressing, he looked at Clint and nodding his head, he grunted, "Good! Good!"

Next, Clint mentioned cutting his hair. At this, the Old Man put up a fuss and would have no part of it. "Flathead warriors do not wear short hair like the white man," he signed, "it is a sign of weakness and slavery." The set of the Old Man's jaw told Clint it was useless to pursue this, so he let it go.

"We'll put this hat on ya and pull the collar on that coat up around yer neck and well...maybe, nobody'll notice ya." In his mind, though, Clint knew it would be hard to have the Old Man live in the hotel. From what he'd seen, most white folks didn't take too kindly to Indians and usually treated them badly. He also knew Indians weren't used to living indoors, they liked to be out and about and seeing what was over the next hill. He was going to have a time on his hands all right, but what could he do?

Speaking more to himself now than to the Old Man, he said "We'll wait 'til sundown and then go on into town. No sense causin' any more commotion than we have to."

CHAPTER 2:
THE OPERATION, FAMILY NEWS, AND MEMPHIS

The operation on Clint's leg took longer than Dr. Gormes had anticipated. The arrowhead was indeed buried in the bone and it took some chiseling to remove it. The bone had begun to calcify around the foreign object; thickening, it had become brittle.

"This leg will give him fits all through his life," the doctor thought as he tied off the last closing stitches. "Probably be a cripple by the time he's forty."

The old Indian had watched the entire operation with keen interest, often getting his face close enough to block the doctor's view. So interested was he, the doctor had to actually push him back out of the way. He didn't so much as flinch when the doctor opened Clint's leg with the scalpel.

Motioning now toward the Old Man, the doctor whispered to his nurse, "Did you notice how seemingly used to the sight of blood he is? He's probably performed an operation or two in his day, if you get my meaning."

The nurse answered, nodding, "But I'd wager, none of his patients survived."

It took two full days for the effects of the laudanum to wear off. In that time, Clint passed in and out of consciousness several times. In this dreamlike state, he saw Storm beckoning to him from across the river. Her raven hair, caught by the gentle wind, blew back from her shoulders in small streaks. She was smiling that special smile he had come to know. The smile that was only for him; the smile that told him she was his woman. God, he loved her--beyond belief he loved her.

Then, he saw them, the riders coming from behind her. Down the river's embankment and through the trees they guided their ponies, war clubs raised, voices screaming. Why didn't she run? She just stood there smiling at him…smiling and waving.

"Run, Storm, run," he screamed but she seemed to pay no attention. "Run, Goddammit, run," he cried.

He knew then he had to reach her, save her before it was too late. With no other way to get there, he dove into the river's swirling water.

"I'm coming," he cried, as he struggled against the raging current.

When at last he dragged himself from the muddy river, he saw her lying on her back, face toward the sky, expressionless eyes staring at the vast nothingness. The side of her head had been bashed in with a war club. Oddly, she still had that same smile on her face.

"I told you to run," he screamed, gathering her up in his arms. "Why didn't you run, why didn't you run?"

In his sobbing, the Old Man shook Clint awake. Then, taking a wet towel, he gently wiped the beads of sweat from Clint's forehead and chest.

"You had a bad dream," he whispered in his native Flathead tongue. "But the fire is leaving your body and you will soon be well." For a moment, he paused. Then, he added "The pain you carry in your leg is great but that which you carry in your heart is far worse. It is a wound that will never heal."

Clint could not understand all of what the Old Man said but his words were spoken quietly and they somehow comforted him. Gently, he nodded off, back into unconsciousness and was once again, standing on the banks of the great river.

#

On the morning of the third day, Dr. Gormes stopped by to call on Clint before going to his office.

"How are we doing, today?" he asked, shaking Clint's limp hand.

"Ugh, fine – fine," Clint whispered, trying to clear the cobwebs from his mind. "I'm doin' fine."

"Good!" the doctor said, pulling back the covers. "Let's just take a look at that leg for a moment and see how it's healing."

In the corner, the old Indian sat sleeping. He was naked except for his loin cloth and the hotel blanket that was wrapped closely about his shoulders. He had piled his clothes and boots in a heap next to him. He looked very uncomfortable with his head hung between his bent-up knees; his breath came in slow, deep snores.

"Doesn't that bother you?" the doctor asked, peeling back the dressing on Clint's leg.

"What?" for a moment he couldn't understand the question. "Oh, you mean the Old Man's snoring? Yeah, it gets real bad sometimes but he's good to help me and I don't fuss with him about it."

Clint wasn't used to making small talk but he felt a need to communicate with someone who understood what he was saying. Once again, he motioned toward the Old Man in the corner.

"He told me he'd been the chief of his people once. Said he was a mighty warrior; took many scalps."

"You wouldn't know it to look at him now," the doctor replied.

"He's walked some hard trails and that's a fact but you don't want to be fooled by his appearance." Clint said. "He's sharp as my knife. Oh yeah, he acts the part of a poor-dog

Injun around those boys down at the saloon but he does it to
survive; he gets his food and whiskey that way."

"Well if I were you, Mr. Jeffries, I'd keep him away
from that saloon and off the streets of St. Louis. A Mister
Patrick Lawson has been spreading the word that he will
personally kill the Old Man and the tall stranger who took his
side the other day." The doctor paused for a moment, looking
directly into Clint's eyes. "I assume that would be you, Mister
Jeffries."

Clint remained quiet.

"Mister Lawson is not a man to trifle with. You see, he is
a coward and they are the worst kind. They're the ones who'll
come out of a dark alley when you're least expecting it and
stick a knife between your ribs."

"Thanks Doc, I'll keep that in mind."

Returning to the business at hand, the doctor re
bandaged Clint's leg. "It seems to be healing nicely, Mister
Jeffries. It won't be long before you're up and around."
Pausing a moment, he went on. However, this time his words
were much more dour. "Mister Jeffries, the injury to your leg
was very serious. Perhaps more so than you think. The bone
was badly damaged and has become somewhat brittle. This
means that if you place any undue stress on your leg, it could
break. And, if it does break, the chances of it being set and
mending are very slim." Again, he paused. "This, of course,
could result in you losing the leg." Clint listened intently to
what the man said.

"My recommendation is to take it easy; walk with a cane
or crutch for a while until the wound is completely healed and
the leg muscles can hold your weight. Also, warm baths and
massage may ease the pain. I do believe, Mister Jeffries, that
you will be troubled by that leg for the rest of your life. Some

doctors wouldn't tell you that but I feel you should understand the seriousness of the situation."

"I appreciate your honesty, Doc. I'll do as you say for as long as I can. But you know as well as I that a man can't run a trap-line or skedaddle from Injuns when he's dependin' on a cane or crutch."

Turning toward the door, the doctor answered him. "Then perhaps you should consider another line of work, sir. Good day!"

#

Clint hobbled from the bed to the window in his room, using a chair to support him. It was the first time he'd actually tried to walk since the operation. The pain in his leg burned like fire but he gritted his teeth and put up with it. After all, it wasn't anything new; he'd been in pain since he was shot that day on the creek. His room was on the second floor and overlooked the main street of the town. The roof of an overhanging porch, which covered the sidewalk in front of the hotel, however, obstructed the view. He noted that one could easily step from the room, through the window and onto the roof of the porch.

He had asked the hotel manager if he'd buy him a cane from the general mercantile store. The man agreed and Clint gave him some money. When the man returned with the cane, he also carried a letter in his hand.

"Sir, I believe this letter is for you," he said, handing Clint a somewhat wrinkled and tarnished envelope. "When you signed your name in the hotel ledger I remembered seeing that name somewhere before. It finally came to me where and I rummaged through the drawer where I keep all the undelivered mail. You see, there are a lot of folks pass through here on their way to the mountains and the prairies. They sometimes drop letters off with me in case their relatives or friends happen by. Mostly they're never delivered but I keep them just the same. I figure if someone took the time to write them, the least I can do is see that they get to the people they're meant for."

Clint thanked the man and after he'd left, set about opening the letter. He'd never received a letter before and could only imagine it to be from his sister. Hell, he didn't have anyone else. Now as he opened it, he noticed that the only legible words on the face of the envelope were his name. The rest had apparently gotten wet, for the ink had severely faded and run and was unreadable. He was happy to see that the letter inside had not suffered the same fate. It read:

My Dearest Clint,

It has been some time since last we spoke. I believe it was at your birthday party. It was then that you told me you were off to the mountains to become a trapper...you were going through St. Louis, you said. I knew of no other way to get this news to you than to address this letter to the Frontier Hotel in St. Louis, praying that you might someday stop by there. If you are reading this, I suppose my prayers have been answered.

It is with heavy heart that I now inform you of your sister's dire situation. Sometime after you left, she met and married a man named Whitney Collier. Mister Collier was an ambitious man with big plans. He borrowed money from several bankers and opened a retail clothing business in the township of Memphis. As he made his way home one evening, he was struck by a run-away carriage and killed. Your sister, Molly, tried to run the business but had not the know-

how nor the strength to do such. The business was soon lost to the bank in a foreclosure and with it, her home as well. Besides this, she is deeply in debt to various creditors.

She is a proud woman and will not accept charity or help from anyone – besides, she says her life is over, now that Whitney is dead. She has become very thin and has taken up residence in Dunbar's Saloon as one of the working girls.

She was for a long time, my best friend – now we hardly speak. She seems ashamed to look me in the eye. I've tried reasoning with her...tried to get her to come and live with us but she won't hear of it. She says that someone of her kind would only bring trouble to my family. When last I saw her, she was drunk and had cuts and bruises on her face.

I fear deeply for her life and pray that this letter reaches you before something terrible happens to her. If you can possibly come to her rescue, do so. I bid you God speed.

Your True Friend, Penny Rae Long

Having not the occasion to read for some time, Clint studied the letter over and over again. Taking his new cane in hand, he rose from the bed and made his way to the door. Once in the hallway, he walked to the top of the stairs. The manager of the hotel was standing behind the main counter.

"Say," he called down. The man looked up at him. "Do you recall when you received this letter and who brought it? I can't read the date on it."

Scratching his head in thought, the man hesitated before answering, "Hmmm! Gotta be three, maybe four years ago"

He said. "Don't exactly remember when and I sure don't remember who brought it. I see so many people, you know... Sorry!"

Clint thanked him and went back to the room.

"Old Man," he called out in Blackfoot. The Indian raised his weathered head.

Now, in sign language, Clint said, "We're going to ride on a big boat. What do you say to that?"

A spark of light flashed in the Old Man's eyes. "Will it take us to my home?" he asked.

"We will take a big boat to your home soon but first we must take this boat to my home." The Old Man smiled and nodded. "When do we do this?" he asked.

"Soon, my friend! Soon!"

#

Clint watched the skyline of St. Louis fade into the landscape as the big riverboat made its way downstream. It would take three or four days to reach Memphis. The doctor had warned him against traveling so soon after the operation but Clint had made up his mind. He realized the letter was several years old and whatever had happened with his sister had probably already occurred. However, he felt a certain urgency that made him believe he might still be in time to help her.

Standing there at the boat's railing, Clint stared down into the green water. It mesmerized him as he watched the currents and eddies roll and boil beneath the surface. His mind was on Storm and a time, not so long ago, when he was the happiest he'd ever been. The roll of the boat reminded him of his time on the Platte, of the make-shift raft he'd spent so many days on. It all played out again and again in his mind. He missed her so badly.

At his elbow, the old Indian propped himself over the rail and watched the country slowly drift by. "Better than riding a horse, ugh?" he laughed. "Not so bumpy." He laughed again, this time moving his hand up and down. Clint nodded and smiled back at him. Through their time together, Clint had learned much of the Old Man's native language. They could converse quite easily now and they enjoyed each other's company.

"The woman is in your thoughts again," the Old Man remarked, without taking his eyes from the shifting landscape.

"My sister, you mean?" Clint asked. "Yes, I'm worried for her..."

The Old Man cut him off. "No," he said, quietly, gesturing with his hand. "The other woman – the one you grieve for."

Reluctantly, Clint answered, dropping his head. "Yes," he said. "She's always there in my mind." The Old Man could feel his friend's sadness and after a long moment, began to speak. His voice was soft and his words came slowly, "Indians look at things differently than white men do," he started. "They have a more realistic understanding of the way the world is. Things live and things die. They are given to us by the Great Spirit and taken from us when he sees fit." Clint listened intently to what the Old Man said. "I once came upon a beautiful wild horse," he went on. "It was the grandest horse I had ever seen. I chased it for three days and when I caught it, it was tired and frightened and tried to kill me. But I loved it and tamed it and taught it to trust me. I rode that horse into many battles and it never let me down. When hunting buffalo, mine was the swiftest horse in our camp. Our tribe sang songs about my bravery and the stamina of the horse. We loved each other, that horse and I." He stopped for a moment, gathering his thoughts. "It was during one of the fall buffalo hunts that I rode the horse too close to the stampeding beasts. One of the young bulls charged out from the mad rush and sank his horn into my horse's belly. We fell into the thundering mass, tumbling and rolling under their hoofs. When I finally awoke, my beautiful horse lay dead before me. I cried for many days over that horse and wondered why the Great Spirit had spared me and taken him. But then, I realized that it is just the way of things and I got another horse." Again, the Old Man paused. But when he began to speak again, he looked deep into Clint's eyes. "It doesn't mean I've forgotten what a wonderful horse he was. Nor does it mean that I love him any less because I got a new horse. No! I love and remember that horse but he was only mine for a little while." Lowering his eyes once more to watch the country go by, he uttered, "I think Indians look at things differently than white men do." Late in the evening of the third day, they saw the lights of Memphis come into view.

CHAPTER 3:
ANGUS DUNBAR, SISTER JOLENE, AND BABY JEREMY

"May I help you?" the man behind the hotel's counter, asked, casting a suspicious eye on the Old Man standing at Clint's side.

"I need a room with two beds," Clint answered.

"Sign here," the man said, pointing to the ledger before him. "Say, he ain't an Indian, is he?" the man asked, again eying up the Old Man.

"No," Clint answered, without looking up. "He's French – royalty, I think he told me. He's related to their King or someone like that."

The man's face eased a bit. "Does he speak any English?"

"Nope! Say, would you happen to know where Dunbar's Saloon is?" Clint asked, quickly changing the subject.

"Two blocks up the street on the left," the man answered, motioning with his head. Then, he continued, "Wanna be careful there, though, it's kind of a rough place." Pausing a moment, he continued. "If it's a girl yer needin' to warm yer belly fer the night, I can arrange for that myself. Uh, that is for a reasonable fee, of course. Then, ya wouldn't have to go to that hell-hole."

Clint smiled at the man and answered, "Thanks, just the same, but I'm supposed to meet someone there."

After moving their things to the room, Clint explained to the old Indian that he needed to go look for his sister and that it would be better if he stayed there in the room rather than go to the saloon. Clint said he would return soon. The Old Man agreed and set about making himself comfortable on one of the beds. "Jeffries, you bring back whiskey, huh?" he said. Clint smiled at him and nodded.

The night air was cold and Clint pulled his collar close about his neck. Putting his hands in his coat pockets, he made his way along the dimly lit street. His breath came out in little warm clouds that floated upward, disappearing over his shoulder. Up ahead, he could hear the tinny voice of an old piano. Accompanying it were the typical bar room sounds of men who'd had too much to drink. Occasionally, the resonance of a woman's laughter rang out above the harsh racket. It made him think of his sister and his belly tightened in a knot. He quickened his pace.

The door of the saloon was heavy but it swung in easily when he twisted the knob. Stepping in from the crisp night air, he was immediately confronted with the harsh smell of humanity. It seemed a curious blend of cigar smoke, whiskey, and cheap perfume. He coughed slightly into his hand and moved forward. For a moment, those nearest the door cast their eyes upon him, assessing his stature, his manner – friend or foe was the self-asked question. Most went back to what they were doing. One set of eyes in the far corner followed Clint's movement to the bar.

"What'll it be, mister?" asked the bar-keep.

"I'll have a whiskey and some information," Clint replied.

"Information's free but the whiskey will cost ya."

Clint laid a dollar on the bar, took the shot of whiskey the man had poured, and swigged it down in one swallow. It burned like a hot poker, bringing tears to his eyes. It nearly took his breath away.

"Phew, Jesus," he mumbled to himself.

As his eyes cleared, he could see the man behind the bar waiting to pour him another. Waving the man away, he choked out, "Thanks anyway, partner but that's enough for me. You can keep the change."

"What about the information?" the man asked without changing his expression.

"Oh yeah," Clint said, again clearing his throat. "I'm looking for a woman named Molly Jeffries or Molly Collier. Do you know her?"

"Never heard of her," the man answered all too quickly.

"She worked here three, maybe four years ago," Clint persisted. "Had long honey-colored hair and blue eyes..."

"I told you I never heard of her," the man interrupted, cutting him off.

"What seems to be the problem here, George?"

Clint turned to see who had asked the question. Behind him stood a man nearly as tall as himself. He was a thin man, almost gaunt in appearance. His dark hair was parted in the middle and hung just above his shoulders, covering the back half of his ears and outlining his narrow, sallow face. His eyes were set very close together and burned with a curious intensity. Below his protruding cheekbones, his face sunk in deeply. "Almost like that of a skeleton," Clint thought. The man's sharp nose gave him a hawk-like appearance and a strange nervous tic tugged at the corner of his thin lips.

He wore a long, black, knee-length jacket that hung loosely over his slender frame. In the poor light of the saloon it looked dirty and unkempt. His tight-fitting trousers were a light brown. Narrow dark stripes ran up and down their length. At his waist was tied some sort of maroon colored sash, Indian, maybe, or Spanish, Clint wasn't sure.

"How do you do, sir?" the man said, offering his hand. "My name is Angus Dunbar but most people call me Scotty. I own this establishment. Is there something I might help you with?"

Clint shook the man's hand. "Jeffries is my name, Clint Jeffries. I came here looking for my sister. I believe she worked here some years back."

For a long moment, the two men stared into each other's eyes, making assessments, drawing conclusions.

"Sir, you'll have to forgive George for his less than courteous attitude. You see, he has his orders. Due to the delicate nature of our business, we never give out information about our female employees. Most of them have a past, if you know what I mean, and it just causes trouble if that past catches up with them." He stopped for a moment and then continued, "However, I can see that you have honest concerns about your sister, sir and therefore, I would be glad to help you in any way I can."

"Thank you, sir," Clint answered, "I appreciate that. What I was saying to your man, is my sister's name is Molly Jeffries or she might be going by the name of Molly Collier. I heard she was employed here, three or four years ago."

"Molly Jeffries or Molly Collier," the man repeated, seeming to stir his memory. "You know, there was a Collier girl working here some time back." He paused, again struggling to remember. "She fits the description you gave but her name wasn't Molly. It was Jolene"

"That would be her," Clint offered. "My sister's middle name is Jolene"

Pausing a moment, the man again began to speak "I guess you're in luck sir," the man smiled "Your sister runs a saloon down on Canal Street. It's called JJ's. One of my finest competitors," he added.

"Thanks," Clint said, again shaking the man's hand.

"Just don't tell her who told you, okay?" The man smiled, "her and me don't see eye-to-eye on a lot of things." Clint nodded and walked out into the street.

JJ's was not as large a place as Dunbar's but the interior was much nicer – cleaner. It smacked of a woman's touch. Clint eased in through the door. Trying not to be noticed, he made his way to an empty table near a side window. Even before he reached the table, he was taken in tow by a lovely, dark-haired girl with smiling eyes.

"Buy me a drink, mister?" she asked, putting her arm through his and moving with him to the table.

"Sure, why not?" he answered.

"My name's Mary Lou," she offered, snapping her finger to get the bartender's attention "Two whiskeys," she said. Then turning her attention back to Clint, she went on "My momma named me after the Virgin Mary. She thought I looked so innocent, I guess." She smiled but looked somewhat troubled when she said it. "Anyway, I'm no virgin and I sure as hell ain't innocent so if you have something special in mind and you have the money to back it up, I can be talked into almost anything." Again, she smiled.

"I'd like to talk to Jolene if she's around."

His words took the girl by surprise. For a moment, her smile lessened. "She's around honey, but she's not one of the workin' girls, if you know what I mean? She doesn't come down here on the floor."

"She's in one of those upstairs rooms then?" Clint asked. "If you'll just point me in the right direction, I'll find her myself." He smiled.

"Nobody goes to her room honey without an invite – that is, unless they want to get the livin' shit beat right out of them." Her voice had taken on a different tone and though she was still smiling, there was a hard, cutting edge to her words.

"Maybe if you told her, her brother was here to see her, it might make a difference."

"Does her brother have a name?" the girl asked, this time offering an obvious sarcastic smile.

"Yeah! My name's Clint. She'll know who I am."

The woman snapped her fingers again, this time at a burly man who stood near the top corner of the stairs, motioning for him to come down. Clint had not seen him when he came in.

"Trace, tell Miss Jo there's a feller here to see her. Says his name's Clint."

"What's he want?" he asked, staring at Clint in an uneasy manner.

"Hell, how should I know what he wants? He says he's her brother – now go tell her."

The man stood motionless for a moment as though sorting out the instructions to make sure he understood. Slowly, he plodded up the stairs.

Clint turned his attention back to the woman seated next to him. "Thank you, ma'am. Here's to good times." He raised his glass. "Good times," she echoed, smiling. They clicked their glasses and slugged the whiskey back.

Above on the landing, Clint detected the opening of a door. Then, there was a sudden swishing of petty-coats accompanying the tac-tac-tac of a woman's heeled shoes coming forward over the rough-sawn pine wood floor.

"Clint? Clint, is that you, darlin'?"

Before he could answer, she answered for him.

"It is you! My brother, my baby brother! I thought you were dead for sure." She hurried down the stairs to meet him and he rose from his chair and walked toward her. As she approached, she suddenly wrinkled her face into a frown, put her hands on her hips and snapped out at him, "Why the hell didn't you write, anyway? The least you could have done was let me know you weren't dead." Seeing the discomfort in his face, she paused a moment, easing up, "Sorry – I've just worried about ya. By the way, where ya stayin'?"

While he was trying to come up with the words to answer her questions, he couldn't help but stare in amazement at this woman. Oh, she was his sister all right but she looked different, way different from the last time he saw her. Gone was the honey-blond hair that hung nearly to her waist. It was now auburn colored and piled high on her head. And, he'd never seen so much makeup on any ten women. Lipstick and eye-paint and powder and such, so deep on her cheeks you could scrape it off with your knife. He guessed that the dress she had on must have been very expensive. It tucked her in here and pushed her out there and did all the things that'd make a man want to leave home. But for all it was worth, it only served to cheapen her. What stunned him the most though, was the hardness of her. Somewhere over the last nine years, she had lost her sweet innocence.

A pang of guilt suddenly shot through him and he began blaming himself for what he saw.

"Jesus, if I'd stayed around things would be different – she would be differ ..."

"Well, ain't ya gonna say somethin' for Christ's sake?" Her voice snapped him back to reality.

"Oh, uh yeah, sure. It's real good to see ya, Molly." He put his arms around her and squeezed her tight.

With that, she smiled and her expression softened. "Haven't been called that in a long while," she said. "I'd almost forgotten..." She seemed lost in thought for a moment. Then, a tear traced a path down across her cheek.

"Now look what you made me do. I swore I'd never shed a tear over another man and now I've gone and broken my own promise." Pulling a handkerchief from her sleeve, she wiped away the tears.

"You didn't' say where you were staying but it doesn't matter, I want you to check out of there and move in here."

Clint began to protest but was quickly overridden "I insist, Clinton," she said. "I won't have my brother staying in some meager hotel room when he can stay here with me at the finest inn in town. And, it's free." Not waiting for his reply, she went on. "Well, there you have it. Trace here, will help you with your bags. When you get settled in, we have a lot of catching-up to do."

Clint nodded his head, smiling. "Come on, Trace, let's go get those bags."

Within an hour, they had collected the luggage and the old Indian and were settling into the suite of rooms Clint's sister had promised. When they arrived, she gave the Old Man some hard looks. She had some obvious questions but thought better of asking them when she looked into her brother's eyes. Oh well! There would be time for that later, when she had Clint to herself.

Excusing himself and the Old Man, Clint said he was very tired and would like to get some sleep. His sister nodded. "We can talk tomorrow" she said. "There are so many things to talk about."

"Oh, by the way," Clint added, "I'd like to buy a bottle of whiskey. I promised the Old Man I'd get him one."

"I don't believe in givin' whiskey to Injuns," she snapped out. "Makes 'em crazy. They go to killin' folks when they git liquored up." Again, she looked into her brother's eyes, searching for his reaction.

"I'll be responsible for him," Clint said in a quiet tone, his voice casting out a slight air of disappointment. "I promised him, you see."

For a long moment, they stood staring at one another, almost as if they were measuring each other's grit. Clint was unwavering, his eyes burned with an intensity she had not seen there before.

"Oh awlright," she conceded. "But if he cuts yer throat when yer sleepin,' it won't be my fault." With that she stomped off toward her room.

"Guess she's used to gettin' her own way," Clint whispered to himself. "Could be a problem. I don't reckon I'll be hangin' around these parts too long."

#

Because they were still tired from their long journey, Clint and the Old Man slept through the morning. In the afternoon, they walked around the city, looking in the windows of the stores, talking and laughing as they went. Occasionally, they bought something to eat from the street vendors. Most of the vendors and store owners gave them curious looks, particularly when they saw the Old Man. They figured him for an Indian but weren't sure because of the white man's clothing he wore.

As they passed before one of the outfitters stores, the Old Man spotted a fine, bone-handled hunting knife in the window. It was a heavy bladed knife, trimmed in brass and cradled in a heavy leather sheath. Fringe adorned the edges of the sheath and fine bead work outlined its shape against the leather. He stopped. Pointing at it, he grabbed Clint's sleeve.

"Look at that knife, tall one," he signed. "A warrior could skin many buffalo, clean many fish, take many scalps with such a weapon, could he not?"

"That he could, my friend," Clint smiled. In his mind, he was thinking, "They never lose their identity, once a warrior, always a warrior. That's good!" Still smiling, he nodded his head as if to confirm what he had just thought.

"Would you like to have that knife?" Clint signed back.

The Old Man stared at him for a long moment without answering, trying to ascertain if he was serious. "Yes," he nodded, understanding the offer was true. "I would very much like to have it."

Upon paying for it, Clint smiled and handed it to the Old Man.

"Here you go!" he said. "I hope you carry this on many hunts and skin many buffalo." Pausing, he then added "Oh yes, I almost forgot. I hope it takes many scalps."

The Old Man held the knife delicately in his outstretched hands, admiring its heft and balance. Two or three times he pulled it from its sheath to examine the finely-honed blade. Seeming satisfied, he then tucked it into his britches behind the thick belt that held them up. Once more grabbing Clint's arm, the Old Man looked into his eyes. He smiled and nodded. Clint understood that it was the Old Man's way of saying thank you. They continued, then, down the street.

#

For many hours, Clint and his sister visited, recalling their childhood on the farm and the good times they had shared as kids. Because of their loud laughter and Molly's piercing voice, many of the working girls and some of the waiters sat around with them and listened to the stories. Business was slow and Molly didn't seem to mind. She had lightened up some since Clint arrived. They guessed it was because he eased her loneliness. It had been a long time since she'd had a man in her life. Yes, a long time since Angus Dunbar had walked out the door and gone out of her life. Since that time, Molly had hardened her heart and her disciplinary measures had become more than harsh, as many a fired bar-keep and prostitute could testify to.

When Clint began talking of his adventures in the mountains, everyone listened intently, for none of them had ever been to that wild country. They had only heard stories of the great high peaks and the vast herds of buffalo and the huge silver coated bears that could tear a man's head off with a single swipe of their great paw. Some of them asked about the Indians and wanted to know if Clint had captured the Old Man during a battle. Clint only laughed and told them he had befriended the Old Man in St. Louis. He didn't go into details. He didn't think it necessary.

He related the story of how he was wounded and described the two friends who had helped him survive. He spoke of the months he spent with the Shoshone and how he had decided to return to St. Louis to have his leg mended. He told them of a great lake he had found high in the mountains, which had hot bubbling water pots at its edge and related how he had soaked his leg in them. He also told of the hill of gold he had found and how a man could just walk along and pick it up. When he mentioned that, many of the men paid very keen attention to his words. Several asked him questions about where the gold was located and did he think he could find it again. He answered that he thought he could but that he had no desire to. He had learned that gold drives men crazy and only brings them trouble. "Everyone's always trying to take it away from you," he explained. "I've had men try to kill me for the gold I was carryin.' I tell ya, it ain't worth it."

Later, when the rest had retired to the action of the saloon, Clint and his sister made time for some personal talk.

"You know, I didn't think I'd ever see you again," she said in a quiet voice. "That day when you stepped aboard the boat and I saw it carry you off, it was like a piece of me had been torn away." She paused, running her finger around the rim of the half-empty glass of whiskey before her. "A lot of things have changed since then." There was a sudden sadness in her voice. But that was the gentle voice Clint remembered.

Hearing it made him feel as though he were home again, back on the farm. He smiled and touched the back of her hand.

After a moment, she asked, "How did you know where I was?"

"By some stroke of luck, I happened to be staying in the Frontier Hotel in St. Louis and the manager remembered the name Clinton Jeffries. He said that some years ago, he had received a letter addressed to me. He had kept it in hopes that the man it was addressed to would pass that way someday. The letter was from Penny Long. She said your husband had been killed and you had fallen on very hard times and she was worried about you. I had to come; had to see if you were alright, even if it was three years later." He paused, smiling, "Better late than never, I guess."

She smiled back, "You always were very protective of me. Remember when Billy Comey had me pinned down on the hay out in the barn. He was just tryin' to get a little kiss and you jabbed him in the butt with a pitchfork. That boy ran all the way home, screamin' at the top of his lungs. I'll bet he didn't dare tell his ma how he got those holes in his backside."

"Molly, you mentioned Angus Dunbar a while ago; said he walked out of your life. What's that all about?"

For a moment, she looked into his eyes, then lowered her gaze to again focus on the glass of whiskey before her. Her reaction told him it was a painful subject and her words came slowly.

"Actually, it was uh...the other way around. I walked out on him. Shortly after Whitney was killed, I found out I was pregnant. There were so many bills and I had very little money. They took all the furniture and threatened to foreclose on the house. I started drinking heavily and even tried a little whoring. It paid the bills but I hated it." She paused, searching his face for some sign of understanding. It was there. "I didn't ever think I'd stoop to that, much less tell you about it. But one does what they have to, sometimes, to get by." Again, she paused, taking a long swallow of the whiskey, letting the burn of it slide down easy.

"Angus saw me on the street trying to pick up men. He told me I would be arrested for soliciting or worse yet, I'd wind up in an alley with my throat cut. Then he asked me to come to work for him; said he would give me a place to stay and that I would be safe with him. Somehow, I trusted him and agreed to the terms. It wasn't long, however, before my condition became very noticeable. It's funny about most men, even if they're drunk, they don't want to make whoopee with a pregnant woman. I wasn't making any money. But instead of throwing me out, like so many other brothel owners would, he let me stay on. He told me I could cook and do chores and clean up the bar for my keep. He was very good to me, Clint, and I became quite fond of him. After the baby was born, Angus bought things for him and did nice things for me. Also, he insisted that I not work as one of the girls anymore and that I remain doing what I had been doing. He loved to play with Jeremy; that was his name, Jeremy. Angus used to tend him for me when I needed rest or if I had to go someplace. Heavens, you'd have thought it was his child. Not long after that, he asked me to marry him. He said he loved me and wanted to take care of the two of us. I had grown to love him too but for some reason, I just could not say yes. I suppose it was too soon after Whitney's death." She paused, gathering her thoughts.

"He said he understood but after that, things were not the same between us. He began to drink heavily and turned mean. I saw him pistol whip two or three men over nothing. I suspected it was because of me and I decided to leave. I really had nowhere to go and I had very little money. I was living in a rented room behind a hardware store up on Main Street but my reputation was following me and no one wanted to hire me. Oh, there were plenty of men who wanted a free one but offered nothing in return. Anyway, I had quit that life." She paused again and took another hit on the whiskey.

Her voice had been soft before but now it grew even softer and Clint had to listen hard to catch what she was saying.

"It was, at this time," she began, "That Whitney's mother arrived in town. She heard through friends that I had conceived a child and she was highly upset that I had not written to her. To tell you the truth, I had never met the woman. I had no idea where she lived and wasn't even sure she was alive. I found out later that she lives back east in Pennsylvania. Whitney once told me she had come to Memphis to visit him. Apparently, she didn't think much of the place and said she would never again return.

Anyway, when she arrived, she found out where I was living and what I had been doing at Dunbar's. Of course, she was appalled and wanted to know if I thought this was any way to bring up a child; particularly, her grandson? I had no answer and I, better than anyone else, knew this was no life for Jeremy. When she offered to take him back to live with her in Pennsylvania, I sharply objected. But then reality set in and I realized she could take much better care of him than I. He would be able to go to good schools, wear fine clothes, and have nice things. Here, there was nothing for him. She offered to set me up in business and pay for everything until I could get on my feet. So, I wound up with this old building and she got my child. I should never have agreed to it." Tears were streaming down her face and her bottom lip trembled uncontrollably.

"Afterward, when Angus found out what had happened, he was furious. He couldn't believe what I had done. He yelled at me and asked how I could have been so stupid. He said he would have taken care of me if I had only let him know. He was right I was stupid; stupid for not marrying him and stupid to give up the baby." Now, Molly was crying full out.

Clint leaned over the table and took his sister in his arms. "C'mon, Molly," he whispered, rocking her gently. "It's all right. People have to make hard decisions sometimes and sometimes their choice isn't always the right one. However, given the circumstances, I don't see that you had any other way you could go." With that, he gently patted her head and kissed her on the cheek. "I love you" he whispered.

She wiped the tears from her eyes and sniffed back her running nose. "If I can just get this place paid for then I can go to Pennsylvania and get my baby back. But I'm in debt. The money Mrs. Collier gave me to get started only bought the building. I had to take out a loan from the Memphis City Bank for everything else." She sneezed and wiped her nose. "Business is good but what with the interest on the note and the day to day expenses, it'll be years before I'm clear of the debt. By then, my baby will be grown." Again, she broke down in a torrent of tears.

"How much is this debt, Molly?" Clint asked.

Between sobs, she answered, "I'm not sure exactly, probably around $2000. I don't know…but it's a lot more than I've got."

"Well, it ain't more'n I got," he said. A little grin tickled the corner of his mouth and he added. "I gotcha covered sis."

"I couldn't ask you to do that," she sniffled. "That's way too much money for me to borrow from you."

"Call it a gift," he smiled. "Hell, I don't expect you to pay me back. The way I look at it, if a man's in a position to help his family when they're in a time of need and he doesn't, then he outta have his ass kicked 'cause he sure nuff ain't much of a man."

"The question is, how're you gonna get the boy back? You know that woman is not going to give him up without a fight."

Molly knew Clint was right. She had seen the longing in her mother-in-law's eyes when she first showed her the baby. She had not wanted to think about the attachment the old woman would form with the boy. She had put it out of her mind. But now, Clint was giving her a chance to get her son back and she would have to face whatever the situation was.

With a grateful smile on her face, she whispered through her tears, "Clint, would you come with me to Pennsylvania to get Jeremy?"

For a long moment, he thought about it. Then sighing, he hesitantly answered, "Sis, if I were to do that, it would just cause more trouble. I'm not polished enough to go and do the talkin' that's gotta be done to get that boy back. I've been in the mountains too long and my way of doin' things wouldn't work. Besides that, I promised the Old Man I'd take him home."

"But you said you would help me," she said, getting ready to cry again.

"And I will," he answered. "I'll do anything I can, you know that. It's just that I think there's a man who could help you more than I."

Silently, they looked at each other, knowing full well what the other was thinking.

"Angus?" she whispered.

"Yeah, Angus," he answered. "I'll speak with him tomorrow, right after we settle up with the bank."

Clint stretched and yawned, "I've gotta go to bed," he said. "Mornin' will be here soon. I suggest you do the same. We have a big day tomorrow and you're gonna need your rest."

"I'm so excited, I'll never be able to go to sleep. Oh Clint, you don't know what this means to me."

He smiled down at her, "Yes, I do," he whispered. "Yes, I do."

CHAPTER 4:
HARSH WORDS, THE REUNION, AND LEAVING MEMPHIS

Angus Dunbar sat alone near the rear of the darkened saloon. His elbows rested comfortably on a scarred wooden table as he hunched forward, staring into the steaming tin of coffee between his hands. His hair hung forward of his shoulders, dangling and looking greasy and uncombed. The shirt he wore was of fine linen but it was wrinkled and reeked of sweat, cigar smoke, and whiskey from the previous night's bar crowd. He had not slept at all. He was a man with too much on his mind.

"Mornin' Angus!" Clint offered, stepping through the saloon's front doorway.

Angus winced at the sudden break of silence and the piercing shafts of sunlight that entered the room, violating his morning solitude. Lifting only his eyes, he stared for a long moment at the silhouetted image before him. Then nodding his recognition, he lowered his eyes, once more, fixing his gaze on the steaming coffee.

"Mind if I sit down? I'd like to have a talk with you," Clint paused for a moment then quickly added, "I've a favor to ask of you."

Again, Angus raised his eyes but this time his drowsy expression changed, taking on a sense of guarded apprehension. Without speaking, he pointed to the chair across the table and motioned for Clint to sit down.

"George! Bring another tin of coffee out here, would ya? We have company." Looking straight at Clint, he continued, "Now, Mr. Jeffries what is it that is so important as to cause you to come lookin' for me at the crack of dawn?" Pausing, he added, "By the way, what time is it anyway?"

"It's eleven o'clock, sir." Clint answered, "I apologize if it's too early. Perhaps I should come back later?"

"No, it's alright. I just had a bad night and it seems earlier to me. Too much whiskey, I guess. Please forgive me. What can I do for you?"

"It's about my sister and her son, Jeremy. She needs to get the boy back."

For the next half-hour, the men sat discussing what Clint and his sister had spoken of the night before. Clint told Angus he had paid off the note on Molly's saloon that morning and now she was free and clear of the debt.

"Perhaps, with your help Angus, Molly can get Jeremy and ...."

"Whoa! Hold up there, friend" Angus interrupted, "What's this business about me helpin' out here? Jolene, uh Molly, doesn't need or want my help. She made that very clear to me some time ago."

"I know! She told me the story last night. She said you'd been very kind to her and the boy; said that you cared for him a great deal. She made a big mistake by turning you down and she knows it. I think ....."

Angus cut him off then, "She didn't make a mistake, Clint. She saw me for what I am, a gambler, a gunfighter, a card-sharp - certainly not the makins' of a good husband or father." He paused, sipped at the coffee, and went on. "Yeah, there for a while I had some crazy idea I could settle down and live a normal life; buy a ranch, raise some cattle, have more kids. But..." he shook his head. "It wouldn't work. Not for someone like me. Probably wouldn't work for Jolene either. She's been at it too long. This life hardens ya. You gotta ask yourself, what kind of a mother would she make?" With that remark, he searched Clint's face for a reaction. There wasn't one.

"This type of life is like a disease, it gets in your blood. You sleep all day and stay up all night. Ya gotta be where the action is; the fightin', the cursin, the gamblin'. Hell, if I hated my life, it'd be different but I don't. I love the smell of cigar smoke and the way the whiskey burns when it rolls down your gullet, warmin' ya up all over. And I crave the attention of the girls, their hands touchin' me as they pass me by. And oh God, the stink of their cheap perfume drives me crazy. I couldn't give up this life, not for Jolene or Jeremy. That's just the way it is..."

Clint stared at Angus a long minute. The corner of his eye twitched slightly and his mouth and jaw tightened. Angus saw it and it made him uncomfortable. He returned his gaze to what was left of the coffee in the tin cup. Slowly, Clint rose, putting his hands on the table. Then, he leaned forward and looked directly into the man's face.

"For what it's worth Angus, I think you're a Goddamn liar. Not only that, I think you're a Goddamn coward to boot. You ain't got the guts to go after what you really want. You're afraid you couldn't stick it out with a wife and kid."

"Nobody talks to me like that, you son-of-a-bitch." He was suddenly on his feet, coming across the table with both fists clenched.

Clint was ready for him and caught him square between the eyes with a hard, right hand. The crack of the blow echoed through the saloon and was quickly followed by the crash of the man's body landing on the hard pine floor.

"Get up, you cowardly bastard and let's see what yer made of." He had hardly gotten the words out of his mouth when he heard the familiar click of a pistol being cocked.

Angus rose from the floor, pointing the small gun directly at Clint's chest. Clint didn't move.

"Now what are you going to do, shoot me?" Without giving the man a chance to answer, he went on. "If that's the case Angus, you're gonna have to shoot me in the back cause I'm walkin' outta here. Hell, I came here offerin' you a chance to have that normal life you talked about. Its right there man, right in front of yer nose. All you gotta do is reach out and take it. But no, you give me some lame-ass excuse about how you love what yer doin' and how ya can't change. To that, I say, bullshit." Clint paused a moment to catch his breath. "You think yer livin' such a great life, well look at yerself. Go on, take a long hard look at yerself in the mirror. Yer a damn mess. Ya stink and you look like shit. Where's yer life goin' man?"

Angus stood there shaking, "I oughta kill you right where you stand."

"Yeah, you oughta but you ain't gonna." With that, Clint turned and walked out the door.

Angus stood there and watched him go. He'd never taken such abuse before, not even from his father, who often beat him when he was a boy. Words had more damaging effects than fists. Bruises and cuts healed – cruel words never did. When the door closed, he let the hammer forward on the gun and dropped it on the table. Slowly, he sank back into the hard, wooden chair. A million thoughts ran through his mind.

"George! Bring me some more coffee."

#

The large German clock sitting in its place of honor behind the bar in Jolene's saloon had just struck the last of five chimes when the front door swung open. The afternoon sun lying low on the horizon silhouetted the tall form that filled the narrow opening. It was Angus Dunbar.

From the far corner of the bar a woman's voice called out to him, "Hey stranger, did ya come to buy a lady a drink?"

191

He knew without looking who the voice belonged to. It was Jolene. Somehow though, it seemed a little tamer than usual and had a definite ring of happiness to it. "Unusual", he thought.

Walking toward her, he answered, "Came here to talk to you and yer brother. I got somethin' to say to the two of you."

His voice and his manner seemed different, not the same Angus she knew. Because of that, Jolene looked at him warily, as the gap between them narrowed. Mostly, she looked at his eyes but there was nothing there that gave her a hint of what he wanted. "No emotion," she thought, "Cold, very cold! That's why he wins at cards."

In the soft light of the saloon, Angus looked unusually handsome to her. He had on a new pair of pants, a pressed white linen shirt with fancy ruffles on the cuffs and up the front, and a new pair of high black boots. Also, he wore a coat she had not seen before – it was new and a silver stick pin in the shape of an arrowhead adorned the left lapel.

"Who died?" she laughed, trying to start up a conversation. "Hell, ya look like yer goin' to a funeral.........or maybe a weddin'."

His eyes flashed and he smiled at her but said nothing.

She went on, "Clint's upstairs! I'll send for him. Trace," she motioned to the man at the foot of the stairs to fetch her brother.

When Clint arrived, Jolene led them to her private table. Angus sat opposite of them.

Even before they had gotten comfortable in their chairs, Angus began. "Jolene, yer brother came to see me today and we had a long talk about me and you and Jeremy."

Her eyes opened wide, "Clint, you didn't say you'd......"

"Let me finish," he interrupted. "You know, you and I are two strange people. We seem to want something special from life but don't know how to go about getting' it." He paused for a moment and looked straight into her eyes. "What I mean is we go in just the opposite direction of what we should be goin' to reach what it is we're tryin' to reach."

Clint and Jolene were each puzzled. "Well, Angus, I'm completely damn tea-totalin' lost as to what in thee hell you're tryin' to say."

"I'm tryin' to say that I love you and that I should have taken you away from this life and married you a long time ago. We should have bought that little farm we used to talk about and raised Jeremy and been a family - together." He took a deep breath and dropped his eyes. "That's what I'm tryin' to say."

Tears welled up in her eyes and she reached across the table, laying her hand on his. "Do you know how long I've waited to hear those words?" she whispered. "Oh, if only we could have......."

Again, he cut her off. "But we still can" he replied. "It's not too late. We'll go get the boy, bring him home, and let someone else run the businesses. Then, we'll buy that farm and ...."

This time, it was she who cut him off. "You'd go with me to get Jeremy?"

In her eyes was a gentleness and longing he'd not seen before.

"Yes, I will" he replied. "We'll go together and get the boy."

Looking then across the table at Clint, Angus went on. "Sometimes it takes a kick in the pants or, in this case, a hard, right hand between the eyes to let you know that you're making a big mistake; that yer makin' a mess of yer life. At the time you receive it, it hurts like hell; not just the physical pain but a greater pain, the pain you feel in yer soul and yer heart, knowin' that what yer bein' told is the God's-honest truth. Men like that...like me, don't often like to look at themselves in the mirror, because then, they might have to face up to what they see. You made me look in the mirror today and I'm grateful."

Clint said not a word but with a smile, nodded. "You're welcome," was the unsaid message.

Clint cleared his throat and rose from his chair. "I uh, need to go check on the Old Man to see if he's doin' alright. I'll be upstairs if you need me." Walking away he smiled "Hell, they don't need me. They got each other."

#

In the days that followed, Angus and Jolene made arrangements to get Jolene's son. They spoke of marriage and that it would be romantic to have the captain of the river boat marry them on their journey. Jolene had washed the dye from her hair and taken off the gaudy makeup. She was now the sister Clint remembered. She asked Clint to run her bar until she returned but he refused, telling her that the mountains called and he had to get back where he belonged.

Clint and the Old Man left Memphis on a river boat ten days before Angus and Jolene were scheduled to leave. The couple came to the dock to say their goodbyes. Once again, Jolene bid farewell to her brother as she had so many years before. There were hugs, kisses, and tears and promises to return. Everyone waved their goodbyes. He didn't let it show but somehow Clint suspected, he would never see his sister again. He had no plans to return to this city, nor any other for that matter. The cities were dirty and filled with people struggling to get ahead, doing whatever they had to; lying, cheating, killing. They were not for him. This time, when he reached the mountains he swore he would stay there forever.

Clint hadn't noticed before but standing along the rail of the boat, some twenty feet away, was a man he recognized. The man was young and small of stature, wearing a strange looking hat with a garish silver pin cast in the shape of a large "V". It fastened the right side of the brim of his hat to the upper part that fit on his head. Clint had never seen a hat worn this way and as he stared at it, the young man spoke.

"Mister Jeffries" he began. "You probably don't remember me but my name is Victor – Victor O'Bannon. That's what the V stands for. My mother gave it to me on my eighteenth birthday and I wear it on my hat. I sweep floors for Mister Dunbar."

Clint nodded, now remembering where he'd seen the lad.

"Yeah, you work for Angus. That's right!"

"Yes sir, I do." He paused a moment then went on, "I listened to your stories about the mountains and the dangers and especially the part about the gold you found, layin' there just waitin' for someone, anyone......me, to pick it up. And, I got to thinkin' that maybe I should go and try to find that gold myself. I mean, I'm never gonna get rich workin' in a saloon......." He shrugged his shoulders, "so what have I got to lose"?

Clint was silent for a long moment. "Son, that gold is out there and you and anyone else is welcome to it, as far as I'm concerned. But, I've got to tell you, the odds are agin ya findin' it and even if you do, yer chances of makin' it back to spend it are slim. You know, there are those who would kill you for bein' white, and those who would kill you for bein' rich, and those who would just plain kill you for no good reason. But when you add the fact that yer packin' gold to any of those reasons, it makes you ten times more of a target. Take it from one who knows."

The young man listened to what Clint said but the look in his eye and the set of his jaw told Clint that whatever he said would not dissuade this young man from his ambition.

"I can see that you're damn bound and determined to go after that gold so I'll tell you what. I'll make you a map, as close as I can remember it. That should help you along yer way."

"Thank you, sir. It's a beautiful day isn't it"?

BOOK 3 – STORM'S STORY

CHAPTER 1:
KEEL BOATS, BAD NEWS, AND LUST

Ned Larch and the two Indian women had ridden many miles down the Missouri, searching for any sign that might lead them to believe Clint was still alive. For two days, they yelled and hollered and rode to high places along the bank, trying to catch sight of their companion. They found nothing.

Storm wanted to go on but Ned convinced her that it was futile and that they must return to the Platte. He still had said nothing to them of the pony tracks he'd seen when he first went looking for Clint. Thinking back on it now, he suddenly believed in his heart that the Indians had probably killed and scalped his friend. "Otherwise," he thought, "he'd have found us."

Ned knew how much Clint and Storm loved each other. He believed her to be Clint's first love and he knew Clint was the only man in her life that had ever brought her happiness; no, he would never have gone on to St. Louis without saying goodbye to her. Now, with tears streaming down her cheeks, Storm accepted Ned's reasoning words. Nodding her agreement, she reluctantly turned her horse around. Except for the muffled sobs and Lou's soft, comforting voice, the ride back was a quiet one.

On the fifth day, after they had returned to the mouth of the Platte, the keel boats came into view. Growing ever larger as they approached, the giant wooden craft swung heavily out of the river's current and headed for the beach, where Ned and the women stood watching. Some of the men cursed and shouted orders at others who pushed with great long poles against the will of the mighty river. Their hardened voices echoed across the water, coming to Ned and the women as

197

though they were right there next to them. Ned saw the uneasiness in the women. "It'll be all right," he assured them, in Blackfoot. "We will make a trade with these men." His words did not remove the concern he saw in their eyes.

When the first boat neared the shore, a man jumped from its deck with a long rope coiled in his hand; one end was attached to the front of the boat. Quickly, he tied the other end to a large willow tree growing near the shore. Once secure, the mighty boat swung easily into the shoreline. Men began to pile off the boat, stretching and throwing bundles and tools onto the sandy beach.

At first, no one seemed to notice the three on-lookers standing quietly back from the water. But then, they suddenly had everyone's attention. "Women!" the cry went out, "Sweet Jesus, there's women ashore."

For a moment, all motion came to a halt. Nothing moved; there was no sound. It was as though the entire world had stopped. Men with heavy loads set them down. Others, maneuvering the boat with long poles, quickly wedged them into the sandy bottom, to hold against the powerful current. All eyes now scanned the shoreline, hoping to catch sight of the women. Then, the silence was broken; on deck, someone began pointing and yelling, "There they are. There they are."

The motion, that had ceased only moments before, was again in action. Now, men were running toward Ned and the women. Frightened, Storm and Lou quickly stepped behind Ned for protection.

"Awlright, that's enough," shouted a voice from the ship's deck. The men stopped dead in their tracks, recognizing Green's sharp tongue. "Ya act like a bunch a God damned heathens. Leave them folks be and git about yer business."

The men grumbled but did as they were told, knowing that if they didn't, they'd pay a dear price. Green Scroggins was no one to trifle with. There wasn't a man-jack of them aboard that could match him in a fight. And besides, if you did happen to get the better of him, he was still the captain of this expedition and could have you hanged if he took a likin' to.

Swinging to the ground, Green walked toward Ned and held out his hand.

"Name's Scroggins," he offered, smiling, "Afton Scroggins, but you can call me Green. You'll have to forgive my men, they get a little crazy sometimes. It's just that they haven't seen a woman since we left St. Louis and it gets mighty lonely here abouts."

Ned eyed the man up and down, taking measure of the way he carried himself. The cold blue eyes and the square set of his jaw marked him as a leader of men - one who could handle this rowdy bunch.

"Howdy!" Ned answered, "I'm Ned Larch and these here are my wives, Lou and Storm." With the lie, he watched the expression on the big man's face to see what it told him. If Green had any thoughts about it one way or another, he kept them hidden.

"Nice to meet ya, ladies" he smiled, nodding his head. "I'll try and keep these men from botherin' ya but I can't guarantee it. They're gonna wanna trade fer one or both of yer women."

"I ain't interested in tradin' either one of 'em" Ned answered.

Looking in his eyes, Green could see that Ned meant what he said. "If that's yer wish, we'll honor it." Then, pausing a moment, he walked back toward the boat and shouted instructions to two men downloading a large trunk.

When he returned, he said, "We're gonna camp here for the night and I'd be pleased to have you join me fer dinner. We're headin' upriver fer the Yellowstone country and beyond to the Great Falls. If'n yer familiar with that part of the world, I'd sure enough like to ask you some questions about it."

"I think I might can help ya out there," Ned answered, smiling. "Anyways, we'd be pleased to sit with you at supper."

When Green returned to the boat, Ned led the women back to the stand of trees where they'd had their camp set up. Motioning to their robes and cooking gear, Ned said, "I'll fetch the horses in, you two pick up our goods. We're gonna move our camp further back from the river, just in case any of them Frenchies decide to come courtin'."

A quarter mile upriver, they located a small meadow tucked in amongst some large cottonwood trees. It lay adjacent to the water with good grass for the horses.

"This'll do," Ned said, sliding from the horse's back.

While they struck a camp, Ned explained what he had told Green about them both being his wife. He said it was for their own protection - a man wasn't as apt to come after a woman if he knew she belonged to another man. Especially if he thought he might get shot doing it.

With that, the women looked at each other and started laughing. "Listen to this one brag," Lou laughed, winking. "He thinks he's the bull of the herd - able to satisfy two squaws and sire many, many children."

Both women then rubbed their stomachs, tossed their heads back, and began moaning "Oh! Ah!, Oh! What a man - what a man." Then, when they could contain themselves no longer, they fell to the ground, rolling with laughter.

"Well awlright then," Ned said, pretending to be angry, "Maybe I'll just trade you both away to those booshwah pork eaters and git myself a new rifle and a fine set of store-bought clothes. Then, I'll find me a woman who appreciates me."

"Please don't trade us, please don't trade us" the women giggled, running to him and throwing their arms around him. "We could not stand to be away from the bull of the herd. We promise to appreciate you more."

"Good," Ned replied, no longer able to keep from smiling. "This'll teach ya." With that, he swept them up, one under each arm and they all tumbled to the ground laughing.

#

Dinner that night was palatable and the men behaved themselves, as Green had promised. In conversation, Green spoke of his employer, John Jacob Astor. He explained it was Astor's dream to send expeditions to the mountains, exploiting their bountiful harvest of furs. These, he would export to the markets of the world and thereby become extremely rich.

Throughout the discourse, Green asked Ned many questions about the country that lay upriver. Mainly, he wanted to know if the tribes of Indians in the area would trade with the white man. Ned told him what he knew of the Crow, the Sioux, the Blackfoot, and the Nez Perce. Also, he spoke of the Flathead who lived more to the north.

Now, as they sat smoking their pipes, the conversation ebbed. In the dancing light of the fire, Ned could see the wanton looks on the faces of the men about him, staring at the women. They reminded him of the wolves that always show up when you kill a buffalo. They just sort of come out of nowhere and surround you, settin' there in a circle watching and waitin' for you to leave or maybe throw 'em a chunk of meat. Many's the time he'd tossed 'em a rib or leg bone just to watch the fun. They'd damn near kill one another - first one would grab it, then a bigger, tougher one would take it away from him, and so on and so forth. Life was hard out here - it seemed that people, just like them wolves, had to fight for every damn thing they got. And then when you got it, you had to fight like hell to keep it 'because some other son-of-a-bitch was always trying to take it away from you. Yup, life was hard.

During dinner, Lou and Storm had not spoken nor had they looked upon any of the men sitting about them; they knew it would only encourage them and invite trouble. Now, however, Storm nudged Ned, pushing at his shoulder and whispering to him in Blackfoot. Her movement caused a sudden stir among the men.

"Alright, alright, I'll ask him," he said, leaning away from her insistence.

"Say Green, on yer trip upriver you didn't happen to come across a feller ridin' a raft, did ya? He's a big man - has a game leg - name's Jeffries, Clint Jeffries."

The stir that had risen among the men suddenly became very still. Storm fixed her eyes on Green, waiting for his reply. She could not understand all the white man's words but she could pick up on the expressions and the facial gestures - she could tell what was being said.

His reply was guarded and it came in the form of a question. "How is it you know Clinton Jeffries?" he asked, looking carefully into Ned Larch's face.

Without taking his eyes from the fire, Ned answered, "Saved my life a while back. Killed some Indians that were about to do me in." Ned let the smoke from his pipe roll out the corner of his mouth and up his cheek. He went on, "We met him this side of the divide and traveled with him to the mouth of the Platte. Somehow or other, we lost touch with him in the dark and haven't seen him since - don't know if he's drowned or maybe got hisself scalped - just wondered if you might have seen him?"

Again, Green's reply was slow coming. "Yeah," he said, nodding his head, "we saw him about a week ago. Loaned him a dugout boat, I did, to get him to St. Lou."

Storm, understood the man's nod to mean yes - he had seen Clint. Clint was alive. A smile came to her lips but she quickly put it away.

Green went on, "I've known Clint since he first came upriver; saw him grow from a boy to a man. A hell-of-a-friend he was too..."

"What do you mean, was?" Ned broke in, sharply.

"Got himself killed he did, over a bag of gold." Seeing the questions in Ned's eyes, he continued. "He offered me gold when I let him have the dugout, he held out a hand full saying he'd pay me for the boat. Hell, I didn't want his gold but there were two no-good sombitches in the crew who did. The next morning, they took one of the other dugouts and went downriver to rob him. When I saw they were missin' and the boat was gone, I dispatched two men to search for Clint. They came back some days later saying they'd found him. The dugout was hung up in a log jam; they told me the animals and birds hadn't left much, so they said a few words over him and dumped what was left in the river. I didn't see him all that often but I'm gonna miss that boy."

Storm sat motionless, waiting for Ned's translation of what she thought she understood the man to say. When he turned to her she saw the pain in his eyes. He did not have to speak. She quickly lowered her face to hide the grief that welled up inside her. The hope that had been there only moments before now ran out of her in a wash of memories and silent tears. How could he be gone? How could he be dead? She loved him so much. What they had together, even though it was only for a short time, had been something she had never felt before - she knew now she would never feel that way again. There could be no other love for her.

Ned did not need to look at Storm's face to realize the anguish she felt. He heard her gasp at his words and felt her fingernails bite into the back of his arm as she fought to hold back the tears.

"It jes' don't seem fair somehow," he whispered to himself, "every time she has a chance for happiness, somethin' comes along to ruin it."

#

Daybreak the next morning found Ned and the women striking camp. With the news of Clint's death, there was no sense staying here. Strapping the last bedroll on the packhorse, he gave a long sigh. "Damn..." was all he said. The women turned from what they were doing, sharing in what he was feeling.

None of them had gotten any rest. The news about Clint had left them devastated. Storm especially, had had a bad night. Her eyes were swollen from the crying; dark circles hung under them, accenting the hollow of her cheeks. Her usually dark skin seemed pale and her lips were drawn in. A loose fitting buckskin bandage wrapped the deep gash that ran from the point of her left shoulder down toward her inner elbow. Neither Ned nor Lou mentioned it.

Last night in the waning light of the campfire, as he and Lou laid in their buffalo robes, Ned saw Storm take up a large skinning knife and quietly slip from camp. He knew what she was about to do. Quietly, he followed her to the meadow where the horses were tethered. He listened as she wailed and sobbed for her dead warrior. Tears ran down his cheeks also but his grief he held in silence. This was a very private thing for Indian women and it would not be good if Storm knew he was watching her. He respected her privacy and wouldn't have followed her except that he worried for her safety. He knew of some women who had gotten carried away in their grief, inflicting mortal wounds on themselves. When their relatives searched for them the following day, they found they had bled to death. He didn't want that to happen to her. If he had to, he'd help her.

In the dull moonlight, he had watched her disrobe. He could barely make out her outline as she knelt and held her arms above her head. In anguish, she chanted to the Great Spirit, asking him to care for her mighty warrior and protect him from the evils of the dark world. She also pleaded with him to take her life for she did not want to live without her man.

Ned could not see the blade in her hand but he knew it was there. When at last she became silent, he knew it was time. He barely saw the motion and then he heard the gasp, as her breath caught in her throat. Again, she held her arms skyward, wailing and crying.

"Gawd," he whispered, feeling totally helpless, "It's so damn dark I can't tell how bad she's cut."

In the darkness, he waited. When it looked as though she were back on her feet and getting dressed, he silently slipped back to the camp.

"Is she all right?" Lou asked in hushed whispers as he climbed in beside her.

"I don't know," he answered. "You better check on her when she comes in."

Moments later, Storm walked into camp and began rummaging through one of the parflieches. "Are you all right, my sister?" Lou asked.

"I have cried for my man and I have bled for him," she answered. "My heart is as empty as the morning sky and I feel there is no reason to live. I asked the Great Spirit to take my life but he would not." She paused then for a long moment; quietly she added, "You sleep now. I will tend to the wound. It is not serious. One cannot lose their life when it has already been taken from them."

#

Ned sat in the saddle, holding the reins of the other horses and waited for the women to mount. They were huddled together near Storm's pony; Lou's voice was muffled as she spoke and he could not understand what they said.

"She's sick," Lou said, walking over to take the reins from his hand. "She threw up what she ate this morning. I think it's the stress of Clint's death."

"I don't doubt that a bit," he answered. "Makes me 'wanna throw up too."

"I'll be along in a moment," Storm said. "You go on; I'll catch up."

"As you wish," Ned replied and spurred his pony. Riding away, he could hear Storm retching.

The day had begun sunny and warm. It was fall, however, and the icy grip of winter was not far off. Now, as the breeze stiffened, its bite caused the riders to lower their faces. The women had each wrapped themselves with a blanket and rode hunkered down against the horses' backs.

The hours passed slowly as they made their way upstream. Only now and then did the keel boats come in sight. Ned planned it that way. He knew, the less they saw of those men, the better off they'd be. In fact, he pushed the horses at a good pace and rode on long after dark in order to put extra distance between them and the boats. The camp spots he chose were far back from the river and usually hidden among thick brush and woods.

"Why do we ride so long?" The women complained. "We are tired and need rest. We have ridden hard for the last five days."

His only answer to them was that winter was coming and they must get to a place that had good shelter and game. Besides, he felt uneasy here and thought that danger was all about. Upon listening to his explanation, the women looked at one another and rolled their eyes. Danger was always about; they knew that. It was nothing new. And yet, Ned was being what they considered extra careful. "Why?" they asked. "Why?"

He was too tired to argue over this and he did not want to try and explain that the men on those boats would likely do anything they could, to lay-up with the women. He knew better than Storm or Lou that a stiff pecker had no conscience. And, there was many a stiff pecker in that bunch.

"Don't argue with me," he lashed out, suddenly spinning around in the saddle, surprising both of them. "Just keep your mouths shut and ride." With that tone in his voice, they recognized this was not something they should continue. And, since it was the Indian way for women to do as their man told them, they lowered their eyes and rode on in silence.

CHAPTER 2:
WITH CHILD, RAPE, AND DEATH

The days dragged on and their fatigue grew worse. Ned knew he had pushed the women pretty hard and, as it had been over a week since they last saw the boats, he conceded to stop for a while and rest. Also, it would give him an opportunity to scare up some fresh meat. Early in the afternoon, they came to a pretty meadow where a small stream entered the river. The water was clear and cold and a good stand of buffalo grass grew all around.

"C'mon," Ned muttered, turning his horse upstream and motioning with his head. "Let's foller this up a ways and see if we can find a good campsite."

"What's wrong with this campsite?" Storm asked. "There's good grass here and we can catch fish in the big river."

"I think it would be better to move back away from the river," he argued "so, let's go."

With those words, Lou quickly came to his side.

"Storm is tired and needs rest," she whispered in low tones.

"Yeah, well I'm tired too," he answered. "But we're still gonna move back away from the river."

"Yes, but you are not carrying a child." She paused, waiting for his reply.

"What?" he said, squinting deeply into his wife's eyes and trying to digest what he'd just heard. "Did you say..."

"You heard me," she said, cutting his words short. "She needs to rest – now!"

"Well, I'll be..." he stammered. "I'm gonna be an uncle." Then, looking at them in a mood of proud understanding, Ned smiled and nodded his head.

"Awlright," he said, "this'll do." Pausing for a moment, he went on, "As long as I'm astride this horse, I'm gonna ride upstream a piece and see who's about - maybe get us a deer if I can." With that, he rode away from the clearing, leaving the women to set up camp.

Near the stream, the underbrush was thick so Ned rode out a ways. Then turning, he continued on a parallel course with it. Looking about, he noticed that the countryside was mostly flat; a rolling prairie that seemed to go on and on. Scattered about, stands of colorful trees and brush added tones of red, yellow, and orange to the otherwise monotonous sea of brownish green, buffalo grass. The afternoon sky was as blue as any he'd ever seen. The biting wind had ceased and the sun shone warm on his face. All, seemed right with the world.

Stopping his horse at the crest of a shallow hill, he stretched upward as far as he could in the saddle to scan the horizon. He cupped his hands above his eyes to shade them from the sun. Far off in the distance he could make out some low hills.

"No damn mountains in this part of the world," he grumbled to himself, "I hate a place that's got no damn mountains."

#

At the river, the two Indian women busily went about setting up camp. They talked and laughed, enjoying each other's company and the peacefulness of the warm October afternoon. In their contentment, they failed to notice the stirring in the brush and the nervousness of their tethered ponies. Now, watchful eyes measured their every move.

Almost before they knew it, the men were among them. The first grabbed Lou from behind, taking her to the ground in one easy motion. Two others came at Storm and she quickly pulled her knife from its sheath and stood her ground. Terrified, she tried to scream but there was a sudden "whack" to the side of her head. The knife flew from her hand as the pain washed over her in a jarring wave. She felt herself falling.

Before her face slammed into the ground, the two men before her caught her and rolled her onto her back. She could hear them talking but she could not see them. Her head swam in an uncontrolled whirl of blackness. She could not open her eyes.

She felt their anxious, groping hands upon her, tearing at her clothes, baring her skin, touching her parts. Someone was holding her arms tightly and she could feel the grass and cold earth against her back and her butt. A warm sucking mouth suddenly closed over one of her nipples and in her battered confusion she imagined it to be Clint. Oh, how she loved him and the way he made her feel; his touch was magic; their love was magic. But he was dead, gone. How could this be?

Now, she felt the sharp sting of the man's entry. He was large and erect and he pounded against her, viciously. For a moment, her eyes came open and she looked up into the spasmed, contorted face. His frantic movement only seemed to add to her confusion. It was his loud release and the pain in her breasts that brought her to full consciousness. The man lay upon her now gasping for breath and biting her about the nipples. She recognized him as one of the men from the keel boat.

She screamed at him to get off her. He could not understand her and would have cared little if he could. He only laughed at her. She then spit at him and tried to knee him in the crotch but he was too strong for her.

The two men who held her arms laughed as their friend arose.

"She's a wildcat, no?" asked one of them. "She'll not be so wild when I introduce her to this," he said, grabbing at his crotch. With that, he took the first man's place and mounted her.

Beyond the pain and disgust of what was happening, Storm suddenly thought of her sister. "Lou, where was Lou?"

She turned her head from side to side trying to see what was happening. She could hear Lou struggling beneath the pile of men that surrounded her. She watched as one after another took their turn.

When the three who raped Storm were through with her, the others who had taken Lou came over and had their way with her also. This went on for what seemed to be forever. One after another, they kept it up. Again, and again, the women were ravaged.

"Where was Ned?" Storm wondered. "Why wasn't he here to help them?"

When the men at last had finished with them, they moved away a short distance. Squatting on their haunches, they formed a loose circle and talked in low tones. Now and then, one would point at the women and the rest would laugh or nod their heads. They spoke in a tongue unfamiliar to Storm. She knew, however, that what they said involved her and her sister. She could only assume they were deciding their fate.

Both women lay still upon the ground. Besides the obvious pain of the rape, Storm felt like she had been kicked by a horse. Every inch of her body cried out in pain. Even the slightest movement caused her to wince.

Slowly turning toward Lou, she tried to speak. "Are you all right, my sister?" Lou said nothing. She moved her arm, gently reaching out toward her sister. "Lou, speak to me. I..."

Her voice was suddenly driven from her throat as the powerful hand closed around her windpipe. She fought for air but none could be had. She tried to struggle but could not move. The bulk of his weight lay upon her. Through her fear, she looked up into the face of death. Her gaze was countered by his, forced back at her with a cold deliberateness she had never seen. In his hand, he held a slender dagger.

"I will go to the Great Spirit now," she thought. "My time here is over."

Slowly he raised the dagger to his lips, as though it were his finger. "Shush," he whispered.

When he at last relaxed his hand, she gasped for air, filling her lungs again and again.

"You like the air, huh?" he grunted and began to tighten his grip once more. Her mind was in a whirl now. Spots of light came and went and she couldn't concentrate. She felt her life sliding away from her.

Even before she heard the crack of the rifle, she saw blood spray from the man's body and felt his hand relax its grip on her throat. He tumbled to her side in a lifeless heap. A warm crimson cloud settled over her face as she once more gulped at the life-giving air. Somewhere in her dim consciousness, she recognized the scrambling sound of men running. Shouts and two more shots filled the air, then a scream and then...only the silence. The noise had gone away.

Many minutes later, Storm felt a hand on her shoulder. She recoiled sharply.

"It's alright, it's me." Ned's voice came in reassuring words. "Are you hurt badly?"

"No," she answered "Look after Lou...see if she's..."

Quickly, he moved to Lou's side. She wasn't moving.

"Lou! Lou!" he cried. "Are you hurt...talk to me, Lou." Ned put his arm under her shoulder, lifting her head up off the ground. It was then that he noticed the blood, staining the ground where she'd lain.

"Goddammit, don't die on me, girl," he cried, gently shaking her. "You can't die...you just can't die." In the failing light of the afternoon sunset, he stared at her, straining to detect any sign, any movement that would convince him otherwise, of what he knew to be true. He had confronted death many times but never like this.

Tears filled his eyes and he drew her close to him. Stroking her hair, he gently rocked back and forth and wept as he had never wept before. Storm gathered what strength she could find and crawled to him. Cradling them both in her arms, she sang softly to the Great Spirit, asking him to spare her sister, to send her back to the ones who needed her. Somewhere, far across the river, an owl hooted a lonely greeting to the approaching night, welcoming the silent stars.

CHAPTER 3:
KILLIN' TIMES

The burial platform took the better part of a day to construct. Storm dressed Lou in her finest buckskins, combed her hair, adorned her face with vermillion, and wrapped her in their best blanket. Together, she and Ned lifted Lou to her final resting place. Trinkets and amulets were hung on the poles of the platform to honor Lou and show the Great Spirit and all who passed what a fine woman she had been.

Through all of this, Ned moved as though he were in a trance. So great was his sorrow, he could not do otherwise. Storm had to be the strong one for both of them. It was she who had directed the building of the funeral pyre and she who had prepared her sister for the final send-off. Storm had never seen this side of Ned, had never realized the tenderness and love that filled this giant man. She felt so sorry for him and tried to tell him so but he only shrugged and went about the necessary preparations. Through the day, she heard his quiet sobs and saw him reach up to wipe away the tears.

When at last the ceremony was ended, Storm and Ned rode silently away, each of them with their own thoughts and remembrances of the wife and sister they had known and loved and lost. It was deep into the night when they at last made camp. They built no fire nor ate no supper. Instead, they wrapped themselves in blankets and tried to sleep.

For Ned, the following day was much the same as it had been the day before. He refused to eat and moved about as in a daze. Storm didn't push it – she knew that it would take time for the realization to set in. She also knew that once Ned regained his senses there would be hell to pay for her sister's death. He was a vengeful man, the worst she'd ever known. She feared that Ned, in his blind rage, would go after the men who did this and be killed, himself. Her fears were justified.

When she awoke the following morning, Ned was gone. Storm broke camp and followed his trail. It wasn't hard to guess where he was heading. His tracks led toward the river.

Since keel boats only gained a few miles per day, it wasn't hard for Ned to locate the hulking boat. Vengeance burned in him as he planned his retribution. Where the current was extremely strong, some men would be put ashore and would have to pull the boat upstream, using long, heavy ropes while the others, on deck, used poles to move the boat forward. Just such a situation was underway as Ned now peered down from a low bluff above the river. Fortunately, the men were ashore on his side of the river.

Noting a protruding stand of willows a few hundred yards ahead of where the men now pulled the boat, Ned worked his way into position. The river at that point must have been shallow for the willows were thick and grew far out from the regular bank. Quickly he made his way to the brushy outgrowth. Near where he planned his attack, he bent several of the willows down, breaking them just above the water level. This was a place to rest his weapons, to ensure his rifle and pistol stayed dry. A few yards more toward the river, he submerged himself beneath the icy water. Only that area above his nose was visible. Gripped tightly in his huge fist, was the deadly knife he had so often called upon to slay his enemies. Now, he could hear the voices of the men as they cursed and strained to move the heavy boat.

"Today they will pay for what they did to my Lou," he whispered.

Ned let five men pass him before making a move. Rising from the murky water, he grabbed the nearest man about the face, silencing his scream. The razor-sharp knife slid in just under the man's ribcage, finding his liver. He collapsed in a heap. The man just behind him, disbelievingly stood with his mouth agape at the sight of this giant hulk rising from the water to kill his friend. Before he could react, Ned sprung upon him, plunging the knife deep into his chest. He screamed as he died.

"Injuns!" The cry went out. Suddenly, there was mass confusion. Most of the men let go of the rope and began swimming to get back to the boat. One of the men who had passed Ned, now ran back towards him through the willows. Seeing the opportunity, Ned crouched and met the man head on.

"This one's for Lou," he screamed as he planted the knife in the man's crotch. Three times he stabbed him, not wanting to kill him outright but rather to make him suffer. The man screamed in agony, still scrambling to get out into the river and back to the boat. Knowing he was done for, Ned let him go.

Seeing what had happened, the others who were ahead of Ned, launched themselves into the swift current and were stroking to get as much river as they could between him and themselves. One of them fired a pistol at Ned before diving in the river. The shot narrowly missed and Ned quickly ran back and grabbed his guns. Advancing to the front of the willows, he shot the closest man to him with his pistol. The man went under and never surfaced again.

Shots now rang out from the boat. Several men on board thinking Indians were attacking, fired into the willows where Ned stood. He could hear the balls clipping the branches behind him. Steadily, he drew a bead on one of the swimmers. Bang! The man disappeared. But now, Ned had to get back to shore to reload. He'd left his powder and possibles high on the riverbank where it was dry.

Above the river on a nearby bluff, Storm had heard the shooting and had seen Ned kill one of the men as he swam for the boat. Quickly, she headed for the place she knew Ned would come ashore. Tying her horse off, she headed into the thick brush to meet him.

"Ned," she whispered. "Where are you?"

"I'm here Storm," he answered. "Just let me finish loading this rifle and we'll get outta…"

"Yer not goin' anywhere except straight to hell," shouted the voice of the man behind him. And with that, he grabbed Ned about the neck and plunged his knife into his back.

"Arrgh," Ned bellowed and grabbed the man's arm. "You've killed me, you son-of-a- bitch, but yer gonna die too." Tossing the loaded pistol to Storm, he gasped "It's loaded. Shoot him. Shoot him for me and Lou."

Ned still had hold of the boatman's arm as he sunk to the ground. The man struggled to get loose but couldn't. When at last he freed himself from the dead-man's grip, he was looking down the barrel of Ned's belt pistol. Storm stood less than four feet from him, her hand trembling

"Well then! What'll it be girlie? Are you gonna shoot ole' Bill or what?" He spoke softly and began to circle to his left, trying to put some brush between he and the girl, trying to catch her off guard.

"I don't think ya got it in ya to pull that trigger," he said, smirking. "That's what I think."

It was then that Storm recognized the man. He was the one who had raped her first. The one who had bit her and left his filthy seed in her. He was one of the men who had killed her sister. Her hand steadied as she extended her arm, bringing the weapon even with the man's heart.

The man saw the sudden recognition in her eyes, saw the uncertainty change to cold determination, and saw the trembling hand become stone solid. All color drained from his face.

"For Lou and Ned," Storm whispered in Blackfoot and squeezed the trigger.

The boat had drifted several hundred yards downstream but those on her decks heard the final shot. Some say it was followed by a man's scream.

#

Fearing that the men on the boat would mount a search party and come looking for their fallen comrades, Storm quickly grabbed the guns and Ned's possibles sack and made for the horses. Before she ran, however, she leaned down and, touching the cheek of her old friend, whispered a final goodbye. They had ridden so many trails together and he had always been there for her and her sister, protecting them and providing for them. Now, he was gone and she was totally alone.

Panic drove her as she made her way upstream and away from the river. She wasn't worried about hiding her tracks, she would do that later. Right now, she had to put as much distance as she could between herself and the men on the boat. As she rode, she cursed herself for not listening to Ned when he had wanted them to camp far back from the river. If they'd have done as he wished, both he and Lou would still be alive.

For two days, she continued to ride, stopping only when necessary. Many times, she fell asleep on the horse's back, leaving him to wander at will. Once, toward the end of the second day, she dozed off and then fell to the ground, landing hard on her right shoulder. The force of the fall knocked the wind out of her and she lay gasping, trying to gain her breath. Fortunately, the horses were well mannered and didn't run off when she fell. Instead, they stood grazing on brown bunch grass some yards away.

As she lay there facing the sky, she thought of Clint and the love they had shared. It had not been that long ago but it seemed like years. Oh, what she wouldn't give to see his smiling face and have him hold her once more in his arms. Thinking of him, she reached down with both hands and placed them on her stomach, rubbing them gently across the small swelling.

"I carry what is left of you my love," she whispered. "He will be a mighty warrior just as you were and he will have your name." Suddenly, she could hold back no longer. The tears welled up in her eyes and she burst out sobbing. Why had things happened the way they did? Everyone she ever loved was gone, never to return. She was suddenly very lonely and very frightened. For a moment, she let a dark thought cross her mind.

"It would have been so much easier if they had just killed her as they did Lou. Then she would not have to suffer the loneliness and heartaches of this life. If the Great Spirit would take me, I would go with him and not look back." But then, remembering the life that stirred inside her, she wiped the tears away.

After several minutes, she tried to get up but the pain in her shoulder forced her to lie back on the ground. "I'll just lie here a while until my shoulder quits hurting," she whispered. With that, she closed her eyes and fell soundly asleep.

The biting cold of the early December evening stirred her from her sleep. She didn't know how long she'd slept but every star in the sky was shining brightly and the night was pitch black. At this time of year when the sun goes down, the temperature drops sharply. As she struggled to get up off the ground, she could see her breath come in small white clouds. Her teeth chattered as she gained her feet. With her eyes adjusting to the night, she moved slowly toward the horses. She had stiffened up while lying on the cold ground and now, as she walked, her muscles and joints cried out in angry torment.

Reaching into one of the parfleches that had fallen with her, she pulled out a heavy blanket. She threw it over her back and shoulders and felt an immediate warming. "I should build a fire and eat something," she thought. "But I am too tired. I must rest." Finding the pack-horse, she untied the heavy buffalo robe from his back and rolled it out upon the ground, fur-side up. On top of this she spread the blanket she had draped over her shoulders. She then laid down on one side of the giant robe and pulled the other side over her. Snuggled between the layers of blanket and warm fur, she let the sleep once more overtake her. It wasn't until late the next morning that she awoke.

CHAPTER 4:
A GIFT AND ARMAND

Several weeks passed and Storm kept riding, steadily northward, up the great river. She was a stranger in this country but she knew the river would lead her to the land of her people. Something inside her told her she must keep going; she must go home. Always keeping it in sight, she used the river as a guide. However, she knew better than to venture near it. The last thing she wanted was to run into the boatmen again.

The days grew shorter as winter approached. Some mornings when she awoke, there was a skiff of snow covering the ground. Generally, it was gone within a few hours but Storm knew there would come a time when it would not melt and everything would freeze. This realization caused her to search out a good camp in which to spend the winter. Getting home would have to wait until spring.

She had come to a rather good sized river that, some distance down-stream ran into the great river. Following it upstream in hopes of finding a good place to cross, she came to a smaller creek that flowed into the stream. It ran out of a narrow canyon in some low-lying hills to the south. Along its banks grew heavy stands of cottonwood trees. She knew their bark would help feed the horses through the winter. Also, there were grassy meadows with wild plum trees outlining their edges. No plums remained on the trees, however, their limbs and the brush that grew in the nearby thickets would afford Storm some decent shelter and plenty of firewood. She immediately set about building a wikiup.

This structure she had learned to build as a child, helping her parents whenever the camp moved. She first cut straight, stout limbs from the heavy brush that grew in the surrounding draws. The limbs at their thickest were about two inches in diameter. These, she arranged in a circle, standing them upright and burying their heavy end about a foot in the ground. This would ensure they were anchored tightly when the strong winter winds came to call. Once they were buried she bent the tops toward the center, tying them securely with rawhide straps where they crossed each other. Other limbs of lesser thickness, she wove and tied around the structure in intervals, parallel to the ground.

That done, she took pieces of cottonwood bark and laid it on its edges around the base of the structure. This, she held in place by banking dirt and stones against it. Two of the three buffalo robes she had, she used to cover the framework. Lashing them securely, she knew they would keep the snow out and the warmth in. She left a small opening in the top to let the smoke escape. Lastly, she made an opening for the door, placing it on the east side, away from the prevailing winds.

Standing back, she smiled and admired her handiwork. Building the shelter had boosted her confidence. She knew the ways of the wilderness and if she applied them correctly, she would survive.

She had been fairly successful in finding food. Mostly, it amounted to birds and small animals such as rabbits, squirrels, and porcupines. Sometimes, she caught fish from the stream. She also dined on wild onion and tubers when she could find them. Soon, before the first major storm, she would go for deer. Ned had taught her to shoot and she believed there might be large numbers of them in the surrounding hills and draws. She would try to kill two or three to get her through the winter. She knew the weather would be cold enough so they wouldn't spoil. Much of the meat she could dry. It stored well that way.

Winter arrived with a vengeance, slipping down from the north and coming full force one night as Storm slept. The previous afternoon had been blustery with the wind pushing the wispy mares-tail clouds up from the south. The moving air had a stinging bite to it and nipped at the edge of Storm's nostrils as she gathered firewood. When she laid down for the evening, there was only the threat of snow in the air. Now, however, as she rose from her sleep and opened the flap of the wikiup, she was blinded by the swirling flakes that danced wildly before the wind's breath.

The storm raged for two solid days without letting up. Worrying about the horses, she went out several times to check on them. Some days earlier, she had fashioned a small corral and had erected a windbreak from brush and logs. When she looked in on them, they seemed peaceful and unfettered by the blowing snow.

When the snow had at last stopped falling, Storm donned the heavy buffalo hide cover that had been Ned's. She had to trim it some to fit her. When finished, she pushed her head through the center hole and set about gathering what she needed for the deer hunt she had been planning. Stopping for a moment, she calculated what all she would take with her. When satisfied that she had what she needed, she climbed aboard her horse and headed up the canyon toward the low, snow packed hills. Better than a foot of snow had fallen and any tracks she came across, she knew would be fresh. Along the way, she encountered a red fox who, she suspected, was looking for food also. Upon seeing her, he scurried away, disappearing in a flurry of snow.

For an hour, Storm rode without seeing any sign of critters at all. Then, in the bottom of a shallow draw, she came across several sets of hoof prints, bunched together and heading west. She recognized them immediately as deer tracks. Following them to the crest of a pointed hill, she scanned the ridges and draws below for any sign of movement. There was nothing and she patiently rode on. A half-hour later, she was standing at the edge of a small stream. Most of its surface was frozen or covered with snow but here and there running water was visible. She held the halter low, letting the horse drink.

The deer had crossed the stream where she stood. Their tracks led away into a brushy ravine some forty yards ahead. The ravine rose sharply for several yards and then seemed to flatten out. As it did so, it angled off to the left. Storm had mounted her horse and was about to cross the small creek when the silence of the tiny valley was broken by a gunshot.

She nearly jumped out of her skin at the unexpected boom. Quickly, she brought the horse about, heading him up the stream to gain the safety of another brushy draw. Dismounting, she held the horse's nose to keep him silent. Then, she listened. There was not the slightest whisper of anything unusual. The brook beneath the snow gurgled over the rocks, providing a constant background sound to the birds and the occasional whine of the wind. But, there was nothing else.

"Who would be shooting," she wondered, her mind questioning itself. "Most Indians in these parts did not have guns. Could it be the men from the boat? Maybe but she doubted it. She had purposely ridden many miles from the big river, in order to stay out of their path."

For several minutes, she waited to see what would happen. Then, curiosity got the best of her. She had to find out who was in her neck of the woods. If it was a war party or the men from the boat she would have to move her camp, for it would only be a matter of time before they found her. Tying the horse securely to a small tree, she made her way through the brush and climbed the steep hill out of the draw. She kept to the brush as it afforded her good cover. The ravine where the deer had run was not far ahead of her and she drew up behind a small evergreen to catch her breath and plan her next move. She saw nothing that looked suspicious. In a low crouching run she proceeded to a place where she could see a good stretch of the ravine as it ran away, down the sloping hill. From this vantage point, she could see a small flat on the other side of the ravine. Standing in that flat was a man.

Instinctively, she crouched lower to better conceal herself. Near him, on the ground, lay a deer. There was a great deal of blood on the snow and she guessed he had already cleaned the animal. This man was the first human being she'd seen since that day on the river and it stirred a spark of loneliness within her. She often got lonely and sometimes even cried because of it. But now, she quickly erased the emotion from her mind. "It is better to be alone," she thought, "than take the chance of being murdered." Quietly, she slipped back to the safety of the thick brush and made her way to the horse.

On her way to camp, she cursed her luck at not killing a deer. Her food was running low and she could have used the meat. She also cursed the fact that there was another in this part of the country who might be an enemy. Mostly, she worried that she may have to leave the campsite she had spent so much time building; the campsite where she planned to give birth to her child. That night, many thoughts ran through her mind as she lay wrapped in the buffalo robe, watching the flicker of the fire dance in uneven patterns upon the wall of her shelter. Before long, she was asleep and dreaming.

Her rest was not calm, however, as her dreams brought back memories of the men on the keel boat. They were staking her to the ground and having their way with her. Then, somehow from somewhere Clint and Ned were there to rescue her; to take revenge on the men for what they did to her and her sister. Her poor sister! Lou, whom she had loved so deeply now lay frozen on an icy burial platform in some remote canyon. Storm could see her sister's face crying to her because she was so cold "Give me a blanket, please," she whispered. "I am so cold – so cold. The wolves come at night and they frighten me. Keep them away, Storm. Please, keep them away. They're coming now. Can you hear them snarling and fighting; don't let them get me, please."

In her dream, Storm could hear the snarling of the wolves but she could not see them. It was terrifying and she struggled to help her sister. But they kept up the growling and yapping and would not stop. Suddenly, she realized the snarling was not in her dream but was coming from just outside her shelter. Throwing some twigs on the hot coals, she soon had a small fire going. She kept some bunches of dry grass handy to use as torches. She lit one and lowered the flap of the wikiup. Morning wasn't far off and its inky sky would be showing first light at any time now.

What she saw with the torch were two large buffalo wolves jumping to get at something that hung in the tree not ten yards from her shelter. Yelling at them to get their attention, Storm charged through the snow waving the torch in one hand and wielding a heavy piece of firewood in the other. This was too much for the wolves and they beat a hasty retreat out into the darkness.

"What were they after?" Storm whispered, examining the packed-down snow where they had been circling and jumping. When she raised the torch, the sight she beheld took her breath away and caused her heart to jump into her throat. There, hanging from two neatly tied rawhide straps was half of the carcass of a deer. She quickly doused the torch and made a dash for the wikiup. Reaching inside, she brought forth the loaded rifle. Then she took shelter near the horse pen. Shivering, she waited there until full light, wondering all the while who had come to her camp and why. The only thing she could surmise was that it had to have been the stranger she witnessed from her hilltop perch. That would answer the who but what about the why? Why had he brought the meat and why did he not say anything? How did he know she was here? Had he been watching her? Her fear turned suddenly to anger. There were too many questions and not enough answers. She would find out who this intruder was and just exactly what he wanted.

The tracks were not hard to follow in the deep snow. They led in a southeast direction, climbing upward toward a small knoll that jutted out sharply above the main ridge of the rounded hills. A mile further brought her to a steep gorge that cut directly across the presumed path the stranger had taken. However, as she approached the cut, she noticed that the horseman had made a sharp right turn and followed the edge of the gorge down into a narrow canyon. The trail then proceeded upward through a grove of trees.

When she emerged from the trees, she couldn't believe her eyes. She was in an oval shaped valley – a big valley. From what she could tell, its floor seemed almost flat. Here and there, meadows ran between scattered groves of thick oak and juniper. The beauty of the place almost took her breath away. She had never seen anything like it. For long moments, she sat motionless, staring at the wonderment before her. The anger she had built up earlier seemed somewhat unimportant now. It surprised her that this place had such a calming effect.

Regaining the trail, she pressed onward. The tracks led along the edge of a long meadow and then curved sharply to the left, skirting out around a point of dense oak and tangled brush. Rounding the point, she found herself at the edge of long narrow lake. The lake only added to the pristine beauty of the valley. Once more, she found herself gazing at the splendor of the place. Her mind was not attuned to her purpose or perhaps she'd have seen him sooner.

Amid the pleasure of the moment, she was suddenly shocked back to reality with the familiar *Click, Click* of a rifle being cocked. Realizing the sound had come from very close behind her, she pulled the pony up sharply and sat motionless, staring straight ahead.

"How could I have been so stupid to fall into this trap," she thought. It was then that she realized, whoever it was behind her, had banked on her woman's curiosity, had known she would follow the tracks that were so easy to see. Now, she knew a rifle was pointed at her and she didn't move.

Slowly, he circled, coming into her view from the left side. He was, perhaps, fifteen feet from her and she felt his eyes upon her, staring, waiting, daring her to move. She wanted to turn to face him, to be furious with him but she could not. She was afraid.

She carried Ned's rifle in one hand, across the horse's back. The barrel faced toward him. As quick as a cat, he covered the fifteen feet that separated them and wrenched the rifle from her hand. The sudden movement caused the pony to sidestep and rear up.

"Whoa," he said in a soothing voice, taking hold of the halter. Storm could then see his face. It was a bearded face, dark skinned like her own but with different features. Obviously, he was not Indian. She stared down at him in disgust and sharply kicked his hand, knocking it away from the horse's halter.

"Ahhg," he said, laughing. "This woman is a wildcat. Hah!"

He spoke in a tongue she had not heard before. She could not understand him. Quickly, he grabbed the halter back and attempted to lead the horse away. Again, she kicked at his hand. But this time, he hung on. His flashing black eyes challenged her and she read their meaning, "Do it again," they offered, "do it again and I will knock you from the horse's back." She let him lead.

Halfway along the edge of the lake, he broke to the left, leading the horse across some open ground to a thick grove of cottonwoods. There, amidst the trees was a small snow-covered meadow. In it, stood a shelter very much the same as the one Storm had built, only bigger. A ribbon of smoke lazily threaded its way skyward, issuing out from the small hole in the wiki's top. Half of a deer hung in the shade of the large trees.

"The other half of the one he left for me," Storm thought, her anger returning.

Pulling the horse up in front of the shelter, he motioned for her to get down. Stubbornly, she sat there as if frozen to the horse.

"Ahh! So, you want to play games, huh?" he laughed, looking up at her. "Well senora, we'll have to do that another day. Right now, I am too tired. If you wish to go, you may." With that, he dropped the halter.

Quickly, Storm wheeled the horse about to escape but he cried out to her and held up Ned's rifle. "You may go but I still have your rifle. You cannot get along without it."

As before, she could not understand one word of what he said but the meaning of the words, coupled with his gestures, was very clear. He had her rifle and she could not get along without it. "Give it to me," she said in Blackfoot. Her tone was filled with anger, "It is mine, give it to me."

"I cannot do that," he answered, in Blackfoot. "If I do, you will shoot me, no?"

He spoke perfect Blackfoot. Storm was surprised and her expression must have shown it.

"Who are you and where do you come from?" she demanded.

He paused, looking into her eyes, "I am Armand Velasquez and I come from a faraway land called Espana." Again, he paused, searching her face for a sign of friendliness. "And who are you?" he queried. "And why are you so angry?" Storm only glared at him and refused to answer.

Seeing her resistance, he asked, "Why don't you climb down from the horse and share some meat with me? I have more than enough in the cook pot for two. You see, I was expecting you." He smiled as he said it. His smile intensified her anger and she suddenly vented the frustration. "I'm not hungry and even if I were, I would not eat with you. I have my own food and I will not take anything from you." Her words did not break his smile and this taunted her all the more. "Why do you have such a silly grin on your face?" she asked. "And who do you think you are coming to my camp in the middle of the night like a cowardly coyote?" She paused for a moment to get her breath. "Now, give me my rifle and let me go."

His smile saddened as he nodded and held up the rifle to her. But before he let go of it, he spoke to her, gently. "I only wanted to be friends with you," he whispered. "And I didn't know another way. I thought a gift might be the best way to begin that friendship. I guess I was wrong. I'm sorry."

Storm snatched the rifle from his hand. For a long moment, she looked at him. Then, in an unwavering voice she said, "If you come again to my camp, I will shoot you." Without answering, he watched her turn the pony to the trail and ride away. It was late in the afternoon when she arrived at her camp. The first thing she did when reaching the camp was to cut the deer down and drag it into the nearby woods. The coyotes could feast on this so-called gift but she would not touch it even if she were starving.

CHAPTER 5:
THE WAR PARTY

Winter had held the land tightly in its frozen grasp but now, the first signs of spring were coming forth. The icy wind that had swept down from the north, bringing with it one blizzard after another, was now tempering its wrath. It still blew, blustery but its breath was not as cold.

Storm grew restless, spending long days inside the wikiup, huddled about the small cook fire. She only ventured outside to tend to the horses or to gather firewood. Because of her increasing girth, she found it ever more difficult to find food. She felt top-heavy and was afraid she would fall and injure the baby. Therefore, the hunting she did was limited to the area near camp. She had managed to shoot and trap some rabbits and birds in the thickets but their numbers seemed to dwindle as the winter worsened. Many nights she had gone to sleep hungry. It crossed her mind that she may have to kill one of the horses in order to survive 'til spring. This she would do, only as a last resort.

She had not seen the stranger again but often wondered if he was still about. Perhaps she had been too hard on him. After all, he had been friendly enough to bring her half of his deer and he had not tried to restrain her when she wanted to leave. And, as she requested, he had not come near her camp again. Sometimes, she wished she had not been so unfriendly to him. It was terribly lonely here and she knew that in the coming months she might need his help.

One morning, Storm was awakened from her sleep by the whinny of a horse. As quickly as she could, she grabbed the rifle and crawled from the wikiup. The morning was cloudless and beautiful and greeted her with its frosty breath. Her lower back ached from the weight of the child and the stiffness of the night. Hunched over, she carefully shuffled along toward the horse corral.

"I feel like an old woman," she mumbled, holding her back with her free hand. Upon reaching the barricade, she saw that the horses were still hobbled. They stood alert, however, with their ears perked on end and their eyes locked on the thicket to the north.

"Be still my friends," she whispered, trying to calm them. "Probably that pack of wolves that's been slinking around here for the last week." She had shot at them once when they caught the scent of the horses and came in too close. She had missed that time but she would not miss again – she would let them get closer.

A slight movement at the edge of the far-off thicket abruptly caught her eye. She strained, rising to her tip-toes and moving her head from side to side to identify it. When he appeared, the rider was like a mirage, materializing from the dense cover. His horse seemed hardly to move and yet he came forward at a surprising rate. "It's him," she muttered, "The stranger! I suppose I should see what he wants and...." The words had scarcely crossed her lips when she saw the other two riders emerge from the same place as the first one. Storm's heart jumped into her throat and she fought to catch her breath. The first man was close enough now that she could see the frightening markings on his face. "A war party," she whispered.

A thought suddenly surfaced in her mind. "If they don't kill me, I'll need the rifle to survive. If they do kill me, it won't matter."

Quickly and without moving, she pitched the rifle into what was left of a deep snowdrift that had blown up against the horse corral. The straps of the powder horn and hunting pouch she slipped from over her head, hurriedly dropping them against the lower logs of the corral. Without taking her eyes from the approaching riders, she kicked snow over the items to hide them.

The Indians approached cautiously, spreading out so as not to make an easy target. The leader, keeping his eye on Storm, motioned for the others to look in the wikiup. Moving to the shelter, they dismounted and went inside. When they were satisfied there was no one else in the camp, they emerged and signaled back to their leader. Without speaking, he nodded and motioned them away. He then gestured with his rifle for Storm to walk back to the shelter. He followed at a close distance.

When she reached the thick hide door of the hut she stopped and turned to face him. In doing so, she clenched her teeth, drew the skin of her forehead tightly back, and lifted her face in defiance, so as not to show the burning fear that was rushing through her.

Seeming unimpressed, he nimbly slid from the horse's back and removed the wolf-hide hat he wore. He was a tall, ugly man with a jutting lower jaw and a thick, bulbous nose. An angry purple scar began just above his right eye and angled sharply downward across his pock-marked cheek, ending near the corner of his lips. His head was shaved on the sides above his ears with only a thick lock of hair growing down the center. At his forehead, the hair was short and stood on end but toward the back of his head, it grew progressively longer and ended in a woven braid which hung well beneath his shoulders. Red, yellow, and black streaks of war paint decorated the man's face and only added to his fearsome ugliness.

Approaching her, he slid the tip of the rifle under the flap of the wikiup and motioned for Storm to enter. She didn't move. He then spoke to her and nodded his head toward the opening. His words were unfamiliar to her and again, she didn't move. Losing his patience, he leaned the rifle against a nearby tree and in one motion, turned and slapped her with the back of his hand, knocking her to the ground. Quickly then, he drew forth his war club and waved it wildly above her head.

"Don't kill me! Don't kill me," she screamed, "I will do as you wish." Painfully, she drew herself up to her knees and crawled into the wikiup.

In the flickering firelight, she watched in horror as he disrobed. She knew what was about to happen and she feared for the small life that grew within her. The man was dressed in a heavy, buffalo-hide coat, leather pants, and knee-length moccasins. He stood over her as he undressed, slowly removing one piece at a time. All the while, he watched her, curiously studying her facial expressions and body language.

When at last he revealed his total body, Storm could see the sinewy muscles of his chest and legs glowing orange in the dim light. His manhood stood in anxious anticipation. Sternly, he motioned for her to undress. The look on his face told her he meant business and she knew he was not above striking her again. She raised up from the robe she had been lying on and removed the heavy coat that had been Ned's. The man watched her, as a hawk watches a field mouse. Eagerly, he waited for her nakedness, each movement she made further aroused him. She too had moccasins and leather pants, all covered by a loose-fitting doeskin dress. When she at last stood naked before him, he reached out and took hold of her arms. In the half-light of the warm dwelling, he slowly drew her towards him. His grip was firm but gentle and it surprised her.

In slow deliberation, he released his grip and moved his hands from her arms to her breasts. Gently, he squeezed and massaged them, teasing the firm nipples that now stood hard and erect. She hated them for betraying her. She wanted to slap him or tear his eyes out or kick him but she knew to refuse him could cost her, her life.

Now, he began to lower one hand from her breast. She knew it would only be a moment before he reached for her crotch. She was about to scream but she was again surprised when he ran his hand around her back and proceeded to lay her down on the soft robe beneath them. Now he was above her. He bent his face toward her and she could feel his hot breath upon her shoulder. As he was about to enter her, he suddenly bumped into her bulging, round belly.

"Whah!" he gasped and backed away. Feeling in the dark, he placed his hand upon her. Quickly, he reached up and pulled the door flap aside. Sunshine came streaming in and he gazed full on at the naked and very pregnant woman trembling before him.

"Ahh!" he shuddered, "Ahhh!" he said again and shook his head. For several minutes, he sat talking to himself, waving his hands about, seemingly asking himself questions, and then shaking his head in what could only be described as self-disgust. Apparently, he had not seen that she was pregnant, what with the heavy coat and the dim light of the wikiup. Storm wondered if he would kill her. She waited.

Suddenly, he grabbed up the doeskin dress and threw it at her, motioning for her to put it on. She didn't hesitate. She quickly pulled it over her head and then set about putting the leather pants back on. As she dressed, he dressed. It took him somewhat longer but when he had finished, he moved the flap full open and stepped outside.

Anxiously waiting his turn, one of the other braves stepped quickly toward the opening of the wikiup.

"No," said the leader. He grabbed the man's arm and turned him away, motioning for him to return to his horse. The man jerked his arm away and an argument quickly ensued. It wasn't long before the other brave came over to join in. They wanted their share of the woman and they would not take no for an answer. Harsh words were exchanged and Storm listened fearfully. It seemed somehow ironic to her, that only moments before she had been cursing the man, praying that he would die. Now, he was the only thing that stood between her and extreme brutality.

Surprisingly, the leader of the small band won over the other two and they all prepared to leave. The other two men were still grumbling, however, when they rode up to where their leader stood, before the wikiup. Storm had not come out. She sat just inside the opening; visible, with the flap up the way it was. The leader turned to her and spoke. She knew not what he said but imagined from the tone of the words and his gestures that he was apologizing. He smiled at her and nodded his head goodbye. Through her fear, she forced a slight smile but drew it back when she saw the others watching her.

As the leader swung up to mount his horse, one of the other men struck him with his war club. The blow caught him solidly above the ear and sent him reeling to the ground.

"YaHaaa!," he cried, leaping from his horse to finish the leader off. With cunning ability, he drew his knife, grabbed a handful of the leader's long braided hair, and attempted to cut his throat. In the struggle, he failed to notice that the leader, in his half-conscious state, had also drawn his knife. When the man rolled him over to finish him, the leader stabbed straight up, plunging the knife in to its hilt, under the man's ribs. Without a sound, the man collapsed and died, falling directly on top of him.

The brave on the horse, seeing what had just happened, quickly cocked his rifle and took aim at his leader, who now struggled to free himself from under the weight of the dead man.

"No," Storm screamed and threw one of the small animal hides that was lying near her at the man's horse. She knew Indian ponies were skittery and would shy away from anything they thought was attacking them. She was right. The horse, hearing her scream and seeing the hairy gray hide fly out of the wikiup, jumped straight in the air and proceeded to buck its rider off. The man's rifle discharged, narrowly missing his leader who still lay in somewhat of a stupor on the ground.

Crashing down on his shoulder, the man had the breath knocked out of him and he was slow to get up. Storm saw her chance. Quickly she dashed to the tree where the leader had leaned his rifle when the men first came to camp. Cocking it, she turned in time to see the man gaining his feet, an empty rifle hanging useless in his hands. In silent disbelief, the man looked at her; a long look that somehow seemed to beg for mercy. It was a wasted emotion, however, and he saw it in her eyes just before he died. Storm, who was no stranger to killing, shot him straight through the heart.

The leader, who had saved her life, now struggled with his own life. The blow that was delivered to the side of his head had split his skull and he was fading fast. Storm managed to get him into the wikiup and tried what she knew to doctor him but he kept slipping in and out of consciousness. Later that night, he stopped breathing.

She cried at his passing and she didn't know why. After all, he'd tried to force himself on her and had she have not been pregnant, he'd have gone through with it. She knew that. She also knew that when he was through with her, the other two would have had their way with her too. Hell, they'd have probably ended up killing her. At that thought, she stopped crying.

She had learned something though from this whole ordeal. Yes! She had learned that lust can turn men against their friends, to the point of killing one another.

"Sex is that important to them," she whispered. "All that fuss for a few moment's pleasure." She shook her head in disbelief.

She also learned that she could not survive in this wilderness alone. She needed help and companionship – especially with the baby coming. Tomorrow, she would search out the stranger and ask for his forgiveness and his help.

CHAPTER 6:
TWINS

At first light, Storm was readying the pony for her journey to the stranger's camp. The horse's long winter coat felt good to her chilled hands. She had not slept well, partly because she was so uncomfortable, but mostly because she hated what she was about to do. "If only I didn't need his help," she muttered, slipping the bridle up over the horse's nose. "I don't need anyone in this life," she muttered once more "Everyone I get to know and love is taken from me......." With that, tears filled her eyes and she thought of Clint, his warm ways, his tender hands. He had been her love and...well, that was over. She harshly wiped the tears from her cheeks and cursed herself for crying. Suddenly, she was taken with a sharp pain. It almost took her to her knees and she felt like throwing up. In a short time, it subsided but it scared her. She had never felt pain like that. She must find the man quickly.

She packed some food and a skin with water in it for the journey. She stood thinking for a moment, deciding if she had everything she needed. "Food, water, powder, balls, knife...yes, it was enough." Now, however, she faced a problem she had not anticipated. It had been some time since she had ridden a horse and, in that time, she had grown much larger in girth. She could not mount the horse. After several minutes of struggling to get up, she finally led the animal to the small coral she'd built, clambered up the stacked logs and slid aboard the pony. Once she had her seat, she wrapped her legs tightly to the horse's sides and knew she could ride. The weight she carried though, made her very uncomfortable as the horse made its way up the draw toward the stranger's camp. Halfway to the top of the hill another sharp pain stabbed at her. She bent over the horse's neck, grabbing its mane with both hands. She wanted to scream but she bit her lip and rode on.

Often, as horses climb, they lunge to gain their footing and can easily unseat a rider. Storm was an excellent horseman but on one of the steep, slippery slopes, the pony stumbled. Trying to keep his footing, he suddenly charged forward. In doing so, Storm lost the hold with her legs and rolled off the back of the horse, crashing to the ground on her left side. It knocked the wind out of her and she thought she was going to die. Many minutes passed before she tried to move. "Oh!" she moaned, trying to sit up. It hurt too badly and she laid back down. "Oh! What am I going to do," she thought, "I'm a long ways from my camp and I can't move. I can't walk, I can't get back on the horse....... But, I've got to do something."

Once more she tried to sit up but could not. She did, however, gain a position that afforded her more comfort. She tried to move again. But this time, instead of trying to sit up, she started to crawl. It worked – she could at least crawl on her hands and knees. She knew she could not make it back to her camp, though. It was too far and she was too weak. Also, she felt funny. Her stomach, the baby, those sharp pains, something, felt out of place. She had done some damage in the fall.

The rifle she had been carrying lay some 15 feet away and she struggled to get to it. Though heavy and cold, it gave her some bit of comfort just holding it. Suddenly, a thought came to her. "I wonder if he could hear a shot? Maybe two or three?" She sat pondering the idea for a long moment. It was worth a try. She aimed the big rifle skyward, tilted it toward the direction of his camp and fired. The boom of its voice filled the small canyon she was in and echoed out across the flat from where she'd come. Quickly, she dumped more powder from the horn into the muzzle of the gun. Without a patch, she started a ball and seated it down with the ramrod. She primed the gun and pulled the trigger. Boom! Again, the deafening roar thundered up and away, disappearing in all directions. Two more times she fired the rifle, using less powder each time to conserve what she had left.

"If the wolves come," she thought, "I should probably save one shot for myself, for I cannot shoot them all and I don't want to be eaten alive." She shuddered at the thought. Once more, she loaded the rifle, aimed it into the air, and was about to shoot.

"Senora, are you hurt?"

The voice startled her so much, she jumped, firing off the rifle. The man had come up from behind her and she tried to roll over to face him. "Oh!" she whimpered, struggling to turn. "Please help me."

He recognized her pain and gently touched her shoulder. Speaking Blackfoot, he whispered "Do not move, woman. I will help you." With those words and his comforting touch, she laid still.

Cutting two long, thin lodge pole pines and cross pieces, it took him no time to construct a travois. "I must ride to your camp to get something to make a pad for the litter," he told her, kneeling at her side. "But I shall come right back."

She took hold of his coat sleeve and pulled him near. "In my shelter, you will find a large beaver skin bag. It contains things I will need for the baby. Please bring it with you."

Within the hour, he returned, carrying the buffalo robe and the beaver skin bag she requested. He laid the robe on the muddy ground next to her. Carefully, he moved her onto it. She helped him as she could and even though she was in pain, did not cry out. Once on the robe, he wrapped it about her and drug the whole thing onto the travois. "I must tie you on here," he said. "That way, you will not fall off. I think you've fallen enough for one day, huh?" He grinned as he said it.

He soon had the travois attached to the pony. He picked up her rifle and the other gear that had spilled out across the ground and lashed them and the bag to the crude framework. Mounted on one horse, he led the other slowly up the draw and across the rim of the low topped hills. Storm was comfortable and warm, wrapped in the buffalo robe and with the swaying of the travois, she soon drifted off to sleep. Something was wrong inside her, however, and she soon came awake with a cry. Another of the sharp pains took hold of her. "Ooooh!"

Hearing this, the man stopped the horses and came to her side. "Are you all right?" he whispered.

"I think it is time for my baby to make his way into the world. Will you help me?"

"Si, Senora," he said, forgetting he was speaking his native tongue. "Uh, yes," he answered in Blackfoot, "I will help you. Can you hold on for a little while longer, as we are nearly to my camp?"

"I cannot," she muttered. "It is time. It is time."

Grabbing his hand, she pulled him near. "You must help me do this – help me get to my feet."

"What?" he answered, "You cannot stand."

"Yes, I can. I must, I will." With that, he quickly untied her and she pulled herself up off the travois. She felt dizzy as she stood and she grabbed his shoulder to steady herself. "Let me see if I can walk," she whispered. She took one step, stopped, swayed forward a little, and took another. Surprisingly, it did not hurt her to walk but she had bad pains in her stomach. At the third step, she felt a sudden gush of warm water rush down both of her legs. "Aaahg!" she moaned, stooping to put her hands on her knees. "Inside the bag, you will find a soft doe-skin and there is another beaver skin in there. Please get them for me." As she tried to move again, she lost her footing and almost fell. He caught her before she hit the ground. As he rolled her over, he saw that she had passed out. He had to get her to his camp. There, he could take care of her.

Effortlessly, he scooped her up into his arms and carried her back to the travois. Lashing her on once more, he made for the camp. This time, he hurried – he had to. When at last he reached his wikiup, he carried her inside. This dwelling was very much like hers only bigger with more hides and skins laid out on the ground. Smoldering embers glowed in the small cook fire that he had left when he heard the shots. "Too many shots, too quickly," he'd thought.

He had heard the woman shoot before and had often watched her from a concealed position, not wanting her to regain her anger and shoot him. He did this because he knew there would come a day when she would need his help. That day was here. But what could he do? He would let nature take its course – somehow that baby would be born whether he helped or not.

Carefully, he laid her down upon a huge buffalo robe. He then threw some wood on the fire and lit two tallow candles to provide more light. As he knelt by her side, Storm cried out in pain and he cradled her in his arms. "Pobrecita!" he whispered, wiping the sweat from her wrinkled forehead. More pain hit and she gritted her teeth and sunk her fingernails into his arm. "Help me," she cried. "Help the baby."

Pulling her dress up, he could see the baby's head. He tried to help but didn't know what to do. Storm grunted and pushed and the baby moved further out. Again, she pushed and again, the baby moved out. "Push again," he said to her, holding her hand. "Push again." He had hold of the baby now and was helping it. "One arm, then the other......that's it now, just get the legs and feet out and.........Wauuuugh!" The baby choked and let out a long squeal. He was so surprised, he nearly dropped it.

His hands were shaking and sweat stood out on his brow but he gently cradled the child and wrapped it in a soft doeskin. "Madre Dios," he sighed. I have not seen the like of this in my whole life. Esta milagro!"

"What is it you say?" Storm asked in a dazed voice.

"I said, it is a miracle," he answered in her tongue. "You have a fine son." He handed the baby to Storm. But just as she took the child in her arms, she tensed and let out another cry of pain. "I think there's another one," she said. "Ooooh!"

And so it went. Within minutes, Storm gave birth to another child. This one was also a boy. With some experience under his belt, Armand knew what to expect and was much more helpful. The second birth seemed to go much easier for both mother and child.

When it was over and the babies were tucked closely to her breast, Storm fell fast asleep. Armand covered them with a soft elk robe and sat near them through the rest of the day and deep into the night, feeding the fire when it threatened to go out. Sometime during that long night, he laid down next to them and drifted off into a welcomed sleep.

Lifting the flap of the wikiup, Armand Velasquez quietly stepped out to meet the coming day. The sky was white and cloudless and the air hung as still as a corpse. Its bite tore at his lungs, causing him to cough violently and hold his hand over his mouth. Some distance away, the hobbled horses searched between the receding patches of snow, feeding on whatever bits of dried grass and humus they could find. A heavy frost had deposited itself on their backs and they almost shimmered as they foraged about. In the dim light, their dark forms were silhouetted against the shiny landscape. He watched them paw and move and paw some more. Their bulk and the steam that blew from their nostrils reminded him of the stories his mother used to read him. Stories about great, fire-breathing dragons and men who rode off on prancing steeds to slay them with lances and swords. He often dreamed of slaying a dragon one day and returning home as a hero.

Yesterday had been a long day. For him it was tough, for the woman, unbearable. He had heard of twins and had once seen twin girls when he was a boy. But, he never dreamed he'd take the part of a midwife at the birth of twins. He was more than happy to have helped this woman out in her time of need but he knew he didn't ever want to do anything like that again if he could help it.

The babies were identical boys and seemed to have fared the ordeal much better than their mother. She had lost a lot of blood and looked very weak and tired in the flickering candlelight. Now, she and the boys were wrapped snugly in the warm elk skin robe and were sleeping peacefully. Armand would have to gather more firewood and more food now that he had guests.

BOOK 4 – BACK TO THE MOUNTAINS

CHAPTER 1:
EMILE TRUDEAU, GREEN, AND A GLIMMER OF HOPE

The trip back to St. Louis was uneventful. Upon their arrival, Clint secured the Old Man in a hotel room and then made his way to the docks along the edge of the river. He made inquiries at the different freight agencies, asking if there were any expeditions or hunting parties heading up the Missouri. He was told that a company of men was being assembled by the Missouri Fur Company to haul supplies up-river to the trappers and outposts far to the north. Heading up that company was a Frenchman named Emile Trudeau. They said he could be found in a riverfront bar called the High Water Pub.

The bar was a dimly-lit, musty place, which smelled of a mixture of river water, burnt tobacco, body odor, and stale beer. The patrons were mostly of French descent and looked to be boatmen by trade. None wore the leather garments of a trapper. Asking of Trudeau's whereabouts, the barkeep motioned Clint toward the back room. There was a lot of noise and laughter coming from the room and it didn't take long to spot Trudeau. He was a large, powerful man with a thick beard and brown curly hair. He had on a heavy, gray woolen shirt - the sleeves of which had been cut off at the armpits. Under it, the arms of his red faded underwear were pushed back just above his elbows. On his left forearm was a tattoo of a naked woman with a snake wrapped about her. His right forearm bore the tattoo of a crucifix and the Lord's name. He wore two gold earrings, one in each ear. The two middle fingers of his right hand were missing.

When Clint first saw him, he was gripping a pint of ale in his left hand, while arm-wrestling another man with his right. From the look on his face, Trudeau seemed to be merely playing with the man, knowing that he could pin him anytime he wanted to. It was a sadistic game and the man writhed in severe agony, feeling the bones in his hand being crushed. The drunken audience was cheering them on and betting wildly – first on one, then on the other. Some favored his opponent but most were betting on Trudeau. The action continued for many minutes, with the frenzied crowd growing louder and louder. Then, as if having grown tired of the game, Trudeau slammed the man's hand down, proclaiming his victory. The man slumped to the floor gripping his injured hand. Everyone cheered and exchanged the money they had bet. Trudeau called for another pint. When things finally settled down, Clint approached the man.

"Excuse me, is your name Trudeau?" Clint began. The man looked at him with a questioning eye but said nothing. "My name's Clinton Jeffries and I was told you were looking for hunters and trappers to hire on for a trip up the river. I have traveled the river before and have knowledge of the country and the Indians who live in the great mountains to the west. In fact, my traveling companion is an Indian. We are both good hunters and trackers and could be of service to you." Again, the man said nothing. Instead, he just stared at Clint, apparently sizing him up.

"Oui, Monsieur, I look for men to go with me on journey up river. But men must be strong and how do you say, dependable......not afraid of hardship, not afraid to fight. Also, we be gone very long time.....one, maybe two years." He then fell silent and again, stared into Clint's face looking for some sign of the man's quality, something that would tell him he might be a man to hire. Clint's calm demeanor, however, offered no clue to his character. He seemed like he'd be alright but Trudeau had to be sure.

"You afraid to fight, Monsieur Jeffries?" Trudeau had a devilish gleam in his eye that Clint hadn't seen there before.

"Was this a test? Probably!" Clint thought. And then he answered. "I don't like to fight, Trudeau, but I've never run away from one yet." There was a noticeable change in the tone of his voice. And, he had looked straight into Trudeau's face while answering. No blink of an eye – no twitch of a nerve.........almost an issued challenge. At least that's how Trudeau saw it.

For a long moment, the two men stared at one another. Then, smiling, Trudeau suddenly said, "Bon! Bon! This is good. We may have room for you."

Clint, wondering what he meant by that, asked, "What do you mean, may have room for me? Either you do or you don't. What's it to be?" Again, he saw the gleam in Trudeau's eye – something was coming.

"I tell you what, Monsieur Jeffries. I want to arm wrestle with you – if you win, you can go with us. But if you lose..............well, too bad. What you say?"

Clint knew there was no way he could beat this man in an arm wrestle but he had no choice. If he wanted to go with this bunch to the mountains he'd have to give it a go.

"Alright," he answered, "if that's the way it has to be." A cheer went up from the crowd and Trudeau smiled......

"You sit there, Monsieur and I will sit here." Trudeau was sitting backwards on the chair and Clint followed suit. He turned the chair around backwards, sat down, and placed his right elbow on the table. Standing a good six foot four inches, Clint was not a small man. But now, as he sat across the table from this Frenchman, he realized how big Trudeau actually was. Probably not any taller, but he had Clint by a good 75 pounds and his neck, shoulders, and arms were massive. When he offered up his hand, Clint thought it more like a paw – a thick, heavy, three-fingered paw.

For a moment, they sat there staring at one another. Then, they clinched their hands together. Trudeau's hand completely enveloped Clint's. His grip was like a vice.

"You say when, Monsieur," Trudeau said grinning.

Clint's only chance was to catch him off guard if that were possible. "Now!" Clint yelled as he put everything he had into the challenge. The big man's arm hardly moved. He just sat there grinning....grinning and gripping. Tighter and tighter his grip became. The missing digits of Trudeau's hand only served to add to the power that was slowly crushing Clint's hand. It was obvious that Trudeau had no intension of ending this thing quickly. Instead, he wanted to break Clint's hand and fingers as he had the other man; wanted to hear him cry out for mercy.

Remembering the heavy knife he kept in his belt, Clint took hold of the elk horn handle with his left hand. Then, quick as a cat, he brought the knife up and slammed the butt of it into Trudeau's forehead, just between his eyes. At the same time, he yanked his hand away from Trudeau's. For a moment, the big man just sat there, not knowing what had hit him. The menacing grin on his face was still there but now the corners of his mouth were beginning to sag and a dribble of spit ran down his beard. A bright reddish-purple circle began to form on Trudeau's forehead and, as if in slow motion, the big man slumped forward. He was out cold.

The group of men around them suddenly became very quiet. Their compatriot was down and they were not happy. Two of them then made a move toward Clint and he flashed the knife near their faces in a cutting motion.

"Do you want some of this too?" he whispered, again waving the knife in front of them. Apparently, no one did because they backed off and gave him space.

"When he wakes up, you tell him he can find me at the Riverside Hotel. I'd be happy to go with him up river if he still needs me." With that, he slowly backed out of the bar. Stepping into the street, he ran as fast as he could back to the hotel. There was no telling what those boys might do if they got together and came after him. Liquor does funny things to men when they've had too much.

#

Two days went by and there was still no word from Trudeau. Clint and the Old Man were just walking out of the hotel that afternoon when one of Trudeau's men showed up. They met him at the doorway. Clint didn't remember the man but the man certainly knew who he was.

"Monsieur Jeffries?" he began. "I've brought word from Monsieur Trudeau that he would be pleased if you would join us on our trip up the Missouri. He wanted me to tell you there are no hard feelings – he was drunk and he apologizes."

"What do you think?" he asked the Old Man in Flathead. "Can we trust this Frenchman?"

The Old Man thought about it for a moment, then answered. "He may not be one to be trusted – he may want revenge for what you did. But we have no other way to get to where we want to go. The two of us alone would never make it to the headwaters of the river. So, I say we go with them and we watch them like a hawk." With that, Clint told the man they would go with them.

"Bon," the man replied. "We leave at sunrise three days from now. Don't be late or we go without you."

#

There was a total of fifty five men hired by the freight company to make the journey. Most were French boatmen. Some were of Spanish descent, while others were a mixture of rag-tag beggars and half-breeds. One man was a black – his name was Charles White. Most of the men were assigned to poling and pulling (when necessary) the four large keel boats that held the supplies. There was also a small herd of about thirty tethered horses traveling along the shoreline, adjacent to the boats. Most often, however, they would get out ahead some distance since the boats made such slow headway. Two Spaniards and the black man, Charles, were responsible for taking care of the horses. Trudeau was the leader of the group.

Besides Clint and the Old Man, there were two other hunters aboard. One was a half-breed named Lame Dog. It seems he had been born with one deformed foot, hence the name. Mostly, the men just called him Crip, short for Cripple – he didn't seem to mind. From the looks of him and the way he handled himself, Crip had had plenty of experience in the wilderness. He knew how to track and could read sign as well as any mountain man Clint had ever known. Also, he was a crack shot and accounted for many of the animals that fed the company along their journey.

The other hunter in the group was a strapping young man named Eldon Foster. Foster had spent most of his young life in the colonies back east and was not wise to the ways of the frontier. Although he was a good shot and was a friendly sort, he often did things that were dangerous and that could get a man killed in this wild country. One thing he did that was particularly dangerous was riding off alone and not telling anyone where he was going. This he did often.

Clint tried to explain the dangers that lurked and the need to be cautious when one was out and about looking for game but the young man could not see it. He would listen intently as though heeding every word Clint said and then go right out and do something stupid. It was only a matter of time until it would catch up with him.

#

One morning as Clint and the other hunters were preparing to leave the boats for a day of hunting one of the crew began to holler and point upriver. Clint couldn't make out what the Frenchman said but he knew something was up. Walking toward the ruckus, he looked across the river to see two keel boats, riding the downstream current and heading straight for them. Trudeau stood waving his arms and shouting "Welcome, Mon Amis, welcome." As the boats drifted nearer, Clint thought he recognized an old friend standing atop the deck of the lead boat. Turning quickly to the other two hunters, Clint shouted, "Crip! You and Foster go on ahead without me and the Old Man. We'll be along directly but right now, I need to meet up with an old friend. "

"Green, is that you?" Clint shouted at the approaching boat. The man on the deck heard his voice and stared at him in stunned disbelief. For a moment, he just stood there without answering. Then, he motioned for the boatmen to make for the shore and come up near the moored boats.

"Well, I'm a son-of-a-bitch," were the first words he uttered. And then he followed with, "I can't believe my eyes. I...I thought you were dead. They told me you were....dead."

"Well, they told you wrong, hoss. It's me, alright." Clint was grinning from ear-to-ear and making his way toward where the keel boat would come ashore. Green didn't wait for the deck hands to tie off the boat. Instead he jumped from the deck into the knee-deep water at the river's edge and made his way ashore.

"Damn, it's good to see you brother." he shouted, throwing his arms around his longtime friend. "Didn't think I'd ever see you again. What are doing with this bunch?"

Clint smiled at the man and answered, "I wanted to get back to the mountains so I hired on as a guide and a hunter." With that he paused a moment then asked, "By the way, who's been spreadin' these tales about me goin' under?"

Smiling, Green slapped him on the shoulder. "Let me get my boats tied off and the men settled and then we'll talk. I've also got a couple of things I need to tell Trudeau. I won't be but a minute or two."

When Green returned, the two men sat and talked about what had happened since the last time they'd met. Green began, "I know you're wonderin' why the hell I acted the way I did and said those things about you dying. But son, I really thought you'd been killed." He paused for a moment and reached down, picking up a small twig from the ground. With it, he drew small circles in the dirt and continued to speak. "The morning after you left, two men from my crew took one of the dugouts and headed downstream. They slipped away during the morning meal, when everyone else was eating. One of the sentries saw them go but didn't think it was anything unusual. When I asked some of the others what happened they said they'd heard the two men talking about your gold and how they'd be mighty well-off if they could get their hands on it."

Clint remembered the two men and what had happened there in the darkness that night. But most of all he remembered the fear that had gripped him then, the sudden, blinding flash of rifle fire, the smell of gunpowder, the sound of a man with his throat cut thrashing about in the bottom of a dugout boat. Yes, all these things came to him in an instant but he said nothing.

Green had again paused but now went on, "I know you can take care of yourself but I was fearful for what those men might do. So, I sent two of my crew to find you and help you if they could. They came back some days later saying they had found a dead man lying in the dugout that you'd taken; the boat was wedged in a log jam down near the big bend. They said the buzzards and other critters had been at the body for some time and it was torn apart, not recognizable. They assumed it was you. They buried the remains on the shoreline and brought back the boat. I figured that was it, they'd robbed and killed you and went on downriver to St. Lou. That's why I acted the way I did.........sorry." Green looked up then to see what response Clint would offer.

He started slow, almost reluctantly. "Yeah, they came at me in the dark, after I'd laid down to sleep. Lucky for me they were not careful to be more quiet or things might have gone different. I shot one of them and ..."

Green could see the torment in Clint's eyes as he spoke and decided that what had happened was over and needn't be spoken of again.

"Hey!" Green interrupted, "I'm just glad to see you and know that you came through it all unhurt. The rest don't matter anyway." With that, he slapped Clint on the knee.

"C'mon! I've got some whiskey on board I've been savin'."

As they walked along the shore, Green suddenly remembered something else. "Say Clint, I almost forgot to tell you. Right after my men came back with that boat, we met up with this big feller; strong lookin' he was; had two Indian women with him. He was askin' if we'd seen you."

Upon hearing this, Clint stopped, grabbing Green by the shoulder. "Where'd they go?" he asked with an almost wild tone to his voice.

"Well, they went on upriver some distance and about two weeks after we lost sight of 'em, we had one hell-of-a run in with them people."

"What do you mean by that," Clint asked. "What happened?"

Green could see the immediate concern in the young man's face. "We were runnin' low on meat and I sent a bunch of my men out to scout around and fetch us up some deer or buffler. They didn't find much meat but they did run onto that feller and his wives." Green paused, taking a swig of the whiskey. He offered the jug to Clint and then went on.

"Bein' as how they hadn't seen a woman for many months, they were all ready to breed. I guess they slipped up on 'em in the brush and grabbed 'em while the man was away from camp. Went at 'em like a twin-peckered Billy goat, I guess. Raped 'em both - over and over again."

Clint couldn't believe what he was hearing. "Jesus, man! Where were you when all this was goin' on?" A tone of blame came through on his voice.

"Why, I was uh, steering the boat, a ways downriver." He answered, almost apologetically. "I did hear the shootin', however."

"There was shootin'?" Clint queried.

"Yeah! Two of my men were killed and another one was wounded." Green took another sip of the whiskey, savoring the burn of it. Then, he went on. "When I asked what had happened, they didn't want to talk much about it but I persuaded them. Seems like the big feller came back to camp and caught 'em having their way with his women. Chased 'em back down river, killin' 'em as they ran." Again, Green paused. "And," he continued, "If that wasn't enough, the crazy bastard laid in wait for us, attacking and killing five more of my men as they were pulling the boat upstream. One of 'em stuck a knife in him though and finished him off. We went ashore to..."

Before Green could finish his statement, Clint anxiously interrupted, "What about the women? What happened to them?"

Green stared at him a long moment before answering. "Well, as I was sayin', we went ashore as quickly as we could to see what the hell had happened. That's when we found what was left of my men and him. There was no sign of the women anywhere. We figured they must have skedaddled when the killin' started."

"Where'd all this take place?" Again, Clint's voice seemed anxious.

"We first met up with those folks near where the Platte runs into the big river. Had dinner with 'em and all. That's where the men got their first look at the women. It was hard to hold 'em back then." He paused a moment, remembering, seeming to run the events through his mind once more, so as not to miss anything. When he spoke again, his voice was more subdued, sensing somehow that these people had meant a great deal to Clint. "It was a good long way above where the rivers join that it all took place. We hadn't seen them in over two weeks; thought they'd gone their own way. I sent hunters out on both banks to see if they could scare up some game. It was one of those parties that came across the women. You know the rest."

Clint sat in silence, staring at nothing, letting the story roll around in his head. It was hard to believe that Storm could still be alive. All this while, he'd thought she was dead. He knew though, that even if she had escaped the wrath of the boat crew, it would be hard for her and her sister to survive in this harsh country. But, she was alive or at least there was some glimmer of hope that she had lived. His thoughts were suddenly interrupted by Green's voice.

"I'm sorry about what happened, Clint. I always try to keep my men in line but it's often an impossible task; especially when they're ashore, out of my sight. They are a wild bunch and they could be doing anything and I wouldn't know it."

Silently, Clint shook his head in agreement with his old friend. "No hard feelings, Green. You're a good man and I know you'd have done what you could to keep this from happening." With that, he shook Green's hand in friendship. Green smiled and nodded. Nothing more was said.

After saying goodbye to his old friend, Clint and the Old Man rode out to join the rest of the hunting party. As they rode, Clint relayed to the Old Man, the story he'd been told, emphasizing the possibility that the women could still be alive. The Old Man listened intently to his young friend and then quietly smiled to himself. A change had come over his young companion, something in his voice, an excitement, an urge, told the Old Man that a darkness had been lifted from his spirit. He continued to smile as they rode on.

CHAPTER 2:
BEARS AND INJUNS

In the weeks that followed, Clint was very unsettled. He wanted to reach the Platte River, the place where he had last seen Storm. He knew that above that confluence was where he would start looking for signs that she had been there. Because of the run-off from the melting snows in the mountains, the river was running high and carrying a lot of debris. The crews on the keel boats had to continually watch for logs and brush, steering away from them if possible. Hence, the boats moved at a snail's pace, not making more than a few miles a day.

Each day, the hunters went far-afield to provide what meat they could for the party. It was understood that Clint would hunt with the Old Man and Foster would hunt with Crip. Each group would head in a different direction, so as to cover more of the country.

Here and there they encountered a few deer or an occasional buffalo but for the most part, game was scarce. They hadn't seen any Indians nor had they come across any recent sign that they might be about. But with the lack of game, they surmised that someone or something had either killed or chased it off. There should be more animals holding in the brushy draws this near the river.

One morning as they were preparing to head out, Foster was complaining that he was tired of hunting with Crip. His reason was that Crip was too careful and would not venture out far enough to find game. In his words, Crip was, "afeared of gettin' his hair lifted." This was an all-out insult, an accusation that Crip was some kind of a coward and it did not set well with him. Crip came about sharply, his hand on the knife in his belt. Seeing this, Clint quickly stepped between the men, pushing them both back.

"Hey now; that's enough. Just back off!" His voice was stern and he tried to keep it down and out of earshot of the boatmen. "We don't need this kind of trouble."

Motioning to the Old Man, he grunted something and gave a quick sign. The Old Man nodded and touched Foster on the shoulder, instructing him to follow. Foster wasn't sure he wanted to do that. He was a little afraid of the old Indian and he couldn't hardly understand what he said or meant. Clint saw the hesitance in his eye and quickly settled the matter.

"You go with the Old Man today, Foster. I'll take Crip with me. Tomorrow we can change up."

Before climbing on his horse, Clint cast one more hard glance at the youngster. "You listen to what he tells you and you'll stay alive. And remember, if you pull any of your dumb-ass stunts and get him hurt or killed, I'll do the same to you." He paused for a long moment, not losing eye contact, and then added, "I mean it, damn it!"

Today, they would hunt the east side of the river. Clint told the Old Man and Foster to hunt upstream until the sun was directly above them. Then, he wanted them to turn to the east. He said that he and Crip would head due east and then break back to the north some and try to meet up with them. If they had no luck today, they would have to stay out until they did, being as how the party was so low on meat. Everyone understood the plan and the two groups rode off in the morning darkness.

Just after sunrise, Crip spotted a small deer. The animal saw him at the same moment and bolted away into a thicket of dense brush. Crip gave a sharp whistle, getting Clint's attention.

"He went in there." Crip mouthed the words and pointed to the thicket. Clint saw what he meant and motioned back that he would circle out around the thicket while Crip went ahead to run the critter out.

All went as planned and when the frightened deer bolted from the brush, a well-placed shot dropped it in its tracks. Clint had ridden up to the animal and was reloading his rifle when Crip came out of the brush.

"Nice shot," he said, then added, "I think there was another one in there with it. I heard it go off that way." I'm gonna swing back through there and see if I can get a crack at it. Then, I'll work back to where my horse is." Clint nodded in agreement and began to dress out the deer.

The heavy brush within the thicket made it difficult to get through. Because of his game leg, it was doubly difficult for Crip. He'd try to walk and the brush would snag his feet and legs. Deer could run through this stuff easily and quietly but he sounded like a herd of buffalo crashing around. Deciding to give it up, he looked for the easiest way out. Off to his right was a small clearing that lay some 20 yards away. The brush wasn't as thick that way. As he approached it, he noticed a brown clump lying in a shallow swale among the weeds and grass. He stopped for a moment, trying to make out what it was. He couldn't tell. At his next step, the brown clump raised up, revealing a huge head with beady eyes and a blocky snout.

"Holy Mother of Christ," he whispered and slowly began backing away. At the first sign of his retreat, the bear was up and running toward him. He knew he couldn't get away and it would only enrage the animal if he shot and wounded it. So, with determined resolve, he decided to stand his ground. He pulled his knife and stood as tall as his puny frame would allow him. Then, he took a deep breath. The bear snorted as it quickly closed the distance between them.

Crip knew it would probably raise up just before it struck him – bears usually did that. And, that's just what it did. He looked steadily into the monster's face and saw the yellowed teeth open and then snap together, issuing their warning. Drops of frothy saliva glistened at the corners of it jowls as it raised up, not five feet from him.

Then, with his hair standing on end, Crip leaped toward the bear, raised his arms as though to tear into it, and let go the loudest growl he could muster. "Aarrrrrrrrrgh," he roared. "Aaaarrrrrrgh!" At the same time, he stuck his chin forward, opened his mouth, baring his teeth. The veins on his forehead and down the sides of his neck stood out like little ridges.

His movement was so sudden and his growl so intense, that it took the bear completely by surprise. Stopping in mid-charge, it just stood there staring. Then, it began backing away. Crip again jumped toward it and let loose another horrifying roar, "Aaaarrrrgh!" That was enough for the bear. In one quick motion, it whirled and disappeared into the thick underbrush.

Crip was sitting with his head in his hands, rocking gently back and forth, when Clint came running up. "What the hell was all that noise? Sounded like a gad-danged demon about to eat somebody up."

Crip, looking like he'd seen a ghost, just rolled his eyes and shook his head. "You dunno how right you are, brother" he sighed. "You just don't know."

#

Later on that day, the two pairs of men met up as they had planned. Clint and Crip had managed to kill one more deer but didn't see anything else in the way of game. The Old Man and Foster had heard animals running in the brush along the river but hadn't been able to get a shot. The Old Man had shot a turkey though. It would be their dinner.

"So where do we go from here?" Foster asked. And without waiting for anyone to answer, added, "We probably should go back and hunt the west side of the river again. At least we saw a few critters over there."

No one said anything. For a few long minutes, the men surveyed the country about them, not knowing which way they might encounter game. Some brush-covered, hilly mounts to the north looked to be the best prospect.

"Maybe Foster's right," Crip said. "It seemed better on that side the last time we hunted."

Again, nobody spoke.

"Tell you what," Clint said, breaking the silence. "Crip, you take these deer back to the boats and butcher them. Meanwhile, the three of us will venture off toward those hills there and see if we can scare somethin' up. It'll be dark by the time you get back to the boats so you can get a night's rest and come meet up with us tomorrow."

Crip nodded his understanding and rode off with the pack horse in tow. The rest of them rode toward the low hills. Clint led the way with Foster close behind. The Old Man brought up the rear. Now and then, he would swing wide of the other two, working in and out of the small draws they encountered.

Three hours had passed since they'd said goodbye to Crip. Now, the sun was sinking in the west, creating long shadows behind the brush and trees. The Old Man had disappeared into one of the side draws and had been gone for some time. Clint reined his horse in and scanned the hillsides for signs of his old friend.

"What are we lookin' for?" Foster asked, seeming not to know that the Old Man had ridden off and was not behind him. Clint didn't answer but kept staring at the last place he'd seen him. He was about to ride over to the draw when he saw the Old Man appear. However, there was something unusual about the way he came on. He was usually unhurried, calm, and deliberate when he rode. But now, he came toward them at a much faster pace, hurrying. Clint had known him long enough to know that something was up. He watched the Old Man carefully and at the same time readied his rifle.

The Old Man didn't stop as he passed them. He only gave a small grunt and a nod, which to Clint meant, "Follow me....and hurry." Foster didn't pick up on it but when Clint spurred his horse to follow the Old Man, Foster did too. The Old Man led them toward the river, back to the west. Hurriedly, he made his way along a small ridge that had steep draws running down each side. The ridge was fairly flat along its top with heavy clumps of brush and small trees.

When they'd ridden for a good ten minutes, the Old Man swung his horse in behind a clump of thick oak and dismounted. "What is it?" Clint asked using sign language. The Old Man answered, saying he'd seen fresh sign of a hunting party. "Maybe eight or ten of them and I think they may have seen us."

"What the hell's goin' on here?" Foster blurted out. "What is it, Injuns – Jesus...are we..."

"Shhh!" Clint whispered. "Be quiet and listen!"

For a while, everything was dead still, no sounds except now and then the call of a robin or the squawk of a jay. But then, slightly behind them and in the draw to their left came a "clunk," the sound of a horse's hoof hitting a rock.

"They know we're here," Clint whispered climbing aboard his horse. "Let's high-tail it for the river and see if we can lose 'em on the way."

No sooner had they begun to gallop away when a blood-curdling war hoop rang out. At the same moment, an arrow sailed over Foster's right shoulder narrowly missing his face.

He spurred his horse on ever faster. The ridge they rode on was beginning to dwindle out, running down into what looked to be a mess of draws, all coming together. The brush in them was thick and hard to get between. It wasn't long before the men had to dismount and lead the horses on foot. Behind them they could hear the Indians doing the same thing.

"Shit man!" Foster let out, "they're right behind us – we're gonna lose our hair."

"Will you shut up?" Clint retorted. "They gotta catch us first. It'll be dark soon and we can give 'em the slip; get back to the river and swim fer the boats."

The chase went on. The white men would find a clear path to ride and they'd take off. Then, the Indians would find the same path and they'd take off after them. This went on until it was too dark to ride. The afternoon had become heavily overcast and now, it made the early evening just that much darker.

Clint and the Old Man began to notice the country now was beginning to fall away in front of them. This could only mean that they were approaching the river. Now, the brush and trees would really become thick again. Once more, they dismounted and led their horses through the entanglement. They were now encountering big logs and trees that the river had carried and deposited during past high-water years. Big snags were everywhere and it was becoming impossible to go any further. The Indians were still pressing them and they, too, were having trouble.

"We gotta leave the horses and go on," Clint whispered. "Get yer possibles off and let 'em go. We'll try to find 'em later." With that, they turned the horses out. On foot, they made for the water's edge. Another fifty yards or so found them wading in water amongst the willows and brush. It was here they came to a large cottonwood that had washed down from somewhere up-river.

"This is as good a place to make a stand as any," Clint whispered. Motioning, he went on, "Foster, you get over there and don't shoot until you absolutely know what you're shootin' at." The Old Man moved some distance along the log, away from Foster. Clint left the two of them and moved back into the brush, toward the river.

Seeing Clint begin to move away, Foster piped up, "Where the hell are you goin'?"

"I'm gonna find us a ride back to camp," he answered and disappeared into the maze of willows.

The evening light was all but gone now. It was hard to make out anything more than ten yards in front of them. The men could hear the Indians stirring in the brush in front of them but the sounds left little to aim for. Foster was nervous and flinched at every little sound. The Old Man tried to calm him. "Shh," he whispered, moving his hand up and down. "You wait, look, make sure...."

The stillness of the night was then broken. "Sssss - thunk". The arrow stuck in the log right in front of Foster.

"Jesus," he hollered and fired into the blackness. The sound of the gunshot was deafening and the flash was so bright, it blinded him and the Old Man. They couldn't see anything. Quickly, he began to reload, feeling for his powder horn. Two more arrows came in, one hit the log and the other whizzed over their heads. Then came the sudden sound of splashing feet - many feet - running towards them. The Indians were charging toward the log, apparently thinking the darkness would conceal them until they were on top of the white men. The Old Man leveled his rifle toward the footsteps and fired. A blood-curdling scream rang out accompanied by the sound of a body splashing into the shallow water. More feet pounded toward them.

The first one to cross over the log was met with the Old Man's rifle barrel across the skull. Foster had his belt pistol in hand and shot another that was only inches from being on top of him. One of them came around the root end of the tree, attempting to get at the two men from the side. Clint, coming back from the river, met him head on in the darkness. The two men grappled with one another and were soon down in the water, flailing about with knives and hatchets. Foster had finished loading his rifle now and sent another round into the darkness, at the on-coming horde. Apparently, that last shot was enough to make them change their minds because the footsteps were now going the other way.

Clint finally got the best of the Indian but not before getting stabbed in the top part of his arm. Disregarding the burning knife wound, he quickly gathered the other two men and made for the river.

"I found another log that should float the three of us outta here," he whispered as they hurried. "We gotta get gone 'fore those bastards realize we've beat it."

The water was deeper now, nearly up to their waists. Clint led them to a beached log he'd found and the three of them pried it loose from the mud. Pushing it into deeper water, it was now afloat and they kicked for all they were worth to move it into the strong current.

"Hang tight, boys," Clint warned, "And don't lose yer rifles."

The power of the river was awesome. It carried the log and the three men along at a fast pace, swirling and turning them about at its will. There was no moon and the night was pitch black.

"Hey Clint! How far you reckon we gotta go 'til we get to the boats?" Foster asked.

Clint thought for a moment then answered, "It's quite some distance I'm thinkin'. Hell, we were a good day's ride to where we were huntin'." Pausing briefly, he went on, "This river's movin' along but it ain't that fast and I don't think we're gonna be able to stay in this water that long. It's too damn cold. We may have to swim for it before long."

The night wore on and the men could feel themselves getting colder by the minute. Once in a while, they caught glimpses of trees along the shoreline and they quickly realized the current had taken them nearer the other shore.

"I don't know about you two but I'm freezin'," Clint whispered. "My legs are goin' numb. Let's all get to one side of this log and see if we can swim it toward shore. We gotta get outta this water."

The struggle to get the log closer to shore warmed them a bit and they felt some of their strength returning. When it looked as though they could make it, the men let go of the log and made for shore. It was rough going, trying to swim with a twelve-pound rifle in your hand and your possibles bag around your neck. But each of them would rather have drowned than lose those precious items. For without them, one wouldn't survive long.

When they at last waded ashore, they realized this bank was no different than the one they'd abandoned upstream. It was muddy, sticky, and strewn with dead logs, clumps of willows, and other such debris. It seemed like an eternity before they found themselves on dry ground.

"TTThink we dare bbuild a ffffire?" Foster asked, his teeth chattering, wildly.

"Yeah!" Clint answered. "But let's get back away from the river some, so's we've got some deep cover. We need to dry these rifles out too in case we have any more visitors."

The sun was high above the eastern horizon when the men finally awoke. It had been a cold, wet night but they had each managed to drift off and get some sleep. They traveled downstream, looking to meet up with the boats, stopping only to kill and cook two willow grouse and a hare that they happened upon. The sun was high overhead when they finally caught sight of the boats.

From atop a low hill, overlooking the river, Clint fired a shot in the air. "Hello, the boat," he cried, waving both hands over his head. The lookouts saw him and it wasn't long before one of the dugouts was on its way to get them.

When the boat arrived, Clint told Foster to go back and tell Trudeau what had happened. Also, he was to get more powder and ball and then return with Crip. He said they'd hunt this shoreline today.

While they waited for the other two hunters to return, Clint and the Old Man scouted up the herd of horses that was brought along to service the company. Three men herded the horses and brought them along as the boat moved upstream. Because they could make better time, the horses were usually somewhat ahead of the boats. That's where Clint and the Old Man figured they would be and that's where they found them. The herders were not happy when they found out that four of the horses had been abandoned in the skirmish with the Indians. Clint explained what happened and said he was sorry and that tomorrow, he'd go look for them. With that, the herders cut out six head for them.

Crip and Foster were waiting for them when they returned. Two of the horses had pack saddles on them and the other four were for riding – the men rode them bareback.

Today, they would try again to bring meat to the camp. Such was the life of the company hunters.

CHAPTER 3:
WINTERIN' WITH THE MANDANS

When the group finally passed the confluence where the Platte ran into the big river, Clint insisted that they hunt only on the west bank. He told Trudeau and the others that the hunting was better on this side of the river and that they would encounter many more buffalo. What he said was true but the Old Man knew the real reason. It had long black hair, dark eyes, and went by the name of Storm. Clint had spoken of her so often that the Old Man thought he'd recognize her if they were ever to meet. He understood Clint's feelings and did not question him when he wanted to scout far ahead of the party. He knew that the young man was searching for any sign that the woman had passed this way.

In their ventures afield, they often ran into small villages. Most were not hostile and were willing to trade furs or horses for the "foofaraw" that the white men brought up-river. A man could get five beaver pelts for one good skinning knife and a few tins of vermilion. They would also offer up their women for such gifts as beads and trinkets. A man could lay up with a squaw if he had a small mirror or a few needles to trade. It was in these matters that a lot of the trouble between the Indians and the boat party occurred. Someone would renege on a trade or a boatman would beat up the woman and there would be trouble. Most of the trouble, however, centered around whiskey.

Indians didn't do well with whiskey. They loved it but it drove them crazy. When white men drank, they mostly would get happy and pass out but with the Indians, it was different. They'd drink and then they'd turn into wild men. They'd give away everything they had for a taste of hard liquor. They'd kill for it. It was sad to see and so Clint and the Old Man avoided the "tradin' days" as they were called.

Clint always managed, however, to sit down with some of the members of the tribe and ask if they had encountered a woman or two women traveling alone. Saying that "......these women come from the mountains far to the north and west and do not speak the language of the plains tribes."

But ask as he might, none of the people had seen anyone like that. Many of them said that two women alone would be easy prey for wild animals or raiding war parties; that they would be killed or taken and used as slaves. The answers were not what he wanted to hear but Clint had to ask. He had to know and he had to find her, if possible.

#

Winter was coming on fast when the party arrived at the Mandan Village. The Mandans were brothers to the Sioux but were more peaceful. Their village was located right on the banks of the river. It was huge, with what appeared to be very large mud huts. Fields of corn and other crops, long past harvested, grew at the edges of the village, seeming to surround it. Several people ran from the huts to greet the keel boats as they made shore. As usual, Trudeau was the first one off the boat and the first to make contact. He always carried gifts for those who came to meet him. As the word spread through the village, more and more people came to see the spectacle.

Clint and the Old Man didn't rush to get off their boat but rather stood watching the gathering crowd. The people seemed friendly enough but at the same time, there was an edge to their demeanor that did not go unnoticed.

"What do you think about this?" Clint said, never taking his eyes off the swarming crowd.

"It appears there is a feeling of mistrust here," the Old Man answered. "Apparently, they have dealt with white men before."

Clint's was the second boat to make land and as he and the Old Man clambered ashore, members of the tribe quickly pushed in around them. They seemed to be sizing up the white men, examining them – particularly the weapons they carried. Hard were the looks they gave the Old Man. Many whispered among themselves as they pointed at him, sneering and shaking their heads.

"What's that all about?" Clint whispered to him.

"I do not recognize this tongue but I would believe they are not trusting of me, being with white men."

Clint paused a moment and then shot the Old Man a sly grin. "Well, you can't be friends to everybody, I guess." The Old Man just smiled and grunted.

Pushing through the crowd, they made their way toward Trudeau and the other boatmen that had brought more gifts ashore. Trudeau was calling for him and the Old Man to come quickly. He wanted them to interpret what they were saying to him and relate back to them what he said.

A blanket had been hurriedly spread out on the ground and Trudeau was motioning to some of the elders of the tribe to sit and join him. One among them stood out from the rest. He didn't look a whole lot different from the others, but the way he carried himself and the reverence the others paid to him told Clint this must be the Chief. Indeed, it was the Chief, Ma-to-toh-pe or Four Bears as he was called in English.

As Trudeau spoke, the Old Man (who understood English fairly well but had a hard time speaking it) signed his words. When the Chief would answer, the Old Man would speak in his tongue to Clint, who would then tell it to Trudeau. This presented a roundabout way of communicating but it seemed to work.

After formal introduction and the "welcome" talk. Trudeau told them that he planned to go up the big river to the tall mountains in the west. There, he would trade his goods for furs and bring them back down the river to the white villages far away. Four Bears seemed to understand what he meant, saying that many French trappers had traded with them in the past and that they welcomed their white brothers.

Trudeau also said there would soon be ice floating in the river and that he could not go onward with the boats – that he would have to camp somewhere near them until spring. He went on to say that his group would trade with them through the winter for any fur or food that they brought in. With that, the mood of the village seemed to ease somewhat.

In the discussions, the Chief indicated that other travelers had spent the winter at a camp spot across the river and north of where they now stood. He motioned in that direction as he spoke, saying they were welcome to use that area. He also told them that other tribes, the Hidatsa and the Arikaras, lived very near. The Hidatsa, he said, were peaceful and would probably be willing to trade with them. He wasn't so sure about the Arikaras. It seemed that the Mandans and the Arikaras had, for a long time, been hostile toward each other. It wasn't an all-out war between them but now and then acts of violence did occur.

So it was then, that the Trudeau Party settled in to winter on the banks of the great river.

#

Shortly after their arrival at the winter camp, Clint and the Old Man began visiting the Mandan and Hidatsa, trading beads, knives, mirrors, and other such goods. As they mingled among the people, Clint would ask if any of them had seen or heard of one or perhaps two women who had, some time ago, passed this way, heading up-river. The answer was always no. Clint wanted to go to the Arikaras camp and ask them about

Storm, but because of what the chief had told them, he decided it was best not to.

As the winter deepened, the river froze completely over, allowing the men to cross with ease. Hunting parties made up of both trappers and Indians often went out together in search of game. Mostly, they would bring back buffalo or deer. Sometimes, they would bring in ducks, geese, and other such fowl.

Clint didn't enjoy hunting in large groups. He rather preferred to go with the Old Man. Sometimes, Crip or Foster accompanied them. And so, it was on one particular day that the four of them struck out across the river, heading west. They left camp in the dark, walking their horses so as not to alarm the other men. They had ridden for over an hour before the first hint of daylight showed in the east.

The morning light was slow to emerge as it struggled against the dark, low-hanging clouds that now threatened snow. With the overcast sky, the temperature had warmed some but the light breeze that scuttled up from the south chilled the air and made the ride most uncomfortable. Steam blew from the horses' nostrils with each breath they exhaled. Foster tugged at the collar of his coat, pulling it up tightly around his ears.

Upstream from their camp, the river made a wide turn, swinging from a northward direction to a more westerly one. Clint usually crossed the river and headed more to the south where he had had some success killing buffalo. Today, however, he led them on a path that followed the river west for several miles. After scanning the surrounding area, he motioned them to cross back over the river toward the north. Here, lay a short stretch of open prairie and just beyond that, some stunted, scrubby hills, which appeared to have some sort of vegetation growing on and about them – a likely place to locate game, Clint thought.

Coming nearer the hills, the men dismounted and scanned the area ahead for any movement. It felt good to get off the horses and hunker down closer to the ground, somewhat evading the wind that blew steady at their backs.

"What do you think?" Clint asked, without looking at the others.

"I'm cold!" Foster answered.

"There could be critters tucked in amongst that brush in the draws." He pointed, wagging his finger back and paying no attention to what Foster had just said.

"Could be," Crip answered, wiping a drop from the end of his runny nose. "Only one way to find out, though," he added, "and that's to go have a look see."

"Think we can build a fire when we get over there?" Foster asked, ending his question with a shiver. Well, he had asked the question but he already knew the answer – they would build a fire after they'd killed some game and not before.

"Crip, you go with the Old Man, head to the west for a piece and then ride for the top of those hills. Me and Foster will go east and then cut back toward the hills. Once yer up there, ride towards us and we'll do the same with you. Maybe we can drive somethin' up and ketch it between us."

Crip nodded and with that, he and the Old Man turned their horses and rode off. Clint and Foster turned the opposite direction and made their way to the east, riding single file through the sparse trees and broken brush. They hadn't ridden but three hundred yards when they came to a sharp drop-off, going down maybe twenty feet. It was the edge of a rather wide arroyo that had been caused by flooding water.

"Whoa, girl!" Clint whispered to his horse, pulling her up sharp.

"We'll have to find a place to get through this," he said, leaning forward in the saddle, surveying the country to either side of them.

"This way, I think," he motioned and turned to the left, toward the hills.

Foster said nothing and turned his horse as Clint had. Fifty yards ahead, there appeared to be place where they could make their way down to the bottom. Clint's horse balked a little as he urged her over the edge but, with a little slippin' and slidin,' she made it without incident. Foster refused to ride down. Dismounting, he led the horse over the edge and soon he too was in the bottom of the wide wash. Clint noticed but said nothing.

"Didn't want to break my neck," Foster offered, and again, Clint said nothing. Now, they had to find a way to get up the other side.

Continuing in the direction toward the hills, they rode on, looking for a place to get out but the wash seemed to be getting more rugged, offering no way up the steep, rock strewn walls.

"Well!" Clint muttered, "we'll have to swing around and go the other way. Maybe there's a place......" He cut short his words, jerking the horse to a stop. At the same time, he held his hand up, motioning to Foster to stop. The slight movement he'd seen in the trees before them he knew was no animal – an Indian for sure.

"What is it?" Foster blurted out.

"Hush, you fool. There's shady doin's here abouts."

Foster could see no reason for alarm but knew better than to go against Clint's orders. The morning air hung still - no movement, no sound. Then suddenly, they were all about, some in front, some in back, and many along each edge of the wash and all were decked out in war paint.

"Holy shit," Foster said, suddenly catching sight of them. Instinctively, he began to raise his rifle. Clint reaching back, pushed the muzzle down.

"Don't get crazy, friend," he whispered. "If they'd wanted to kill us, we'd already be dead so just sit tight and let's see what they're up to."

For a few moments, the Indians did nothing, only stare at the two white men.

"Who are they?" Foster whispered.

"Arikaree, I think" he answered. "Notice the hawk bone woven in their hair; they do that when they become a man."

A large Indian with a nasty scar on his neck rode forward. Stopping a few yards in front of them, he said something to them, which neither man understood. Clint answered back in the language the Old Man had taught him. He knew the Indian would not understand him but it might show the man that he was familiar with their ways. At the same time he spoke, he began to sign. The Indian stared at the familiar motions he made. A look of understanding came over his face.

"We come as hunters," Clint said. "We only seek to find meat for our group."

"What group?" the other man signed.

"There are many of us," Clint answered. "We stay with the Mandan and Hidatsa."

With that, the Indian was silent, looking about at his braves, seemingly wondering what to do next. Then, with a scowl on his face, he turned back to the white men and began signing.

"You are part of the men who came up the mother river in large canoes." He nodded a little, as though agreeing with himself. Then with extreme motion, he went on, "You are not welcome here. This is our hunting ground and we will not allow you to take our game. Collect the other two that hunt with you and go. And, do not return."

Clint was thinking fast now and signed back. "You do not remember me, do you?" This caught the Indian off guard. Stunned, he looked deeper into Clint's face.

"I was here, in your camp, many moons ago. I came up the mother river on the big boats and brought many gifts to your people. We shared meat and traded. Your chief said we could return any time." Clint hoped the man would remember when that first group had been here. It had been some years, though.

"I remember," he signed. "We did trade and share meat and it was a good time. But there have been other white men who were not good, who cheated us and brought us grief and sickness." He paused a moment and then went on. "Now, we do not welcome white men to our land so you must go and not return."

"If I were to come alone and bring gifts to your chief and you, might I be welcome in your camp one more time?"

The question hung on the man's ear for a long moment, causing him to make a decision.

Hesitating a bit, he nodded, "Yes! If you come alone, you will be welcome."

With that, the man turned to his braves, motioning them to go. As silently as they had come, they disappeared into the scrubby landscape.

"Jee-sus Key-rist," Foster exclaimed, "I thought we were wolf bait for sure. Who are those guys and what'd that sombitch want anyway?

"They're Rees! They want us to get the hell off their land and that's just what we're gonna do." Spurring the mare, he added, "C'mon let's find the Old Man and skedaddle on outta here fore they change their mind."

After meeting the others, they rode back across the river and continued hunting where they'd hunted in days past. Clint told the Old Man what had happened and what was said. The Old Man listened intently. Then, in a low voice he asked, "Did you ask him?"

"Ask him!" Clint answered, seemingly ignorant of what the Old Man meant. "Ask him what?"

"Did you ask him about the woman? That is why you want to visit their camp, is it not?"

Nodding slowly and dropping his eyes, Clint answered, "Yeah! That's why! Maybe they've seen her or know her whereabouts. Could be, she came this way."

The Old Man nodding, whispered "Could be..........Could be!"

#

Three days after the encounter with the Rees, Clint was on his way to their camp. He'd gotten directions from some of the Mandans who visited their group to trade. He'd also gotten warnings from some of them not to go. Last spring, it seems there had been some trouble over a man's squaw being involved with a French trapper. The trapper had promised certain gifts to the man in exchange for sexual favors from his wife. This was a common practice among the Indians and there would have been no trouble, had the trapper held up his end of the bargain. But, as it sometimes goes, the man had given the Indian whiskey, hoping he'd get drunk enough to forget the gifts promised to him. The Indian didn't forget, however, and they'd gotten into a fight. When the trapper started to get the best of the Indian, the Indian pulled a knife. Being no stranger to knife fighting, the trapper grabbed his own knife and the two of them went at each other. The Indian was getting the best of him, cutting the man several times on the hands and arms. But then, he made a fatal mistake and lunged at the trapper, trying to skewer him. The trapper feigned one way and then side-stepped the other, catching the Indian off balance and burying his knife clean into the hilt. The Indian hung there, suspended from the long blade lodged in his liver. The trapper gave it one final twist and the Indian fell; dead, before he hit the ground. Those of the camp that watched were horrified and, now that their brother had fallen, were out for blood. They swarmed over the trapper like ants, pummeling him with their fists, clubs, and knives. He was almost done for when they pulled him to a nearby tree. Here, they boosted him up off the ground, tying his feet to one tree and his hands to another. Suspended face down, they gathered grass, twigs, and limbs, quickly building a fire under him. He didn't last long but his final moments were filled with unimaginable pain and suffering. They said his screams could be heard from a great distance.

Clint realized that incidents like that are not easily forgotten and that many in the Ree camp would just as soon lift his hair as look at him. But he had to find out if Storm had come this way. Hope was fading that he'd ever see her again and he had to know.

As he rode into the camp, dogs barked at the horses' ankles, women grabbed their children, dragging them away to safety, and several braves came forward, war axes at the ready. He knew he must show no fear and so he rode on. At the center of the camp was a large hut, bigger by far than the others surrounding it.

"Must be the Chief's," he thought to himself.

Bringing the horse to a stop, he climbed down. He brought the pack horse alongside his mount and tied them both to a post in the front of the hut. People hurriedly gathered about him but none approached too close. The Indian with the scarred neck came through the crowd to face him.

"You came," he signed. "I didn't think you would. Many here, me included, would kill you if we had our way. But then, we'd have to deal with the rest of the white men in your camp. There would be much death." He paused for a moment but did not look away. "What do you want, white man?"

Clint took his time. Indians didn't like to come right to the point, he'd learned that in dealing with them.

"First, I want to offer gifts to my friends, the Arikara. I know there has been blood spilled between the whites and your people. I do not wish to be any trouble to you." Pointing to the pack horse, he went on. "I have gifts here for them and gifts for your chief." He paused, "will he speak with me?"

With a grunt, the man turned and motioned for Clint to follow him. Reaching into a parfliech on the pack horse, Clint took out a small package, wrapped in doeskin. He followed the Indian to the large hut. Inside, the smell of smoke was very strong. Mixed in with it, was the odor of raw meat, musk, and sweat. It was dimly lit and a small cook fire danced in the center, casting eerie shadows on the earthen walls and the faces that surrounded him. The scarred one led him near the fire and motioned for him to sit. He rolled one leg down and sat cross-legged at the place he'd been directed.

Across the fire and somewhat back sat an old man, huddled in a bright blanket. His shoulders drooped slightly and his countenance was that of one who'd seen hard times and much dying. His eyes, though, burned with an intensity that Clint could only decipher as hatred. Hatred of the man and his kind that now sat before him.

Clint looked straight on at the chief, unflinching.

"I brought you these," he signed, handing the doeskin packet to the scarred Indian who immediately set it before the chief. The chief didn't look at the gift but continued to search the face of the white man.

"They are of the finest quality," Clint went on, pointing to the gift.

Seeing this, the man's concentration was broken and he looked down at what lay before him. Slowly, he folded back the doeskin, revealing a pair of matched, engraved, skinning knives. They were the finest England had to offer.

Along with the knives, was a leather pouch containing tobacco, a small mirror, and an ivory comb, carved from the tusk of a walrus. These things Clint had gathered for just such an occasion.

The old chief studied the gifts and then raised his eyes again to face Clint.

"I appreciate the gifts," he signed, "but they will not buy my friendship toward you or your people."

"I only want one thing from you," Clint answered. "I need to know if a woman came by this way. She is a woman of a different tribe, one that lives far up the mother river, far to the north." He paused for a moment, trying to think of a way to describe her. "She is tall and thin," he signed. "Very pretty but with sad eyes." What else could he say?

The old chief sat there, digesting what had just been said. Clint could tell he had no remembrance of a lone woman traveling to the camp.

"Maybe there were two women," he added, "one tall, and the other one, more round."

Some of the onlookers in the back laughed at his description. No one said anything. There was only stillness. But then, a stirring went about through the group in the rear. The chief listened for a moment and then called for one of the people to come forward. It was a woman. Words were spoken between her and the chief and then the scarred Indian said something.

"It seems," the chief signed, "that there was a woman in the company of a trapper. There was only one woman, though. I did not see her and this is the first I've heard of her but they say she was very pretty. They also say she had two babies with her. Twins maybe."

"She was very sick so they stayed here for a few days but then they went up the river. No one has seen them since."

Upon hearing this, Clint's hopes sunk and he lowered his eyes. The chief recognized the disappointment in the man.

"I'm sorry if this is not what you wanted to hear but it is the truth."

"Thank you," Clint signed and turned to go.

"White man," the chief said in broken English. "Do not come here again or...." With that he ended by making a gesture of scalping an enemy.

Clint got the point and nodded his agreement. When he had passed out the gifts he'd brought, he rode away slowly. He had always held out hope that somehow, somewhere he'd find her or at least find out what happened to her. Now, though, he faced the grim truth that he would never see her again. It was a long, cold ride back to the encampment.

CHAPTER 4:
UPRIVER TO THE ROCHE JAUNE

Winter was a long time going. Clint spent most of his days off hunting. It helped him deal with the heartache. When at last the river began to thaw, he was anxious to be underway; to get the hell out of this stinking camp and away to a place where there weren't so many people.

Initially, it was dangerous to put the boats out on the water because of the ice floes that continually floated on the high, roiling current. Many times, they had to get the boats to shore and camp there until the waters were again passable. Clint found himself spending more time riding horseback than being aboard the keel boats. He and the Old Man would hunt and survey the surrounding landscape, leaving what game they killed hanging near the river, where the boats could pick it up.

Months passed and the party finally reached a large river that ran in from the southwest. The French trappers in the area called it "Roche Jaune," which, when translated, meant Yellow Rock or Yellowstone. A trading post, of sorts, had been erected just up from the bank of the river. Mountain men, most of them working for the Rocky Mountain Fur Company, came and went, depositing their furs and getting powder, ball, traps, and other such provisions in return. The local Indian tribes did the same. Trudeau's boats were scheduled to stop here for a while before going on up-river to the great falls.

Clint and the other hunters found that game was scarce near the trading post. The area had been hunted out years before and so they traveled great distances in search of elk, buffalo, and deer – meat for the trade company men.

Even though he'd come to the resolution that he would never see her again, whenever he was around the trappers, he inquired if they'd seen any Indian women who were living on their own. Mostly, he got strange looks from the men when he asked the question. Women, as they knew them, were never on their own. They belonged to somebody, a buck or some trapper who'd traded for them. Whether they be a wife, a squaw, or a slave, they were never on their own.

Sometimes when he'd ask about Storm, he'd begin describing her. At this, the men would usually start laughing. Hell, didn't he know they all looked alike? All of them had black hair, dark eyes, and dark skin – most all wore buckskins, moccasins, and braids in their hair. He soon quit asking.

One night while sitting at their campfire, Clint began discussing his dilemma with the Old Man. He seemed more to be talking to himself than to the other. "You know," he said, "I think that maybe the men are right. No women out here are on their own." Pausing for a moment, as if in deep thought, he went on, "So...., she must have taken up with someone." He immediately thought back to what the Ree Chief had said, that there had been a woman in the company of a trapper.

"Nah! Couldn't be!" he thought. "That one had two babies."

He then became aware that the Old Man was speaking.

"What if you're right?" he asked. "What if she has taken up with another man? If that's the case, the chance of finding her is.........." He paused for a long moment. "Well, it's just unlikely that you'll ever find her. And perhaps, she does not want to be found. She may be happy in the life she now has." He didn't say what was really in his heart – he didn't say that he believed she was dead.

"I know that," Clint answered, "but I promised her I would meet her after my leg was mended and that we would be together. And, that's hard for me to let go of. I'm going on upriver to the three forks to see if I can find her. She told me once her village was very near there so I have to see for myself." With that, both men sat silent, staring at the fire until they could no longer hold their eyes open. "Night!" Clint whispered. But the Old Man did not answer. He was sound asleep.

After more than a week's stay on the Yellowstone, Trudeau was anxious to get the crew moving on upriver. He told Clint and the rest of the hunters to go on ahead and see what game they could find. Clint agreed and along with Crip, Foster, and the Old Man, he struck out at daylight.

The land around the river had taken on a different look now. It was hillier with different kinds of trees and brush growing in and around the banks. Thick patches of cedar carpeted the hillsides in a dark green pattern. Tall, thick cottonwoods mixed in with chokecherry and river birch abounded along the small creeks and rills that ran into the main river. Groves of wild plum grew in profusion in the wide gullies.

Although there was good cover and abundant food for wildlife in these canyons and gullies, the men found very little game. In fact, they came across few tracks and no fresh droppings. This forced them to travel further and further from the river. Clint didn't mind that they had to do this, for he loved to see new country. The problem was it made them vulnerable to Indian attack. There would be no help for them if they encountered a large war party. They'd have to fight it out themselves.

Another problem was, it took a long time to carry meat back to where the boatmen could find it and sometimes it was hard to tell if the boats had already passed. Therefore, it was agreed that the captain would put a rider out along the shore. His job was to leave markers every half mile or so. This would tell whoever brought the meat back if the boat was ahead or behind. If he found no marker when he rode upstream, he knew the boat hadn't gotten that far and he would leave the meat in a conspicuous place. If he found a marker, he would then ride up the river until he came upon the boats. Since the boats moved rather slowly, this method worked very well.

It was generally left up to Crip or Foster to carry what meat they'd killed back to the boats. They took turns at this, usually traveling every four or five days, depending on how much game had been killed. Crip was amiable about doing this but Foster always complained. He didn't like having to ride that far leading pack animals and being alone. Also, he didn't like having to search out the hunting party when he returned. He wasn't that good of a tracker and felt very uneasy in the wilderness. Clint would always make it very clear to them as to which direction they would hunt and about where they would meet them. Most of the time, they had little trouble finding the hunters.

It was on one of the return trips that Foster ran headlong into a large grizzly, feeding on ants in an old tree trunk. The bear was as startled as Foster, rolling away from the tree and coming up onto its hind legs ready to do battle. At this, Foster's horse whinnied and reared, dumping him flat on his back, not ten yards from the bear. His horse and the two pack horses tore off through the trees in a wild frenzy, snorting wildly as they ran. In the excitement, Foster's rifle had gone flying and was now lying some distance away, to his right. In his mind, Foster knew this bear was going to tear him apart. But the animal didn't advance toward him. It dropped onto all fours and was now facing him, trying to catch his scent. He thought about trying to get to the rifle but knew if he moved toward it, the bear would attack.

Slowly, he rolled onto his stomach and then came up on his hands and knees, turning to face the giant bruin. Fear poured out of him and he could feel a cold sweat breaking on his forehead and upper lip. He fought back the urge to throw up.

"Shit," he murmured, "I'm a dead man."

Clint had always told him that bears were unpredictable. Sometimes, they'd leave you be but most of the time, they didn't let you off that easy. If they charged, and if they got to you, you were a goner. All these things ran through Foster's mind and what he'd managed to hold down before, now came rushing up, spewing vomit all down the front of him. Over and over he wretched, each convulsion bringing forth a fountain of half-digested food.

The bear didn't seem to know what it was facing – this thing's scent was nothing it'd ever smelled before. Slowly, it began to advance, sniffing, plodding. When it was close enough to touch, the bear leaned forward and licked Foster's face. Apparently, it didn't care for what it tasted and with a snort, turned and retreated into the woods.

It was over then. However, in his still frightened state, Foster continued to wretch and finally, letting everything go, he shit himself. When at last his senses returned, he crawled to the rifle and slowly rose to his feet. He then cleaned himself up and set off to find the horses. This episode convinced him that he was not cut out for this life and he vowed to himself he'd be on the next boat heading for St. Louis.

CHAPTER 5:
THE GREAT FALLS, CLINT'S OUTPOST, AND MORAH

Upon reaching the Great Falls, Clint had bid farewell to Trudeau, Crip, and Foster. He and the Old Man took what goods were coming to them, along with two fine horses, and proceeded up the river below the confluence of the three forks. Here, they set up a somewhat permanent camp and went about the business of trapping and hunting.

Clint became familiar with the tribes that lived in the local area. He often went out to visit them and trade for furs. He was, unlike many of the trappers of the time, fair with them. He didn't cheat them and never traded whiskey for their goods. He soon learned, however, that trapping was not the way of the future. Trading was where the money was to be made. So, with some help from Trudeau and others in the shipping business, Clint started up his own trading post.

At first, the enterprise was slow to get off the ground. But Clint had a reputation of being fair and the word soon got around. Within a two-year span, his outpost was trading better than many of the others up and down the river. He had a problem though, in that there was not much river travel coming from the large settlement below and so, when he needed to resupply his post or sell his pelts, he had to use a pack train to move them. Later on, when he could, he would acquire a large canoe or flat boat to move them but, for now, it was the pack train.

The Old Man had gone off to seek out his people and take up his place among them. This meant that the days were long and lonely. Clint was used to having someone to talk with but now there was no one. Occasionally, a trapper or explorer or group of Indians would come to the outpost asking directions or needing supplies. These visits he cherished, engaging the visitors in conversation, asking about the latest gossip or news. He had quit asking about Storm but always kept his eyes and ears open in hopes of seeing her or hearing of her.

In between the times, he spent trading, he went to cutting timbers and fashioning a large cabin in which to trade with customers and store his goods. It would be a good place where he could spend the winter and stay warm and dry. Behind the cabin, he built a large corral to house his horses. When that was finished, he cut and hauled wood to the cabin to be used for heating and cook fires.

The months passed and seasons came and went. It had been nearly sixteen years since Clint had come up river from St. Louis. In that time, he had done a lot of trapping and traveling through the mountains. He pretty much knew them as one would know his own home. He'd also learned the languages of many of the tribes of Indians that frequented the area. He loved it here. It was his home.

It was while he was scouting some new trapping country to the west that Clint came upon a village of Shoshoni. "Northern Shoshoni from the look of it," he thought. Most of the Shoshoni people he'd dealt with were friendly but he'd not been to this village and it wasn't a good idea to ride into their camp without an invitation. He thought he'd like to establish some trade with these folks but he had to be careful.

For two hours, he sat back in the trees watching the movement in the camp. When at last he saw two men mount their horses and ride out, he decided he'd try to meet them and perhaps trade some of the goods he carried on his pack horse.

He followed them for some time and when they stopped at a small stream to water their horses, he rode toward them. He deliberately made noise so they would know he was there.

"No sense takin' 'em by surprise" he thought. "I wanna be friends. I don't wanna get scalped."

"Pehnaho," Clint said, holding his right hand up. This meant hello and was used to show friendship.

For a moment, the two braves said nothing. They studied him carefully, all the while looking to see if there were others with him.

"My name is Jeffries. I come in peace to trade with my brothers the Shoshoni." Still, the men said nothing. Clint went on, "I have blankets, knives, cloth… "

One of the men then spoke, cutting Clint off. "Jeffries! Ah, the man who has the trading post near the big river." He nodded his head as if giving some sort of approval. "We have heard of you. You have ridden a long way."

Clint was about to answer when the other man suddenly blurted out, "Perhaps you have ridden a long way, only to die." A sinister grin then made its way across his face and his hand tightened on the lance he carried at his side.

Clint gave his horse a gentle nudge forward, riding straight up to the man. He stopped some six feet away and stared directly at him. In a low, controlling voice he said, "I came here to trade, not to fight." He paused a moment and then went on, "But if that's what you'd like…" Suddenly, Clint's belt pistol was in his hand and pointed straight at the man's face. "You'll be the first one to die."

The man did not expect this – it happened so fast. Looking down the muzzle of the heavy pistol, he knew this white man could kill him. The bravado he'd shown a moment before was now gone and he dropped his eyes in submission and lowered his lance.

"Wait! Wait!" the other man spoke up, holding his hands out, as though to stop Clint. "My friend's brother was killed by a white man and he carries a vengeance within him. Please, do not kill him."

For a long minute, Clint sat staring at the man, keeping his pistol aimed at him. "Awlright!" he said, nodding his head. "It's like I said before, I came here to trade."

"Perhaps we should ride back to our village. Our women would like some of your goods.

By the way, my name is Nopape Kwii. My friend is Behawate Pehe. We are cousins." Clint just nodded at the man's words and kept his eye on the one named Pehe.

People in the village were delighted by the things Clint had brought but he was soon out of goods and many people went away with nothing. He was, however, invited to share their food and spend the night with them. It was during the meal that he was approached by one of the men of the tribe and asked if he'd trade his knife. Clint didn't like to trade the knife he carried but he always kept an extra on hand in case he needed it.

"What do you have to trade?" Clint asked.

"My woman," came the answer. "You can have my woman for the night. She will make you very happy."

At first Clint shook his head and said he didn't want to trade. But shortly, the man brought forth the woman and pleaded with Clint to trade. Clint loved Storm and always would but it had been a long time since he'd been with a woman and besides, she was attractive. After more prodding by the man, Clint agreed. As he handed over the knife, the woman took his hand and motioned for him to come with her. Together, they walked to her lodge.

As soon as they were inside, the woman began undressing. When she had dropped her clothing, she came to Clint and began tugging at his shirt.

"Whoa! Whoa! Wait a minute" he said, pushing her back. "Ain't we gonna get acquainted first or something?' Hell, I'm not one to talk yer ear off but I would like to get to know ya fore we go at it."

The woman paused then and backed away. "My name is Morah," she said, curtly, "and I have been traded to you for this night."

Clint looked at her expression in the dancing firelight. She didn't look happy. "I know you didn't have much say in this, so if you'd rather not, we can just talk and sleep."

"No!" she said. "I must do this because my husband directed me to."

"If it's about the knife, I'm willin' to…"

"It's not about the knife," she said, sharply, cutting him off. "He has many knives." she paused a moment. "No! It is something else but I don't know what. I was told to bring you to our lodge and lay down with you… keep you entertained."

Suddenly, Clint had a very bad feeling about what was happening. Indians often traded their women for goods or favors but something here didn't feel right. Looking around, his eyes fell upon a large piece of wood that had been stacked just inside the doorway, to be used for the night's fire.

"Why don't you crawl under that robe and I'll be right with you," he said to Morah. Without questioning, she turned and did as he asked. He then took the piece of wood and tamped the fire down, causing it to dim somewhat. Making his way to where Morah lay, he said, "Moan a little."

"What?" she said.

"Moan a little, as if you're having a good time. She looked at him as if he were crazy but did as she was told.

"Oooh! Aaah!"

"Louder," Clint said. "Make it sound like it's the best thing that's ever happened to ya."

294

"Ooooh...Ooooh." She kept it up and with each moan, she increased the volume.

It was then that the flap covering the door was slid back and a shadowy figure silently came in and dropped to the floor. Making his way to where Morah lay, the man raised up, yanked the robe back, and attempted to plunge a knife into the man he suspected was there. Seeing only the woman, he lowered the knife. It was then that the heavy piece of firewood found its mark at his temple and he crashed to the floor, unconscious.

Seeing the man above her with a knife, Morah had screamed and leaped to get out from under his falling body. Clint quickly grabbed the knife from the man's hand. Turning him over, it was hard to see who he was, although Clint suspected it was Morah's husband.

"Who is this?" Clint asked, turning the man's face more to the firelight.

"It's Pehe, my husband's cousin. Do you know him?" she asked.

"I sort of had a run-in with him today. I guess he wanted to get even. One thing's for sure, he's gonna have a hell of a headache."

Just then the flap opened again and it was Morah's husband, he too carried a knife – the knife that Clint had traded to him.

"It is your night to die, White Man," he whispered, bringing the knife to bear. "Your night to pay for all the pain and grief that you and your kind have brought on my people." Slowly, he made his way toward Clint feigning a lunge, first one way and then another. He was very quick but each time, Clint shifted to counter the man's move. Now, however, his back was being pressed ever nearer to the wall of the lodge. Soon, he would have to make a move or die. He was not sure if the man knew he had a knife. In the dark, it was hard to see and he had not brandished it in his own defense.

"Well, this is it," Clint thought. Setting himself for the charge, he held the knife in his left hand, near his thigh, still out of sight. He knew what to do. Somehow it was instinctive – he had been here before. Just then, there was a commotion in the dark, accompanied by a hollow thump. The man's legs collapsed under him and he fell in a heap. Standing behind him, naked as the day she was born, was Morah. The piece of firewood dangling from her hand.

"Jesus Christ," Clint whispered. Morah then dropped the wood and reached for the clothing she had abandoned only minutes before.

"Why did you hit him?" Clint asked.

"Because you would have killed him," she answered without looking at him "And I would have been the one to pay for it when his cousin awoke. Oh, make no mistake, I will suffer a beating for what I did to him but at least he won't kill me as his cousin would have."

"Does he beat you often?' Clint asked.

"Often!" she answered. "Now, you had better go. And, take your knife with you. The trade was not completed."

Clint picked up his knife and stuffed it in his belt. Walking out of the lodge, he said nothing. In a moment, he was back, carrying a woven length of buckskin rope.

"What are you doing?" Morah asked. "You need to go."

"A trade's a trade," he whispered, tying the rope about the two unconscious men. She said nothing more as she undressed and crawled again, under the warm buffalo robe.

"Is there room in there for me?" he asked.

"Of course, there is. After all, a trade's a trade."

It was still dark when Clint rose and slipped out the door of the lodge. He told Morah goodbye, saying he'd return with more goods to trade with the village. He also left the knife laying on the robe next to the warming fire. "A trade's a trade," he thought, "and damn well worth it."

The two bound men were still unconscious and Clint knew he'd have to deal with them again when he returned. The scuffle that had occurred the night before had not been heard by any of the people so there had been no outside commotion. Now, as he rode out, the camp was quiet except for a few dogs voicing their unease.

CHAPTER 6:
TRADIN' AND TROUBLE

A month passed and though he planned to return to the Shoshoni camp, he had been busy with the trading at the outpost. A pack train from the settlement had arrived with supplies and he was busy putting things away and gathering the furs and other trade goods to pay for the supplies. Also, many of the goods he received had to be transported to a secret cache he'd built on the ridge above. He didn't fully trust the Indians who passed by or came to trade, to stay out of the outpost when he was not there.

When things finally slowed down a bit, he loaded three pack horses with trade goods and lit out for the Shoshoni camp. It was a three or four day ride to get there but he took his time, stopping to fish and hunt a little on the way. In the back of his mind he worried about the two he'd had the run-in with. He had not just beaten them at their own game but had embarrassed them also. Nobody, but especially Indians, liked to be embarrassed and he knew those boys were out for blood. This would be tricky!

When he arrived at where the camp was supposed to be, he found that they'd moved. This wasn't uncommon. Villages often moved, following game, or to gain better weather, or just because they want to. Their trail wasn't hard to follow, however, and within two days, he'd caught up with them. Riding into the camp, he kept a careful eye out for the two men he knew wanted him dead. Within minutes he was surrounded by people who recognized him and remembered he'd promised to return with more trade goods. It was customary and polite to meet with the Chief first and gain his permission to deal with the people. And so, Clint made his way to the leader's lodge, presenting him with a trade blanket, a new knife, and a jar of preserved peaches.

Near the center of the village, he spread a bright new blanket on the ground and proceeded to lay out the goods. The tribal members examined and handled the things but were very respectful and took their turn in line to trade. Concentrating on the action at hand, Clint let down his guard. He knew the two men were probably about but there was too much going on to worry about them. It was then that they struck.

Morah's husband was the first to gain Clint's attention, pretending to trade a packet of skins for a blanket, a metal pot, and a mirror. Dickering over what Clint would give him, he began causing a commotion and accusing Clint of being a cheat. With his attention drawn to the man, Clint didn't see the other man come up from behind him. He did see, however, two women standing in front of him avert their eyes to the apparent danger. With that, he quickly rolled to his right, avoiding the hatchet blow that whizzed past his ear and sliced through his leggings. Blood erupted from the cut on his leg.

Clint had not totally been unprepared for the assault and had laid his belt pistol on the blanket beside him. As he rolled away, his hand found the pistol. Cocking it, he brought it to bear just as Morah's husband leaped upon him. The loud boom of the gun's report was somewhat muffled as it went off at point blank range, killing the man instantly. The other man had regained his stance and was about to deliver another blow with the hatchet.

Clint lay helpless with an empty gun and a dead man pinning him down. It was then that the crowd reacted, grabbing the man and disarming him. He kicked and reeled against those that held him, cursing and threatening them. Pushing the dead man off of him, Clint gained his feet.

"Let him go," Clint directed, putting his hands out, motioning for the man to come to him. "Let him go," he repeated. Hearing that, the villagers released him.

Feeling his freedom, the man then came at Clint, screaming his rage. Clint set himself for the attack and met the man full on. Using the other's weight against him, Clint side-stepped the charge and grabbed the man's shirt, slamming him to the ground. Breathless, the man laid there not knowing what had just happened. It was then that the stone-hard fist came down upon him, smashing his nose and breaking his cheekbone. The second fist took out some teeth and split his lip in three places. There was no need for a third blow and Clint held back. The man was out cold and would be for several hours.

Clint told the crowd that the trading was over for the day but would resume the next morning. Meanwhile, he wrapped a piece of blanket around the cut on his leg and went to find Morah. When he got to her lodge he found that she had been tied up and gagged. Untying her, he asked if she could sew up the gash on his leg.

#

It was late morning when Clint returned to the trading. After the fight, the Chief had instructed that the white man's goods would not be touched until he returned. The members of the village honored his words and were standing in line when Clint got there. The slice to his leg had not been deep and was closed with a few stiches. It would leave a nasty scar but it would be just one of many.

Morah's husband's body had been removed by his family and presumably taken to a burial place. Morah did not go with them but stayed near Clint during the trading. When it was finished, he thanked her for her help.

"You will leave in the morning?" she asked, without looking at him.

Nodding his head, he answered, "Yes! And, what of you? What will you do?"

"With my husband dead, I will soon have nothing. His family will come to take everything. A wife has no claim to anything that belonged to her man."

"I guess you could come with me," Clint offered. "Stay at my outpost..."

"Or, you could stay here....with me!" she countered.

"Can't do that," he answered, without further explanation.

"I suppose then, there is no solution. I cannot leave and you cannot stay." She paused a moment and then went on. "These are my people and I belong with them. I have an uncle, Gray Eagle, who has often made me a proposition to move in with he and his wives. I think I will do that. I think I have no choice."

Before the first hint of daylight graced the eastern horizon, Clint, with pack animals in tow, navigated the lonely trail back to his outpost. He could not get Morah out of his mind.

CHAPTER 7:
THE OLD MAN RETURNS WITH LONG TIME COMING

Winter had shown its bitter face now with a dusting of snow on the higher peaks. Mornings were covered in heavy frost and ice formed at the edges of the small creeks. It wouldn't be long before the land was locked in its frigid grip. Clint was prepared though and had no doubts that he could live in comfort through the long days to follow.

He was outside, gathering grass for the animals when he heard them coming from far off. Their horses snorted in the icy air and their hooves clomped upon the frozen ground. Clint wasted no time. With rifle in hand and horse at the ready, he concealed himself in the trees that lay directly behind the log cabin. When they rode into the clearing that lay before the cabin, he couldn't believe his eyes. It was the Old Man. But who were those two with him? Dressed in the heavy furs they wore, it was hard to tell if they were white men or Indians.

As he came forward to greet them, Clint heard the Old Man speak to the two others. He spoke in his native tongue, which Clint had become fluent in. And, judging from the words, Clint could only assume the two others were Indian also. Drawing closer, he saw the almond shaped eyes and the round tan cheeks. They were Indian alright...and female.

"Get down," the Old Man whispered, "we have arrived."

"Well my hell, I didn't think I'd ever see you again," Clint said, smiling at his old friend. "Figured they'd make you chief again and you'd spend the rest of yer days takin' it easy; lettin' all them young bucks and maidens wait on ya."

Turning around, the Old Man smiled and shook his head. "No! Things change, you know. They never are as you left them." He paused a moment and then went on. "I didn't fit in there anymore. Guess I spent too many days bein' a white man." Again, he paused. "I did bring you a present, though." This time, a big smile crossed his face. Motioning one of the other riders forward, he pulled the hood back that covered her face and said, "This one is for you."

Clint stood there for a long moment trying to digest the words that had just been thrown at him. "What do you mean?" he asked.

"I know how lonely you have been, longing for that woman. So, I brought you one to replace her." With that, he pushed the girl toward Clint. "Her name is Long Time Coming. They call her that because her mother had such a long, hard time having her. It almost killed her. She couldn't have any more children after that. I traded a skinning knife, a wool kapote, and some powder for her." He paused for a moment, looking at his young friend, trying to read his expression. "She's pretty, huh? You like her, huh? Will keep you warm on winter nights."

Clint didn't know what to say. So, he just nodded and grunted a little. He'd have to think about this for a while. He didn't want to hurt the Old Man's feelings and after all, she was a gift to him but he couldn't forget the woman he'd grown so close to, the one he loved so deeply. There was no way this one could take her place.

Tying his horse up, Clint motioned to the others, "Come into the cabin. Let's get outta this weather. There's a warm fire inside."

#

Over time, Clint got used to having the girl around although he never did become romantic with her. She was short in stature, thin at the waist with an ample bosom, and somewhat square shoulders. Her hair was not braided and hung down her back and along the sides of her round face. A thin strip of soft deerskin was used as a headband to control it.

She was pretty and had a nice smile. She didn't say much and made no sexual advances towards Clint. Sometimes though, he'd catch her looking at him. When that happened, she'd turn away quickly, pretending not to have noticed him. It was always a boost to his manly ego but he never did anything about it.

She was a very hard worker. Besides all the normal chores that were expected of a woman, she would do anything he asked of her. He took to calling her "Shorty" because of her height and she answered to it without question.

The other woman whom the Old Man had brought back was named "Shesutem" which meant "little girl." She was somewhat older than Shorty but about the same size. Unlike Shorty, however, she was accustomed to whining about work and having to do chores. The Old Man indulged her and she often got her way with him. For that, he gained a permanent bed partner.

As time went on, however, Shesutem became more and more demanding and less and less helpful with the daily chores. She refused to help with the pelts and would not aid in caring for the horses. She also would not do any of the cooking nor cleaning. The only thing she would do was melt snow to provide them water.

One day, after a particularly nasty fight between her and Shorty, a small band of Indians came to the post to trade. They had a horse, some hand-woven blankets, a basket of corn, and two packets of furs. Clint looked at their goods and told them he would not accept the horse or the blankets but would take their furs and the corn.

What the Indians wanted in trade was worth far more than the corn and packets of furs were worth. They insisted that the value of the horse, the corn, and handmade blankets would make up the difference. Clint said he didn't want the horse because it was lame and the blankets they offered had been used so much that they had holes in them. Plus, they were infested with lice. The corn he could feed to the livestock.

Because they could not come to terms, there was a standoff. So, the Indians prepared to leave. It was then that the Old Man pulled Clint aside to have a word with him.

"I know how we can resolve this," he uttered. Clint was all ears so the Old Man went on. "Take the furs, and the other things and give them the goods they want."

"But I don't want those things and they're certainly not worth what I'm giving them in return."

"So then, you must sweeten the deal" the old one said, exhibiting a sly smile.

"What? Give them something else. Are you cra...."

"Shh!" the Old Man interrupted, this time pulling Clint near to whisper in his ear.

As the old one spoke, Clint listened. Then, with a smile, he nodded and said, "That would be a good trade."

In the end, Clint took what they offered and they, in return, got the goods they wanted plus one other thing.... Shesutem! She had to be part of the deal. When they threatened to make her walk, Clint gave them back the lame horse. She was crying when she rode away with them.

"I took a beatin' on that trade," he said to the Old Man. "But at least we can have some peace and quiet around here." Later on, he built a fire behind the outpost and burned the blankets.

#

The Old Man could not get comfortable sleeping in the cabin so when he got the chance, he'd go into the forest and search out long, thin pine trees. Using a white man's ax, he'd cut them down, remove the limbs and bark, and set them aside to dry. When he'd gathered twenty-five or so of them, he had Clint and the women help him erect them as the framework for a large teepee. He used buffalo hides to cover the framework and soon had a comfortable place of his own. It was so comfortable, in fact, that Clint and Shorty soon took up residence there also.

It was not long after the Old Man had built his teepee that a group of Northern Shoshone came to the outpost to do some trading. They wanted blankets and knives and other such items not easily found in the mountains. Upon discovering they had easy access to much of the white man's goods, they decided to make the outpost their permanent home. Within days, there were three additional teepees standing across the meadow from the outpost.

Clint was not averse to this because it gave the Old Man and Shorty a new set of friends, someone they could converse with and share their own cultural thoughts and beliefs. Besides, these people were good hunters and trappers and could, if need be, help in any attack on the outpost.

The Old Man still went with Clint when he hunted and fished but he was bothered by rheumatism and it sometimes hurt him to ride. Also, his eyesight was not what it once was and it frustrated him. Therefore, he spent much of his time inside the teepee entertaining Shorty or over at the Shoshone camp swapping stories and telling lies. He seemed very comfortable there.

Some months had passed and Clint noticed that Shorty was gone more than she was around. His suspicions were that she had found someone she cared for among the Shoshone and that she was spending time with him. It wasn't long before his suspicions were confirmed.

One morning as Clint was doing some repairs to his outpost, a young Shoshone brave rode across the large clearing. He was leading a young filly and carrying a bundle in his arms. He dismounted and tied his horse and the filly to the nearby hitching post. He carried the bundle in both arms and approached Clint as he worked. Solemnly, he handed Clint the bundle and then stepped back.

"I am called Mato Maska of the great Shoshone People. I have come here to ask your permission to marry Long Time Coming."

"Who?" Clint asked. "Oh yeah, you mean Shorty."

The boy had never heard her called Shorty before and didn't know what to think.

He went on, "This blanket and knife are gifts for you along with that fine pony." He pointed to the filly.

Clint stood head and shoulders above him. And although his appearance was very intimidating, the young man, stood tall and looked him directly in the eye. Apparently, Shorty had been watching for his arrival and now came forward to stand at his side. She would not look Clint in the eye.

Clint wanted to smile but he kept it in. "Hmm!" he said, seemingly sizing the boy up.

"Do you like her?" he asked.

"I love her," the boy answered, quickly.

"Yeah, but do you like her?" And without giving the other the chance to answer, he went on. "You know? Do you like the way she smells and the way she talks and walks and all the little things she does? Do you like the way she says your name and the way she dresses and wears her hair and the way she cuddles up next to you?" He paused for a moment and then added, "It's not enough to just love someone, you have to like them too. If you don't like them and the way they are you won't stay in love with them."

The young man hardly knew what to say. He had not expected these questions and now stood at a loss for words.

"Yes! Yes, I do like her and in so many more ways than you mentioned." Turning to the girl, he took up her hands in his. "She is my life," he whispered.

Clint shook his head and smiled, "You have my permission then," he said. "All I ask is that you be good to her. She deserves it."

BOOK 5 – KITCHI AND KEME

CHAPTER 1:
THE RAIDING PARTY

"Don't play so rough!" Storm scolded, watching her two boys tumble about on the scattered buffalo robes that covered the floor of the large teepee. It had been nearly five winters since she bore them and she never ceased to be amazed at how quickly they grew. They were very alike and for someone who was not around them much, it was hard to identify one from the other. She named them Kitchi, meaning brave, and Keme, meaning thunder.

She had endured much pain and sickness at their birth but looking at them now, she smiled and knew it was all worth it. Except for their olive skin color and dark eyes, they looked very much like their father. She sighed then, remembering and thinking it was such a shame that he never had a chance to see them. She thought of Clint often.

If it hadn't been for Armand, her and the children would surely have perished. He was good to her and good to the boys and they looked to him as a father. He was mostly gone from them though, coming back only when his travels allowed it. He had originally come to the mountains to earn a living as a trapper, just as many others had done. However, he had found it increasingly difficult to find beaver and therefore had to travel further and further away to where the streams and lakes had not been trapped out. It didn't take him long to find out there was a better way to make money.

In his travels to the north, he had become friends with a Frenchman who was bringing in trade goods from Europe. Among the goods were blankets, knives, and trinkets, all of which were coveted by the various tribes in the area. Also, there was whiskey! This commodity, above all others, was highly sought after by the Indians and very valuable when trading for pelts or horses. Armand would travel from village to village, leading a string of pack animals laden with these things. When he had bartered all of his goods, he'd strike out for one of the ever-increasing trading posts that were springing up along the big river. Then, before heading north again, he'd swing by the village where Storm and the boys were. After resting and restocking his supply of clothing, pemmican, ball, and powder, he would be off again, disappearing into the mountains, to be gone for several months.

The village where Storm and the boys stayed was spread out along the banks of a small river; one that was slow moving and deep. The village was somewhat of a trading post itself, having a mixture of trappers, Indians, and tradesman. Most of the Indians living there were Nez Pierce. They all knew that Storm was from the Piegan tribe, an offshoot of the fearsome Blackfoot, and therefore had little to do with her. She had made some friends, however, and so her life wasn't one of total loneliness. She and some of the other young mothers would often take their children to a small creek behind the village and let them play in the sparkling water while they talked and laughed about things in their lives.

Life was good here in the summer but winters were a different story. Without a steady man around to bring in food and help gather wood, it was sometimes very difficult to survive. There were men in the village who did nothing but hunt, thereby providing food for the local inhabitants. Others would spend their time gathering firewood for the village. They did, however, require payment of a sort. Nothing was free. Armand always made sure there were plenty of items to trade when he was away so that Storm and the boys would always have food and wood to burn.

Summer had been hot and the fall also warm. But the winds that now blew in from the south had a bite to their breath that meant things were about to change. The leaves on the hillsides had donned their vibrant robes of color and the daylight grew shorter and shorter with each passing sunset.

It was earlier than usual when Storm stepped from the teepee. A thick layer of morning frost blanketed everything about and a dense cloud of steam rose above the ever-rolling river. The sharp chill in the air bit at her lungs as she made her way to the nearby creek to fetch water for the day. Waiting for the jug to fill, she glanced back through the village, watching the smoke roll up and away from the tops of the scattered lodges. Somewhere near the river, a dog barked and then barked again; more intense the second time. Its bark though, ended in a shrill yelp as though it had been cut short. It was nothing new for the village dogs to bark. Usually, there were several of them that joined in, once one of them broke the silence. But the way the dog's bark was suddenly cut off aroused her concern. And why weren't the others barking?

Seeing that the jug was now full, she dismissed her concern and lifted it up from the cold stream. Hurriedly, she made her way back to the lodge. The boys were still asleep, tucked under the heavy skins that kept them warm. She suddenly became aware of a growing commotion outside. People were shouting, yelling, rushing about. What was it?

Quickly, she poked her head out the flap of the teepee to see what was happening. She gasped when she saw the riders making their way through the village. They were of a different tribe than what she'd ever seen. Most had their faces painted in various patterns of black, with here and there a white slash or circle. Around their arms, they wore bracelets of teeth and bones which created an eerie rattle as they rode. Strange adornments of woven hair, feathers, and beads hung from their ears, dangling against their shoulders. Their heads were shaved except for a standing strip of hair which ran from their foreheads back across the top and down to their necks.

Most of the village people were outside their lodges. The riders dismounted and were circulating among them, pushing and shoving them, threatening them with their axes; going into their lodges. They seemed to be taking things from the people. There had been no screaming or shooting but the way they were herding the villagers meant there was trouble afoot.

Storm quickly gathered the rifle, pistol and hatchet Armand had given her and shoved them out under the back edge of the lodge. Anything else she thought might be taken from her, she also shoved outside. Lastly, she made sure the boys were covered as they tended to kick the heavy buffalo robe off when they got too hot.

A loud voice then called into the lodge in a language she did not understand. At the same time, something whacked the side of the lodge. She stepped out into the morning sun, facing the ominous warrior that sat his horse, just in front of the lodge. She felt the fear well up in her but she also felt a burning hatred growing toward these strangers. The skin across her forehead tightened and her jaw clenched.

"What do you want?" she said in her native tongue – signing the question at the same time.

The figure atop the horse said nothing but looked down at her with a grimace of disdain. Just then, two others from the group ran up. One grabbed Storm by the arm and pulled her away from the lodge. Violently, she jerked her arm away and yelled for him to let go of her. She then stepped to regain her position in front of the lodge, standing her ground. The second man called her a name and without hesitation, slapped her across the face, knocking her to the ground. The blow was dizzying and as she tried to get up, the first warrior she had pulled away from, kicked her hard in the stomach. She fell back to the ground, gasping for air. Her head was reeling and she thought she was going to pass out.

She watched as both men then entered the lodge. She tried crawling toward the open flap but the mounted warrior cut her off with his horse. There were sounds of screaming then - her boys! Again, she tried to rise but could not. One of the warriors then pushed through the flap, a screaming, kicking, child in each hand. He had them by the hair, laughing as he pushed them ahead of him. Once outside, he threw them toward their mother. Quickly, she gathered them to her and held them away from harm. She scooted backward for several feet and waited to see what would happen next.

The man that had brought the boys out returned to the lodge. When he reappeared, he was carrying robes and her cooking utensils. The second man had the leather sacks that contained all of their food. They piled the goods on the ground in front of her and went back for whatever was left. They came out with clothing, extra moccasins, bullet molds, and the tools Armand used for sharpening knives - anything they thought would be of value. All this, they piled onto one of several travois', being pulled through the village by horses. Horses that they'd taken from some of the villagers. Everyone's belongings were being stolen and nobody had lifted a hand to fight back. Storm had a knife tucked inside her leggings, beneath her coat but she knew that if she tried to fight them, they would kill her.

The warrior on the horse then motioned to the others and as quietly as they had ridden in, they began to ride off. Before he went, however, he signed to Storm and the other villagers, warning them that if they tried to follow or take up arms against them, they would return and kill everyone in the village. No one said a thing.

When they had ridden away and were out of sight, Storm hurried the boys back inside to the warmth of the lodge. Looking around, she saw they had taken almost everything. Everything the family would need to survive the coming winter. Quickly, she dashed from the lodge and ran around behind to see if the weapons were still there – they were! Next, she made her way out through the trees to a small clearing where her horse had been hobbled. She could not see him and she began to panic. It was bad to have your food stolen and bad to have no weapons but one could not survive without a horse. Just then, a shallow whinny caught her ear. Turning, she saw the horse walking toward her. It had wandered off into the trees, seeking shelter. She breathed a sigh of relief. Stroking the horse's nose, she leaned close to his ear and whispered, "At least I have you, plus a rifle to shoot game and a hatchet to chop wood. I'm very lucky!" She knew that winter would be hard though and hoped that Armand would soon return.

#

Once the commotion had settled, the villagers gathered to talk. From the discussions, it appeared these renegade Indians had stripped the village, taking everyone's belongings and all the food. They had also taken many of the horses. Some of the men wanted to go after them but without adequate weapons and horses they would be slaughtered.

Taking store of what was left, one of the men, a trapper who often took the role of village leader, asked everyone what they had left. Storm was hesitant to mention that she had a rifle and pistol but knew that if it came to hunting for game she would have to offer them up. When everything was accounted for, the combined store of food they had left would not last them more than 5 days.

"Well, they've about wiped us out and we've got to go for food from one of the trading posts down river." Storm listened to the leader's words and though she understood some English, she couldn't totally make out what was being said. The man, realizing that most of the Indians didn't catch what he was saying, repeated it using sign language. He then went on, saying that before the snows came, it would be wise if the entire village moved closer to a trading post – a place where they could get food and provisions. A murmur went up through the crowd and though there was much discussion on the issue, everyone agreed it was the prudent thing to do.

"Good! We are agreed then. We will move out first thing in the morning. With the horses we have left, we'll build travois' to carry the lodges and our goods. Old people and children can ride on them also. The rest of us, however, will have to walk. It will take us several days to reach the nearest outpost."

Shortly after dawn the following morning, Storm had the horse tethered with the travois, the lodge down and folded and what remained of her belongings loaded. Others in the village brought their goods to load with hers. She quickly fed the boys, what small amount of food she had left and bundled them inside a ragged old buffalo robe the thieves had left behind. She nestled them in among the items on the travois and then took her place among the assembled group. Together, they began the long journey toward what they hoped would be a safe haven in which to spend the winter.

CHAPTER 2:
SAVED BY WHISKEY

Armand Velasquez sat atop his horse watching the long line of riders with their attached travois make their way along the narrow mountain trail. He was very familiar with most of the tribes that inhabited the area but he didn't recognize this bunch. Their clothing, their markings, and even their manner were not familiar to him. It was probably a tribe on their way to new hunting grounds to spend the winter.

He had been far into Canada trading with the Indians and had 3 pack horses loaded with prime furs, enough to bring him a handsome profit when bartered at one of the trading posts along the big river. Also, he had another pack horse loaded with what little food he had left and what remained of his trade goods. These, he reasoned could be traded with this group for enough food to get him where he needed to go. Among these items were two jugs of whiskey that he'd saved for special trading, in case he ran across something that particularly caught his eye or something that he just had to have.

He watched them and decided that he'd wait 'til they made camp that afternoon before he approached them. Even though he didn't recognize them, he had no fear of them. He had traded with most of the tribes in the region and had always been welcomed at their fires. He did, however, think better of leading the 3 pack horses with the furs into their camp. It might look like he had "too much" and that didn't set well with Indians. They liked being on even ground when they went to trading. If you had too much they were suspicious of you and would not make as good a trade.

When the sun was about to disappear behind the mountain tops and the shadows had grown long, he made his way toward the glowing cook fires. He'd tethered the pack horses in a small clearing some ways back so that their whinnies and neighing could not be heard.

"Yatahe!" He said, as he rode in among them, raising his hand, "I come in peace to make a trade."

Immediately, the Indians were on their feet, weapons at the ready. One of them rushed toward him, grabbing the reins of the horse. Another, jumping up from behind, threw his arms around Armand and pulled him to the ground.

Armand tried to recognize the language they used but could not. He spoke to them in the words of the local tribes but none of them seemed to recognize what he said. Finally, he shook free of the man long enough to sign a greeting. He told them he was a trader and that he only wanted to barter with them for some food. With that understanding, they seemed to relax some. He then took a blanket from his horse and spread it near the biggest cook fire. Upon it, he began placing some of his goods. Knives, beads, foofaraw of all sorts. Before long, the entire group surrounded him. It was then he noticed there were no women among them.

"This must be a raiding party," he thought, trying to conceal the worry that now crept up his spine, causing the hair at the back of his neck to stand on end.

Their leader was a tall, slender man, lithe and long of limb. His complexion was light but a dark countenance loomed in his eyes. The man watched him as he lay the trade goods before them. A slight smile curled up one side of his mouth. Then, he began to sign.

"White man, why do you put these things before me as if you want to trade?"

Armand paused for a moment, selecting his words carefully. He signed back.

"That is what a friend does when he wishes to trade for food." He paused for a moment and then added, "I am very hungry and have not eaten any meat for several days."

The man eyed him very closely, seemingly searching for some sign of fear in his eyes or his voice.

"You know I am going to take these things away from you and give you nothing in return?"

Armand looked straight into the man's face and without a quiver of his eye or voice, answered, "I expected you might. But I also expected you might give me something to eat. Men of honor do those things." With that, he waited.

Again, the man stared at him, measuring him, assessing the situation. Then, he began signing.

"As you will see white man, I am not an honorable man and you are a very unlucky one."

Then, motioning to the others, he suddenly stood up. Two of the braves grabbed Armand by the arms, dragging him closer to the fire. They quickly stripped him of his personal items and all of his clothes. He stood naked before them, trembling.

"We are taking these things and your horse, also. Dead men do not need such things." A wicked smile crossed his face as he finished signing.

The same two braves that had grabbed him now came at him with war clubs drawn.

"Wait!" Armand cried out, "I have whiskey."

Even if they didn't understand any English at all, there was one word that every Indian understood. That word was whiskey.

Quickly, he pulled away from them and made his way to his horse. He pulled back the skin at the edge of the riding saddle and brought forth two, one quart jugs that held the precious liquid. Just as quickly, the leader jerked one of them from Armand's hand and proceeded to remove the cork stopper at the top. He then raised it and took a huge swig. The others all seemed to be hanging on his expression as he brought the jug away from his mouth.

"Aaahg!" Was all he said. A loud cheer then went up from the group as they clamored nearer to get a taste. At least for the moment, Armand was forgotten.

Seeing his chance, Armand tossed the other jug into the air. The Indians scrambling to catch it lost their concentration. Quickly, he mounted the horse and kicked at its flank. The animal bolted forward in a frenzy, knocking one of the men who had held him, flat on his back. Another man grabbed at the animal but Armand kicked him under the chin and sent him reeling backward.

In three bounds, the horse was away from the camp and disappearing fast into the fading light. The leader yelled to his men to get their horses and take after the man. Fortunately, for Armand, the group had settled in for the night and their horses were not readily available. It was minutes before they could take up the chase.

In that time, Armand had managed to put a good distance between himself and his pursuers. He had deliberately not ridden toward where he'd tethered the other pack horses. He knew it would be very hard to track him in the dark and so he swung the horse in an arching circle, back to where the other animals were.

They were not hard to find but by the time he reached them, the cold had him shaking uncontrollably. Fortunately, he had another set of leather britches and a buckskin shirt to put on. After dressing, he brought up the pack animals, snubbed them head to tail, and began a hasty retreat in the direction from which he'd come. If he rode carefully and continued on through the night, they'd have a hard time catching up to him. Besides, they were a raiding party and would not spend too much time looking for one man. They took everything he had anyway so there was no reason to come after him except to kill him. This last thought is what kept him going.

By sun-up, he'd covered many miles and now stood at the banks of a large stream. He knew if he followed the stream toward its headwaters, he would only have to climb up and over the south ridge and he'd be back at his home camp. It would be good to see Storm and the boys again and get some food.

It was late in the afternoon when he at last rode into the campsite. Everything and everyone was gone. From the look of the travois drag marks, he could see that they were headed downriver toward the nearest trading post that lay many miles to the south east. But why had they gone? Upon closer inspection, he could see other drag marks made by other travois' going in the opposite direction. The same direction his captors had been going.

Kneeling at the tracks, he ran his fingers over the deep ruts and voiced the words, "They must have come through here, taking everything that the camp had. It doesn't look as though there was a fight – no bodies, no blood - must have taken them by surprise." He paused, then nodded, "That's why they left."

He mounted his horse and set off in the direction of the trading post.

"It shouldn't take long to overtake them." And then, in a fleeting thought, he whispered, "Madre Dios, I'm so hungry."

CHAPTER 3:
PARALYZED

As the years passed, Storm told Armand that she wished to move closer to her people, that she wanted to be near them. He agreed, and moved them to a village located many miles north of the confluence of the Yellowstone and the big river which people now called the Missouri.

She found comfort being among her own people and spent the days talking and visiting with old friends. The boys too, were happy here. They had grown into fine young warriors and were always up for a good hunt. Even though their hair and skin was somewhat lighter than that of the other boys in the village, they were taller and more muscular and always won the games they played at. Therefore, they had been accepted as members of the tribe and were treated as such.

Armand got along with the boys but he was never around much and so any fatherly instruction was left to other men in the tribe. It was late into the summer when he told Storm that he was leaving to trade with the French and the tribes that lay far to the north. He had visited them before and found them to be friendly and eager to trade.

As he prepared for the journey, the boys took a keen interest in what he was doing and where he planned to go. They had never before asked to accompany him and he would have turned them down if they had. But they were older now and could pull their own weight. Besides, a group of men was not such easy prey as one man alone. So, when they asked if they could go along with him, he told them they could if it was alright with their mother. She was concerned over this because she knew that Armand was often gone for months at a time and, although he never told her about his wanderings, she saw the scars and scabs on him and knew he'd had some trouble.

She also knew that her sons were growing up and she could not always protect them. So, it was with some reluctance that she said yes. It didn't take them long to get their things together and before the following morning's light touched the mountain tops, they were off. Armand always carried a long rifle and a pistol. The boys were excellent marksmen with the bow and arrow and that was their weapon of choice. Also, each boy carried a knife and a hatchet. They rode single file behind Armand who held the lead rope of the three pack horses.

Along their way, they met camps of French trappers and small bands of Indians, mostly Cree and Assiniboine. Trading was good and they soon found it necessary to get another horse to carry the pelts and goods they'd acquired. The animal they selected seemed like a gentle sort and not prone to cause trouble. Armand fashioned a pack-saddle for the animal and they set about loading it up.

All went well for a few days, but as they were about to make camp one afternoon, the breeze that had been gentle throughout the day suddenly turned nasty. The horses, tethered on a line at the edge of camp, began snorting and pulling at the tether.

"We better hurry and unload the horses," Armand said. "Those clouds are building into a bad storm and it will soon be raining."

The boys hurried to help and soon they had all but the new horse unloaded. As they approached it, a clap of thunder echoed across the mountains and the all-ready skittish horse pitched backwards, raring with eyes white and rolling.

"Whoa! Whoa!" Armand grabbed at the lead rope of the horse, trying to settle it down. The boys managed to get most of the goods off the animal but another heavy boom of thunder sent the animal over the edge, kicking and bucking and charging about. The tether that was stretched between two trees gave way on one end, allowing the horse more latitude. Screaming wildly, the animal ran head long in blind panic. Coming to the end of the tether, which was still attached at one end, it gave a loud snort and lost its footing, landing flat on its back, smashing the pack saddle and what was left of the attached goods.

Armand, seeing what was happening, tried to get the horse up and recover what was left of its load. As the horse flailed to regain its feet, it kicked back, hitting Armand square in the middle of his back. The impact of the blow sent him flying. The boys, who'd scrambled out of the way of the crazed animal, rushed to help him as he lay unmoving.

"Is he dead?" Kitchi asked.

"If he isn't, he should be," Keme answered. "I've never seen anyone get kicked that hard."

Both of them huddled over the limp figure, wondering what to do. In a moment, they realized he wasn't dead.

"Ahhh! Ahhh! My...my back."

"He's alive. He's.....Armand! Armand! What can we do to help?" they asked.

He didn't answer them. Instead, he kept moaning and reaching for his back. Drifting in and out of consciousness, he seemed to be in terrible pain. Sometimes he'd try to raise up on his elbows but then he'd collapse and pass out again. As if all of this weren't enough, it began to rain – hard!

"We need to get him under cover."

Before the accident, they had bent a young sapling down and tied it to the trunk of another larger tree. Over this, they planned to drape a buffalo robe, staking it at the sides to form a shelter. When they tried to move Armand to the shelter, he screamed out in pain.

"We can't move him over there," Keme said. "Bring the robe here and we'll all get under it."

The storm raged on through the night, pouring a deluge of rain on the huddled trio. Needless to say, neither boy got any sleep. Armand too tossed and turned, sometimes writhing in pain and screaming.

Finally, as the first light was breaking over the eastern horizon, the rain stopped. The air was cold and damp and all about them was ankle-deep mud.

Crawling out from under the heavy, rain-soaked hide, the boys cast an eye about for the horses. The horse that had kicked Armand had so violently tried to get away that it had tangled itself in the tether rope and now lay at the base of a large pine, soaking wet and looking like a whipped pup. The other horses, also spooked by the storm, were gone to God knows where.

Kitchi got up and walked over to where some of their supplies were. Reaching into one of the skin bags, he brought forth a handful of dried meat.

"Here," he said, tossing a large chunk to his brother.

For a long time, they sat chewing on the meat without speaking. Then, Keme asked, "What are we going to do? We are a very long way from our camp and if Armand doesn't wake up, we'll never get back. I know I couldn't find my way."

"He'll wake up!" Kitchi answered. "Right now, though, we need to build a fire and dry out."

It was a full two days before Armand regained consciousness.

"Here, help me sit up," he said. "It's hard for me to breath lying down like this."

Keme gave Armand his hand and helped him raise up. Kitche took a pack of their pelts and propped them up under him.

"Is that better?" Keme asked.

"Yes," he answered, then added, "but I can't feel my legs." He suddenly hit himself on the leg with his fist. Nothing – no feeling! A grim look came over his face but he said nothing.

The boys looked at him and then at each other. Worry was written on their brow.

"You just need to rest and then you'll feel better," Kitchi offered.

"Maybe," was all Armand said. He then closed his eyes and drifted off to sleep.

It was dark when he finally woke up. The boys had built a shelter from the buffalo robes and they had a warm fire going. They handed Armand the skin bag that carried their water and offered him some dried meat. He ate and drank vigorously. Not much was said. Each of them seemed to be lost in their own thoughts, as they watched the dancing flames of the fire.

It was Armand who finally broke the silence.

Without turning his eyes from the flames, he began, "Tomorrow we must build a travois for me to ride on. With no feeling in my legs, I cannot sit a horse and I don't know when or if I'll be able to ride again." Both boys looked at each other with grave concern but said nothing.

"We have about done what trading we can and should start back anyway." He paused for a moment. "We have a long way to go and we should get started soon."

#

Riding on the travois was rough. The ups and downs of the countryside and the accompanying rocks, bumps, and trees jolted Armand, causing him to cry out occasionally. Because of the rough ride, he kept slipping downward and they ended up tying him to the framework.

As the days went by, Armand seemed to be regaining some of the feeling in his legs – his right more than his left. His bowels, though, were the main problem. He couldn't tell when he had to go and it just happened. It caused him great embarrassment when the boys had to clean up after him but they were good about it. Often, when they came to a small stream or river, they would help him bathe and clean himself. He hesitated to eat, knowing that it caused him to have to go, so he began to lose weight. By the time they reached their camp, Armand was little more than skin and bones.

Storm, rushing out to greet her men, quickly saw that something was wrong and hurried to help. Armand began to weep when he saw her. Her questioning eyes went quickly from Armand to the boys. Before she could ask, Keme spoke up.

"There was a storm – a bad storm. The horses were going crazy. Armand tried to calm one of them. It...it kicked him! It kicked him hard...in the back. He cannot walk...his legs...."

She got the picture. Then, kneeling, she moved next to him and cradled his head in her arms, gently comforting him.

"Quickly," she said, "Help me get him into the lodge. He must rest."

As the days passed, Armand's condition showed little improvement. What was worse was his attitude. The smallest thing angered him, causing him to fly into a rage, cursing at Storm or the boys. Storm would console him and try to make things better. She explained to the boys that he didn't mean the bad things he said and that it was his not being able to move that caused him to get mad. They seemed to understand.

With their supplies getting low, it was decided that the furs and goods that Armand and the boys had collected from the tribes they traded with needed to be taken to one of the outposts and exchanged for the necessary things they needed. Since Armand could not go, it fell to Kitchi and Keme to get it done. But Armand was not happy about it and said so.

"I don't like sending the boys off to do the trading. Somebody will cheat them out of their goods and we will have nothing."

"I think the boys have enough sense to make a good trade," she answered, scowling defensively. "Besides, they have to learn sometime and since you cannot go, they have to." She paused for a moment and then added, "We have come to depend on many goods that the white men provide. As I see it, we will become more dependent on them in the future and therefore, the boys must learn to deal with them." Nothing more was said.

Kitchi and Keme had the pack horses loaded and were gathering the last of their personal things to make the long journey down to the big river. Armand had gotten no better and so, as their mother had said, they would take the furs and other goods to a trading post and barter for the things they needed. Storm wanted some new blankets and cloth, if they could get it. Also, a new comb for her hair – she'd seen some of the other women with them and she fancied one herself. Armand wanted tobacco, powder, ball, and flints, and two skinning knives. Also, if they had a wool kapote he would like one of those. As they were about to leave, Armand spoke to them. "Be careful what you do around the white men. They are a different sort and will take advantage of you if they can." He paused. "Also, do not let them tempt you with whiskey. They will try to get you drunk and then steal everything you have. Be watchful..."

The boys nodded and told him they would be careful. As they rode away, their mother could see they were excited to be going. She worried for them, though, because she knew they were going to a world they had never seen. The white trappers and the riverboat men were a hard lot. She hoped they would be safe.

BOOK 6 – TRADING

CHAPTER 1:
REMEMBERING VICTOR

Clint was sweeping the hewn log floor of the trading post when he heard the rustle of horses outside. In a few moments, three Indians came through the door. They seemed hesitant at first, for none of them had ever been inside a white man's structure. There were small windows along the side of the building, which let in a bit of sunlight. Also, Clint had a coal oil lamp burning and it, too, cast a decent light. But, the place was deeply shadowed and it lent to the men's nervous hesitation.

Clint had spent many years with the Indians and spoke their languages fluently. So, when they approached him asking about trading their furs, he answered them in their own tongue. They wanted to trade what pelts and skins they had for the usual things, beads, mirrors, knives, cloth and vermillion. Mostly though, they wanted whiskey.

"I don't trade whiskey," Clint said. "I will trade with you for anything you see here but not whiskey."

Hearing this, they grumbled and told him that other white men downriver had traded whiskey with them before and they would go there to do their trading.

"As you wish," he said, "but be watchful they do not cheat you. There are many traders on this river who will get you drunk and steal your goods. I will not do that. I will make you a fair bargain and you will go away happy."

The Indians walked outside and were debating if they should trade with Clint or go on to another post. In the end, they decided to do their trading there. As they brought forth the skins they'd collected, Clint noticed something unusual, pinned to the front of one of the men's deerskin shirt. It seemed to be made of silver, although in a very tarnished condition. Because it was turned nearly upside down, it was hard for him to make out what it was but then it came to him. It was the letter "V," a letter he'd seen so many years ago adorning the side of a young man's hat.

"Victor," he whispered, "Victor O'Bannon." The boy he'd said goodbye to on the banks of the Platte River.

"Very nice," Clint said, pointing to the silver ornament on the man's shirt. "Where did you get that?"

The Indian looked at him guardedly and then answered.

"I found it," he said, not looking directly at Clint.

"Oh, I see," Clint answered. "And where would such a lucky man find an ornament like that?"

The Indian didn't seem to like the questioning but answered anyway.

"I would like to tell you that I took it from an enemy that I fought and killed in battle. But that would not be true. Some years ago, I found a man's bones near the big lake in the land of roaring water. This was attached to a piece of old cloth, wrapped about his skull. I think the spirits that live in that place took his life."

"Would you like to trade that?" Clint asked.

"No! No!" the man answered, shaking his head. "Since the spirits left it with the dead man, it must have great magic and I could not trade it, not for anything." Pausing a moment, he then looked at Clint, knowing the white man wanted the ornament. Quickly he added, "But if you had some whiskey, I might make a trade with you."

Clint thought for a long moment before answering. "Alright, but just this one time," he said. He made his way into the back of the trading post and when he returned he carried a small jug of the coveted liquid. Before he handed it over, however, he told the man again. "I will never trade whiskey with you again. The only reason I trade now is because that ornament once belonged to a friend of mine."

"It is a trade, then," the Indian said, handing Clint the ornament and snatching the jug from his grasp. Whooping and hollering, they ran out, mounted their horses, and galloped away.

"They'll be through that jug in no time," he thought. "Hope they don't come back lookin' for more."

Taking the silver ornament to the back of the store, Clint doused a piece of cloth in some coal oil and set about rubbing the finish to remove the tarnish. The years and the elements had darkened and pitted it but, with the hard, rubbing motion, the ornament regained some of its brightness. Nodding his head, he whispered, "There, that's better! I think Victor would be happy knowing that it ended up here, with me." With that, he placed it on the shelf behind him, leaning it against the log wall where it could be seen.

CHAPTER 2:
MORAH

Trading had been good through the year and now Clint was preparing the load he would take to meet the boats on the big river. It was a five-day journey to the landing. Those boats brought the needed supplies he would trade his pelts for and, in turn, trade to the Indians for their pelts. Beaver was the top trading item these days. The hides were used to make tri-cornered hats and the more popular top hats for gentlemen. They were especially popular in Europe.

The Old Man was late to rise and so Clint went about the work himself. Even though the old Indian moved slowly, he was still a lot of help to Clint. He knew a lot about pelts and loading horses and was always interesting to listen to. He would often recount tales of his youth, emphasizing his bravery and cunning while counting coup on an enemy. Clint listened intently and never questioned the Old Man's stories. He'd just nod in agreement and now and then throw in a gasp as if he were stunned at the heroism he'd just heard. It seemed to please the Old Man and that, in turn, pleased Clint, for he cared deeply for the old Indian. They had ridden many trails together and had become the best of friends.

When all the skins were loaded, Clint went to the Old Man's quarters to roust him out.

"Come on old friend – time to go. We have a long journey ahead of us."

"Go ahead" he answered. "I'll catch up with you on the trail."

With that, Clint climbed on his horse and, leading the pack train, made his way onto the trail that lead away from his trading post. It was a fine morning and as he rode, he took in the countryside; the hills, the draws, the pine groves and the sagebrush flats, looking for movement, watching for danger or anything that seemed out of place. That was the way of the mountain man. Those were the rules you lived by. If you didn't obey those rules, you didn't last long.

He had been riding for a few hours and the Old Man hadn't yet caught up so he decided to stop near a small stream and wait.

"He'll be along," he thought. He tied the lead horse of the pack animals to a small aspen tree in the middle of a grassy area on the stream bank. The horses could graze here and there was water if they needed it. His horse, he tied to another tree. Pulling a chunk of dried meat from the parfliech that hung on his saddle, he sat leaning his back against the side of a fallen tree. The sun felt good as its warm rays washed over his face and he closed his eyes. In a dreamlike state, he suddenly thought about Storm. Memories of her came into mind and he smiled. What had happened to her? Where had she gone?

Drifting deeper into his reverie he could see her, moving toward him, smiling, beckoning, and calling his name.

"Clint! Clint!"

"Clint!" The voice jolted him awake. Grabbing the rifle at his side, he struggled to focus on the one who had called his name. And, there she was, like an angel, silhouetted against the bright sun, speaking his name. He couldn't believe his eyes, it was Storm.

"Storm," he cried. "Storm!" There was silence for a moment and then a voice answered.

"No! No, it is I....Morah."

"Morah!" Jesus Christ where did she come from? How the hell......? Where was the Old Man?

Seeing the confusion in his eyes, Morah moved toward him.

"Forgive me," she whispered, "I did not mean to startle you. I came to your place this morning but your friend told me you were taking furs to trade. He said if I wanted to, he would take me to you."

It was then that Clint saw the Old Man, tying his horse near the pack animals.

"What are you doing here, Morah? Where is Gray Eagle?"

Dropping her face, she answered, "He is dead. He died three days ago, in his sleep." She paused for a moment, then went on. "When the others in the tribe learned of his death, they came to the lodge and took everything he had. They left me nothing except one horse and a robe. I had nowhere else to go so I came to you."

"I'm sorry to hear about Gray Eagle. He was a brave warrior and a fine man. You are welcome to ride with us. I must tell you, though, it is a long way to the place we meet the boats."

"Thank you," she said, "I will not be any trouble."

The Old Man walked over to join them. He had a sly smile on his face as he approached.

"A fine woman, my friend," he said, his smile broadening. "The great spirit smiles on you today. Most men would have to search long and hard for such a woman. But you, you have them searching for you."

Clint eyed the Old Man as he looked for a place to rest his old bones. "Yer always trying to hook me up with a squaw, ain't ya?" He shook his head and smiled at his aged friend. The Old Man grinned at him but said nothing.

The ride downriver took many days. To pass the time, each of them told tales of their youth and exploits. They shot rabbits and grouse for food and now and then they ate a fat trout from one of the many streams along their way.

When at last they reached their destination, Clint was amazed at how much it grown since the last time he was there. What had been a single trading post before had grown into a small village, with a blacksmith, a farrier, a gunsmith and some pelt storage shelters. A dock had been fashioned at the river's edge to accommodate the boats that arrived. A short way back from the compound, stood a half dozen lodges. Indian children were busy chasing and swinging sticks at a deer skin ball.

"We'll tie 'em up here," Clint said, dismounting in front of the trading post. Morah and the Old Man followed his lead. Just then, two men in uniform stepped from the trading post, nearly running into Clint.

"Watch where you're goin,' Injun," one of them said, pushing him aside. "Jesus, he's a big one," the other one remarked. "Don't think I've seen an Injun that tall before." They laughed and went on.

Clint, struck by what they'd said, thought for a moment and then realized, he did look like an Indian. His hair was long, although not black and his skin was weathered and tanned. And of course, he wore deer skin leggings, moccasins, and a fringed buckskin shirt. The giveaway would have been his eyes. They were a bright blue. But then, the men didn't pay that close of attention to him. Just another dirty Indian they thought. They did however, pay close attention to Morah, making insulting comments and gestures. She paid them no mind.

Clint, Morah, and the Old Man walked into the trading post, eagerly looking about at the many things that adorned the tables and shelves. Morah had never seen such things and she wandered about in amazement. The Old Man too looked over what was there and focused his attention on the rifles and pistols that lay across one of the tables near the back.

335

Clint approached the man he believed to be in charge, telling him he had several packets of furs and goods that he'd like to trade.

"Good!" the man answered. "I can get to you in two days. You see, I have several others ahead of you that are lookin' to do the same thing. So, if you would, put your name there on that list and I'll get to you soon as I can." He paused for a moment and then, casting a disparaging look toward Morah and the Old Man, he added, "Don't bring them damned Injuns back in here with you – they steal everything that ain't nailed down."

Clint was quick to answer. "Not these two," he said, "they don't steal nothin' and it riles me to hear somebody like you accuse them of that."

"What the hell do you mean, somebody like me?" His eyes squinted in and Clint could see he was hot.

"Yeah! Somebody like you who takes advantage of these people every damn day. You know, well as I, that most white traders, you included, get their furs and their makins for little or nothin'."

Just then another voice interrupted. "Whoa! Calm down, you two!" It was another man that had been working near the rear of the post.

"What's this all about, George?" he asked.

"This feller claims that we ain't doin' right by these Injuns when we trade with 'em. Sez we're cheatin' 'em."

"Is that so, mister?" He looked directly at Clint, expecting an answer.

"I've heard stories," Clint said. "Stories about you tradin' whiskey for pelts and moccasins and whatever these folks have to trade. You get their goods. They get a belly full of rot-gut and a bad headache for all their hard work. Don't seem exactly fair."

"Well, if you owned a tradin' post, you'd..."

Clint cut him short! "I do own a tradin' post, upriver, five day's ride. Name's Jeffries, Clint Jeffries, and I trade with these folks all the time. I don't trade whiskey though. They don't like to come here to trade but some of 'em have no choice. They say you get 'em drunk and take their goods."

The man glared at Clint but answered calmly. "It's true, I do trade whiskey but I figure these are grown men who know what they're doin' and if it's whiskey they want, it's whiskey I give 'em. It ain't against the law."

For a long minute, Clint just looked at the man. Then, shaking his head, he said, "Guess what they told me is true. Guess I was right about you." With that he turned and walked out, taking Morah and the Old Man with him. "C'mon!" he told them, "let's go make camp."

When they were out of earshot, the owner told his man "When that feller comes in to trade his goods, don't trade with him. We got plenty of other trappers to trade with and fill our lot. We don't need him or his pelts."

Leaving the settlement, the trio rode some distance down the river to make camp.

"I don't think I want to be too near that outfit," Clint told them. "They're a nest of snakes and I wouldn't put anything past them."

Morah, who didn't understand English, had no idea what had been said and couldn't understand why they had to leave. She wanted to stay and look around at all the strange new things in the post. Clint assured her that they would return and she could look further.

There was something about the trading post and the surrounding village that bothered Clint. It was the soldiers. They'd seen them when they arrived at the post. Why were there soldiers here? Back in St. Louis, Clint had seen soldiers but he hadn't paid much attention to them and hadn't even given it a second thought. But here? Why? He'd have to ask some of the other villagers and see what was going on.

After a short ride, they came to a grassy flat that sat back some distance from the river. There was plenty of grass for the horses to graze on and enough cover to block the wind.

"This will do," Clint remarked, swinging off the horse to the ground. They unloaded the heavy packs, hobbled the horses, and began gathering wood for the evening fire. The Old Man and Morah spread out some buffalo robes and set about laying a fire up for the evening.

"I'm goin' down to the river and see if I can catch us some dinner," Clint said, taking up a small bag from his kit. When he approached the rolling water he found a sturdy willow and cut it to make a pole. After stripping the willow of its leafs and twigs, he reached into his bag and brought forth a length of horsehair woven line – thin, but strong. At the end of the line was a hook he'd bought in St. Louis. It was made of metal and was much better than the bone hooks the Indians used. He then walked up the bank away from the river and began looking through the bushes and grass for something to put on the hook for bait. In a few minutes, he had caught several grasshoppers. Pinching their heads so they couldn't get away, he carried them down to where the fish pole lay. Carefully, he surveyed the river, looking for a likely spot where a fish might be feeding. Forty or fifty yards downstream, he spied a fallen tree, it's dry, leafless limbs stretched out into the stream some ten or fifteen feet, creating a swirling eddy. Quietly, he moved to a place above the tree and hunkered in behind its gnarled trunk, trying not to make any commotion. With the willow in one hand, he gently tossed the baited hook and line out into the current. No sooner had the grasshopper hit the surface than a nice trout rolled on it and was hooked.

Within an hour, Clint was back in camp with three fish. Seeing this, Mohra said she would cook them. Clint nodded and she grabbed up a small skin from her pack and went to the river. She was soon back, carrying the skin which was filled with mud. Laying the skin next to the fire, she took up the fish and covered each one with a thick coat of mud. These, she laid in the coals at the edge of the fire.

"They will be cooked soon," she said. When the fish were done baking, each of them took a fish and broke away the hardened mud. As the mud came away, so also did part of the skin of the trout. They picked the meat from the bones and ate heartily. Along with the fish, Clint had some ground corn and wild onion that he'd gotten from a Hidatsa Woman. To these, he added water and a little salt, making a small cake-like patty. He placed them on a flat rock he'd laid in the fire's coals. Before long, they had cooked into a flat biscuit. Morah and the Old Man watched as he did this and ate them up when he offered each a serving. When finished, they retired for the evening. They laid near one another in their buffalo robes. For a while they talked of the day and what tomorrow would bring. The talk soon faded to quiet but before drifting off, Clint thought to himself, "It is good to have a full belly, caring friends, and a warm place to spend the night."

As they slept, a million stars clustered in the heavens above and a gentle breeze flowed up from the river, bringing with it the sweet smell of cottonwoods. Far away, a prairie wolf howled at the rising moon, shouting his loneliness.

CHAPTER 3:
"DIRTY SHIRT" JOHNSON

The white sky of morning found Clint washing himself in the river and donning a clean linen shirt - the only one he owned. It had not been cold sleeping, but now, the morning air carried a sharpness to it that foretold of the coming fall. Soon, the days would become shorter, the leaves would be changing their color, and he would be riding to hunt the buffalo. The animals he killed and the meat they rendered would be what kept them alive over the winter. With the furs he accumulated, he could trade for flour and beans and other such goods; things he, himself, could use to barter with at his trading post.

Morah and the Old Man were awake and stirring about the camp when Clint returned. Dipping into the leather bag she carried, she threw a chunk of dried meat his way. "Here," she said, "this should fill your stomach until I can make some corn cakes and fatback."

Clint caught the meat and began gnawing on it as he put away his personals. He shaved whenever he could because he knew the Indians didn't like beards. He'd heard them refer to men who wore beards as "hair-faces." Thus, it made it much easier to trade with them if he was clean shaven. When they'd finished eating and packed up their camp, they rode back to the settlement.

There were many lean-tos erected along their way, each of which belonged to a white trader or an Indian peddling their wares. Morah had dismounted and now moved from one to another, gazing in amazement at the array of goods that lay on the tables and trade blankets. Clint watched her as she went, thinking, "She's just like the children in the candy stores back in St. Louis." A small smile made its way across his face.

Ahead and slightly set back from the rest of the traders was a large canvas tent. Stacks of pelts and buffalo robes were carelessly stacked along its edges. An old ragged figure of a man sat rocking and smoking a cob pipe just inside the flaps of the tent. A small, hand-scribbled sign reading, "Trade Goods" hung lop-sided just above him. Clint recognized him immediately. They had come up river together, scouting and hunting for the boat crew. His name was Clarence Johnson but everyone called him "Dirty Shirt." And, they had good reason. Johnson always wore the same shirt, which at one time had been the top half of a pair of long johns. No one ever knew what became of the bottom half. Most agreed that they had probably rotted away. If they were anything like the top half, they must have been horrible. Johnson, like most of the other mountain men, was not keen on cleanliness. In fact, you didn't want to get down-wind of him for very long, else you might just puke.

"Got anything worth havin' in there?" Clint asked.

Without looking up, the huddled figure replied, "Got plenty worth havin' if you got anything worth tradin'."

"Don't know as I'd want to trade anything with the likes of you. Ya look kinda crooked to me."

This got the man's attention and he raised up trying to focus on the varmint who'd had just insulted him. The pipe still hung in the corner of his mouth, allowing a thin stream of smoke to curl up around his head. He coughed once and brushed the smoke away from his eyes, straining to make out the stranger's face.

"Well, I'll be dipped in shit! Jeffries, you ole sombitch! Ain't seen you in a month a Sundays. Climb on down and set a spell."

"Hello Johnson," Clint shot back, offering the man his hand. Nodding his head, he answered, "Yup, it's been a while.

341

Last time I saw you, some big old squaw had you down and was kickin' the shit out of you. That was down on Yellerstone, right?" He paused a moment thinking, then went on. "Yeah, ya ended up marryin' her, didn't ya?"

Slow to answer, the man said, "Uh huh! I did marry her and I tell ya, she had some hard bark on her. She liked to work me over about every other day. I loved her though. She was a damn good cook and a better lover and she could skin critters with the best of 'em." He paused and drew another lung full of smoke, reminiscing. "I took up tradin' here on the river and after a while, she got tired of it. Said she wanted to move back north with her people. She took up with some buck that told her he'd take her back home, so she packed up and pulled out. Left me high and dry. I miss her, sometimes."

"You tradin' furs fer goods, Johnson?" Clint queried.

"Yessir! I am. Whatcha got?"

"I've got a pretty good string of horses loaded with prime pelts. They're staked back in the trees, there. But I half-assed told that pecker head up the hill there, that I'd trade with him."

"Well, suit yerself brother, he's probably got more trade goods than I do but I'll match his price for your pelts. Sides that, he's got so many men lined up, it'll take you a week to do business with him." He paused for a moment and then went on, "You know, he trades whiskey to the Injuns." Clint nodded.

Johnson went on, "I used to do that myself but they get that shit in 'em and they go plumb crazy....shootin' up the place, fightin', killin'. I give it up and that's why you don't see big stacks a pelts here abouts. I guess I shouldn't care about 'em but I do. We've brought a poison into these mountains and it's killin' these folks. Between the whiskey and the white man's sickness, it won't be long fore they're all gone."

Changing the subject, Clint asked, "What are soldiers doin' up here?"

"Yeah that!" the man answered, "One more thing to do away with our red brothers. I guess some of the tradin' companies were gettin' nervous about the Indians along the river. There had been some troubles - like always. Anyway, they bitched to the government and the government sent along a detachment of dragoons. They claim they're here to explore and make maps of the surrounding country. Maybe they're doin' that but I ain't seen one map or anybody tryin' to draw one. Seems to me, their presence will do more harm than good." Taking another long drag on his pipe, he put his hand on Clint's shoulder. "Go get them horses and let's have a look at those pelts."

Once the tradin' was done, Clint was ready to pack up and head back but Morah and the Old Man wanted to stay a while and look things over. Clint knew what the Old Man wanted to do and he tried to discourage him. But, like other members of his race, the Old Man had a taste for whiskey. Morah too had been gettin' her nose wet, tradin' what little she had for a cup full of the fire water. Clint kept an eye on them, making sure they didn't get too drunk, and keeping them out of trouble.

It was on the fourth night of their stay that they heard a big commotion in the settlement. They were camped some distance away when they heard the shooting and hollering. Usually, if an altercation broke out, there was a lot of yelling and maybe one or two shots. But, this was different. Several gunshots filled the night air and there was the sound of stampeding horses. Clint stood listening.

"Maybe we should go see what's happening," the Old Man said. "We could probably help somebody and then we could get some whiskey." Morah nodded in agreement.

"You two have had enough whiskey and I ain't of a mind to be stickin' my nose into someone else's fight. I can see where this whiskey thing could become a problem so tomorrow, we're headin' back. I wanna go early so you need to get some rest." With that, they all rolled up in the buffalo robes and went to sleep.

CHAPTER 4:
STARTLING NEWS

Daylight found the three of them readying themselves for the long journey home. Johnson had made Clint a good deal on his furs and provided most of the trade goods they'd need to get through another year. There were still some things, though, that Clint required and they would therefore have to stop and pick them up before they left the settlement.

Pulling up in front of the trading post they'd first come to, Clint dismounted. Before going in, he told Morah and the Old Man to stay there. "If you come with me," he said, "they'll be trouble. They don't like Injuns." The Old Man was used to the insults and the poor treatment that white men issued out and was therefore, not offended with what Clint told them. Morah, however, was not accustomed to their treatment and insisted on going with Clint.

"Okay," Clint motioned, "but stay close to me and don't touch anything." She nodded.

The building was musty and dark and smelled of smoke, blood, and salted hides. Barely able to see, the two of them made their way to the counter at the rear. The same man Clint had talked to before was there. He looked half asleep as they approached him. His eyes were shut and his chin rested heavily on his propped arms. His head nodded slightly to one side and then the other, with little jerking motions.

Clint walked right up to the man before he spoke. "I was in here the other day and told you I'd like to trade my furs." This startled the man, causing him to jump.

"Wha...what?" He said, trying to focus on the man in front of him. "Oh, it's you," he uttered. "What the hell are you doin' here?"

Casting aside the man's rudeness, Clint answered, "I wanted to tell you that I traded my furs to Johnson so I won't be tradin' with you. I do need a few things, however, and I'll pay....." The man cut him off, mid-sentence.

"You think I give a shit what you need?" He stopped short, looking directly at Morah. "I told you not to bring in those thievin' sons-a-bitches, didn't I? Now, get her the hell outta here." he paused a moment and then went on. "Besides, you got a real set of balls on you, comin' in here after what your Goddamn kids did to this town last night. They shot and wounded one of the trappers and liked to have killed everybody else. If it hadn't been for those army boys, they might have...." This time it was Clint who interrupted.

"What kids?" he shouted. "What are you saying?"

"I'm saying your Goddamn kids came in here wantin' to trade some pelts. Said they needed some goods. I told 'em no, that they'd have to wait and take their turn. Or, I'd trade 'em some whiskey right then and there. Then the bastards began raisin' hell, threatenin' me in Injun. They started to pick up some of my trade goods and that's when I lit into 'em. Gave one of 'em a pretty good thrashing too, til the other one hit me over the head with a club. That's when I pulled my pistol and took a shot at 'em. Two other men, comin' through the door, also fired on 'em. Don't think we hit 'em, though, but if they come back here, we'll be waitin' for 'em and this time, we won't miss."

Clint looked befuddled. He couldn't figure out why this man said they were his sons. "Why did you say they're my kin?" he asked.

"Well Jesus man, they look just like ya, same face, same build, same size, same set to their jaw. Yeah, they're your boys alright. You'll see when the army brings 'em in."

"What do you mean?" Clint asked.

"You think they're gonna get away with what happened last night? No sir, they're not. Those dragoons lit out fer 'em at daylight. And when they catch up to 'em, there'll be hell to pay."

"Which way did they go?" Clint asked.

"Ya think I'd tell ya that, ya dumb son of a bitch...so's you could go warn 'em. Ain't no way!"

Taking Morah outside, Clint rushed to the horses. As he climbed aboard, he told the Old Man to take Morah and start back. He didn't explain anything other than to say he had something to do and that he would catch up to them along the trail. The Old Man nodded and turned his horse about but Morah didn't want to leave Clint and said so.

"No Morah!" Clint said in a harsh voice, a voice she had not heard before. "You can't go with me. I have to travel fast and you'd only hold me back. Go with the Old Man and I will catch up with you." The tone of his voice told her there was no use arguing so, reluctantly, she turned her pony to follow the Old Man and the pack string.

Clint wheeled his horse around and headed for Johnson's tent. Johnson was awake, but barely. Luckily, he had seen what happened and witnessed the boys' getaway. As Clint was about to ride off, Johnson cried out to him, "Didn't know you had it in ya, to sire such good lookin' boys." This caused Clint to pull up sharp.

"You saw them?" he asked.

"Sure as hell did. Came right through here where yer settin'. I got a good look at 'em. Twins, I'd reckon. Looked like you did when we first come up the river..........seems like a hundred year ago. If ya plan on catchin' up to 'em, ya best ride through the creek there and up around the west side of that mountain." He pointed off in the direction where Clint was heading. "I've hunted this country a lot and you'll cut off a good distance from follerin' the trail they're on. They gotta go through that pass yonder in order to make it to the north country. Do that and you may just catch up to 'em."

'Thanks Johnson!" Clint shouted back over his shoulder. To himself he whispered, "I've gotta see what the hell this is all about."

CHAPTER 5:
THE BOYS AND THE ARMY

Going the way Johnson had suggested wasn't easy. There was no defined trail and the country was strewn with large boulders. A grove of white-barked aspen surrounded him, causing him to zigzag between the trees and rocks. At last, he came to a defined game trail which led up a wide draw. He could see that the path ahead would bring him up over a small saddle between two hills and would place him somewhere near where Johnson said the main trail north would be.

When he finally came to the trail, he dismounted and knelt to examine the many tracks that had been pounded into it. Several horses had passed this way, and not long ago. Some of them were shod. Since Indian ponies were not shod, he knew they were the tracks the soldiers had left. Remounting, he urged his horse forward, hoping to catch up to them.

Nearly two hours had passed and he still hadn't caught up to the soldiers. The trail led ever-upward. When finally he came to the place it crossed through the pass, he noticed that the trail split, going two different directions. He also noticed the soldiers had divided their numbers and were following each trail. As near as he could figure, there were six or eight of them. Presumably, three or four of them went each direction.

He could see what was happening here. These boys, whoever they were, had been taught well in the ways of delusion. He'd seen Indians do this many times; split up, lay a false trail, divide whoever it was who followed you and then double back and lay in wait to attack. Since, as Johnson had said, there were only two of the boys, he believed they would probably not attack the soldiers but would more likely try to lose them. Unless these blue-coats had any tracking experience, they'd never find the boys.

Clint took the trail to the right, moving slowly, watching for any sign that might indicate where the boys had gone. He knew he could find the soldiers; that wouldn't be hard, but he wanted to find the boys before they skedaddled out of the country.

The trail he followed angled downward toward a thick set of pines. On the right side, the hillside angled upward, rising some distance. "That's where they'll try to lose the soldiers" he whispered. Angling to the right, off the trail, he selected a route that would take him parallel to the trail but higher up in the pines. After some distance, he dismounted and tied his horse to a low bush. Silently, he made his way among the trees, watching for movement or anything out of the ordinary. He made his way toward a small clearing that lay ahead of him and off to the right. At this point, he was a long way above the trail.

Pausing a moment, he noticed a slight movement near the edge of the clearing. It was a horse's tail, flicking at flies. "So! This is where they're hiding." he whispered to himself. "Just as I figured."

Taking up a position where he could watch the clearing and anyone who approached from below, he waited. For some time, he sat listening and watching, knowing they had to return. Then from far down in the woods, a shot rang out, echoing through the trees. Before the echo had died, he was up and running toward where the shot came from. As he ran, he could hear men yelling and horses clamoring. Something bad was happening, someone was going to die.

When he caught sight of the men ahead, he slowed his run to a walk, trying to ascertain what was happening. Silently, he slipped in behind a fallen tree. That's when he saw one of the boys. He lay face down on the ground. One soldier had his foot planted on the back of his neck while another tied his hands behind him.

"Quit yer squirmin,' ya little bastard," one of them yelled and forced his foot down harder on the boy's neck.

Then, from further back in the woods, a voice yelled out, "We've got the other one."

Clint watched as two other soldiers brought the other boy along. They had a rope around his neck and were dragging him behind their horses. He struggled to free himself but there was no chance.

"What the hell we gonna do with these two?" one of the soldiers asked. The soldier that seemed to be in charge answered, "We're gonna take 'em back, try 'em for what they did, and then make an example of 'em." Smiling down at the two lying there before him, he added, "They'll probably hang."

One of the other soldiers spoke up then, "Hell, they're just kids. And, they didn't kill anyone."

"One of 'em shot Jack Parker," the leader said.

"Yeah, but he didn't die. He was only grazed on the shoulder."

"Don't make any difference," the other one said. It'll teach 'em they can't come into a white man's settlement and act like savages. Now, let's pack 'em up and get on outta here."

If he let them ride off, Clint knew he'd not be able to catch up with them before they met the rest of their troops. Then, he'd never be able to help them. He didn't know whether he could take four of them or not but he had to do something.

As they had no extra horses, the soldiers were going to double up one of their men and put the two boys on one horse.

They had tied the boys' hands in front of them and had also tied their feet together under the horse's belly. By doing that, the boys could still ride but they couldn't climb off and run.

When they were about to move out, Clint saw his chance. Running as hard as he could, he lept through the air, catching the lead soldier smack on the side of the head with his rifle butt. The man crashed to the ground, unconscious. The horse he was riding reared up, kicking and snorting. This sent the other horses into a frenzy, dumping one of the other soldiers flat on his back. The soldier leading the horse the boys were on dropped the reins and reached for his pistol.

"Don't!" Clint said, pointing his rifle at the man.

"Alright, alright!" the man said and put his hands in the air. "Don't shoot."

Seeing this, the other two put their hands in the air also.

"Now," Clint said, "lay on the ground face down." The three were slow to respond so Clint kicked one of them behind the knee and yelled, "Get yer asses down there or I'll kill every one of ya."

With that, the men laid right down.

Tossing his knife up to the boys and motioning, he called to them in the language he thought they'd understand. "Cut yourself loose and come and help me tie these men up." When they didn't respond, he quickly signed what he meant. With that, they jumped to do as he said.

After they'd secured the men, they all stood and looked at each other. In all the excitement, they hadn't had time to do this before, but now they stood there gazing in amazement. What Johnson and the other outfitter said was true. These two looked just like Clint. They were every bit his height but thinner, not as heavily muscled; the same features, the same demeanor, their eyes were dark brown though, while his were blue. But for all he could see, they looked just like him.

The boys, too, were astonished. Who was this man? Why did he look so much like them? Where did he come from? Then, Clint noticing their clothing, moccasins, and markings, tried speaking to them in a different tongue, one he had not used in a very long time.

"Do you speak the language of the Blackfoot or Piegan?' he queried. Their faces brightened as they answered.

"Yes, we are of the Piegan people." They smiled proudly as they answered.

From down on the ground the lead soldier had regained his senses and yelled up at them.

"Yeah, yer gonna be of the dead people when the rest of my troop gets here."

"He's right," Clint said. "They'll be coming this way soon so we must leave. But before we go, answer me this. Did you shoot a man at the white settlement last night?"

"We could not have shot anyone. We do not have guns."

Clint then spoke to the men on the ground. "These boys claim they couldn't have shot anyone last night because they don't have guns. So, if anyone was shot, as you say. it was someone else who did the shootin'."

One of the soldiers then spoke up. "Yeah, Sarge, we didn't find any guns with 'em."

"Shut yer mouth," the lead man said.

"I've spared your lives and these boys had nothing to do with the shooting so I don't expect you to come looking for us." Clint said. He paused for a moment and then, kneeling down close to them, he whispered, "If you are foolish enough to do so, you will die." With that, they headed off in a direction away from where their horses were tied. Leaving no sign of their path, they doubled back, arriving at the horses some hours later. It was late afternoon when they arrived at a small stream. Sure that they'd evaded the soldiers, they stopped to rest.

Dismounting, they let the horses drink their fill. Clint took out a small skin bag and brought forth a piece of dried meat for each of them. It was time for introductions. Clint was the first to speak. "What are your names" he asked.

"We are called Kitchi and Keme. That means thunder, one of them said.

"I know what it means," Clint answered. "The other means brave one."

"You look like us," one of them offered. "What is your name?"

"My name is Jeffries, Clinton Jeffries."

With that, both of the boys' eyes got very large and they seemed extremely frightened, staring first at one another and then back at Clint.

"What is it?" Clint asked, noticing their sudden change of demeanor.

"You are dead," one of them remarked, "A ghost warrior."

Suddenly, they were on their feet making for their horses.

"Wait," Clint said. "I'm no ghost warrior. Who said I was dead." But try as he might, he could not stop them. Mounting their horses, they spun to face him.

"We thank you for your help, mighty spirit, and will not speak of you to others, as it is forbidden to speak of the dead. Your name is sacred to us."

"Wait," Clint tried again but in vain. Their horses were at a gallop and, within the blink of an eye, they were out of sight.

"Damn," he thought. "Scared as they are, wouldn't do me any good to try to follow them."

With that, he decided to go back and meet up with the Old Man and Morah. Maybe he'd run into those boys again sometime and they could sit and talk. Seeing them as they were, he felt a certain kinship with them, as if they might be his children. He thought on this for a moment but then dismissed it as coincidence. It was a long ride back and he had to get going.

"Better keep a sharp eye out so as not to meet up with those soldiers. They'd have a good time with me."

BOOK 7 – FAMILY IS EVERYTHING

CHAPTER 1:
ROBBED AND BEATEN

After an hour's ride Kitchi pulled his horse to a stop. Turning to face his brother, he asked "Was he really a ghost warrior? He appeared out of nowhere and...."

"He looked like a real man," Keme answered quickly, cutting off his brother's words. "But he looked so much like us, he had to have been a ghost or our..." he stopped then, not saying the word that hung on the end of his tongue. Instead, he said, "The old ones say the Ghost Warrior can take on different shapes and faces. He must have taken on our appearance. We must not speak of him to anyone."

"What will we do about the trade goods? We still have the pelts and our other things. We can't go back to camp without trading them for what we need and we can't go back to that trading place. What then?"

"We search for another such place to trade our goods. Armand said there are many such places along the river." The other boy nodded his head in agreement.

Before they rode on, Keme looked at his brother and asked, "Mother told us that Jeffries had died, right?"

"Yes," his brother nodded. Turning back on a path toward the river, they urged their horses to a gallop.

Two days later, the boys were standing at the river's edge, some distance downstream from the place they'd had the trouble. There was nobody or nothing in sight. The only movement was the endless current rolling silently past.

"Perhaps we should go further downstream," Keme said.

"Maybe," his brother answered, unsure of what he was saying.

"Well, we either go up or we go down and I don't think up is a good idea. I'd bet they're still looking for us."

"I'm sure they are," his brother agreed. "So, that leaves us to go downstream." On they rode.

Several hours passed and the pair had found nothing. Because of the thick brush and willows growing at the river's edge, they were forced to ride on the low hills above, keeping a watchful eye on the river and what lay about them.

Suddenly, Kitchi pulled his horse to a halt. "What's that?" he said, pointing at a thick patch of pines some distance away.

"What?" Keme said, "I see nothing."

"There, right there! At the edge of those trees."

"Oh yes, I see it now." Keme said. "Some sort of lodge, I think."

"You circle back and come up on the other side of it and I'll slip up through the brush on this side."

Keme did as his brother said, tying his horse back in the trees and coming up behind the shelter. Meanwhile, Kitchi crawled toward the lodge, keeping a thin stand of willows between him and whatever the strange looking thing was. It was round shaped with no pointed top, like a teepee and appeared to be made from willows, like those growing along the river. A skin flap hung over the entrance.

As he watched, a woman appeared from inside. She was carrying a large skin and some pottery. She spread the skin on the ground and set the pottery pieces on it. Then, she returned to the shelter and once again came forth with her arms full of something. After she'd placed those things down, she sat cross-legged at the edge of the skin. She was looking directly at where he lay hidden.

Suddenly, she yelled to him and began motioning for him to come there. He couldn't fully understand what she said but he knew what she meant. For a long minute, he laid there, wondering if this was some sort of trap. But when she motioned to him again, he stood up and began cautiously walking toward her. There was an assortment of food laid out on the skin. This is what she had retrieved from the lodge.

Again, she said something to him and motioned for him to sit. Taking up a place directly across from her, he let himself down to the ground. She motioned for him to eat, bringing her hand up from the food to her mouth and then pointing for him to do the same.

Before he did anything, he began signing. "Who are you and where do you come from?"

She answered him, saying "We are of the Arikaree Tribe. We come here from far downriver."

"Are you here alone?" Kitchi asked, adding quickly, "Where is your man?"

"We were set upon by white men some time ago. Many of my people, including my husband, were killed. Our village was plundered and burned." Tears flowed from the woman's eyes as she related the tragedy that had befallen her people.

"Call in the other one," she signed, "The one back there in the trees."

Apparently, she had seen them before they'd seen her.

"Alright," Kitchi signed. And with that he yelled to Keme to come join them.

"Are there only the two of you?" she signed.

"Yes!" he nodded, then signed back, "We are grateful for this food. We are very hungry."

Keme appeared from around the edge of the strange looking lodge and joined them. As they ate, they signed, asking each other questions. They found out her name was Liela and that she'd traveled here some time ago with her brother. Apparently, he was off hunting.

"So, what are you doing this far from your home?" she asked.

Keme answered her, "We have furs and other items we wish to trade for but we are having a hard time finding someone to trade us for the things we need."

"But where are your goods?" She queried, "I don't see them anywhere about."

"We have them tied up a ways back there with our horses" he answered.

"And, what about weapons?" she asked. "Do you not have guns?"

This seemed like a strange question to Kitchi. "Why would she ask that," he thought to himself.

In his own tongue, he said to Keme, "I think something is wrong here. Why would she ask about weap....?" He suddenly stopped short of what he was saying, looking at the armed men that now surrounded them. Each man carried a spear or war club. Two of them had guns. He saw one of them coming fast toward his brother.

"Run, Keme," he yelled. But it was too late. As Keme raised up to get away, the man's club found its mark behind his ear and he crumpled to the ground. This happened only moments before he too felt the sharp crack to his skull. The last thing he saw was the skin with the food on it coming up to hit him in the face.

When they at last came to, it was full dark and they were bound hand to foot, their knees against their chests and their backs pressed up to a large pine tree; one on one side, one on the other. Besides that, each of them had a noose tightly coiled about his neck, which ran around the tree, lashing them directly to it. The only light at all was cast by the sliver of moon, hanging in the western sky.

"Ohhh!" Keme moaned. "My head! Ohhh!"

"You are awake, finally!" Kitchi whispered. "Can you get free?"

"No!" was the reply. "Ohhh! I feel like I was kicked."

"Be quiet! Try to move your hands...get them loose." Kitchi kept at him.

"There is a piece of sharp rock in the medicine bag I carry around my neck." Keme whispered. "It was the first arrowhead I ever made and I kept it. If I can somehow reach the bag....."

For hours Keme strained at the rope, trying to reach the small pouch that hung near his throat. Blood ran from where the binding cut into his wrists. Finally, he managed to get the small deerskin bag in his hands. Bringing it to his teeth he worked at opening it.

Though the arrowhead was small, it was extremely sharp. It didn't take long to get through their bindings. They were free.

"Come, we must run from here. I think the river is our best chance to get away from them."

"But what about our horses and our goods?" Kitchi asked.

"Let me remind you, brother," Keme said, disgustedly, "We have no weapons and we are outnumbered. Now run!"

Hurriedly, they made for the river. The water was cold but it felt good on the rope burns which encircled their wrists and ankles.

"Let's swim downstream," Kitchi said. "The river is too swift and too wide to cross."

"They'll know we went downstream," Keme answered.

"Yes, but if we go a long way, they won't come looking for us. Anyway, they have everything we own. I don't think they'll track us down for the pleasure of just seeing us die."

"I hope you're right," Keme said as he swam on.

Daylight found them many miles downriver from where they'd been ambushed. By this time, they were so tired they could hardly move.

"I need to rest, brother," Kitchi said. "We must find a place back from the river and leave no sign getting there."

Carefully, they made their way through the thick undergrowth at the river's edge and up the steep bank, trying hard to not leave any trace that they'd passed that way. After skirting the edge of a small hill, they dropped into a brushy draw. Moving cautiously, they took a piece of the brush and dusted away their footprints. They hadn't noticed that the morning sky above was cloudy and threatening rain. It was only after they'd found a safe place to stay that the first raindrop hit Keme in the face. "Crawl in under those trees, Kitchi," he said. "It should stay dry there and we need to sleep."

CHAPTER 2:
LIEUTENANT DUNBAR

Clint had managed to skirt around the soldiers that were looking for him and was now on the trail back to his trading lodge. He hadn't caught up to the Old Man and Morah but he knew he could make better time than they so he figured it wouldn't be long before he met them.

Meanwhile, the soldiers he'd had the run-in with had made it back to the settlement. It didn't take long for their story to circulate. Some of the trappers there had seen Clint and knew that he was camped outside the post with an old man and a young Indian woman. This information, they passed on to the soldiers.

The man from the trading post spoke up. "The old man and the girl are the same two who left here yesterday morning. Rode right past me. They were heading on the main trail up-river. He'll probly slip around this place and go join up with 'em." Pausing a moment, he added, "Shouldn't be tough to track him down. He told me that he has a place five day's ride from here."

There was much flurry within the soldier's ranks and it didn't take a genius to see that they were making preparations for a long ride. One man, sitting astride a chestnut mare, out of sight near the edge of the post, held a particular interest in what was taking place. When there was no question that the soldiers planned to go after Clint, the man struck out for the trail, wanting to get out ahead of them. Dirty-shirt Johnson was on his way to warn his friend.

#

Within two days, Clint had caught up to the Old Man and Morah.

"Thought you might have gone under," the Old Man said. "Was kinda hopin' so. Then I could have this fine woman for my own." He smiled at Clint and then at Morah. Clint squinted his eyes at the Old Man in a half smile but said nothing. Another day passed and near dark, that day, Johnson came upon the three of them.

"Hello, the camp," Johnson called out, so as not to startle them.

Recognizing his friend, Clint called back. "Johnson! Stop, drop, and set a spell. We were just fixin' to eat. You're welcome to join us."

Johnson dismounted and walked his horse to the small clearing where the other horses were tethered. After tying his horse, he walked back.

"What brings ya this way?" Clint queried. "Thought ya pretty much stayed put at that settlement."

"Came to warn ya," Johnson answered. "Peers as though you had some sort of a run-in with those military boys. Pissed 'em off real bad, so they're comin' after ya."

"Hmm!" Clint answered, studying what he'd just heard. "How'd they know where to find me?"

"That feller at the tradin' post, the ornery one, told 'em. Said that you said you had a place up this way and that you should be easy to ketch." Pausing to catch his breath, he then continued, "I think they're probly a half-day behind me. I got out ahead of 'em and I been ridin' hard. Too dark for 'em to travel tonight but they'll be here by tomorrow."

"Thanks for the warnin'. I need to think on this a while. In the meantime, help yerself to a hunk of that elk meat. It's young calf and it's fresh."

Johnson walked to the fire and cut off a large piece of the hind quarter that was skewered on a thick willow, suspended over the glowing coals. Then, he settled in to gnawing at it, smacking his lips and licking at his fingers as the juicy meat disappeared down his gullet. The Old Man and Morah had not made a sound since he'd arrived but now, as they sat across the fire from him, they ate and talked.

"You understand what they say?" Johnson asked.

"Yeah, I do." Clint answered, "It's Blackfoot mostly with some Shoshoni thrown in there."

"She yer woman?" he asked again.

"She's a woman but not mine." Clint answered. "Had her a man up until a week or so ago but he died and left her alone. She had nowhere or no one to go to so she ended up comin' to my place. I've known her for some time now. She's a good person."

After they'd finished eating, they sat by the fire, watching the dying flames dance over the glowing embers. Not much was said. Johnson had stoked his pipe and seemed nearly to be asleep. Every now and then he'd cast an eye toward Morah. She saw him watching her and moved closer to Clint.

"He looks at me like I'm another piece of meat he's about to devour," she whispered. "He is so dirty and he smells."

"What'd she say?" Johnson asked.

"Said yer dirty and ya stink. I don't think she likes ya much."

"Hmm," was all Johnson uttered, taking a long drag on the cob pipe.

At dawn, Clint was up and about, still trying to decide what to do about the soldiers. He knew he could lose them but he also knew that he had to keep on good terms with them if he wanted to continue his trade business. Johnson, the Old Man, and Morah were also busying themselves, getting ready for the long ride ahead. Johnson mounted his horse and rode to where Clint stood, loading the pack animals.

"Well pard, did ya figure out how to handle this?"

"I think so," Clint answered. "Let me ask ya...were there still some soldiers left at the settlement or are they all on my trail?

"Yeah, their leader, a lieutenant I think, is still there with maybe four or five other soldiers. Why do ya ask?"

"Well, I've got to face up to this now or become a fugitive. So, I'm goin' back and turn myself in."

"I wouldn't do that, given the state of mind those boys were in when I last saw 'em. You'll never make it back to the settlement alive."

"I know that. That's why I'm goin' back to the settlement, to the Captain. He should treat me fairly. After all, no one was killed."

"I hope yer right," Johnson said. "Be damn careful, though."

Clint then approached the Old Man who seemed to have been waiting for him to talk to, alone.

"What is it you plan to do, my friend? I hope you are not going to try to talk to these bluecoats."

Nodding his head, Clint answered, "If I want to live in peace in this country, I must talk to them and explain to them what happened. I plan to go to the settlement and talk to their chief. I think he will listen to me."

"They will not listen to you."

"I must try," Clint answered. "Take Morah and our goods and go to the cache in the cave, high on the ridge. Stay there. Do not go to our trading place. These soldiers who follow us will surely go to our place. When they don't find me there, they will take out their hate on anything or anyone who is there, so stay away. I will return as soon as I can."

"Look after yourself," the Old Man muttered.

"Want me to ride with ya?" Johnson asked. "I'm goin' back anyway."

"Sure! But we'll be takin' a different path."

After the Old Man left, Clint and Johnson headed toward the river. This far upstream, it was not as deep or wide as near the settlement. Once there, Clint pointed out a place they could cross without too much danger. The river was low now and they should not have trouble. When they had crossed, they rode far back into the forest and began their long ride back to the settlement.

They made good time following an old Indian trail and, in three days, they were on the banks of the river across from the settlement.

There was a large raft that was tethered to a tree on the far bank. If you fired a shot and waved to the raftsman, he'd come over and take you across. He did this, through the use of two heavy ropes, each one secured to the raft and at the same time, secured to the far bank. The raftsman would let loose the raft from its tether, letting the current take it across to the far shore. Then, he'd attach the line from the other shore to the raft and let the current take it back. It worked well.

When Clint appeared in the settlement some of the trappers and the locals recognized him as the one the soldiers were after. No one said anything, however, and he walked straight to the Captain's Tent.

"The orderly posted outside the tent stopped him and asked him his business.

"I need to talk to the Captain," Clint said, politely.

"He's not a Captain, sir. He's a lieutenant."

"Very well, then. May I please speak to the lieutenant?"

"What is it, Myers?" came the voice from inside.

"A man wishes to speak with you, sir."

"Come in, come in," voiced the young officer. "What can I do for you?"

"My name is Jeffries," Clint said. "Clinton Jeffries. I'm the one your men are searching for."

"I see!" he remarked, eyeing Clint over. "I guess you realize you're in some serious trouble, Mister Jeffries? I sent a troop out looking for you."

"I was hoping I wouldn't be sir, being as how the only thing I'm guilty of is keeping your men from stretching the necks of two young boys who only came here to this post to do some trading. That jackass across the way there, beat one of 'em up and took a shot at 'em. They weren't carrying any guns and I suspect the trapper who was wounded was shot by one of these yahoos, here abouts."

"Do you know these young men, Mister Jeffries? The ones you helped out."

"No sir, I don't," Clint answered.

"And, do you always go about "helping" other people, Mister Jeffries?" His voice had a sly tone to it.

"When I can, Lieutenant."

"That's not what I am given to understand. You see, I know firsthand that you always help those who are in need."

Clint didn't know what to make of the young man sitting before him who was now rising up from his chair."

"You don't recognize me, do you Mister Jeffries? But then, how could you?" Smiling, he offered his hand.

"My name is Jeremy Dunbar." He stopped, waiting for Clint's reaction. None came. "My mother is your sister, sir."

Clint didn't know what to say. This was his nephew, his kin. Jeremy read the expression on Clint's face, which was one of complete shock. "I have heard stories of you for as long as I can remember," he said. "Mother and Dad always spoke highly of my Uncle Clint."

"You'll have to excuse me son, I wasn't ready for this kind of welcome. I thought I might be locked in irons." He paused then, looking at his nephew's face, a man's face. The boy had grown up. "How are your folks, anyway?" Clint asked, still trying to get his mind around it.

"Good!" he answered. "At least the last time I saw them." he added. "They sold their saloons and bought a small farm back in Virginia. That's where I grew up. I got a good education there and managed to get into a fine military academy. I graduated at the top of my class and then joined the Army. When I saw that they were asking for volunteers to travel to the mountains to aid in regulating Indian problems, I signed up. I thought, somehow, I might just meet up with you and sure enough, here you are."

"Damn, I'm glad to see you, Jeremy. I never believed I'd see any of my kin again. It's funny how fate has a way of putting' ya in the way of someone."

The young man thought about that for a moment and then, smiling said, "I never looked at it like that but I guess fate did have a hand in it."

For hours, the two of them sat talking, sharing stories, and getting acquainted. There was much to say and much to learn about each other. Through the passing years, they would come to love and respect one another. After all, they were kin.

CHAPTER 3:
CHAINED TO A WAGON

The Old Man did as Clint had instructed, taking refuge in the hidden cave they had found on one of their excursions. It was located some distance from their trading post and was safe from whatever the soldiers did. Morah was not happy, having to stay alone with the Old Man in the cave but she kept her mouth shut and kept to herself.

In his discussion with Jeremy, Clint explained what had happened and told him how and why he'd rescued the two young men from the soldiers. He also described them as being the "spittin' image" of himself. He went on to say that they spoke little, if any, English and that he thought they'd definitely been raised Indian but he wasn't sure they were Indian.

"Your men ain't too happy with me," Clint said. "Especially that sergeant! I had to whack him up- side the head. "

"I suppose he'll get over it, Uncle Clint. In fact, I'll see that he does."

"Thank you, son. If it's all the same to you, Jeremy, I'm gonna go look for those Injun boys and see if I can talk to 'em. Maybe I can learn something about 'em."

Jeremy agreed and, within the hour, Clint stood before Johnson's tent. The flap was down so he called out to the man. "You in there, Johnson?"

"Yup!" came the reply. "What do ya want this time?" he asked.

"Wondered if ya wanted to take a ride with me...see if we can track down them boys I helped out."

"Trail's cold as ice by now; slim chance, if any, that we'd run onto 'em."

"I know but there's some things I need to talk to them about. Side's that, there ain't too many trappers left to trade with ya. Most have gone back to the mountains." Clint paused for a moment, then added, "But hell, if'n ya don't want to go, I understand."

"Now just hold yer water a sec, nobody said they weren't interested in goin'. Gimme time to pack my possibles and a little hardtack and pemmican and I'll join ya."

When Johnson stepped from the tent, Clint almost fell out of his saddle. "Jesus! Is that you Johnson? What the..."

"I decided to clean myself up a bit so I took a bath in the river and put on fresh duds - hell, I even tried to comb my hair."

"Did ya throw that damn dirty shirt away?" Clint asked.

"Hell no! Couldn't stand to part with it. But, I did wash it out some."

"Oh my god, you've gone and poisoned all the damn fish in the river." Clint laughed. "Prob'ly kill everyone in St. Lou too."

Johnson then took on a serious tone. "I felt bad that that Indian woman of yours thought so poorly of me, saying I was dirty and stinky."

"Well, she was just sayin' what everyone else was thinkin' and, I told ya before, she ain't my woman."

"I know, I know! But it makes a man start thinkin' about takin' up with another squaw; a full-time night woman. I been lonely a long time so I figured if I cleaned up, maybe she might not think so badly of me and maybe..."

"Get on yer horse, would ya, I ain't got time to sit here and palaver about yer love life."

Grousing about Clint cutting him off, Johnson mounted. Within minutes, they were on the trail, riding up toward the ridge to cross through the gap, the last place he'd seen the boys.

#

Kitchi and Keme awoke to a dark sky and a steady wind. The rain had stopped but the heavy, thick clouds still threatened. Even though they had slept, they were very tired from their ordeal with the Rees but they had to move, had to make a decision, had to leave this place. It was not safe here.

"Where do we go, brother?" Keme asked. "It is a long way back to our village and we have no food."

Kitchi thought a moment and then answered, "Yes! And, we know little of what lies downriver from here." He paused a moment and then went on. "But upriver, there is the settlement. They have food and horses. I don't think we have any other choice, however, we must pass near those who captured us and to keep from being captured again, we should keep a great distance away from them. They may be looking for us now."

His brother agreed and they started off. It would take them many hours to skirt around the area where they had been captured. Before they left, they took a sharp stone and cut two thick willows at the river's edge. These, they stripped the limbs and leaves from and again, with a sharp stone, fashioned a point at the heavy end. Spears! "Not the best, they thought. But good enough to defend themselves if it came to that."

By day's end, they'd traveled a great distance, staying far back in the mountains as they had planned. They managed to kill a forest grouse but had no fire to roast it, so they ate it raw, gagging down the stringy meat and flavoring it with wild onion. At least it was something to put on their stomachs.

Two more days passed and they thought they had come far enough so that they could make their way back to the river's edge. They were starving by this time. They had found some edible plants and a few grasshoppers and worms along the way but nothing substantial. Fortunately, they discovered a few small springs, which provided them water. If they could just make it to the river and stay out of sight, there was a better chance of finding food. At least there would be frogs and small critters that came to drink. Also, they might get lucky and spear some fish. These things would hold them over until they could reach the settlement and steal what they could.

At last they came to edge of the small trading settlement, watching it from a distance. "Horses might be easy to steal," they thought, "since they were tethered and hobbled some distance from the nearest dwelling. Food, however, was another thing." They would have to slip into one of the tents or lean-tos to get that. The problem was, all of the men in those tents and lean-tos had guns and knew how to shoot. If they were caught, they would probably die. But right now, it was better than starving to death.

At the near side of the post, close to the river's bank, they discovered a meat curing house. A light smoke wafted out its sooty, black, pointed roof vent, dancing on the breeze and scattering its magnificent smell in and around the forest and buildings. The boys could hardly stand it. Their mouth's watered as they breathed in the smoky odor.

"We must wait until dark," Kitchi whispered. "Then we can slip in and help ourselves."

"I don't know if I can wait that long," Keme answered. "The sun is still high in the sky. It will be a long time before it is dark enough. I'm so hungry."

"Well, it is risky but I'm hungry too. Maybe we can slip inside and get some food, without being seen."

With that, they crawled to a place where they could see if anyone was coming. When they thought they were safe, they made for the large teepee shaped structure, pulling aside the heavy buffalo robe that covered its entrance. As they moved to step inside, they were immediately engulfed in a whoosh of acrid smoke that roared forth out of the open door. They could neither see nor breathe. Both boys began a coughing fit, choking and gasping for air. Keme reeled backward and tried to pull the heavy robe back over the opening but the smoke was unbearable. He let it go and grabbed his brother's arm. "Run!" he choked, "Run!"

"I can't run," Kitchi replied, "I can't see." Stumbling away, they made it to a thick patch of brush. There, they laid on the ground and continued to cough.

The smoke from the curing house was generally barely visible, coming from the high opening. But now, it was pouring from the door, creating a grey cloud of smoke that everyone in the settlement could see. The sound of commotion then caught the boys' ears. People were running toward the smoke. Two men were out ahead of the others, shouting. "It's probly that damn bear again, tryin' to get himself a free meal."

Although the boys themselves were concealed, they couldn't control or silence the coughing spasms that their lungs were putting them through. Thus, when the men arrived, expecting to chase off the suspected bear, they couldn't help but hear the choking and gagging that was happening some yards away. They were quick to investigate and quicker to apprehend the two rascals. The two boys were handled roughly and brought up the street to the Army Headquarters tent. One man on either side of them had hold of an arm. One man walked behind each of them, holding a handful of their hair. Their feet barely touched the ground as they were dragged along. One man whispered from the crowd, "Say, ain't these the same two that raised hell the other night in Terrel's tradin' post? The ones the Army's been after." Another man, standing near him, answered, "I surely believe it is. They look half starved. Probly just wanted somethin' to eat."

When they were brought before the Lieutenant, he immediately noticed the likeness of their faces to his uncle Clint. He asked them their names and where their tribe was but he could see very quickly they didn't understand a thing he said. He was not in the mood to pursue the questioning for he knew that Clint would return in a few days and he could handle the situation. So, he instructed the Corporal to clap them in irons and secure them to the supply wagon. As they were being led away, he said, "Corporal, before you chain them to that wagon, get them something to eat and drink. And make sure each of them has a blanket."

#

Two days passed and Clint had not arrived back at the post. Looking out the flap of his tent, Lieutenant Dunbar called to his first sergeant. "Sergeant, I want those boys released. They haven't really done anything wrong and I can't see holding them here in these conditions. Make sure they each have a canteen of water and a ration of food and send them on their way."

"May I remind the Lieutenant that they tried to steal the meat in the smokehouse?"

"Of course they did, sergeant, they were hungry."

"And sir, they are accused of shooting one of the men in camp and...."

The Lieutenant cut him off. "Sergeant, they had no weapons so I doubt they shot anyone. Now, follow my orders and turn them loose."

"Yes sir!"

At first, the boys thought they were going to be beaten or shot or, they knew not what. But when the soldiers gave them food and water and released them from the manacles, they realized they were free and could go. It took them no time to depart the settlement, leaving on the trail that led north, up the ridge and over the pass, the same way Clint had gone.

Meanwhile, Clint and Johnson made their way along a trail that Clint thought the boys might have taken but they found nothing to indicate they had been there. They had been looking for over a week and were now becoming somewhat discouraged.

"How far north are you plannin' to travel?" Johnson asked.

"Don't know," came the reply.

"We ain't seen hide nor hair of those boys and this is mighty big country. And, the farther north we go, the deeper we get into Blackfoot territory and I sure as hell don't want to run on to any of them fellers." Pausing a moment, Johnson went on, "Didn't you say them young boys spoke Piegan? They's blood brothers to the Blackfoot, ya know.....murderin' bastards, every one of 'em." Clint didn't answer but he appeared to be assessing what Johnson had just said. After a long moment, he spoke up.

"I suppose yer right. We got a slim chance of comin' on to 'em. Best head on back to the outpost."

"Say, who do you suppose those boys are anyway?" Johnson querried. "My God, they look enough like you to be yer kin. You think you got some kids you don't know about?"

"I think I'd know," Clint answered but in his mind, there was a spark of doubt. He tried to recall the women he'd laid up with and the possibility that one of them had gotten pregnant by him. But, these boys were older. If they were his offspring, it had to have happened many years ago. Probably back around the time that he was with... Storm. When his mind spoke her name, a rush came over him like an invisible blanket and his breath caught short in his throat.

"Jesus, what if those...those boys are my sons," he thought. "That would mean she didn't die." The thought of that possibility caused him again, to gasp for air. His mind raced, not dwelling on any one thing but trying to discern every notion that it could be true. What if...

Johnson, wanting to be sure they were calling off the search, spoke up, his voice breaking Clint's reverie and snapping him back to reality. "We're a good long ways from my camp at the outpost, Clint. If we turn back now it'll take us three days to get back. I think we need to give it up."

"Yup! Yer right," was all Clint said, turning his horse about.

#

It was full dark when Clint and Johnson rode into the outpost. Clint spent the night in camp but refused to sleep in Johnson's tent. At dawn, he rolled up his sleeping robes, saddled his horse, and made his way to the soldier's quarters. He wanted to visit with his nephew.

"Yer up early," the young man said, wiping the sleep from his eyes.

"Uh huh! I don't fancy burnin' daylight. Besides, I need to be on my way."

"Are you going back up river to your place or are you still going to look for those boys?" Without giving Clint a chance to answer, he added. "They were here, you know. Tried takin' meat outta the smokehouse but we caught 'em. They were half starved."

"Where are they now?" Clint asked.

"Gone! I held them for two days, thinking you'd return. But when you didn't, I had to let them go."

"When was that?" Clint asked.

"Three days ago! I made sure they had water and some food and sent them on their way. I don't think you'd catch up to them now even though they're afoot."

"Yer probly right! I'd have liked to talk to them and found out who they are and where they came from but maybe I'll run onto 'em some other time." Pausing a moment, he changed the subject. "Are you staying in these parts permanently?"

"No! I have orders to start back down the river before winter and anyway, there's nothing here for us to do."

"Then, please tell your ma and pa hello for me. I really don't think I'll ever get back that way again. I don't fit in there so well."

"I'll do that, Uncle Clint." Then shaking hands, Clint slid onto the back of his horse and rode out.

"See ya, Jeremy," he said over his shoulder. "Keep yer nose to the wind and yer eye along the skyline."

The morning was crisp and bright with sunlight filtering through the shadowing pines. Steam blew from the horse's nostrils as they made their way along the winding trail. The river, some hundred yards away, rolled quietly. Up ahead a squirrel chattered, sounding the alarm that a stranger approached. Everything was peaceful and right with the world.

An hour passed and then two. The trail had gotten away from the river and now rose at a steep angle up a small rise. The trees had thinned some in this area allowing Clint to see quite a ways up the trail. It was then that he caught the movement. He brought the horse to a halt, watching ahead and watching the horse. Horses could often see, hear, and smell trouble before a man could.

"Maybe an elk," he thought. "Or a deer or..." Suddenly, the horse brought his ears up and Clint could see his nose sifting the air currents. "Trouble, for sure" he thought.

This was a bad place to try to maneuver his horse, steep and rocky. He'd have to turn clear around to make a run for it if he was ambushed. As he was about to do just that, a figure stepped from the trees, onto the trail, waving a hand in peace and beckoning for him to come forward. The man was completely shaded by the forest and except for his waving hand, his features were not clear.

Clint did not move except to cock his rifle and ready the pistol he carried at his belt. What to do? He had an idea. Without making a threatening move, he raised his hand and motioned for the man to come to him. Almost immediately, the man came forward. But then, another stepped from the trees and began following the first one.

"Jesus!" Clint whispered. "What the..."

As the first figure broke from the shade and into the sunlight, Clint breathed a sigh of relief. It was one of the Indian boys. His brother, walking behind, quickly caught up.

"Ghost warrior," the first boy yelled, in his native tongue. "We need to ask for your help."

Clint lowered the hammer on the rifle and rode forward to meet them. Dismounting, he tied the horse off to a small aspen. He greeted the boys with the traditional Indian friendship sign, smiling as he did so.

"Why do you call me Ghost Warrior?" he asked. "I'm not a ghost. I'm as real as you are."

"When you saved us from the soldiers, you said your name was Clint Jeffries. We were told long ago that you had died and were in the spirit world. When you attacked the soldiers, you came out of nowhere and we thought you had come from that world to save us."

"Who told you these things?" Clint asked.

"Our mother," they said in unison. Clint's thoughts raced. He kept questioning.

"What is your mother's name?" he asked, "And where is she?"

"WaNeha-eo is her name. It means...."

"I know what it means." Clint cut in, his words shaky. He was looking directly at the boys but his mind was searching back over the years, all those years he'd searched for her, all those years praying that she was alive but thinking she was dead....all the tears!

The boy's voice suddenly shook him back to the present. "She lives far to the north with our people in a small village. She has a man. His name is Armand - he is like our father."

The words, "our father" hung in Clint's ear, grating sharply across his senses. The realization hit him then. These boys had to be his sons. There was no doubt. But he could not accept it until he heard the words from her lips. He knew the boys dared not ask the one big question that he knew they longed to know. He could see it in their eyes. But then, like the crash of a falling tree, the words spilled forth.

"Are you our father?" Their voices again coming in unison but soft and with longing.

He was being asked a question that he would have never dreamed in a thousand years that he'd be asked. And yet, there it was. What could he say? Hell, he didn't know for sure if they were his children. They certainly looked to be but.....

Quietly, they waited but no words answered their question.

"We just..." Keme began.

"I know! I know!" Clint replied. Then taking a deep breath, he looked straight into their eyes. "I would be very proud to have sons like you for I think you are fine men but I am not sure if I am truly your father. Only your mother knows for sure." He paused for a moment but then added, "So we will ask her."

With that, the boys cheered, slapping each other on the shoulders. Seemingly, a huge burden had been lifted from them. Somehow, in that moment, they had all completely changed. Not just the boys but the man also - the father.

"When can we leave for our village?" Kitchi asked, eagerly.

"I'm afraid it will have to wait a while," Clint answered. "Winter is not far off and we must gather the meat we will need to feed us. So, we shall first hunt the buffalo and then travel to your village."

Four days later they arrived at Clint's outpost. They had taken turns riding the horse and so had not made very good time. Along the way, the boys told him of their misfortune at the hands of the river pirates, losing everything they had. They also told him of Armand's accident and how he and their mother were depending on them to bring home the food and goods they would need to survive.

The Old Man was sitting on a blanket in the sun, combing his hair. At the sound of the approaching horse, Morah ran from the shelter. "Clint, oh Clint, I'm glad to see you." She was somewhat shocked to see the two young braves that accompanied him.

When he dismounted, she ran to him and jumped into his arms. "I have missed you," she said. "Have you brought me any presents, any whiskey?"

For a moment, Clint just stood there, puzzled. "Whiskey," he said. "Why would you ask me for whiskey, Morah?"

"Because there isn't any more inside," she answered, dropping back from him.

Clint looked sharply to the Old Man. "What the hell's goin' on?" he asked. "We had six jugs. Enough to last through winter. Did you let her into that stuff?"

The Old Man hesitated to answer but then began to speak. "I had some whiskey when we first got back and I made the mistake of showing her where it was kept. She has a nose for it you know and when I was sleeping, she would sneak in and drink it." Looking down, he went on, "It is my fault and I am sorry."

The Old Man could sense his disappointment. It was a long minute before Clint spoke. "Well I guess we'll just have to make do."

CHAPTER 4:
HUNTIN' BUFFLER AND EATIN' BOUDINS

The days were growing ever shorter and the leaves had taken on their bright fall colors. Mornings were frigid with a heavy coat of rime blanketing the landscape. Even the horses had a coat of white over them. It was time to go for buffalo.

Before leaving Johnson's camp, Clint had arranged to meet him for a buffalo hunt. It was decided that Johnson would ride to Clint's outpost and from there, they'd make their way up river to a place east of the three forks. Clint had hunted there before and was very familiar with the lay of the land and the migration trails of the animals that lived there.

It was more than a week after Clint and the boys had returned to his outpost when Johnson rode in. He was sitting atop a big bay horse and leading three mules. Morah was the first one to meet Johnson. She was pleasantly surprised to see that he had cleaned himself up. She spoke to him in her native tongue, telling him she was glad to see that he was clean. He didn't understand what she said so he just smiled and nodded his head.

"Hey, Johnson!" Clint said, approaching the man with his hand out. "Looks like yer ready to go."

"Yes, I am," Johnson replied, shaking his hand. "Haven't hunted buffler fer a couple a years now. It'll be good to taste some fresh meat."

"Drop on down here and rest for a while, Johnson. We're all packed and ready; just need to load our things on the horses and then we can go. I want ya to meet somebody first, though." With that, Clint hollered for the boys to come out from the shelter, where they'd been readying themselves for the hunt.

"Whoa! Now whatta we got here?" Johnson squealed. "A couple a fine braves if I ever seed 'em."

"These are my sons, Johnson. Keme and Kitchi." There was a prideful tone in his voice. "They're goin' with us."

"Good! We can use all the help we can get. But, it's kinda late in the day, Clint. Maybe it'd be better to strike out at first light - wadaya think?"

"We could make a few miles fore dark but if you'd rather wait 'til mornin', it's okay by me. I shot a cow elk the other day so we can sup on that later tonight."

"Sounds good!" Johnson remarked. "Roasted elk, maybe some flat bread, and a cup a whiskey. A man'd think he died and gone to heaven."

"Yeah, well ya won't find any whiskey here bein' as how a couple of Injun friends of mine helped their selves to all I had."

"Well, not to worry there, ole hoss, I got a jug in my pack."

At the word "whiskey", Morah's eyes lit up. She moved toward Johnson. "Whiskey? You?" She said, pointing at him.

"I'll be your friend, give you anything you want, for a taste of whiskey." These words she spoke in her native tongue and Johnson couldn't understand all the words. But he did understand the meaning.

"Say, Clint! Is she your woman? You know, do you bed up with her?"

"No! I used to see her once in a while when she lived with her tribe but now-a-days she just lives here and does the cookin'."

"So, you wouldn't mind if I.....?"

"Help yerself, Johnson. But, ya better keep an eye on yer possibles and, most of all, that whiskey."

#

It was just breaking light when the four of them rode out. The Old Man had excused himself from going, saying that his back and legs were bothering him. Clint told him where they'd be if he decided to come and hunt with them. The Old Man nodded and then went back to bed.

Clint had given the boys two horses from his remuda and outfitted them with kapotes, knives and hatchets. He had one extra rifle but decided the boys didn't have any experience shooting and he sure as hell didn't want anyone hurt. He lashed the extra rifle in its leather boot to one of the pack animals.

It would take them two days to get to the prairie where Clint had always been successful. They'd travel upriver near to the confluence of the Madison, Jefferson, and Gallatin, then swing east between the rugged, barren hills and make their way onto the grassland prairie.

You had to be careful here. There were many buffalo but there were also many different people hunting them. Clint had often run onto hunting parties of Mandans and Hidatsas and had had no trouble from them. Hell, he'd even camped and hunted with them. The Sioux, however, were a different story. He worried the most about them and kept a constant vigil. They were not fond of anyone hunting on land they considered theirs and would hunt you down and kill you. Other tribes in the area were just as fierce but seldom came this far west to hunt.

When they neared the edge of the prairie grasslands, Clint motioned them into a small draw on the south side of a low hill. Here, they tethered the horses and proceeded up the draw to a rising rock cliff that shown a bright yellowish tan against the bleak gray shades of the brushy hillside.

"This way," he motioned to the others, edging along the bottom of the cliff's face. "We're gonna watch from here for a while to see if we can locate some buffler and also look to see if anyone's about."

"Johnson, you watch out ahead and to the south, along those brushy edges. I'll take these two and go further around the hill so we can see what's off to the north. Come git me if ya spot anything."

Kitchi and Keme followed Clint as he made his way through the rubble of rock that had long ago fallen from the face of the cliff. From here, they had a good view of what lay ahead on the plain and they were well hidden. Earlier, before they'd left the river's edge, the boys had cut long, straight pieces of river birch to fashion themselves some spears. They certainly didn't want to go on a buffalo hunt with no weapons. So now, as they sat watching, they skived the bark and small twigs away from the inner wood, using their knives and sharp stones that lay about them. This area was well known by the different tribes to contain chert, agate, and the black chards of obsidian, which were used for arrowheads, skinning knives, awls and, in this case, spearheads. They had long ago learned the art of knapping and could fashion a piece of rock into a weapon very quickly.

As Clint watched them, he realized these boys had been taught the ways of the warrior and though he considered them just boys, he knew they had the wherewithal to wage war, kill, and scalp their enemies. Again, a sense of pride filled him and a gentle tear made its way from the corner of his eye. Quickly, he turned his head away so they would not see.

For several hours, they sat watching but nothing appeared. It would soon be dark so they made their way back to the horses.

As they mounted, Clint said, "Back behind us a ways, there's a good camp spot...hidden, with some grass for the animals. It should be a good place to spend the night." This, he had to repeat in English to Johnson. Since he'd had the boys with him, he spoke more in their tongue than his own. This often left Johnson wondering what the hell he'd said. But he just followed along and most of the time, it worked out.

Thinking it unwise to build a fire, they kept a cold camp that night and ate pieces of dried elk and hard flatbread that Morah had fixed for them. This they washed down with water from their flasks and canteens. It was now time to relax to talk; to share their thoughts; to speak of past deeds and victories. Clint wanted to talk to the boys and so, before addressing them, he apologized to Johnson, telling him there were things he had to know about them and their mother. Johnson understood and sat quietly smoking his pipe.

"Tell me about your mother," Clint began. "Is she well?"

"Yes!" answered Keme, "She is well but she works very, very hard. Our other father was kicked by a horse some time ago and cannot move his legs. Now, she has to do everything."

"That is why," Kitchi chimed in, "we brought skins and other goods to the trading post. Normally, it would have been him that did the trading but it was left to us and we failed. We lost everything and there will be nothing for them to live on when winter comes."

"We won't let that happen," Clint whispered. "We'll get plenty of meat and I can let you have other goods that you will need."

"But we have nothing to give you," Kitchi stated. "We don't....."

"Don't you worry about that," Clint interrupted. "You can pay me back some other time. What we need to concentrate on now is finding the buffs." He suddenly felt very tired and though he wanted to know everything about Storm, he thought it best to go slowly. After all, they were telling him things about their mother and even though he felt close to them, he thought his questions might seem too personal.

"We'll find buffalo tomorrow," he said and rolled over to go to sleep.

At dawn, they again made their way to the perch they'd sat on the day before. This made the boys and Johnson unhappy.

"Shouldn't we be out on the plain lookin' fer tracks and sign?" Johnson asked, pointing in that direction. The boys didn't understand his words but they grasped what he meant. They too looked at Clint with eyes that wanted an explanation.

"No! We watch from here. It's safer and when we see the animals, we can better plan how to get to them. You must be patient."

There was some low grumbling but no other questions were posed. In the meantime, the boys had finished their spears, attaching the sharpened spear points with strips of rawhide that Clint provided. A deep notch was cut into the heavy end of the spear and the sharpened stone was placed in it. They wet the rawhide, making it soft and pliable. Then, wrapping it tightly around the shaft of the spear they secured the point and tied off the rawhide. As it dried, the wetted skin shrunk and tightened the head of the spear to the shaft. They were ready.

Hours passed and still, there was no sign of buffalo. Giving up the vigil, the boys had found a comfortable place in the shade of a rock overhang and were sound asleep. Johnson was tired of sitting on the hill and so walked around the cliff face to complain to Clint.

"Shit! We're wastin' our time up here. I say we pull off a this here hump and go search up somethin' to shoot." Clint didn't reply for some time. Finally, he spoke.

"Look out across that prairie and tell me what ya see."

"Well, just like yesterday and this mornin', I don't see a Goddamn thing. They's nothin' there."

"Right! And how far ya reckon ya can see out there? Eight maybe ten miles!"

"Yeah, I guess so." Johnson answered even though he didn't know where this conversation was going.

"Well, it's damn near half-day's ride out to the place you can see from here. Then, when ya get there, where ya gonna go? We ain't seen nothin' between here and there so ya won't have fresh sign to follow. Besides if you run into some Injun trouble, you'll be fightin' 'em in the open; runnin' and gunnin'." He paused for a while hoping that what he said would sink into Johnson's mind. "I'm tellin' ya, the buffalo will show up here and when they do, we'll take 'em. I've done this other years and they eventually come this way."

Johnson just grumbled as he turned and walked back to his watch place. "Hell, we'll likely be old men fore they show up.....probly be too damn old to go get 'em."

At first, it looked like a small dust-devil rising off the plain far to the northeast. Clint noticed it but then dismissed it as just that. The boys were still asleep and he hadn't heard any more out of Johnson. He glanced back now, to see if the dust had gone away. It hadn't. Instead, it seemed to have increased.

"Could be buff," he thought to himself but he couldn't make out what was causing it. He waited.

Some time passed and the dust disappeared. "Probably just wind that kicked it up," he thought. "Maybe the buff won't come this year. Need to give it more time, though."

He leaned back against a large tilted rock and gazed up at the bright autumn sky. Here and there, thin, wispy clouds were stretched out, being pushed along toward the east. The sun was warm against his face and he closed his eyes. His thoughts centered on the boys and their mother. How he longed to see her and hold her and tell her all the things he'd saved up for so many years. To express the love he held for her and....

"Wake up!" A nervous hand was shaking Clint's shoulder and he quickly came awake. It was Keme. "Look," he whispered, pointing. There before them, a herd of some thirty or forty buffalo walked, grazing as they went. They had come up from the direction Clint had seen the dust. It was then he noticed the bright red paint on the faces of his boys. War paint! Apparently, the Old Man had given it to them before they left. It was an Indian thing

"Let's get to the horses," Clint whispered, saying nothing about their adornment. They picked up Johnson on their way around the cliff face and scurried down the draw to where they'd hobbled the horses. When they were mounted, they made their way along the edge of the hill, staying back so the approaching animals wouldn't see them. In the rush, Johnson grabbed Clint's arm. "What the hell's them boys got on their faces?" he asked.

"War paint, I reckon. Injuns do that before they go into battle or before they hunt. They believe it puts fear in their enemy and helps them to conquer the animals they're after. Sorta puts 'em in good standing with the Great Spirit, I guess."

"You don't believe that shit, do ya?" Johnson asked.

"Doesn't matter what I believe," Clint snapped. "It's their way and they believe it."

Holding his hand up, Clint got their attention. "There's a low swale out beyond us." He began, "Usually, the buffs will try to stay as far from this hill as possible and that will take them down into that swale. When they go in, they will be gone from our sight and that's when we move. Johnson, you go to the south, that way. I'll take one of the boys north with me. We'll drive them toward you. Kill what you can. This may be the only chance we have."

When the herd was almost even with them, the buffalo did as Clint had said. They fed down into the swale. When they were finally out of sight, Johnson made a beeline to the south and found himself a vantage point, which placed his back against a shallow rise. Both his rifles were primed and loaded. One he laid next to him, the other he held in his hand at the ready. In front of him were a pair of crossed sticks. These, he would use as a rest to steady his aim. His horse, he tied to a stand of brush back behind the edge of the small hill.

Clint explained to the boys about what to do. He took Kitchi with him and they rode to the north to get behind and around the lolling herd. Keme followed along the rise just outside their view. Clint also had both his rifles loaded and primed. One he held, the other was lashed crosswise to his saddle with a piece of leather thong.

When it was time to move, Kitchi came in directly behind the animals. Clint had circled out a ways and came at them from the east side. They rode slowly at first not wanting to alarm the beasts until they were good and close. Kitchi kept an eye on Clint and when he saw him wave to come in, he put his heels to the horse and charged toward the buffalo. Clint did the same, coming up sharply on the side of one of the unsuspecting cows that was at the rear of the herd. She broke into a full run but only went a few yards when the ball from Clint's rifle passed through her and she tumbled in a dusty heap. At the shot, the others took off in a thundering stampede.

Hearing the shot and the pounding hoofs, Keme rode over the edge and into the swale. He was suddenly right in among the frightened buffalo. The spear he'd made, he now carried in his right hand, held high above his head, poised to strike.

Ahead, he saw a smaller cow running at the edge of the herd. Quickly, he kicked at the horse, bringing it to a full gallop alongside the charging animal. With all his strength, he thrust the spear into the cow just behind her front shoulder. It did not penetrate deeply; he'd hit a rib. Pulling the spear back, he again urged his pony on, coming up close to the animal and this time, aiming higher on its body, he drove the heavy spear into it. The force of his attack paid off. The spear pierced downward into the animal's lung and it began to stumble.

He was still clinging tightly to the spear and when the buffalo finally collapsed, his grip on the spear yanked him from the back of the horse, sending him sprawling, headlong into the ground. With the wind knocked out of him, he tried to sit up but couldn't. One of the charging buffalo, coming from behind leaped over the dying animal, narrowly missing Keme. He couldn't catch his breath and he tried to rise again.

Johnson had shot two buffalo and was going down to begin cleaning them when he saw Keme struggling to get up. Grabbing his horse, he mounted and rode back to help the boy. When he got there, Keme was up, sitting on the cow he'd killed, spitting dirt and trying to clear the dust from his eyes. Some of the paint the he'd put on his face was smeared down his cheek and small pieces of grass and dung clung to it.

Johnson smiled at him and clapped him on the back. "Damn boy! I've never seen anyone take down a buff like that. You got the hair a the bear in ya."

Keme could not understand what Johnson said but he knew what he meant. He smiled back at Johnson and in his own tongue, said, "The Great Spirit smiled on me today. This is my first buffalo."

When the dust finally settled, Clint and Kitchi rode back to where they saw Johnson and Keme.

"You alright?" Clint asked, smiling at the dust covered young man.

"I am fine." he replied. "This is my first buffalo."

"And a fine one it is," Clint replied. "All told, it looks like we brought down six animals. So, we've got our work cut out for us."

Through the rest of the day, they skinned and parted the meat into large chunks. Much of it they lashed to the pack saddles on Johnson's mules. The rest they loaded on to two travois they attached to Kitchi and Keme's horses. It was nearly dark when they left and a circle of buffalo wolves surrounded them, waiting for the men to leave so they could have at the carcasses. Riding away, they could hear the growling and fighting as the wolves gorged themselves on what was left.

The wolves were not the only ones who ate good that night. The four of them took their fill of fresh "hump," tongue, and loin meat. This, they roasted over the coals of their fire. Clint even took some of the intestines. These he cut into chunks and turned them inside out. After washing them good, they were thrown on a spit over the fire. They sizzled and crackled, dripping their fat onto the hot coals.

When he thought them to be done enough, he tossed a piece to Johnson and each of the boys. "Boudins" he said, popping a piece into his mouth. To the boys, he explained that among mountain men, boudins were always a good time. Once cooked, they stretched the intestine out. One man would start eating on one end and another man would start at the other end. Somewhere in the middle was a knot. The first one to eat his way to the middle was the winner. The trick was, you couldn't use your hands. You just had to start eating. This

meant that the men couldn't chew off pieces and eat them fast
enough, so they'd just chew and swallow, chew and swallow.
Sometimes, when one man thought the other was getting the
best of him, he'd clamp down with his teeth and jerk his head
backward, thus pulling two or three feet of half-eaten boudin
out of the other man's gullet. There was a lot of gaggin' and
chokin' but everyone had a good time.

CHAPTER 5:
PAWNEE TROUBLE

It took three full days to bone out the meat and cut it into chunks they could load on the travois. Much of it, Clint salted with a sack of salt he'd brought along. Their camp lay at the side of a stream so there was plenty of fresh water and grass for the horses. During the day, three of them would do the butchering and the other would stand watch. They took turns. When they had a few moments to spare, Clint educated the boys in the use of a rifle. He showed them how to load, cock, aim, and fire the weapon; also, how to clean it. When it was their turn to stand watch, he let them take the extra rifle.

They had completed most of the work on the meat and were getting ready to load up and return to Clint's outpost. It was mid-morning and Keme was standing watch. From where he stood, he could look back on the way they'd come and could also see far out onto the surrounding countryside. Peering back to the east, his eye picked up on something moving. It was far off and not discernable.

"Perhaps an elk or a buffalo," he thought. But as he continued to watch, he could make out the riders. There were five of them and they were coming this way. Quickly he got down to his pony that was tied in the brush below and raced to warn the others.

Upon hearing this, Clint started issuing instructions, "Johnson, take your rifles and get in those willows. If you have to shoot, make it count." Turning to Kitchi and pointing to the opposite side of the camp, he said. "Take my other rifle and go to those rocks. Stay down and don't let them see you. If you have to shoot, kill the closest man to you." He then handed Keme his pistol. "Tuck this in your belt and stay here by me. When they come in, move slowly toward that fallen tree but don't turn away. Keep a sharp eye. If you have to shoot, wait until they are almost upon you or else you'll miss."

It was more than ten minutes before the riders came in. Three of them rode forward while the other two held back. Clint wasn't sure but he thought them to be Pawnee. "Probably a hunting party," he thought. "They aren't decked out in war paint and they've got pack horses."

Their leader was a stocky man, not tall but muscular and very dark skinned. He had a rather square jaw and his lips seemed to be tightly stretched across his mouth. One of his front teeth was missing. His hair was in a single, long braid which draped forward over his right shoulder. A piece of bright orange cloth was woven through the end of the braid. A medicine bag hung at his throat and a powder horn with its attaching strap was slung over his left shoulder. He appeared to have the only rifle in the group. The rest carried bows, arrows, and spears. The two warriors in the back had their bows fitted with arrows and were ready to use them.

Sitting atop his horse, the man's keen eyes surveyed the camp. In a soft voice, he turned partially, speaking to the others. "There are too many horses here for just two men. There must be others about. Be watchful."

Then, turning his attention back to Clint, he inched his horse forward a few steps. "Why do you come here to steal our buffalo, white man? This is our land and you don't belong here. I think we will take back what belongs to us."

In a quiet but stern voice Clint answered him. "This is not your land and these are not your buffalo and if you try to take this meat, you will die." He paused for a moment and then went on, "This land belongs to the Great Spirit. And the buffalo that walk on it, he gives to all his children. We took this meat with his permission and he has smiled on us."

The man was shocked when Clint answered him in his own tongue.

"And, you are right," Clint added. "There are more of us than just what you see and we are ready to fight if need be."

When Clint said that, the men suddenly became very nervous, looking all around to see if there were others hiding in ambush.

"You do not want to make an enemy of me or the Great Spirit. So, I say to you, go out on the prairie and kill your own buffalo. There are many of them to be taken. If you persist in trying to steal from others, then the Great Spirit will be displeased and will deal harshly with you."

The man did not know what to say but it was clear that he was embarrassed by the way Clint had stood up to him. Clint could tell that his words had bitten deep into the man's ego and he waited to see what would come next.

"Alright," the leader began, "Call in your other men and we will help you pack your horses and see you safely on your way."

Upon hearing this, Clint spoke out in Blackfoot, "Kitche, this man intends to kill us and take our goods. When he makes his move, shoot him."

The man could not fully understand what had been said. He sat listening for any reply that might be coming from those who the white man had obviously been talking to. Thinking it a bluff, he said with a snide laugh.

"It appears that those you supposedly talked to have vanished and that you stand here alone with this boy. So, Great Spirit or not, I think we'll take what is ours."

"Don't make that mistake," Clint warned, "Or you will..."

From out of nowhere, the man produced a hatchet and kicked his horse forward. As he raised it to hit Clint, a shot rang out in a deafening roar, knocking the man over, sending him crashing to the ground. The others stood aghast, not knowing if they should fight or run.

"Stay as you are," Clint yelled to them. "If you move or try to kill us, you will suffer the same fate as your leader." Then, motioning for them to come forward, he said "Come! Take him to a place of burial. We do not wish any harm to come to you."

For a moment, the others waited, looking at each other with questioning eyes. Finally, one of them said something to the others and two of them came forward and loaded their fallen comrade on his horse. One of the men picked up the leader's rifle but before he could carry it off, Clint snatched it from his hand, leaned over the dead man and tapped him on the head with it. "There! I count coup on your brother and for that, I take his rifle."

Clint could see the hatred burning in the man's eyes but the man climbed on his horse and the group turned and rode quietly back in the direction from which they'd come. When they'd gone, Clint called to Johnson and Kitchi to come in.

"Nice shot," he said to Kitchi. Then, tossing him the fallen man's rifle he said, "Here! This is yours now. You earned it."

With the meat loaded, the hunters steered their mounts toward the far-off outpost. Both boys rode proudly with their heads held high, knowing that they had proven themselves as men but more than that, knowing they'd proven themselves to their father.

BOOK 8 – GOING TO MEET STORM

CHAPTER 1:
BACK FROM THE DEAD

When the hunters finally arrived at Clint's outpost they were greeted warmly by Morah and the Old Man.

"It looks as though the Great Spirit has smiled on us," uttered the Old Man. "We will have food in our bellies this winter and skins to make clothing."

"I killed my first buffalo," Keme said, prideful.

"And I killed my first enemy," Kitchi chimed in, "and here is his rifle."

Morah cheered the boys' victories and then bid them to come inside and share the dinner she'd fixed.

"Go ahead," Clint told the boys and Johnson. "I'll take care of the horses. The Old Man can help me."

When they'd all gone inside, the Old Man turned to Clint. His voice was solemn. "You had trouble?" He whispered. "Someone was killed?"

"Yes! We had a run-in with a hunting party; Pawnee, I think. There were five of them and they wanted to take the meat we'd killed." He paused for a moment then looked the Old Man straight in the eye. "We had no choice. Their leader attacked me and Kitchi shot him. It was as simple as that and it had to be done."

"But it is not simple, my friend. There will be a price to pay for that man's life. A vendetta - blood for blood." Clint said nothing and the Old Man went on. "You have been riding many horses and dragging two travois loaded with meat, leaving a trail a blind man could follow and that trail leads right here. If it were the old days and we didn't have the outpost, I wouldn't worry. They'd never find us. But, we live here and trade here and we're easy to find. "

"I hear what you say and your words are wise but it was either them or us. We sent them on their way with their dead leader. I doubt they will want to follow us. But just in case, you should take Morah, Johnson, and the boys to our cache on the ridge, above camp and stay the night. Explain why and tell them where I am and what I'm doing. That way, if any trouble comes, you won't be here to meet it. Now, come, let us eat with the rest and be happy." Even though he was smiling, an uneasy feeling was coming over Clint. The Old Man's warning was valid. There may be a "get even" time coming. Tomorrow he'd ride their back trail and see if anyone had followed them.

#

Clint was up and gone before the first hint of daylight appeared. He'd told the boys the night before that he had something to do in the morning but that he'd be back before nightfall. They, of course, wanted to know what and where and if they could go along. He told them it was something he had to do alone. They accepted that and nothing more was said. He then instructed the Old Man to take the others and ride to their secret cache on the ridge. Also, he'd best warn the Shoshone encampment across the meadow that there may be trouble coming.

As he rode the trail they'd used, he could see what the Old Man said was true. Even in the dark, the drag marks of the travois were visible. Hopefully, the Pawnee would return to their village and their hunting and let it go. His mind said that but, in his gut, he knew they would not forget what happened.

At sunrise, he led his horse off the right side of the trail, zig-zagging through thick sage until he came to a deep wash. To his right was a place where the bank had caved in and he thought he could cross there. Once across, he rode to the edge of a grove of thick aspen trees and dismounted. He then led the horse into the trees a short distance, just enough to conceal himself, but close enough so he could peer across the flat and watch for anyone traveling that way.

He walked very slowly, looking for any sign of movement. Everything seemed normal. Birds sang, crickets chirped; it was a beautiful fall day. He was then taken back to a time when another peaceful, serene day suddenly turned into a violent barrage of arrows, one of which had found its way to his leg. At the thought of it, he reached down and rubbed the old wound.

Hours passed and he'd gone quite a distance up the long valley. He was in the place now where the trail they'd traveled turned more to the east, entering a narrow gap between two hills. Ahead of him was a dense pine forest, one that would be hard to negotiate because of the thick deadfall. The hill on the other side had some pine pockets but was mostly aspen. It would be much easier to travel there than what lay ahead. It meant he'd have to, once again, find a way across the deep wash. He mounted the horse and picked his way through the sage to the edge of the wash. It was just as deep here as before, with sharp sides dropping down some ten or twelve feet.

"I'll follow it a ways," he thought. "Maybe there'll be a place to cross near the pines." Instead, the wash began to turn to the right, not the direction Clint wanted to go.

"Damn! I wonder how far I'm gonna have to ride before I can cross this thing."

Following the wash, he'd gone only a few hundred yards when he heard a horse whinny. The sound came from across the valley, in the direction of the trail he'd been watching. Just ahead of him was a small grove of aspen. He spurred the horse forward, dodging in behind the trees. He quickly dismounted and cradled the mare's nose in his hands. "Shh," he whispered, caressing her and rubbing her cheek. "Shh."

Within minutes, a figure appeared, coming down the trail into the valley. The man pulled his horse to a stop and sat listening and watching. Clint could not make out who he was, only that he was Indian. Apparently satisfied with what he saw, the man raised his hand, motioning for others to come forward. Three other riders came down the trail, leading more horses behind them. Clint recognized one of the horses being led as the one the dead Pawnee had been riding.

"They have come for us," he thought. "Blood for blood."

Checking both his rifles, he waited until they were a ways down the trail. He then mounted up and began following them, riding up next to the aspen grove. When he was nearly even with them, he yelled out. "Have you come seeking vengeance for your fallen brother?" His words shattered the silence, startling the group. They quickly jerked their ponies to a halt. Clint went on, "If you have come to kill me and get even for what has happened, you may find that it is a fool's quest. Some or all of you will surely die if you continue this. I want no trouble from you." His words seemed to have no effect on the men. They looked at him and finally recognizing who he was, gave a loud war hoop and charged toward him, not realizing there was a deep wash ahead. Clint, seeing their intensions, acted as though he was going to run away. But then, he suddenly, whirled the horse about and began charging them. This surprised the men.

Pulling up short of the deep wash, he dismounted. He quickly turned the horse sideways, laying his rifle across her withers, zeroing in on the lead rider. At the sound of the shot, the man crumpled, dropping his bow, he crashed to the ground. Quickly, Clint pulled the other rifle from its sheath and again, taking a dead rest across the horse's withers, sighted in on the next rider.

Seeing their brother killed, the three remaining braves began to dismount and come forward on foot.

However, they were not quite fast enough and a second man met the same fate as the first. Clint quickly mounted before the remaining Indians could get within bow range. He knew the wash would slow them down.

Gaining the safety of the trees, he quickly bailed off the mare and reloaded both rifles. He could not now see them but he knew they were coming for him. He also knew that if they tried to cross the wash, they'd not make it. It was too deep and too steep. Grabbing a rifle in each hand, he made for the thick sage, crouching and running at the same time. When he'd reached the heavy cover, he knelt down, listening. Sure enough, one, or both of them had tried to cross the wash and was trapped between its steep sides.

Clint came forward, slowly, quietly. The struggling was coming from somewhere off to his right. When he could see the edge of the wash, he began to crawl. Peering in over the edge he could see one of them was trying to get out and the other was lying on his stomach, holding his spear down, trying to help him. The man in the bottom was frantic, knowing that he was trapped.

Cocking his rifle, Clint suddenly stood up, pointing it at the man who was trying to help the other.

"Stop," he yelled, in a tongue he thought they'd understand. Both men froze, not moving.

"Three of your brothers have already died and you are about to join them if you do not stop this blood vengeance you pursue." The men remained motionless. There was no indication they understood him. Clint did not want to kill these two but, if it came to that, he would not hesitate.

"Do you understand what I say? If you do, you'd better speak up or I will shoot you now."

After a moment's hesitation, one of them said, "We understand some of what you say and we do not want to die." The man hesitated a moment and then went on. "You killed our friend. That is why we came here. We wanted to kill you."

"Your friend attacked me and that is why he died. He was trying to steal meat from us instead of hunting for it himself. That was wrong and dishonorable. Now, two more of your brothers are dead, trying to do a dishonorable thing. Do you want to join them?"

Neither man spoke but fear was written on each of their faces. Then, the man that was lying down spoke. "If we have to die, white man, we will, to avenge our brothers."

"But you do not have to die. I do not want to kill you. I want to go in peace and have you do the same. I want this to end here and now; no more killing."

The man who'd spoken put his hands under him and started to get to his feet. The sagebrush was nearly up to his shoulders. As he rose, he began to speak. "How can we return to our village with any honor when we ride in unharmed and three of our brothers are dead? We cannot do that. They would stone us to death."

When the Indian stood up, he lifted the spear out of the grasp of the man in the wash.

"I intend to put this spear through your heart, white man." With that, he suddenly ducked down and backed away, disappearing from Clint's sight. Clint could hear rustling as the man skulked away through the tall brush. Clint quickly did the same. As he backed away from the wash, he noticed a small clearing on his right. In its center was a huge ant hill. Everything had been eaten by the ants for several feet around the pile. These ants were big and delivered a painful bite but

Clint could not be concerned by that now. There was a man in front of him who wanted him dead.

The Indian in the wash was calling out to his friend to give it up; saying he didn't want to die and that the white man "has given us chance to live." There was no answer from the man with the spear. Suddenly, a wailing voice could be heard, rising from the wash. It was a death song.

Clint knew the man with the spear had to get close in order to deliver it. Even though he had a rifle, and had the apparent edge, he knew the accuracy and deadliness the Indians had with this weapon. He had to be alert.

Across from him and slightly to the left he heard what he thought was the snap of a twig. He didn't know if it was the Indian or whether the man was trying to get him to commit to the sound and shoot. Then he could deliver the deadly throw, thus killing Clint and ending the fight. Clint wondered if the man realized he had two rifles. Probably, but..... in the heat of battle, sometimes those things don't register.

Clint looked around for a rock. Two could play at this game if, in fact, that's what it was. Taking up two small stones from the edge of the clearing, he tossed one to his left. Then, very quickly he tossed the second in the same place. "Might make him think I'm over there," he thought.

From across the wash, he then heard another snap. Pointing the rifle in that direction, he fired. At the same time, he rolled from the clearing, bringing the other rifle to bear. When the Indian heard the shot and saw the plume of smoke rise, he charged toward it, spear raised. Clint was surprised at how close he was but not as surprised as the man was when he saw the rifle pointed at him. He was thinking that the white man was where the shot had come from and was going to throw the spear there. So, when he finally saw Clint, he made a half-hearted attempt to adjust his aim. The spear didn't even leave his hand when the bullet went through him. He dropped into the brush.

The man in the wash ceased his death song when he heard the two shots. But, when he saw Clint walk to the edge of the wash, above him, he started in again; this time with more vigor.

"Stop that!" Clint said, in a stern voice.

"I don't want to die, please. I don't want to die," the man cried.

"You're not going to die," Clint said. "Now come over here and take hold of this." Lying down, Clint lowered the rifle barrel down to the man. "Hang on to this and climb up here."

At first the man seemed reluctant but he knew if the white man was going to kill him, he would have already done it. So, taking hold of the barrel he pulled himself up onto the edge of the wash. Clint could see that the man was scared. He could also see that he wasn't much older than his own sons. "Just a boy," he thought.

Motioning to the young man, Clint said, "Come! My horse is over here."

Right at that moment, there was a sudden rushing sound behind them followed by a blood curdling, "Aieee." The spear narrowly missed Clint as he whirled to see the tortured face of the man he thought he'd killed just minutes before. The man seemed to hang there for a moment and then he collapsed.

There was total silence now. No one spoke. Then, "Whew! That was a close one," Clint said. "Damn near got me." As he turned to face the young brave, his eyes fell upon a terrible sight. The spear had missed him but had gone completely through the boy. He lay on his side, his life's blood staining the brush and ground beneath him. Placing the boy's head in his lap, Clint took his hand and whispered, "Let go, son. Let it go."

The boy gasped once or twice, trying to gulp air and offset the blood that poured into his lungs, but it was no use and it ended very quickly. In that moment, Clint thought of the boys, his children, and how he'd feel if it was one of them lying there in his lap. It was too much. A wave of overwhelming sadness washed over him, completely enveloping his being. Tears and sobbing rocked his body. He cried until he could cry no longer. Oh, the sadness....

He had no idea how long he had sat there. It was nearly dark and both of his legs had gone to sleep. He felt completely exhausted. His throat hurt and his eyes burned. He gained his feet, staggering at first, and tried to locate his horse. She was quietly grazing at the edge of the trees.

Fearing that the wolves and coyotes would make a meal of the boy, he pulled the spear from him and moved him to the cover of the trees. In the morning, he would perform a proper burial for the boy. Clint dared not build a fire, fearing that he may fall victim to other Indians who might be in the area so he sat through the night, watching the stars and listening to the critters fighting over the remains of the men he'd killed. None came near the boy.

At dawn, Clint worked, gathering enough logs and sticks to build a platform. It should have been higher, he knew that, but he could not lift the body very high. And so, he built it near to six feet high, lashing it together with the rawhide rope he had on his horse. Before placing the boy there, he took a blanket from his pack and laid it across the platform. He then placed the boy on the blanket and wrapped it about him, securing it with rawhide thongs. The boy's head he faced in a southerly direction. And from his head, Clint cut a lock of hair, tying it with a piece of cloth, taken from the edge of the blanket. This he attached to a tree branch that hung next to the platform. The spear that had killed the boy, he placed alongside him. With that, he added his own hatchet, knowing that a warrior should not enter the land of the dead without weapons.

For an hour, Clint knelt at the side of the platform, wailing the death song he'd so often heard. When he rode away, he only turned around once to look on the boy. Facing back then, he whispered, "Goodbye, son."

#

Since he'd instructed the Old Man to take Morah, Johnson, and the boys to their secret cache on the ridge, that is where he rode. As he approached, the boys saw him and came running to greet him.

"Where did you go?" they asked. "We were worried when the Old Man made us come here."

In a calm voice, he answered, "I had to make sure that the Pawnee we had trouble with did not follow us and try to seek revenge."

"Did you meet them or have trouble with them?" they asked.

"No, I did not see any sign of them. I searched for fresh pony tracks but there were none. I would suppose they went on their way, knowing that it would be foolish to attack such mighty warriors as you two." For a moment, they didn't know what to make of that. They were not used to being teased. Then, when they saw the twinkle in his eye and his mischievous smile, they knew he was playing with them and they broke into laughter.

"I don't know about you two, but I'm half starved. Did Morah cook up any of that good flat bread she makes?"

"Morah is not here," Keme said. "She left with Johnson. He said he would rather go back to his place at the settlement than come up here. He asked her if she wanted to go and she accepted."

Clint thought about what had just been said and then slowly nodded his head. In English, he whispered to himself, "Damn that Johnson, he should have stayed here in case those Pawnee had got past me."

"Guess we better fend for ourselves then, boys." he shouted. "Did you bring any of that dried elk meat with you?"

"Yes, and we do have some flat bread that Morah made up for us before she left."

"Good! Then let's have it."

Later that afternoon, they packed up the camp and started back for Clint's outpost. The boys rode out ahead of them. When they were far enough out of earshot, the Old Man asked if there had been trouble. Clint's answer was brief. "Yes, but they won't bother us again."

The Old Man nodded his understanding. It would never be spoken of again. They rode on.

CHAPTER 2:
FIRST MEETING

The morning was brisk, with a chilly wind coming in from the south. "Storm coming," whispered the Old Man. "Be here soon."

The four of them had been working for three full days, cutting up the buffalo they'd killed. The meat had to be sliced into thin strips, in order to dry and cure properly. Clint had made a special area near the outpost for drying the meat. It was an enclosure of a sort, built to keep the critters out, who would gorge on the meat if given the chance. It did not, however, keep the flies or yellow jackets away and when the men took fresh piles of the sliced meat into the enclosure to dry it, they were immediately immersed in a cloud of buzzing, stinging insects.

While Clint and the boys sliced up the meat, the Old Man busied himself making pemmican. This he did by pounding the driest of the jerky meat between two large rocks. This pulverized meat he then seasoned, using his own recipe ingredients. This concoction was then stuffed into a large rawhide bag and drenched it in a mixture of melted marrow and tallow, which had been salvaged from the slain animals. The rawhide bag was then sewn shut. As it began to cool and harden, the Old Man had the boys walk on the bag to flatten it.

"It's easier to store or to carry that way," he explained. Understanding the Old Man's meaning, the boys nodded their heads.

"You listen to that Old Man and you'll learn a lot," Clint told them. "He's very wise."

When the work was done for the day and all the meat had been prepared, they all sat around the fire, roasting chunks of loin they'd saved for their dinner.

"When do we ride for our village?" Kitchi asked.

"Two, maybe three more days," Clint answered. "We'll pack what we can of this meat and the other goods you'll need, onto the horses. That means we'll have to walk until we get to the settlement. From there, Johnson should let us use some of his horses so we'll be able to ride the rest of the way.

Rain was threatening when Clint and the boys left the outpost. They'd dressed warm because of the impending storm and the cold wind blowing in from the west. It would take them the better part of five days to reach the settlement where they could meet up with Johnson. The Old Man had begged off the trip, saying that he wasn't up to the long walk. He said he'd stay at the outpost and take care of what was needed. Clint didn't like leaving him but there was no other way. Besides, he'd have the women and the Shoshoni people to help him if need be.

From the time he'd learned that Storm was alive, Clint hadn't been able to concentrate on anything else. He was excited but at the same time nervous. He had no idea what to say to her or how she would react to seeing him. After all, it had been many years since the day he'd climbed on that raft and waved goodbye to her. Hell, she may not even remember him at all. People do change!

He didn't want to seem overly inquisitive with the boys but every now and then, when they were talking, he'd throw in a question about their mother. Some little inconsequential thing like, "Does she still have that lock of hair that falls down over one eye or does she still walk a little bow legged?" Simple questions, but the answers to them would help paint a fresh picture of the woman he was riding to meet.

He was also excited to see his nephew, Jeremy, again and talk about family things. They would share the stories of the past with each other. Stories of Clint's childhood, where he and his sister, Molly grew up, the pranks they'd played, the dreams they'd shared. And, in turn, Jeremy would talk of his childhood, his friends and the things he liked to do. Clint was looking forward to their meeting again.

When they finally reached the settlement, Clint was quick to notice the obvious lack of activity about. When he was here the last time, there was a lot of trading going on; many more trappers, and much more hustle and bustle. But now, the place seemed empty, devoid of people. The rafts and keelboats that had lined the edge of the river were gone. The hitching rails that always tethered many horses and mules were empty. Most of all, he noticed that the Army Headquarters tent was missing.

Without stopping, Clint and the boys walked straight on to Johnson's tent. "You in there?" Clint yelled, tying the pack animals to a nearby post. Morah was the first to poke her head out the canvas flap.

"Clint," she said, smiling. "We've been expecting you." Even though she seemed happy to see them, she would not look Clint in the eye. Just then, Johnson pushed the flap aside and walked out.

"Glad to see you made it, pard. The Old Man said you'd gone back to see if them Pawnee had follered us." He paused a moment, then asked. "Well...."

"Yeah! We met up."

"They give ya some trouble, did they?"

"A bit! But after a time, I convinced 'em they should leave me be." Saying no more about that, Clint then asked about the settlement and why it was so quiet.

"Most of the trappers have gone back to the hills and the boats packed up and left two days, ago."

"What about the Army?"

"They were gone when I got here. Word is, they received orders to go back to St. Lou. That young lieutenant asked me to give you his regards and say he was sorry he couldn't say goodbye in person. Said he'd catch up with you the next time around."

Clint nodded and was about to ask Johnson if they could borrow some horses. But Johnson spoke first, before Clint could get it out.

"Say, about me leavin' with Morah, I wanted to set that straight with ya."

"There's nothin' ya have to set straight, Clarence." Clint's tone was sharp. "I have no claim on her. She can come and go as she pleases. Apparently, she wanted to come here with you and so as far as I'm concerned, that's that."

Johnson felt the keen edge of the words that had just been spoken to him. He could feel Clint's ire. Hell, it was the only time Clint had ever called him by his first name.

"Well, I just wanted..."

"No need for words," Clint interrupted. "What I do need is to borrow three horses from ya. I'll pay you for the use of 'em and I'll take good care of 'em. I'll see to it they're fed and watered proper."

"Hell, what can I say but yes," Johnson thought. "I owe him that much."

"Sure," Johnson whispered in a half-voice. "Not a problem, Clint. I'll cut three of 'em out for ya." He paused a moment and then spoke again. "Seems like yer awful sore at me for something, Hell, I told you I fancied that woman and you..."

Clint cut him off right there. "Ain't the woman, Johnson," he said, his voice a little more forgiving, "It's the fact that you pulled out and left the Old Man and the boys there alone to face those Pawnee if they'd a come a callin'. Yeah, I'm sore at ya but it all worked out and I'll get over it. I just wanted ya to know."

"We friends again, then?" Johnson asked, holding out his hand.

"Never was anything but," Clint replied and shook his friend's hand.

#

It was good to be setting a horse again. Clint didn't mind the walking they'd done but riding a horse beat walkin'. Keme had taken the lead when they rode from the settlement. His brother followed and Clint brought up the rear. Each of the boys led a pack horse and Clint led two. Single file, they made their way up through the divide and over the pass. Their path took them in a north, northeast direction.

It was deep into autumn now and most of the colorful oak brush and hardwood leaves had fallen. The dark green pines, growing in great, tall clusters seemed even darker as they added contrast to the endless landscape. The aspen trees, for the most part, had assumed their whitish gray, winter appearance. Here and there, a patch of brilliant yellow leaves still clung to their mother tree, trembling, and then falling away with each small wisp of a breeze. Winter was not far off.

Late in the morning of their fourth day out, Keme and Kitchi brought their horses to a halt, waiting for Clint to join them. The boys then pointed off to the east toward a long valley. It was not only long but wide as well, with a good-sized river running its length. About midway through it, dusty gray pillars of smoke rose from out the surrounding trees. The tops of lodges were visible and a herd of horses fed on a nearby plain. From this vantage point, Clint could make out some activity in the village. He thought to himself, "It's no wonder I never found her...not clear up here."

"There! There is our home," Keme said, smiling. "We will be there soon."

It was not long before they were approached by the lookouts who kept watch for enemies. As they rode up, they quickly recognized the boys and there was much laughter and loud talk. They were somewhat suspicious of Clint but when the boys introduced him as their father, he was immediately accepted.

Kitchi then turned to Clint and said, "We want to ride ahead and tell mother that we're here and that we have a big surprise for her."

"Go ahead," he answered, "I'll find my way."

"It's gonna be a big surprise alright," he thought to himself and he could feel his stomach tightening.

\#

Storm was not at the lodge when the boys came riding in. She had taken some skin bags to the river to fetch water. The boys got off their horses and rushed through the flap on the lodge calling out to her. Armand greeted them with warmth and told them their mother would be back soon. They could see that he was having trouble moving and guessed it was because of the accident.

"We were so worried about you," he said. "We thought you had lost your way or had been captured or killed. It is so good to see you. Your mother will be happy that her sons have returned."

The boys began to tell him of their adventures and he sat listening with excitement at what they said.

Clint had almost lost sight of the boys as they sped into the village. As he rode among the lodges, he received wary looks from many of the village people. None approached him, however. Seeing the boys' horses in front of one of the lodges, he dismounted and was tying the horses to a tethering pole when he saw her. At about the same time he saw her, she saw him. A sudden look of fear and shock crossed her face and she dropped the water skins she'd been carrying. Tears welled up in her eyes and she put her hand to her mouth to hide the small whimper that issued forth.

"Hello, Storm," he said in a quiet voice, hoping to ease the feelings that raced through her.

"It can't be," she whispered. "It can't be...you're dead...they, they killed you."

"No," he answered, still in a quiet voice. "They never did catch me. I....I missed you in the darkness, wound up on the river, I looked for....thought you were dead." Clint couldn't get the words out. They were tumbling over each other and made little sense. It was then that he noticed a small tear make its way down his cheek. His throat tightened and he didn't know if he could speak again.

God, it had been so long and he'd come to the realization that he'd never see her again and now, here she was, looking the same as he remembered, just as beautiful, just as warm, just as womanly as she had been all those years ago, on the banks of the Platte. He wanted to rush to her and sweep her up in his arms.

"I live with a man now," she murmured, wiping the tears away. "He is my husband."

"I know. The boys told me about him."

"Then, you have met my sons," she asked. "Where are they?"

"I rode here with them. They showed me the way. They're in your lodge."

Quickly, she turned and made her way to the lodge, calling their names as she ran. There were loud sounds of rejoicing as the boys greeted their mother. Clint didn't know what to do. He just stood there wondering what would come next. He bent down and retrieved the leaking water skins and carried them to the edge of the lodge. He didn't attempt to go in. It was only after Kitchi came through the door flap and took him by the arm that he felt he should enter.

Armand greeted him as he came through the small opening. When the flap closed, shutting out the sunlight, it was very hard to see. The small fire that burned in the center of the lodge added some light but not much. Soon though, his eyes became accustomed to the darkness and he could see much better.

Armand did not speak good English and so addressed Clint in Blackfoot.

"I apologize for not getting up but I had an accident some time ago and it has left me to the point that I cannot stand."

Clint acknowledged the man's apology. "That's alright," he said, "Kitchi and Keme told me what happened. I'm sorry about your misfortune and I hope you get well soon."

"I will not get well at all," he remarked. "In fact, my ability to move gets worse each day. I...." His voice trailed off then, causing him to choke up.

"Forgive me. I get feeling sorry for myself sometimes and it gets me down. If it wasn't for my wife, here, I would surely perish." With that, he reached out and took Storm's hand. She bowed her head but said nothing. She did not look at Clint.

The silent sadness was suddenly broken by Keme. Lifting the flap aside, he laughingly said, "You must come and see the things we've brought. We have plenty of meat for the winter, blankets, knives, and some special gifts for both of you." For a moment, he again became serious. "All this, we have because of one person, our father." Then looking quickly to Storm he said, "He is our father, right?"

She said nothing, only nodded and gave him a smile.

They helped Armand out of the lodge and propped him up so he could see. Many of the villagers had gathered around to greet the boys and see what they'd brought on the pack horses. As they began unloading the animals, the now gathering crowd would cheer as each parfliech of meat or sack of pemican was unloaded. When it came to the gifts that the boys had gotten for their mother and Armand, everyone oohed and aahed as the boys brought them forth.

With the crowd milling about, Clint went to attend the horses. Storm approached him then. She had composed herself and needed to talk with him. Seeing her advance toward him, Clint turned to face her.

"I have something for you," he said, reaching into the small pocket of his shirt. "Here! This is in remembrance of a time when you and I loved one another." Taking her wrist in his hand, he brought forth a delicate horse-hair bracelet, much like the one she'd given him. Gently, he tied it about her wrist. The touch of her was almost too much to bear and he took a step backward.

"I've never stopped loving you," she whispered. "You were my one and only. But, I thought you were dead and then when Ned and Lou..." she stopped for a moment, wiping a tear away, gathering her thoughts. "After Ned and Lou were gone, I was alone; pregnant and alone. I did anything I could to survive. That's when I met Armand. He saved my life and our sons' lives. Had it not been for him, the three of us would have perished. He was there for me. And now, in his time of need, I must be and will be there for him."

She had laid it out for him, her story, and her life. Feeling that he must do the same, he began. "On the day I lost you, there was a hunting party of warriors who caught sight of me on the raft. I tried to stay out in the middle of the river, out of bow range. They knew they would lose a man or two if they tried to take me so they kept their distance. I was worried about you, Ned, and Lou, thinking that you might try to come back and check on me. Anyway, they finally rode away. I was very tired and must have drifted off to sleep. When I awoke, it was pitch black, there was no moon. A strong wind was blowing and waves were hitting me in the face. I looked for your fire but there was no light anywhere. I tried to get the raft ashore but I couldn't fight the current. That's when I realized I had been swept onto the big river..." Clint paused for a moment, trying to remember the details of what happened. Then, he went on.

"When I finally made it back to the place you'd waited, I found many tracks of ponies around the place you'd built the signal fire. I searched high and low for days hoping to find any sign of you but there was nothing. I, like you, believed that you and the others had perished at the hands of a hunting party. When I could look no further, I climbed on the raft and paddled downstream. It was there that I met a river boat. The captain of that boat was my friend and he loaned me a small boat to get me back to St. Louis. You remember that I was going there to get my leg mended and that's what I did." He stopped for a minute, stepped forward to where he'd been and reached out for her hand. She gave it willingly. Then he went on.

"Once my leg had healed, I hired on with the fur company as a hunter and came back up the river. For years, I searched for you, asking Indian and white man alike if they'd seen you. I was once told that a white man with an Indian wife, who fit your description and two twin boys had spent a time in one of the villages but I didn't think it was you, not with two children. And, as you and I had said we'd someday go there to live, I went to the place where the three rivers meet and waited for you. I have a trading post there now. Of course, you had no idea about that."

When he mentioned the three rivers and their promise to live there forever, she hung her head and began to weep. Just then, Kitchi came through the crowd and interrupted them.

"How long will you stay with us, father?" he asked. Clint was suddenly startled but pleased. It was the first time one of the boys had called him father. A silent pride boiled up inside him and he then knew what it meant to have children, to love them and have them love you. That pride was then torn away when he realized the gravity of the situation. He had so wanted to come here, to see Storm, to express his love to her. But now, all he could think of was how badly he wanted to leave.

Letting go of her hand, he answered the question. "Winter's comin' on fast, son, and I dare not let it catch me this far from home." Saying the word "home" suddenly struck a place in his mind that reminded him how badly he wanted a home, and sons, and....Storm.

"I'll stay the night and then I must leave. I've got to get Johnson's horses back to him and then I need to get back and check on the Old Man. He's not been feelin' too well lately."

"Then we want to come with you," Kitchi said.

Clint looked down, a small sigh escaped him as he answered. "What about your mother?" he asked. "How do you think she and Armand will make it through the winter? Someone needs to be here to help them, to be the men of the family." He paused then, looking at Storm. "When spring has come and the trials of winter are behind us, I will come for you and your brother; then we can hunt and fish and see new country together."

The boy thought about what his father had said and realized that it was true. Someone had to take care of the home front. Resignedly, he said, "I still wish you would stay awhile with us."

Looking the boy in the eye, he whispered, "I can't, son. It'd be too hard on me and everyone else. Someday you'll understand."

When the boy left to rejoin his friends, Storm whispered, "Thank you for that. You are such a good man." She walked to Clint and taking his face in her hands, kissed him gently on the lips. It was too much. He could restrain himself no longer. His arms were suddenly about her, drawing her to him, embracing her, caressing her. God, she was warm and soft, just as he remembered. He wanted this moment to last forever. Then...

"I must go," she whispered. "If we are seen like this, there will be much gossip in the village and it will go bad for the boys and me."

"I love you, Storm," he said, as she pulled away from him to join her sons.

There was a great feast that night to celebrate the boys' return. Young braves, including the boys, painted their faces and danced wildly to the heavy drum beats. Everyone ate well, gorging on buffalo and gnawing on the roasted ribs. Clint was invited to spend the night in the lodge but begged off, telling them he'd rather sleep under the stars.

As he laid there, thoughts ran in and out of his mind. Often, the tears streamed down his face. All these years, all this time.... he'd lost her once back on the banks of the Platt and now, he was losing her again. He could not sleep.

Inside the lodge, Storm was going through much the same thing. She had loved him and lost him and believed for so long that he was dead and then...then, there he was standing before her, so big, so handsome, so loving. She rolled over, trying to fight back the tears and the sobs that racked her body.

When the sun rose the next morning, Clint was gone. Unable to rest, he'd readied the horses and struck out on the trail for home. A few dogs had barked at his leaving but other than that, the village was silent.

Kitchi and Keme were very disappointed that he had gone without saying goodbye. "I guess he really doesn't care for us," Keme said, sadly. "Of course, he cares for us," Kitchi retorted. "Why would he have done all the things he's done for us if he didn't. You just don't know what's going on. I will explain later when we are alone."

Storm's eyes and face were swollen and red from crying all night. Armand said nothing as she rose and walked past him. He understood the situation. She went about the motions of feeding the boys and Armand but her mind was on other things and she could not eat. Village life was hard, what with the lack of food and wood and water, and trying to keep from freezing to death. It was hard. Now, for Storm, it would be a whole lot harder.

CHAPTER 3:
JIM TUCKER – WHITE DEATH

The first snow of the year was falling when Clint rode into the settlement. His first stop would be at Johnson's place to return the horses he'd borrowed. He was somewhat shocked to see the empty space where Johnson's tent used to stand.

"Well I'll be," he whispered. "Didn't think he'd ever pull outta here."

"You must be Jeffries," a voice said, from behind him. Turning, he saw a grizzled looking fellow with long white hair and a beard to match.

"He told me you'd be comin' this way. Said you'd be bringing back his horses."

"Yup, that's what I'm doin'. And who might you be, sir?"

"Name's Lemuel Porter."

"Pleased to meet ya, Lemuel," Clint said, reaching down to shake the man's outstretched hand. "Any idea where Johnson took off to?"

"Told me he was headin' fer yer place. Gonna stay up that way fer a spell....said for ya to just bring those horses along."

"Well, I guess I can do that alright," Clint said. And then looking down the main road, he asked,

"Say Lemuel, is there someplace here where a feller might get some food? My belly button's rubbin' a sore spot on my backbone. I'm about half starved."

"No formal place to eat, like those sit-down rest-ee-rants," he answered, "But if ya don't mind some good ole Injun cookin,' I can get my old lady to fix us up somethin'."

"Sure would appreciate it. I can pay ya...."

"No, ya can't," he answered, cutting Clint off. "Yer money's no good with me."

422

As they ate, they talked about the usual things on the frontier; trapping, Injun trouble, who's come up the river, who got killed, things like that. It was in that conversation that Porter mentioned there was a prospector who was looking for men who could lead him up to the three-forks area and then south to the red rock country. He said he had a map that he got from an old Indian, showing the location of a pure vein of gold.

"He's lookin' fer men who know the country and can lead him there."

"When's he plannin' on startin' this journey?" Clint asked.

"From the sound of it, he's goin' purty soon."

Clint smiled, "From the sound of it, he's some kinda fool or maybe a greenhorn. This ain't no time to be headin' into the mountains to look for somethin' that probably ain't there. Hell, winters comin'."

Porter went on, "Says he thinks he can git fer enuff south to escape the winter."

Clint shook his head and kept on eating. "I tell ya, some folks got no brains. They're dumber than a yard a shit."

"Well, one good thing......he's got a feller who he says knows all that country. Says he's been there before."

"Say! Who are these fellers anyway?" Clint asked.

"The prospector's named Wallace - a big man, kinda fat. The other feller's name escapes me." Scratching his head, Porter fumbled for the other name. "Let's see, it's Turner, no that ain't it, um Tasler, Thomas, um...um Tulmer. No, it's Tucker. That's it, Tucker."

"Not Jim Tucker?" Clint asked.

"I believe that's it, alright. Yes sir, it's Jim Tucker."

"Good hell!" Clint whispered to himself. "Old Jim! Where are these two stayin'?"

"Got 'em a couple a lodges set up east of here, in the clearing next to that bunch of Injuns out there."

"Uh, no offense darlin,'" Porter said, trying to calm the hard looks he was receiving from his wife.

"She knows some English words," Porter whispered to Clint, "and Injun ain't one of her favorite ones."

"Guess I'll drop around and say hello," Clint said. "Tucker's an old friend of mine."

#

Clint thanked Porter and his wife for their hospitality. Then, leading the pack horses east, he rode from the settlement to the large clearing. This was the same clearing that he, Morah, and the Old Man had camped in. It was empty then, but now there were many lodges scattered about. He rode slow, looking them over for any sign of his old friend. He was about to stop and ask someone if they would show him where the white man was living when he caught sight of a leather-clad figure lying before a lodge on a large buffalo robe. A rolled-up pelt was stuffed under his head and his hat was pulled down over his eyes. A long-stemmed pipe hung from the corner of his mouth, issuing forth a thin column of gray smoke.

Clint dropped the reins of the pack animals and rode slowly up to the man.

"What'll it be?" the man asked in Shoshone, not bothering to look up.

Answering him, Clint said, "What are you burning in that pipe? It smells like a mixture of corral dirt and bird droppin's."

With that, the man lifted the brim of the hat and gazed up at the stranger looking down at him.

"Who the hell are you?" he spouted, this time in English.

"Well, I guess I've changed some," Clint answered. "But you ain't. You're still the lazy, ornery, skinny, old son-of-a-bitch that I remember."

"Clint! Clint, is that you?" Suddenly, the man was getting to his feet. "Well, Goddam, I don't believe it. Last time I saw you, ya was hobblin' off to St. Lou to get yer peg fixed. Didn't think you'd ever come back to the mountains."

"Yeah, I was gone fer a spell but I couldn't leave all this beautiful country to the likes of you."

"Drop down off that nag and set a spell," Jim said. "Would ya like a shot a whiskey? Got a jug of it inside." Before Clint could answer, Jim spoke out, again. "Bring us out some whiskey, woman."

When she appeared, Clint thought she looked familiar. "Isn't that..."

"Yep!" Jim answered before Clint could finish. "It's Black Elk's youngest daughter, Nineksa. She's been with me all this time. One hell-of-a-woman, I tell ya, but mean, mean. She can kick my ass around a tree any time she wants to but she usually doesn't have to bein' as how I'm so lovable and all."

"Ain't lost yer sense a humor any, I see. But what's this I hear about you and this Wallace feller strikin' out to find some Injun gold? You do realize that winter's gonna be here soon?" He looked at Jim, awaiting an answer.

"Yeah, I do and I think if we leave now we can beat the big storms and get to the red rock country where it doesn't snow much. Supposedly, that's where this Injun gold is...a whole mountain of it, he says. Says we'll all be rich."

"You'll all be dead if'n ya start now. There's no way you can do that, Jim. It's too far. Hell, yer talkin' a three or four-month journey and that's if the weather's good. In another month, it'll...." Clint paused for a moment. "Hell, have you ever even been there? I mean all the way to the red rock country?"

"I once went as far as that lake that tastes like salt," Jim answered. "Damndest thing, Clint! All the rivers and creeks that run into it are fresh, sweet, drinkable water but you try to take a drink a that lake and it'll choke ya." He paused then, scratching his head. "Never did see any red rock, though. Saw plenty of black rock....but Wallace has a map and says he knows where he's goin'."

"What about her?" Clint asked, nodding toward the lodge.

"Guess she'll be goin' with me," Tucker answered. "She's faithful! Goes everywhere I do."

"Yeah! Well, I wish ya luck, Jim. Be careful out there." With that, Clint climbed on his horse and started across the clearing.

"Wouldn't want to come along would ya?" Jim yelled, "We're gonna be rich."

Clint didn't even turn around. He just waved his hand and rode on.

It was full dark and freezing cold when Clint finally arrived at his outpost. The orange glow of a dying cook fire bounced off the surrounding pines, creating ghostly dancing shadows. Somewhere in the darkness, a pony whinnied, sounding an alarm and announcing his arrival. Surprisingly, it was the Old Man who first appeared from his lodge to see who was there.

"Is that you, tall one?" the Old Man queried, his breath streaming forth in a small cloud.

"Yes, it is, my friend."

"Are the boys with you....and what of the woman?"

The words hit him like a punch in the gut. "The woman!" he thought. With those two words, he was suddenly thrown back into the memory of her and it almost took his breath away. He closed his eyes and sighed, not wanting to remember.

"Let me put these horses up and then we'll talk," he answered.

This satisfied the Old Man and he returned to the warmth of his lodge.

For many hours, the two of them talked. Clint related what had happened and where things stood. The Old Man listened intently, offering no suggestions or advice. Now and then he would nod and grunt his approval or disapproval, whichever way the conversation went. When Clint had finished, the Old Man looked long and hard at him. "I must sleep now," was all he said. Pulling the heavy robe about his shoulders, he rolled over and went to sleep.

#

The snow was unusually heavy. Coming early and borne on the howling northwest wind, one storm after another pelted their fury on the surrounding mountain tops, hiding everything under a thick, heavy, white blanket. The valleys too, suffered the same freezing milieu, filling up to the depth of a horse's belly. Wallace and his small crew of travelers were snowed in.

It had been nearly a month since they left their camp at the settlement. They had not anticipated the storms would come as quickly nor be as harsh as they were. At that moment, they had plenty to eat and had found adequate shelter in a thick grove of pines. The horses were the ones suffering, having to scrape away the deep snow to forage on the frozen grasses that lay below.

Jim had convinced Wallace that they must turn back. Wallace was not happy about it but agreed they could not go ahead.

"When do we start?" he asked Jim.

"I think we stay put here for a while until the storms quit. The going will be hard but we need to get out of these mountains, get to lower ground." Wallace agreed to the plan and so they sat, waiting for a break in the weather.

When it finally came, they lead off, going single file. First, Jim would take a turn breaking trail and when he was worn out, Wallace or one of the other Indian bearers would take his place. Most of the equipment they had, had been carried on travois but, with the depth of the snow, that was no longer possible. They packed the horses with what they could and left the things they didn't need. Wallace insisted they place those goods in a sheltered place in the trees where he could find and retrieve them in the spring.

For five days, they trudged through the frozen mass, struggling for every foot they gained. Because of the biting wind that visited them daily, the snow would drift, sometimes being two feet deep and other times, six feet deep. Jim fashioned a pair of snow shoes from some nearby willows and went in front of the group with a long pole measuring the depth of the snow, steering them around and away from the deep drifts.

On the sixth day, two of their horses had to be put down. A lack of food and the terrible cold had taken its toll on them and they collapsed in their tracks. It became more and more evident that they could not make any headway with the horses. So, it was decided they would all make snowshoes and carry the food and other necessities on their backs.

For Jim and the Indians, walking on snowshoes was not a problem but Wallace was an extremely large man and he kept breaking through the top, frozen crust. The others wanted to leave him but Jim insisted they stay and help him.

When the last horse finally gave in, they butchered the loins from its back and divided the meat among them. They ate well that night and dug snow caves to keep out of the howling wind. Jim's wife had held up well and that night, wrapped in their buffalo robes, she asked him if they were going to make it out alive. He answered, telling her not to worry; that they would all be safe and everything would be alright. As he told her this, lying there in the darkness, he wondered if they really would make it. The situation was bleak and they had a long way to go.

Climbing from the snow cave, Jim looked up at the large snowflakes falling gently from the sky. In any other situation, he would have considered them beautiful. But now, they were just more of the thing that was killing them. He and his wife chewed on a frozen piece of horse meat, washing it down with handfuls of snow. Wallace had not surfaced. Neither had the Indians.

"Wallace! Hey Wallace! It's time we got started."

"Not today," he answered. "No more! I can't go on. I'm just too tired and cold. Just leave me."

Jim cast a worried look to his wife. "Aw, c'mon Wallace. Get those snowshoes on, have a bite a that horse and let's get kickin'. There's more snow comin' and we need to move out."

"I told ya, I ain't goin' and that's that."

"You'll die here, man," Jim waited for a reply but none came. "Okay! I'm sorry Wallace."

By this time the two Indian bearers had climbed up out of their holes and were strapping on their snowshoes. A few minutes later, they were all on their way. Without Wallace to slow them down, they made good time. "Going at this pace," Jim said, "we should be near one of the big rivers soon; out of the high country; out of the deep snow." They trekked on.

About midday, they arrived, as Jim had said, at a rather large river. The snow here was not as deep but it wasn't frozen as hard either and they found themselves breaking through the crust, slowing their progress. Ahead of them, a thick grove of pine came down off the steep mountainside, growing right to the river's edge. It looked impossible to get through and there was no way to go around. They'd just have to navigate a path through the trees and hope they didn't lose their footing and slide into the river. Jim told Nineksa to stay back and let him and the other two men search out a path for them to take.

While the men disappeared into the thick forest, Jim's wife took the welcome opportunity to pee without them looking on. She then found a sheltered place out of the snowfall and proceeded to chew on a piece of the frozen horse meat. She was feeling better about their situation. She believed they might actually make it out of this without dying. She leaned back against a large pine and drifted off to sleep.

It started out with a sharp crack, almost like the sound of a rifle, but then a low rumble quickly followed. She was suddenly awake and sitting straight up, wondering what was happening. The sound got louder and she tried to see through the falling snow but it was useless. It was the terrifying sound of the huge pine trees snapping off and being consumed by the racing, roaring white mass that approached from above, which sent her into a panic. In an instant, she was running, back the way she'd come. Her legs tore into the knee-deep snow trying to gain traction, trying to get away. It was then she felt the tremendous surge of wind from behind her. Stronger and stronger it came, finally lifting her from her feet and propelling her into a large tree. The force of the blow caused her to wrap almost around it, twisting and coming to rest behind the tree and away from the force of the avalanche.

She had no idea how long she'd laid there. Hitting the tree had knocked her unconscious. She felt the pain rush through her body as she tried to stand. Nothing seemed broken, however. All about her, the snow was very deep and hard as a rock. She could walk on it without sinking. It was then she remembered Jim. He had gone into the trees to find a path for them. Now, there were no trees, just a giant mass of snow clogging up the river, forming an unimaginable wall of ice and broken timber and brush. Everything in its path had been crushed.

She began to call for him, climbing over broken trees and huge rocks. She screamed until she could scream no more. Her voice had given out. Finally, she retreated to a thick stand of pines behind her and away from the slide. She gathered some dead pine needles and twigs and soon had a warm fire burning.

"Jim will see this fire and know that I am safe. He will come for me and we will eat and lie down together....and tomorrow we will..." A twig snapped in the fire, causing a hot cinder to land on her cheek. Her mind was then jarred back to the reality of the situation. Jim was gone.

"But what of the other two?" she said to herself. "Would they not have answered when she was calling out?" She hung her head. "They too, were gone."

Through the night, she fed the tiny fire and sang the death song. In the morning, she would again look for Jim and the others.

CHAPTER 4:
NINEKSA

Johnson had set up his tent not far from the Old Man's. He was knocking the loose snow off it when Clint appeared from his outpost. Clint had, for a long time, slept in the Old Man's Lodge but now, he preferred the solitude of the log dwelling. In there, he didn't have to put up with the Old Man's questions concerning Storm and the boys. He didn't need those right now.

"Colder than a whore's heart this mornin'," Johnson yelled. Clint just nodded to him and proceeded to walk around the corner of the outpost to pee.

"Looks like you didn't walk far enough," Morah said, standing there watching him and grinning.

"Jesus, a man can't even pee around here without company," he replied. "It's gettin' too damn crowded. I'd like as not to move on outta these parts and find some solitude."

"You couldn't look at me then," she said, flirting with him, "and you know you like to."

He did too. But he'd never admit it, especially now that she was living with Johnson. "Say, where you goin' anyway?" he asked.

"I'm tired of melting snow for water. I'm going to the river and get some real water."

"Well, don't fall in," he said.

Johnson had finished what he was doing and walked to Clint's outpost. Stomping the snow from his feet, he entered. "Cozy warm in here brother," he said. "A might dark though." Without giving Clint a chance to say anything, Johnson went on. "About time we was setting' up some trap lines don't ya think?"

Clint nodded, "Well, I ain't much on trappin' these days. Too much work and the water's too damn cold to wade in, settin' them traps. I'd just as soon let them other fools ketch 'em and then trade 'em to me. I make money and I don't have to get wet. Besides, there's lots of snow to deal with."

"You calling' me a fool?" Johnson said, laughing.

"Yup! But yer a likeable fool," Clint answered. "Tell ya what though, we'll have to travel some distance away, being as how that bunch across the way there will be doing' the same damn thing and they'll have everything trapped out that's close by." He raised a finger, casting it in the direction of the Indian lodges on the far side of the clearing.

"Ya ever think about runnin' 'em off?"

Clint shook his head, "Nah!" he answered, "Hell, this is their country. If anyone was to get run off, it oughta be us. We're the trespassers."

Johnson just nodded, thinking about what Clint had just said. Then, he changed the subject. "I been greasin' my traps and could be ready to head out in just a short while."

"Alright then!" Clint said. "Ya talked me into it. Gimme an hour or so and I'll be ready. I'll ask the Old Man to keep an eye on things here, so's my goods don't wander off."

#

They elected to ride upstream from the outpost. When they reached the confluence of the three forks, Clint followed the branch that came in from the east. He had always done well with his trap lines in that area.

Since many different Indian bands frequented the same area to hunt, fish, and gather stone for arrow and spear points, he and Johnson had to be very watchful. Many of the Indians that were of a local nature, knew Clint and had traded at his outpost. But there were groups that passed in and out of the area who were very war-like and would lift your hair in a second.

On the fourth day out, they had still not located any decent trapping waters. Oh, there were a few beaver around but they had been harassed so much that they were very trap-wise. Even the castor scent the trappers used to lure them to the set would alert them and scare them off. And so, it was, that the men had to travel further and further up the river to find an unspoiled location.

While following one rather large stream, they began to see more and more sign that the area had not been trapped at all. They decided this was a good place and they would set up a concealed camp; one they could use as a base from which to trap this river and other small streams in the surrounding area. There was quite a bit of snow and it was impossible to move about and not leave tracks. They built their camp at the edge of a small side-water of the main river. This, they could ride their horses into and then move to the main stream, leaving no tracks directly to their camp. Once in the main stream, they could ride up or downstream a good way, before exiting to work a trap line.

They had set traps above and below the camp and had had good success. On this particular morning, Clint told Johnson he thought they should travel further upstream and find a new campsite. Johnson agreed and so before the sun cast its first light in the eastern sky, the two of them were underway. It was a clear, cold morning with only a sliver of moon to provide any light. The horses had been this way many times in the past few weeks and knew their way through the darkness.

The men had ridden some distance up the river and were searching about to find a decent camp when suddenly, Johnson held his hand out, stopping Clint. "You smell that?" he whispered. Clint said nothing, simply nodding. It was the smell of smoke, a campfire.

"Let's back on outta here and high-tail it back down river," Johnson whispered, starting to turn his horse.

"Wait a minute," Clint answered, "let's have a look."

"Are you crazy?" Johnson shot back, terror in his voice. "If they ketch us, they'll cook us over that damn fire."

"Calm down! This ain't no big camp or there'd be more fires. Also, there ain't no horses about or they'd be fussin'. C'mon!"

"Shit!" Johnson muttered, climbing down from his horse.

When both men had dismounted, they tied their horses, and proceeded forward to see who it was. The sky above was still dark but was brightening with the coming sunrise. In that waning darkness, an orange glow filtered out through the trees; embers of a campfire. Now and then a small flame would flicker, casting more light on the scene. In that light, the men could make out a blanketed figure, slumped over and huddled near the fire.

"Peers to be just one of 'em," Johnson whispered. "Let's go!"

"Shh! Keep quiet. Let's watch for a bit."

After a while, the figure moved, picking up small twigs and limbs from a near-by pile of firewood. With the addition of fresh wood, the fire leaped to life, lighting up the surrounding area to a brightness that enabled the men to more closely view the blanketed figure. At the same time, the figure adjusted the blanket about itself.

"Jesus Christ, it's a girl," Johnson blurted out, raising up to get a better look.

Boom!!! The pistol ball whizzed past his ear, causing him to drop flat on his belly once again.

"Son-of-a-bitch, that was close," Johnson squealed, pulling his rifle up to shoot.

"Hold on now," Clint shouted, forcing the barrel down.

"We mean you no harm," Clint shouted to the figure that hurriedly struggled to reload the pistol.

"Get down Clint," Johnson screamed, "She'll put the next one between yer eyes."

At the sound of Johnson saying Clint, the girl stopped reloading and stood looking at the men.

"Kinnt?" She asked, trying to mouth his name.

"Nineksa?" Clint answered, this time in the Shoshone tongue.

Suddenly, she was in tears, dropping the pistol and running toward him.

"Oh Kinnt, he's dead, he's dead," she sobbed, falling into his arms

"What happened?" he asked, cuddling her against his chest, "tell me!"

Between fits of tears, she managed to get the story out, describing the terrible crashing of the snow and boulders. How she'd searched the whole slide area over and over and found nothing. Finally, when all hope was gone, she had begun walking, following the river, eating anything she could find. Her face was gaunt and she looked half starved. When offered dried meat from the men's packs, she gorged herself.

"We'll stay here for a while," Clint told Johnson. "She needs to get some food in her and get some rest. If we keep the fire to a minimum we shouldn't be bothered."

"We're not goin' back, are we?' Johnson queried.

"No! We're not goin' back. We've come too far and there's good fur to be taken here. She'll just have to go along with us until we've got the pelts we need."

When Clint explained it to her, Nineksa nodded and agreed to stay with the men. In reality, she had no choice. She knew she would be killed or freeze to death if she struck out on her own. In their packs, each man had extra clothing.

Some of this, they modified to fit the woman. It didn't look the best but it would get her through the trapping season.

For protection from the weather, they fashioned a lean-to from hewn aspens, tying them with buckskin and covering the whole thing with pine boughs. Facing away from the prevailing wind and with a fire pit near the opening, it afforded them warmth and protection from the storms.

Clint and Johnson each had a large buffalo robe to sleep in. Nineksa only had her blanket. With it wrapped tightly about her, she spent several nights next to the fire, feeding it and trying to stay warm. During the day, while the men were away, she would gather wood, stacking it near the fire pit. Then, she would crawl into the shelter, under the robes and sleep through the day. Eventually, however, the nights became too frigid so she slept with Clint in his robe. One night, Johnson offered her to sleep with him but she promptly refused. For two days, she would not even look at him.

"What the hell's got into her?" Johnson asked Clint. "She won't even look at me. All I did was ask her if she wanted to sleep with me that night."

Clint chuckled a little when he answered. "Well, I don't think it was the fact that you asked, but more the way that you asked. Hell, you was bare-assed naked when you pulled that robe back. Scared her, scared me, and damn near sent the horses into a stampede. No wonder she wouldn't climb in with ya. Ya looked like a plucked chicken."

"That ain't funny, Goddamit. All I was wantin' was a little affection, you know?"

"Yeah, I know.....I know." Then, with a stern face, he turned to look Johnson straight in the eye.

"Jesus man, what's wrong with you? She just lost her husband and you pull that kinda shit."

"Yeah, well I hear those strange noises and all that movin' comin' from inside yer robe. You think I don't know what's goin' on?"

"Well, you don't know what's goin' on," Clint retorted. "Those sounds, as you call 'em, are comin' from her cryin'. She cries herself to sleep every night. And that movin' is her havin' nightmares about seein' her man swallowed up in a snow slide. She tosses and turns, tryin' to erase those thoughts."

With that, Johnson had nothing more to say. From then on, the men were cordial with each other and with the woman but a wedge, of a sort, had been driven between Clint and Johnson.

CHAPTER 5:
TROUBLE AT THE OUTPOST

By the time they'd finished their trapping, the snow was on the melt and the ice at the edges of the streams was gone. The river levels hadn't risen too high and so the small streams were still passable. It wouldn't be long though before the major run-off would have them outside their banks. Clint wanted to be back at his outpost before that happened.

As they were finishing loading the pelts on the pack animals, Clint spoke to Nineksa, "You can ride with me. The horse can easily carry both of us."

"I'm not going with you," she answered. "I've decided that I must go and find Jim and give him a proper burial; a warrior's burial."

Clint was taken aback for a moment but he wasn't surprised. He knew how she was hurting, how she longed for her lost love. Feelings he well understood.

"You may not be able to find him," Clint said quietly, trying to dissuade her.

"I will look until I do," she answered, with firm resolve.

He knew it was no use talking to her. She had made up her mind.

"Alright then, let me help you put some things together for your journey."

Clint took one of the parfliches off his pack horse and began filling it with things he thought she might need. Besides a good ration of dried meat, he added what was left of the beans he'd brought. Also, he placed in it one of his skinning knives and an extra shirt and hat.

"You have makins' for startin' fires don't ya," he asked.

She nodded and then said, "You don't have to give me all of this. You won't have enough for yourself."

"I'll manage," he answered.

As he handed the parfliche to her, he took her in his arms and hugged her tightly.

"Are you sure of this?" he whispered.

"Yes!" she answered. "Thank you for all you've done for me."

With that, she turned and walked away from the camp.

Johnson, who had been busy making his own preparations, had not been privy to what had been said and just then noticed the woman walking away.

"Where the hell's she goin'?" he queried. "We're fixin' to leave and she's goin' the other way."

"She's not goin' with us, Johnson," Clint answered. "She's goin' to find Jim and give him a proper burial."

"What? Hell, she'll never find him. He's either buried deep or the animals have been at him, or..."

Clint cut him off then. "She knows what she's doin'," he said.

"You know she'll die, don't ya?" Johnson said, watching her disappear into the forest.

Without answering, Clint took up the reins of the pack animals and mounted his horse, "Giddup" he said.

#

It was mostly a silent ride back to the outpost. The men addressed each other only when there was a decision to be made regarding the trail or the direction they were traveling. Clint had given a good portion of his food to Nineksa so he had to ration out everything he ate in order to make it last. He'd be damned if he'd ask Johnson for any of his food. Anyway, Johnson didn't offer any either.

By the third day of their return, Clint was out of food and was getting mighty hungry. He scanned the forest for any kind of bird or animal that might provide a meal but none were to be found. As he rode, he reached down and sliced off a piece of leather from the top of the heavy winter moccasin on his right foot. This, he chewed on, trying to gain any amount of nourishment he could. He also ate snow, taking handfuls from the branches of the aspens when he could reach it.

At one point along their path, they came to a rather large clearing where they rode out and away from the surrounding forest. Once in the open, they were immediately startled by the sudden whoosh of wings and the deafening caws emitted from the cloud of crows and magpies that rose from the half-eaten elk carcass.

"Well, whadda we got here?" Johnson said, pulling his horse to a halt. "Some bit a winter kill I reckon. Makin' a meal for the birds, looks like."

"I'm gonna have a look myself," Clint said, climbing down from his horse.

"Whoa, that'd be some rotten shit now. What the hell ya plannin' on doin' anyway."

Clint didn't answer. He tied his horse and the pack horses to a heavy sagebrush and made his way through the knee-deep snow over to where the elk lay. The snow there was trampled and bloody. Wolves and coyotes had been gorging on the remains along with the birds and other vermin that were about. Clint suspected the elk was old and had probably died during the arduous winter and then had been frozen. Since the spring thaw was now in full swing, the snow had melted, revealing the dead animal to all the scavengers that roamed the woods. At the rate it was being consumed, it would soon be a mere pile of bones.

"Looks like they've left enough for this ole hoss," Clint whispered, pulling the knife from his belt.

The odor was terrible and he held his breath as he worked at cutting away what meat remained.

"Damn good thing it's so cold or the bees and the flies would be takin' their share too."

Out of curiosity Johnson had tied his horses and was making his way toward the bloody mess.

"Jesus Christ, yer not eatin' that are ya?"

"I'm gonna," Clint said as he kept cutting and trimming to find what might be edible.

"Goddam Jeffries, that looks putrefyin'. Don't know as I'd eat that if I were you."

"Yeah! Well you ain't me and I'm damn hungry. The way I look at it, meat's meat and this'll do."

Walking back to the horses, he quickly secured an empty parfliche. This, he filled with the half-frozen chunks of the bloody meat.

"Johnson, you can go on if ya want but I'm gonna stop for a while and cook me up some of this elk."

"Ain't no hurry," Johnson said. "I could do with a warm fire myself."

They moved from the clearing and into the trees and it wasn't long before Clint had stacked a pile of wood and was setting it to flame. He cut a low branch from a nearby pine and trimmed the twigs and needles away to form a roasting stick; the end, he whittled to a sharp point. After skinning the bark back from the point, he skewered a few thin slices of meat on the stick and set to roasting it over the now dancing flames. It began to sizzle as it turned from dark red to brown. The aroma it cast off was too much for him to bear and he yanked the meat from the stick, burning his hands in the process. He didn't care. Juggling the sizzling mass from hand to hand, he blew on it to cool it. It was still too hot so he dipped it into the snow. A moment later it was in his mouth and he was chewing, savoring the life-saving morsels. "I'm just another goddam scavenger," he whispered. "But I'll live to see another day. Meat's meat, by god."

Through the rest of that day and into the night he fed the fire and hung the remaining meat near the flames to dry. By morning, he had nearly a bag full of the semi-dried meat. It wasn't the best but it was food and would last him until he got back. Six days later they arrived at the outpost.

#

It was mid-morning when Clint and Johnson rode into the clearing that held their encampment. The sun was high in the clear blue sky and was working on the remaining snow, turning it to a gooey mess. Clint pulled up at the rear of his outpost and began tending to his horses. Johnson rode on to his tent.

Dismounting, he approached the tent and pushed his head through the flap, calling to Morah. She wasn't there. He went back to the horses, took up the reins, and began leading them toward Clint's outpost where he would unload and store the furs. His path took him directly in front of the Old Man's lodge and as he passed, he heard laughing coming from inside and recognized it to be Morah's. He dropped the reins and walked over to the lodge. Pulling back the skin door cover, he bent and looked in. It was dark inside but the sun coming in through the opening made it easy to see. What he saw enraged him. Morah was naked, straddled atop the Old Man and going for all she was worth. Her large breasts bounced up and down and she was giggling.

"Son-of-a-bitch," Johnson cried and stepped into the lodge. As quick as a cat, he grabbed Morah by the hair and yanked her backward, throwing her out through the opening into the icy mud. She let out a blood-curdling scream and flung herself back into the lodge.

Clint heard the scream and came running to see what had happened. He arrived just in time to see Morah again come flying backward through the teepee's doorway. Her nose was bleeding and she'd had the breath knocked out of her. She lay in the mud gasping for air.

Clint rushed past her and stepped through the doorway. There in the half-light he could see the Old Man crouched against the rear of the lodge, a large knife in his hand. Johnson was circling slowly toward him. He too, held a knife.

"I'm gonna cut yer balls out," he said, moving in closer, about to spring.

Clint could see this was going to get very ugly very fast. "Don't do this, Johnson," he said.

"Stay outta this, Jeffries," he retorted, "I'm gonna nut this bastard."

With that, Clint grabbed the large knife at his belt and turning the blade away, hit Johnson with the butt of the handle just above the right ear, sending him crashing to the ground and out cold. He quickly pried the knife from Johnson's hand and threw it outside. Seeing his chance, the Old Man lunged toward the prone figure, knife poised for the kill.

"Whoa! Hold on there," Clint shouted and caught the Old Man in mid stride. "It's over. Let him be," he said, straining to keep from getting stabbed himself. The two of them were face to face now. Hate was painted all over the Old Man's face. "Calm down now," Clint whispered, trying to ease the situation.

The Old Man relaxed then and backed away.

"It is not good to leave an enemy alive," he said, now scrambling to get his clothes on. "Alive, they can come at you again when you least expect it and kill you."

"What the hell's going on, anyway?" he asked the Old Man.

"You know what's going on," he answered. "She was lonely and afraid to be by herself. She came to my lodge and asked if she could stay. I told her it was alright with me and....well, you know the rest. She is a handsome women and very willing."

"You better go to my outpost and stay there until he comes to. I'll see if I can deal with him."

With that, the Old Man slid into his moccasins and made his way toward the outpost. Clint found some of Morah's clothing and a trade blanket that was laying on the floor. Gathering them up, he stepped through the opening and threw them at her. "Get these on and then go to my place," he directed, "and don't come out."

It was some time before Johnson regained consciousness. When he did, he was moaning and gently caressing the goose egg above his right ear. Clint sat across the lodge from him, feeding the small fire that kept the place warm. The men's' features were painted in the yellowish-orange glow it emitted and in that dimness, they stared at one another. Clint's loaded pistol lay at his side, just in case.

"What'd ya hit me for?" Johnson queried. "I was gonna teach that bastard a lesson."

"Yeah, and what lesson would that be," he answered, and then added, "the one about being true to your mate? Seems to me you weren't thinkin' about Morah much when you were tryin' to coax Nineksa to lay up with ya. But I guess that's different, huh?"

"Well it just riled my fur to see her screwin' that old man. Him gettin' what otta be mine and her enjoyin' it."

"Johnson, you know as well as I that Morah's been passed from man to man. And as much as I hate to say it, I was one of 'em. I guess what I'm tryin' to say is that she's never gonna be a one-man woman. Enjoy her for what she can bring to yer life but don't scorn her for bein' what she was when ya met her."

Those words seemed to take the fire out of him and for a long moment, Johnson sat, staring at the floor and contemplating Clint's words. Then, he spoke.

"I can't stay here now. I can't be around that old man, knowing what happened. I want ya to take those pelts I brought in and gimme what they're worth in money and trade goods. Then I'll be on my way."

"Can't give ya much money," Clint remarked, "but I can fix ya up with the goods ya need. Those are fine pelts and you'll do well by 'em." He paused for a moment and then asked, "Where ya gonna go?"

"Down river! Fort Union maybe. Got no family back in the settlements. They all died from the fever some years back." He paused a moment, then asked, "You think Morah will come with me, Clint?"

"I don't know, Johnson. You need to ask her. Anyway, I'm sorry to see ya go but you know best."

When Clint returned to the outpost, the Old Man and Morah were sitting near the fire in silence. Morah had gotten most of the mud off her and the Old Man was fully dressed.

"You two better stay in here tonight. Johnson's still riled up some and he needs more time to calm down."

"Is he still mad at me?" Morah asked, without lifting her eyes from the fire.

"What do you think?" Clint answered. She had no reply.

"He says he's leavin' here, goin' down river. I imagine he'll be pullin' out tomorrow as soon as he gits his gear packed up."

Hearing this, Morah suddenly had a grave look of concern on her face. Clint wondered what was going through her mind but he kept silent and didn't ask. By mid-morning the next day, Johnson had settled up with Clint on the furs, had broken camp, and had loaded his pack horses. He waved goodbye to Clint as he rode past the outpost. Morah rode next to him.

CHAPTER 6:
THE POX

Since Clint had left them in the fall, he had never gotten Storm or the boys out of his mind. He had promised to return in the spring and he fully intended to do just that. Now that Johnson and Morah were gone, the Old Man seemed lonely and spent much time hanging around with Clint. Sometimes to the point that he became tiresome.

"I miss that woman," he said to Clint.

"Wha...what?" Clint answered, trying to tabulate the furs he had been taking in.

"Morah! I miss her."

"Yeah! Well she almost got you killed," Clint remarked.

"I know but I would have killed him if you hadn't butted in."

Clint didn't say anything further he just shook his head and sighed. The Old Man went on, "Think I'll go see my brothers across the way there and smoke a pipe with them."

"Good idea," Clint said, nodding his agreement. Now, maybe he could finish getting these pelts counted and bundled. Then, he'd prepare to make the long trip north to see his sons and their mother. It took him the better part of three days to finish what had to be done around camp. Some of the goods in the outpost, he transported to the hidden cache he kept on the upper ridge. He had never had anything stolen before but there had been more Indians move into the clearing and he didn't know if they'd come snooping around when he wasn't there. Better not to take the chance.

With plenty of firewood stacked by the outpost and enough grass and cottonwood bark to feed the Old Man's horses, Clint figured he could leave the Old Man there alone and not worry about him.

"I'll be back before the next full moon," he said. "Keep yer nose to the wind and watch over our place."

The Old Man nodded and held his hand up, "The trail you travel leads to the one's you love but it is a lengthy journey with many dangers along the way. Don't let the love you have for those people cloud your mind and narrow your vision. If you do, you may not return."

"I will be careful," he answered.

The Old Man watched as his friend and the four pack animals he led disappeared into the forest at the other side of the clearing. Then he wrapped his blanket tighter about his shoulder and walked to his lodge. "I wish Morah had stayed," he whispered to himself.

A day and half into his journey, Clint stopped to rest and get a drink at a small spring. He tied off the horses, leaving them to forage on whatever grass or moss they could find beneath the fast melting snow. He had not slept well the night before and now found himself yawning and somewhat sleepy. A light breeze brushed across his cheek as he sat down, straddling an old fallen tree and leaning his back against one of its protruding limbs. The sun's warmth beat down on him and he was soon fast asleep.

In his slumber, he thought about Storm. How beautiful she looked when he had at last found her. And their sons, what fine young men they were. He wanted so much to be part of their lives, to be a family. It had been so long since he'd lost his own family that he only had a vague remembrance of that life. He had, since that time, led somewhat of a solitary existence but he enjoyed the company of others and unlike many of the reclusive mountain men, who spent their entire lives alone, he needed to be around people; to laugh and converse and feel the warmth of companionship. He would go to Storm and the boys and take them to his heart. He would love them and care for them and....

The snort of his horse suddenly had him on his feet, snatching up his rifle and scurrying for cover. Someone was coming. There was no immediate sound to be heard but his horses had their heads up and were all looking the same direction.

"Injuns!" he thought, "They can smell 'em."

Quickly, he made his way to the horses, leading them back into the trees. If he had to make a run for it he'd probably have to leave the pack string behind. "Shit!" he whispered. "A whole year's work lost."

He was back away from the trail a ways but whoever was coming would see his tracks in the snow and be able to ride right to him. He waited! The faint clomp of horses' hooves echoed through the trees, getting louder as the riders approached. Then, the muffled sound of voices reached his ears and he listened to determine how many of them there were and who they might be. "Two voices," he thought as he listened ever more intently. If he wasn't mistaken one of them was speaking English; the other, Shoshone.

Easing his horse out from the trees, he slowly made his way to a place where he could see the trail. He dismounted and cuddled the horse's nose, not wanting it to whinny. When the riders came into view he quickly recognized them. It was Johnson and Morah. "What the hell?" he thought.

"Hey, yer goin' the wrong way," he shouted as he rode up to them.

"Clint! Jesus, you gave me a start."

"What happened? Did ya get turned around or somethin'?"

"No! We're headed back because there's pox all up and down the river."

"Pox!" Clint uttered, "You mean small pox?"

"Smallpox," Johnson said. "Some Frenchie boatman carried it up river, infectin' everybody and now people are droppin' like flies. They warned us off from the settlement, sayin' we'd die if'n we stayed, so we decided to high tail it back to yer place where it's safe."

"Has it gotten out to the tribes?"

Johnson nodded, "They said it's killin' 'em off real bad, the Mandans and Hidatsa downriver and the Blackfeet; especially the Blackfeet. Probably won't have to deal with those mean sons-a-bitches anymore bein' as how most of 'em will be dead."

Clint was deep in thought and didn't seem to hear what Johnson was saying. Then, Johnson spoke again, "Say, you got a couple of boys up in that area. I hope they don't ketch that shit."

"Johnson," Clint said with urgency, "take my pack animals with you to my outpost. Tell the Old Man what's happened and get him to help you unload the furs and other goods. Also, he must warn the Injuns that are camped in the clearing not to go to any of the trading posts along the river nor mix with any wandering bands that may come by. If you and Morah want to live in my place, you're welcome to until I come back."

"Are you goin' for the boys then?" Johnson queried.

"Yes, and God willin' I'm not too late."

Clint separated the pack animals, taking the two that held food and his possibles. The other three he took to Morah, handing the lead rope up to her.

"Think you can take care of these for me?" He said, smiling.

She nodded and said, "I will take good care of your things.'

451

Clint mounted his horse but before he left them he turned directly to Johnson. "I want you to pay attention to what I'm gonna tell ya now," he said, pointing his finger at the man. "If you harm one hair on that old man's head, I'll hunt you down and kill ya and I promise, you won't die an easy death."

Johnson could see that Clint was dead serious. In a softened voice, he replied, "Alright! I'll not cause any problems."

"Good! Then I'll see ya soon." Giving his horse a kick of his heels, he hurried away, down the trail.

He rode all the rest of the day and into the night before stopping. Before daybreak, he was up and at it again. He didn't want to go through the settlement and use the ferry but the runoff in the river was too high to allow him to ford it so he had no other choice. He thought if he could use the ferry at the first light of day, he would not encounter any of the residents there and could be safely on his way.

His plan worked and he had no problem with the crossing. Now, it was up the trail and over the divide. Soon, he would be at Storm's side and he could protect her and the boys. The snow here, except in the shadiest parts, was only a few inches deep but the melting of it had caused the ground to be very muddy. The horses were having a time keeping their footing in the mud as he climbed the steep trail.

What would he do if he found them all dead? It was a question he didn't want to deal with. He'd never seen the pox before but he'd heard tales of people having it and what it did to their bodies. He knew that most people who contracted the disease died from it. If they were dead, he couldn't even give them a decent burial. He wouldn't dare go near them. Instead, they'd be left to the critters and the insects.

He continually watched the trail for tracks, human or horse. But so far, all he'd seen were a few deer tracks. He knew though, that other well-traveled trails joined the one he was on, so he would soon know if riders had been traveling this way.

The skies were clear and with the light of the now, full moon, he could follow the trail long after the sun had set. Rising before full daylight, he would take a handful of dried meat and eat it as he rode. He would only stop to pee or relieve his bowels. By doing this, he shortened the time getting to the camp. Before, it had taken him four full days to ride from the settlement to the Indian camp but now, he arrived mid-morning of the third day.

He was hoping the camp hadn't moved and that Storm and boys had not relocated their lodge. Upon reaching the camp, he didn't ride straight in. Rather, he made a slow sweeping circle out a ways from the perimeter, watching for any activity. No one moved within the camp. Smoke rose from some of the lodges but not all of them. This was troubling, fore the weather was still damn cold and one would need a fire to keep the lodge warm. He did notice, that the forest was bare of all deadfall, meaning that the tribe had gleaned whatever firewood was available.

Finally, he came abreast of what appeared to be Storm's lodge. A small ribbon of smoke exited the vent at the top. He dismounted and tied the horses to a tree. Then, making his way slowly into the camp, he watched for any movement. He had to pass by one lodge to get to the one he wanted and as he passed, he noticed there were few tracks leading in or out of the doorway and the tracks that were there, were old.

He approached the lodge from the side. The opening lay to his right. He stopped a few feet from the edge of the lodge and quietly called out, "Storm! Kitchi! Keme! Are you in

453

there? Are you alright?" He could hear stirring inside then and a voice called back, "Who is out there? Go away! Do not come in here."

"It's me, Clint," he said, raising his voice a bit. "I've come as I said I would. Are you sick? Are any of you sick?"

The skin covering the entrance opened and Kitchi stuck his head out. "Father," he whispered, "there is much sickness about. You should leave this camp before you..."

Clint cut him off. "But, are any of you sick?"

"No!" the boy replied, "but we don't want to get near other people who are."

"May I come in?" He asked, He could hear Storm talking to the boy.

"Only if you have not been around the sick ones."

"I haven't! I heard that a great sickness had fallen on your people and I came to take you away."

With that, the boy motioned for him to come in. It took a minute for his eyes to adjust to the dim light within but when they did he could see Storm sitting across the fire from him, feeding it small twigs. The boys rushed to embrace him. When they did, he experienced a feeling he'd never known, a feeling of fatherly love. So strong was it, that tears welled up in his eyes and his voice was not to be found.

"Must be the smoke," he whispered, wiping the tears from his cheeks.

"We have missed you so," they said.

"And I, you," he answered, looking past the boys to their mother.

Her eyes then flashed, that old familiar flash, meeting his, not turning. In a moment, she said, "Hello Jeffries."

He nodded, acknowledging her, "Storm!"

Casting an eye around, he could make out the form of the man she lived with, lying under a buffalo robe. He looked pale and his eyes were set deep in his face. A heavy beard wrapped about his thin cheeks and chin and he coughed as he pulled the heavy robe up to cover his shoulders.

Before Clint could ask, Storm spoke up. "He does not have the sickness but he is not well. He has never recovered from the accident. His legs do not work and he cannot walk. I think his back is broken." Armand said nothing as she talked about him.

"What of this sickness?" Clint asked. "Are there many in the camp who have it?"

"Many!" she answered. "Several have died. We hear the death songs nearly every night. It breaks my heart to see my people perish this way."

"We've got to get out of here, Storm. We need to get away from this sickness. It's only a matter of time before it comes to your lodge and you all will die."

"I cannot go but you can take the boys and ride far away from here."

"What do you mean, you can't go?" he said, then added, "You have to go. I won't leave you here."

"And what about Armand?" she said. "He is in no condition to travel. It would kill him."

"Yes, it might kill him but if he stays here, he will surely die and you will die alongside him."

She thought about what he had just said and it made sense.

Clint spoke up again, "I and the boys can build a travois for him. That way, he can be comfortable as we travel." He waited a moment and then went on. "Storm, we must leave this place. Death is all around."

With that, she nodded, "Alright! I'll get things ready and we can leave in the morning."

"No!" Clint answered, "We're leaving today....as soon as we can."

With the boys in tow, Clint made his way back to where the horses were tied. "Come on," he said we'll cut some new poles for the travois.

Kitchi spoke up then, "There are poles laying there by that other lodge. The people who lived there are dead and no longer have a need for them."

Shaking his head, Clint answered the boy, "No! We're going to cut fresh ones. Those may have the sickness on them. We cannot take a chance with them." Pausing a moment, he asked, "Where are your horses? We will need them."

"I'll bring them," Keme said, eager to help his father.

"Do not speak to anyone or go near them. If there are men with the horses, leave them and come back and we'll make do with what I have here."

In a matter of minutes the boy returned with two horses. While Clint and Keme fashioned the travois, Kitchi helped his mother get their things ready to go.

"I hate leaving this lodge," Storm whispered. "I've had it for so many years. It's my home." He could see the sadness in her face. Laying his hand on her shoulder, he said, "I'll make you a new one."

Getting Armand out of the lodge and onto the travois was difficult and painful. The boys helped but Clint finally picked him up and carried him to it. Once loaded, they wrapped heavy robes about him to cushion the ride and keep him warm. When Clint tucked in the last robe about him, Armand raised his head and took hold of Clint's arm. "Thank you," he whispered, "You are doing the right thing. You know I'll never make it out of these mountains alive. That horse did me in. So, when I die, please bury me in the ground. I don't want to be laid out on a platform like her people do it. Promise me you'll do that."

Clint nodded, "I promise," he said.

It was late afternoon when the group finally rode away from the camp. A small group of people, standing some distance away, watched them go. Storm looked longingly back as the lodges disappeared from view. "I no longer have a home," she thought. "I will not be with my people again."

#

Several hours had passed since they'd left the village. The melting winter snow that remained on the ground was heavy with water and made travel difficult. Even the horses struggled to keep their footing. Armand groaned with discomfort every time the travois bumped over a hidden stone or log. He kept slipping downward, causing Clint and the boys to lift him up and tie him in place. This only added to his discomfort.

"We need to stop," Storm announced. "I am wet and tired and Armand needs attention."

Clint agreed and motioned to the boys who moved ahead of them. Pointing off to their left, he said, "See if you can find us a place in amongst that stand of pines where we can hole up for a while."

They nodded and angled their horses to the place he'd pointed. In a matter of minutes, they had stomped and pushed away enough snow to make a clearing in which to build a fire. The ground under the canopy of each tree was mostly clear of snow and provided them with dry twigs and pine needles. The boys scurried about, bringing in armloads of wood and they soon had a fire blazing.

Clearing away more of the snow, Clint spread two of the buffalo robes on the ground. He helped Storm with Armand, moving him from the travois to one of the robes and the warmth of the fire. Armand looked pale and haggard but he managed a smile and thanked them. Storm kneeled down beside him and wrapped a blanket about herself.

Clint tied a picket line between two trees and secured the horses to it, leaving them enough tether to reach the ground and paw for food. Before joining the group at the fire, he retrieved a handful of dried meat from his pack. This, he passed out to each of them. Silently, they ate the meat and peered into the dancing flames before them.

When things had settled, the boys began to make small talk with their father. Clint answered their questions and laughed when they said something funny. He never imagined the joy that came to him now as he conversed with them, sharing small snippets of his life; adventures and stories of his years in the mountains. He was beginning to tell them how he'd met their mother when suddenly, she blurted out angrily, "We should never have left the village. Traveling here was crazy. We should go back."

Everything got suddenly quiet. For a long moment, Clint stared at her, not speaking. Even the boys were shocked to hear their mother speak so.

Clint then broke the silence. Raising up from the comfort of the fire, he whispered, "Storm, could I have a word with you over here?" He moved toward the horses.

Looking up, she saw the set of his jaw tighten and a small twitch work at the corner of his eye. In a moment, she rose from the ground, tightened the blanket around her, and followed him to a place just out of earshot of the others. She knew what was coming and so, was the first to speak.

"You know we should have never left the village," she repeated. "This is going to kill Armand and..."

Clint suddenly interrupted her. "Yeah and what about you and your sons? Would you rather have stayed in that festering hole and watched them die and then perish yourself? What the hell is wrong with you?"

"I left my lodge, most of my belongings, and all of my friends," she snapped. "And besides, you don't know if the sickness would have touched us."

"You know damn good and well you'd have gotten sick. Within a week, everyone in that village will be dead. No one will escape the pox. Hell, we might get it yet."

"And what about Armand?" she said, raising her voice in anger. "This will probably kill him."

Clint cut her off again. "Armand is going to die," he said, bluntly. "You know it, I know it, and he knows it. It's not this trip that'll kill him. It's whatever came from being kicked by that damn horse. Hell, he hasn't been able to move since then and he's wasting away to nothing." Pausing a moment, he went on, "I think you need to stop bitchin' about your situation and be thankful that you're here with your sons and the two men who deeply love you and want you to be safe."

Glaring at him, she tightened the blanket closer to her chest, "I know Armand loves me," she retorted, "but I hardly know you. It's been a long time since we were together. I really don't know what's in your heart. I see your affection for the boys but....."

Shaking his head, Clint lowered his voice, turned, and looked her straight in the eye. He knew it was the frustration of leaving her home and the worry about Armand that was causing her to act this way but he just couldn't hold back.

"What about the last time we met, when I brought the boys to your lodge? I kissed you and held you and told you how much I loved you? My God, Storm, I've loved you from the very first time I saw you. All the days we shared and those special moments on our short journey along that river have kept me going all these years. And, for all these years, I've traveled across God's Creation, looking high and low for you, hoping beyond hope that you were still alive and that I'd find you, and all the while nursing a broken heart. If you can't see that, can't see what's in my heart, then something in your heart has died. And for that, I'm truly sorry."

Well, there it was! The words he'd been longing to say had just poured out in a fit of anger and frustration; not the way he had hoped to say them. But, what the hell, he was never one to sugar coat things and had little patience for those who knew the truth but were afraid to face it. Now, he wondered if he'd come on too strong. He turned to walk away but then stopped and turned back to her.

"Look," he said softly, "I will get you to safety and see to it that you have what you need. When the sickness passes, I will return you to your village and you can go back to the life you love."

Listening to his words and watching him pour his heart out she suddenly realized how deeply he loved her and how badly she had hurt him. She also realized that the love she had had for him so long ago was now stronger than ever. She was suddenly very sorry for the way she'd acted and wanted to tell him so but he had returned to the fire.

For a long time, she stood gazing off into the bleakness of the forest, letting what had just happened pour over her. His words had been harsh yet true and although she was still confused about her situation, there was a kind of peacefulness about it. She knew where she stood with him and she also knew that whatever happened, he would be there for her. After a while, she returned to the warmth of the fire.

BOOK 9 – CLINT BRINGS HIS FAMILY HOME

CHAPTER 1:
JEALOUSY CAN GET YOU KILLED

The Old Man was skinning a rabbit he'd shot when he saw the riders enter the flat in front of the outpost. He recognized Morah and knew it was Johnson that rode by her side. They led the same pack-train they'd left with.

"That's curious," he thought. "They were supposed to be riding downriver to Fort Union."

Morah was the first to ride up. The Old Man kept about his work, tugging at the skin until it released. Not looking up, he whispered in Shoshone, "You missed me, huh?"

"No!" she answered. "There's bad sickness up and down the river; many people are dying. Jeffries thought it best if we came back here and waited until the sickness is over."

The Old Man said nothing. He just nodded and proceeded to pull the entrails from the rabbit.

"What'd you say to him?" Johnson blurted out, his horse coming to a stop right in front of the Old Man.

"I told him of the sickness and that Jeffries told us to come here where we would be safe."

"Yeah, well you better tell him somethin' else. Tell him not to come nosin' around you or he's a dead man. His protector isn't around now."

A shallow smile crossed the Old Man's face then. Johnson didn't know it but over the years, the Old Man had learned the white man's tongue. He didn't speak it well but he understood every word that Johnson spoke. Morah then began to translate in her native tongue of Shoshone but the Old Man waved her off.

"I know what he said," he whispered. "He's very jealous of me. It is because he knows I am a better man and a better lover than he." He paused a moment and then smiled at her. "You know it too."

She said nothing but turned the horse toward the outpost. "Come Johnson! We will place our lodge on the other side of the outpost, away from his."

#

After that initial meeting, the Old Man kept pretty much to himself. He would often go to the village across the clearing but he stayed away from Morah and remained on his side of the outpost. Johnson too, was careful not to cross any lines but he could not forget what he'd seen that night in his lodge and it ate at him. Therefore, he kept a close eye on Morah. He didn't trust her and he knew how the Old Man felt about her. This constant uneasiness agitated him until he could hardly stand it. The Old Man could often here him ranting in his anger at Morah, over one thing or another. Once, he heard her cries when Johnson took to slapping her around.

Even though the Old Man had said nothing to either of them, he knew that Johnson was just looking for an excuse to kill him. If he was right, Johnson would make his move soon, before Clint returned. The Old Man began hatching a plan.

Through the days that followed, the Old Man took to riding his pony away from camp. Sometimes he'd leave at daylight, sometimes late in the morning. Never going the same direction. On each occasion, he would ride just beyond the edge of the trees and stop. From there, he could watch the camp. And, every day he did this, he would see Johnson mount his horse and come out the same way he'd ridden. The Old Man would then lose him in the woods and slip back into camp from another direction. It had almost become a game with him but he knew it was no game to Johnson. He fully intended to kill the Old Man, if and when he got the chance.

In the back of the outpost, hanging on the wall behind the counter, were two old bear traps. Clint had taken them in on trade from a trapper who'd been plagued by a grizzly. Once the bear had been disposed of, there was no need to keep the traps so he'd brought them in to trade for other goods. It was nearly all one man could do to lift them. They were made of thick iron with huge jaws that could hold the biggest bear. Straining under their weight, the Old Man loaded them onto a pack horse. Along with them, he piled on some rope, a heavy hammer, some metal stakes, and a spade. On top of it all, he placed some old meat that hadn't been smoked and was rotting.

Riding out, he rode close to Johnson's lodge, making as much noise as he could. He knew Johnson would hear the ruckus and see him leaving. He would be curious about what he was doing. Sure enough, Johnson came to the opening of the lodge and peered out. The Old Man saw him and with a slight smile pointed at the traps. "Bear," he said, "Big bear. Bad! Up near cache." With that, he kept riding. He knew that Johnson knew where their hidden cache was. He'd been there before.

Morah was just waking up when she heard Johnson rummaging around in the lodge. He found what he was after and slipped out through the door. She walked to the opening and peered out. Johnson was saddling his horse.

"Where you go?" she whispered, in broken English.

"Thought I'd see if I can shoot some fresh meat for us. I'll be back before dark."

He intentionally rode the opposite direction from that which the Old Man had ridden, just in case anyone had been looking. When he reached the forest, he rode into the trees some 200 yards and then made a sharp turn, heading for the ridge where the cache was. As he rode, he checked the prime on his rifle, "Good!" he whispered.

The Old Man was not careful to hide his tracks. In fact, if he saw a patch of lingering snow, he would deliberately ride through it, ensuring Johnson would know which way he had come. When he at last reached the ridge where the cache was hidden he veered slightly to his left, taking a dim trail down through a shallow canyon and then up to the next ridge line. He had long ago found that he could watch the cache from there and see anyone who approached it.

When he arrived at the place he wanted to be, he tethered the horses and went about his work. The traps were heavy and he struggled to get them where he wanted them. Jeffries had shown him how to set them, using two heavy iron bars. But a man had to be careful. One mistake and you could lose a limb or even your life. When he'd finished placing the traps he sat back in the shade of the tree and watched the ridge where the cache was.

A half hour passed before he saw Johnson, rifle in hand, sneaking along the edge of the woods, toward the cache. Quickly, the Old Man grabbed the hammer and one of the stakes he'd brought and began pounding the stake into the ground to secure the trap. Hearing the ping of the hammer on the steel stake, Johnson quickly moved to a place where he could see what was going on. He witnessed the Old Man setting the traps in the middle of a game trail. Patiently, he watched. Once staked out, the traps were carefully concealed with dirt and leaves and then baited with the rotting meat. The Old Man hung the meat in a blown-down tree directly ahead of the traps. After that, he gathered brush and piled it along the trail on both sides thereby forming a sort of narrow chute that an animal would have to traverse to get to the meat. Once he was finished, he walked up the trail away from where Johnson watched and disappeared over the rise of the ridge.

Johnson sat there for a very long time, thinking the Old Man would be coming back his way but he seemed to have vanished. "Where is that old sombitch?" he whispered, easing down the trail where the Old Man had set the traps. "Probably restin' in the shade over that rise."

As he neared the place where the traps had been set, he stopped, assessing the situation, listening. It looked like the Old Man had made a good set, for the traps were well hidden on the trail. One of them he could see but the other must be better hidden he thought. "Best move over," he whispered, "don't wanna step in one of those bastards." Moving to his right, he cocked the hammer on his rifle.

Just then, he heard another ping from the hammer. It was just ahead of him; just out of sight. Quietly, he stepped forward, making his way between two large pine trees. So intent was he, that he didn't see the rawhide trigger hidden in the pine straw where he walked. Moving slowly, he felt the slight tug of it on his right toe. He glanced down and realized in that moment what he'd done. A second later, the suspended log hurtled down from its hidden position, slamming into his head, killing him instantly.

When he heard the crash of the log, the Old Man made his way to where Johnson lay. For a long while he stood looking at him, canting his head one way and then the other. "The Indian way of trapping a bear works just as good as the white man's way," he whispered.

It took him until dark to pick up the traps, retrieve the rope, load the horse, and return to his lodge. He rode back the same way he'd ridden out and saw no one. The glow of firelight from within, lit up the sides of Johnson's lodge as he passed. He assumed Morah would be waiting inside for

Johnson to return. Tying his horses to the rail in front of the outpost, he lugged the traps back inside and returned them to their place on the rear wall. He did the same with the hammer, stakes, and the rope. He then hobbled the horses, turning them out to graze and made his way to his lodge. He was cold and exhausted when he crawled beneath the heavy buffalo robe. He would not awaken until mid-morning.

CHAPTER 2:
RIDERS APPROACHING AND TWO BURIALS

Two days had passed since Johnson had left to go hunting. On the third day, Morah, who was worried that something had happened to him, approached the Old Man and asked for his help in finding him. The Old Man told her that Johnson had probably had to travel long distances to find game and that she shouldn't be concerned. But when Johnson's horse showed up the next morning, grazing in front of the lodges with the rest of the horses, she knew that something was definitely wrong.

The Old Man had seen the horse come in and figured that whatever Johnson had tied it to, had not been strong enough to hold it or perhaps the reins had broken. Whatever the case, Morah was readying her horse to go search for him.

"Do you want me to go with you?" the Old Man asked, approaching her from behind.

"Two of us could cover more area than me by myself," she replied, without turning.

"Alright! I'll get my things."

A half hour later, they were riding out of the clearing together.

"Can we backtrack his horse?" Morah asked.

"Maybe," the Old Man replied, "but there are so many horse tracks in the clearing it may be difficult."

"Perhaps he was up on the ridge near where Jeffries has his cache," she offered. "We could search there first."

"Perhaps," the Old Man answered, "but I would be more inclined to think he followed the river, hunting the draws where the south slopes will be bare of snow and have new grass for the elk and deer to eat."

"Yes!" she said, nodding her head. "That makes more sense. But if we don't see tracks or pick up sign of his being there, we can make our way up to the ridge." The Old Man said nothing. He just nodded his head in agreement.

Three days of searching brought them no closer to finding Johnson. They had camped out at night and resumed the search early the next morning. The Old Man had tried his best to stay interested and act as though he was truly searching. But by the sixth day, his enthusiasm was waning. They had gone where he suggested, following the river and searching the draws that made their way down off the surrounding mountains but there had not been one track or any other sign that Johnson had come that way. Morah was ready to go back.

"I don't think we're going to find him," she said. "The country is too big, too many canyons. And, I'm tired." Pausing then, she turned the horse around. "Let's go back to camp."

In the days that followed, the Old Man kept his distance, not going near Morah's lodge. She was the first to break the tension that had been there between them, spreading a large blanket on the ground and offering him a pot of boiled meat with wild onion.

"I am tired of eating alone," she said, "so I thought you might like to join me."

"Yes, I would." he answered, joining her on the blanket. He then dipped into the steaming pot and pulled forth a thick chunk of meat.

Gazing off across the meadow, she gnawed on a small piece of rib. "What do you think happened to him?" she whispered.

"Do you really care?" the Old Man answered. This took her aback.

"Of course, I care." she answered, turning to face him. "Why would you say that? Of course, I care. He was a hard man to understand but he took care of me and I liked the way he got jealous when other men looked at me." She paused then, and finally added, "like he did when he caught us together."

The Old Man continued to eat but said nothing. After a while, he thanked her and made his way to his lodge. This too, took her aback. She was used to the Old Man sweet talking her, trying to get her clothes off. This wasn't like him at all. She didn't know what to think but she let it slide. Later that night, she would come to his lodge.

#

The Old Man sat astride his pony on the hillside above the outpost, watching a small group of wayward Indians make their way across the large clearing. There appeared to be four riders with pack animals; one pulling a travois. "Another group of wayward souls," the Old Man thought. It wasn't unusual since members of many of the local tribes had joined the ever-growing village across from the trading post.

He spurred the horse, driving her downhill and out into the clearing. He must go and tell them to camp with the other Indians and not near the outpost. Johnson had told him of the disease and warned that they must be wary of any travelers coming this way who might have the "pox."

He had ridden but halfway to them when he recognized the leader. He spurred the horse even harder.

"I see that you have cheated death one more time," he said, holding out his hand to greet his old friend. "You still have your hair and no arrow or no pox has found you."

"Not yet," Clint answered, taking the Old Man's hand in his own.

"Aiyee," the Old Man yelled, pulling his hand back. "Your grip is strong."

"Your's isn't so bad either," Clint retorted. This made the Old Man smile.

"So, I guess Morah and Johnson made it back to tell you about the sickness?"

"Yes, they did. We have not encountered anyone that seemed sick or had marks on their skin."

"Good!" Clint answered. "We have an injured man here who needs lookin' after. I need to get him to the outpost. You remember the boys, here?" Clint said, motioning to Keme and Kitchi who had ridden forward to their father's side. "And, that's Storm and Armand." The Old Man nodded and smiled.

"Looks like Johnson put his lodge on the other side of the outpost, away from yours." He paused a moment and then smiled. "Good!" he said, "Saves a lot of trouble."

As they came nearer the outpost, Morah stepped from the lodge, waving and calling his name.

"Hey Morah," Clint answered. "Where's Johnson?"

When he said that, she quickly lowered her head and became quiet. The Old Man then spoke up.

"He is gone."

"What do you mean, gone?" he asked.

"Gone," the Old Man repeated. "He left to go hunting and never came back. We looked for him but could not find him." Clint watched the Old Man's face as he talked. Nodding, he said, "You can tell me about it later."

They moved Armand first, taking him from the travois to a pallet in the back of the outpost. He was very frail and it seemed, as they lifted him, that he weighed nothing. "Skin and bones," Clint thought. "Won't be long."

Clint set about making a place for Storm, alongside of Armand. He folded a heavy buffalo hide in two as a base then covered it with another. On top of that he placed two trade blankets for covers. "There," he said, "That should be a comfortable bed for you."

"Thank you," she whispered.

Storm didn't know what to make of the outpost. She'd never been inside a white man's structure and it was somewhat frightening. It was so big. However, it felt safe to her and having Clint there made her feel even safer. Within the dim light surrounding her, she dropped onto the bed he'd made and sighed heavily. Tears suddenly welled up in her eyes. She was not one to cry but her life had been shattered and the trip here had taken a toll on her. She'd lost her people and....and Armand! Oh Armand! He was dying and she knew it and it was too much to bear. She buried her face in the blankets, sobbing uncontrollably.

In the meantime, the Old Man had offered Kitchi and Keme a place in his lodge. They said they would like that but that they would have to ask their father if it was alright. Clint told them yes but warned them of the Old Man's snoring.

Once he'd settled everyone in, Clint went looking for the Old Man. He found him sitting on a robe, in the sun, talking to the boys. As he approached, he spoke. "I think you boys ought to go tend to your mother. I heard her crying a while ago. This journey had been very hard on her and she could probably use some tenderness from her sons." He paused a moment and then went on, "Besides, I need to talk with my friend, here." With that, the boys said goodbye to the Old Man and retreated to find their mother.

The Old Man scooted to one side of the large robe, patting it with his hand, for Clint to sit down. He knew what was coming. Clint settled in, bringing his legs up to his chest and wrapping his arms about them. Both men sat, looking toward the encampment across the way, not speaking. Several minutes passed before the Old Man broke the silence.

Pointing to the lodges across the flat, he said, "Seems like there's more and more of them coming here every day."

"Yeah! Well, it's a nice area and close to our post. Makes for easy tradin'."

Again, there was a long period of silence. Finally.....

"Want to tell me what happened?" Clint said, "about Johnson, I mean."

The Old Man spoke quietly but did not look at his young friend. "Johnson is dead," he uttered. "I killed him."

Clint waited for the explanation that he knew would follow.

"I stayed away from him and Morah as he told me to but I knew he hadn't forgotten what happened between her and me. I could see the hatred in his face." The Old Man paused for a long while, then went on, "Every time I went out to hunt he would follow me. It was almost like a game, I would leave, he would follow, I would lose him in the forest, and I would come back to camp. He would come in sometime later. I knew it was only a matter of time when he would try to kill me. So, I set a trap for him and he walked right into it. It was over very quickly."

Clint was quiet for a few moments, trying to digest what he'd just heard. "Does Morah know?"

"I think she suspects that he's dead since he hasn't come back from the hunting trip he was supposed to be on. I don't think though, she suspects that I had anything to do with it."

"What did you do with his body?"

"I left it for the animals. I knew they would take care of it. I can take you to it if you wish."

"Yes! I will have you do that. He was my friend and he deserves a Christian burial."

"I'm sorry it happened," the Old Man said, this time looking directly at Clint. "But it was him or me. I hope you understand."

"I believe you," Clint answered. "Johnson could be a hothead sometimes. We'll go tomorrow."

Through the night, Clint tossed and turned. Sleep evaded him. All he could think of was the way the Old Man had openly admitted killing Johnson. His manner, when he said it, was so nonchalant and uncaring. It was as if life had no value to him. Was that because he was an Indian or was he just a cold-blooded killer? When those last three words crossed his mind so did a sudden dark shadow of conscience. He had done the same thing many times and had always justified it as the Old Man had, "It was him or me." And, most of the time, that had been the case. But it was after the deed had been done that was now eating at him. He couldn't remember if he'd ever been sorry for anyone he'd killed.

The morning light was barely visible over the eastern peaks when Clint stepped outside. His throat was dry and he needed a drink. In the waning darkness, he made his way to the water barrel that sat at the edge of the outpost.

"You are an early riser," came a soft voice. He nearly jumped out of his skin but he knew immediately who it was.

"Yes!" he replied, "And it appears, you are too."

"I am not used to the white man's lodge," she whispered. "I could not sleep so I thought I would come and visit the stars." She paused momentarily, then went on, "They are beautiful don't you think?"

"Yes! Yes, they are," he whispered, squatting against the building, near where she sat. "They remind me of a time long ago on the banks of that far-off river when..."

She suddenly cut him off then, saying, "That was a long time ago. It was a wonderful time but much has happened since then. The Great Spirit chose different paths for each of us to follow."

"Perhaps," he answered, "but those paths have crossed once more and we are, once again, in each other's lives. I guess we'll have to see what the Great Spirit will do now." He did not give her a chance to answer. Instead, he rose quickly and walked on to the water barrel.

#

When the Old Man finally came out of his lodge, Clint had the horses ready to go. He had loaded some dried meat and a water skin for their journey. He had also lashed an old buffalo robe, a short length of rope, and a shovel to one of the pack animals. The boys were still asleep and he was glad for it. He didn't want them going along and he sure hadn't relished the thought of explaining why they couldn't.

Without speaking, they rode side by side, through the flat, and up the trail that led to the cache. When they finally reached the ridge, the Old Man broke the silence.

"It's this way," he grunted, turning off to the left, guiding his horse down the dim trail. Clint followed close behind. Before they had reached the bottom of the hollow, a sickening smell rose to greet them. Clint recognized it immediately. It was the smell of death - human death.

"No other animal stinks like a man does when it dies," he thought. The horses too had smelled it and were now getting skittish, not wanting to go on.

"Let's tie 'em up here," he told the Old Man. Dismounting, he went to the pack horse and removed the robe and shovel. "We can walk the rest of the way," he said.

Although the smell of death was strong when they reached the place Johnson had fallen, there was not a whole lot left of him. What was left, was scattered about. The meat-eating critters had had their way with him and except for a few pieces of bone and the old dirty shirt he always wore, there wasn't much to bury.

They wrapped his remains in the buffalo robe and tied it up with the rope. In a small clearing, they took turns digging a shallow grave. When they'd finished burying him, they piled rocks on the grave to keep the animals from digging up what was left. Before he walked away, Clint kneeled down and whispered, "Who knows when one trail will end and another begin. We don't - but He does! God keep you safe Johnson."

#

Within a week, there was another burial to contend with. Armand, in his frail condition, had passed away. It had, for all purposes, been a peaceful death. He simply went to sleep and never woke up. Storm was heartbroken, as were the boys. He had been a husband and provider to her and the only father the boys had ever known. It was a grievous time of mourning for them all.

Storm wanted him buried in the traditional way of her people on a platform, high in the air. When Clint told her that Armand had asked to be buried as a white man, she would not hear of it.

"He will be buried as a warrior should be buried, in the way of our ancestors," she said, "or he cannot be welcomed by the Great Spirit." Seeing her insistence, Clint let it go.

"Oh well! Dead's, dead," he thought. "Probly don't matter if yer buried in the ground or up in the air." Still, there was the promise he'd made to Armand. The promise he'd made to a dying man. He couldn't take that lightly. He'd have to see it through.

Storm and the boys selected a site for the burial. It was at the edge of small clearing and was about an hour's ride from the outpost. They set about cutting the necessary trees to build the platform that would hold Armand's body. When they had finished, they went back to the outpost to fetch his remains. Storm wrapped him in a fine new blanket that Clint had given her. Next to his body, she placed several small personal items, his pipe, a knife, his tobacco pouch, and an old broken watch that had been his father's. Finally, he was tightly wrapped in a buffalo robe, leaving the skin side out. Long pieces of rawhide were then wetted and tied about the hide to keep it in place. He was loaded aboard a travois and taken to the platform. Storm didn't want Clint to be there so only her and the boys made the journey and performed the ceremony.

During all of this, Storm had wailed the death song and had inflicted cuts on both her arms. It bothered Clint greatly but he said nothing. He was worried that in her grief she might cut too deeply and sever an artery, thereby bleeding to death. But it didn't happen and after a while, things seemed to calm down. In the weeks that followed, Clint kept his distance from Storm, only speaking when spoken to. It was uncomfortable for him but he dealt with it.

The boys had come around within a few days and were once again, after him to hunt and fish and teach them to speak English. Clint usually spoke Blackfoot but the boys had heard him talk to Johnson and the English language he used intrigued them. Now, they both wanted to learn it.

Once, while hunting, Clint had mentioned Armand to the boys. They had then become very untalkative and would not look at him.

"Did I say something wrong?" Clint asked, "Was I not supposed to speak of Armand?"

For a moment, they were both silent. Then, Keme spoke up, "It is not polite to speak of one who has gone to the Great Spirit."

"I'm sorry," Clint said, "I meant no disrespect. It will not happen again."

Several weeks had passed since Armand's death. But Clint had not forgotten his promise. It was then, in the pre-dawn hours that he made his way toward the burial platform. A shovel was lashed to the side of horse. He knew that Storm or the boys would not find out that he had moved Armand to a grave, being as how Indians never went near burial grounds once their deceased had been placed there.

It was nearly noon when he finished what had to be done. Again, he knelt at the graveside and whispered a small prayer. Solemnly, he rode back to camp.

EPILOGUE

As the years passed, things changed in the mountains. The market for beaver had all but disappeared, bringing an end to the era of the mountain man. More and more people were moving up the river and through the mountains on their way to Oregon and the gold fields of California. Things changed in Clint and Storm's lives also.

After Armand's death, Storm mourned deeply for some time but came to once more fall in love with the man who had, early on, captured her heart. The boys had grown into men and had each chosen a different path in life. Keme spoke English much better than his brother and opted to travel to the settlements to get an education in the white man's schools. To the dismay of his mother, he cut his hair and added his father's last name to his own. Keme Jeffries was how he would be addressed but people had a hard time with Keme and started calling him Ken. He liked the sound of it and would be known by that name all his life. He graduated from McKendree University in Lebanon, Illinois with a degree in health professions. Later he attended a medical school in the east to become a doctor. During the years when the Civil War raged, he attended the wounded Union troops, doctoring them as best he could. After the war, he took up residency in Chicago and became a well-known surgeon. He never returned to the mountains.

His brother, Kitchi, kept to the Indian ways and married a Crow girl from the encampment across from the outpost. He had become good friends with his cousin, Jeremy Dunbar, now a captain in the U.S. Calvary. Dunbar, leading a company of troopers, had returned to the trading post on the river to keep order in the area. When the Army at last ordered him to go back downriver to Fort Union, he offered Kitchi a position as an infantry scout. The pay was $13 per month.

Kitchi packed his belongings and with his wife, said goodbye to his parents.

There was talk of a great civil war coming, something to do with slavery. Clint warned Kitchi that, if at all possible, "Keep ta hell out of it. It ain't yer fight." Kitchi stayed with the Army for many years but when the Civil War ended and the Indian hostilities wound down, he returned to live near his parents. He had 5 children, four boys and a girl. Although they were given Indian names, they had Jeffries as their last name.

When Johnson didn't return, Morah became lonely and took up once more with the Old Man. His health was poor and with the idea in his mind that he would soon die, he coaxed her to return with him to the land of his forefathers. Before leaving, he came to Clint's lodge to smoke one last pipe. For a long time, they sat in silence. Then, the Old Man spoke, "We have walked many trails together, you and me. They have not all been easy. And although we did not always see things the same way, we never let our judgments come between us." He stopped then, inhaling again on the pipe. "You are and have always been my friend and you know I would stay here and protect you if I could, but I am old and I feel the weight of my years bearing down on me. It is time for me to return to my people and meet the Great Spirit in the land of my father."

"You did that once before," Clint said, trying to dissuade him, "and it didn't work out. I think you should stay here with Storm and me. Besides, it's a long way from here to your peoples' camp."

The Old Man listened to his friend's words and thought on them for some time. "Before, when I left," he said, "it was to lead my people. I had once been their chief and I thought it could be that way again. I was wrong. In my absence, they had found a new chief, a younger chief, a wiser chief and they did not need me. I thought to myself, they don't need me but Jeffries does. So, I came back to spend these years with you. And that was a good thing." He took a deep breath then and went on, "This time, I am going back to die. Don't feel bad, for it is as it should be. We all come to that time. I will always remember you and I hope you do the same about me." The Old Man could then see the tears welling up in Clint's eyes. He knew how his friend felt about him. He reached across the space between them and placed his hand on Clint's shoulder. "Be brave my friend. Warriors do not shed tears and you are a great warrior." With that, he took one last drag on the pipe, handed it to Clint and stepped from the lodge.

The next morning, Clint helped with packing up the Old Man's belongings. As he and Morah were about to leave, Clint waved and yelled out to him, "Hey, Old Man what is your name? Through all of our years together I have never known your name." The Old Man turned to him and smiling, said, "Black Wolf! But I prefer Old Man." Clint and Storm looked on until they were out of sight.

"Do you have something in your eye?" she asked, looking up at him.

"Must have gotten some dust in it," he answered, wiping away the tear that ran down his cheek.

#

With friends and family gone, and the fur trade at an end, Clint and Storm decided to sell the outpost and move further north into Canada. Many of the Piegan and Blackfoot people had moved there and Storm wanted to spend her life near them.

The outpost was bought by a preacher from Kentucky who said he wanted to bring the word of God to the indigenous tribes of the area. He painted the front of the outpost white and erected a large wooden cross in the front. Unfortunately, a small bunch of Shoshone who were passing through, stopped by the post to see Clint and Storm. They were surprised with the look of the place and the new owner who appeared at the door. He was a slightly rotund fellow, clothed in a full length black robe that was tied at the waist by a fancy rope-like belt. A white collar fit tightly around his neck. Upon his chest lay a large metal cross, dangling from a beaded necklace. The sight of him was strange and the Indians whispered and motioned among themselves. This made him nervous and he tried speaking to them. He was, however, not well versed in their language and was having a hard time making them understand that the post was now his and that his mission was to bring the teachings of the Lord to them. The more he spoke, the more suspicious he seemed to the Indians. Suddenly, they were off their horses and approaching him. In their curiosity, one of them reached out to touch the cross. His reaction, driven mostly by fear, was to yank the cross from the man's hand. This infuriated the Indian and he pressed forward even more.

"Stop!" the man yelled at them. Then raising the cross from his chest, he thrust it forward, screaming, "Back! Back, ye sons of Satan." The deafening roar of his voice and his sudden actions caused the Indians to back away. Thinking him crazy, they mounted their horses and made a hasty retreat but not before letting loose a few arrows in his direction. None of the arrows found their mark but it was enough to convince the man that he would be better served to preach the gospel to people who were not so hostile. Within a week, he had packed his things and was on his way back to the settlements. The outpost lay unoccupied for many years except for the occasional hunter or traveler who happened by to spend the night. The cross fell into disrepair and eventually was toppled by a strong wind. Due to a lack of available firewood, it was dismantled and burned.

With their move north, Clint and Storm joined up with her people and enjoyed the company of new friends. There were still many confrontations between the U.S. Calvary and the tribes to the south. But there was little, if any, trouble in the Canadian Territory. It was rumored throughout the tribe that Chief Joseph of the Nez Perce had made a run for Canada but was overtaken by the Army before he could make it. Many of his people had died or been killed in their attempt to escape. The rest were returned to a reservation.

#

Clint and Storm's life together was all he had hoped for. Together, they spent each day fishing, hunting, or simply watching their grandchildren play their games. In between those times, Storm busied herself with the normal, everyday work that was the plight of most Indian women. She had many friends though and they would often get together, working and gossiping. They would joke and tell wild and funny stories of their girlhood or swoon over some young brave that was coming of age.

At night, when the last of the cook fires had died to smoldering embers and the village was quiet, Clint and Storm would sit together, holding hands and looking up at the stars. The crickets, frogs, and the low hum of the insects provided a soothing background symphony to the surrounding peacefulness.

On one such night, the moon had been slow to rise but now, as it peeked over the distant mountains, Clint put his arm around her and pulled her close to his chest, sheltering her against the coolness of the evening.

"Isn't it beautiful?" she whispered, snuggling closer to him.

"You're beautiful," he answered.

She smiled and raised her face close to his. "Do you know how much I love you?" she said, again in a whisper.

"I do," he answered. "Yes, I do!"

For a long while they just sat there, holding one another. When sleep was almost upon them, Clint stood up and lifted her in his arms. Walking into their lodge, he whispered, "Tomorrow's another day. Now, it's time for sleep."

CPSIA information can be obtained
at www.ICGtesting.com
Printed in the USA
LVOW10s0759060417
529840LV00002BA/2/P